ANOTHER SMALL KINGDOM

JAMES GREEN

Published by Accent Press Ltd – 2012

ISBN 9781908262899

Printed and bound in the UK

Cover design by Sarah Ann Davies

Foreword

In July 1790 the US Congress established the Contingent Fund of Foreign Intercourse in response to a request from President George Washington for funds to finance intelligence operations. The Fund was granted $40,000 which, within three years had grown to $1 million, more than 10% of the Federal Budget. Successive administrations developed and expanded this Fund until, in 1947, President Harry Truman signed into law the National Security Act – and the CIA was born.

Chapter One

PARIS 1802

PARIS 1802

February 23rd

The Office of Maurice de Talleyrand, Foreign Minister to the French Republic.

Ambassador Livingston was trying very hard to keep the hate from his eyes and the anger from his voice. Had he been able, like Samson, to bring the Tuileries Palace down on himself, but more especially on the head of the man sitting opposite him, he would have done so willingly.

'Monsieur Talleyrand, if the American Republic is to expand, and it must expand ...'

'Grow or die, eh, Monsieur Ambassador? How very Napoleonic.'

'There is no question of America dying, that is never going to happen. Ask the British if you doubt it.'

'Of course I do not doubt it. But there is a question over whether it will grow, is there not?'

'No, there is not. America will grow and will take its rightful place among the nations of the world.'

'And that place will be?'

'At any table where decisions are made which might affect America.'

'So, America will be here, there and everywhere for, as we know, all decisions great or small affect all other decisions in some way or another. When the wine growers meet to discuss the vintage, America will be there. When farmers meet to discuss the harvest, America will be there. When the mistress of the house meets with the cook to discuss the menus for the week, America will be there. Very well. But tell me, Monsieur Ambassador

Livingston, how many Americans do you think will be left in America while so many are away sitting at all these tables where decisions are made?'

'Monsieur Foreign Secretary, you may choose to make a joke of my words if it pleases you to do so. But I know you understand my meaning. The fact that you play with the issue instead of discussing it shows you understand it very well indeed, and understand its importance. Make something look ridiculous and no one will take it seriously. Perhaps that works well enough with smaller issues but it will not work with this one, Monsieur Talleyrand, and no amount of wit nor clever words will make it otherwise. America will expand and America will sit at the Council Tables where the great nations meet.'

'Monsieur Livingston, if you as the Ambassador of President Jefferson say that it will be so, then I am sure it will be as you say. One day, I am sure, America will be great in all senses of the word. The question I ask is, when will that day be?'

'America will expand, Talleyrand, and it will be sooner rather than later.'

'Ah, then you have come to some arrangement with the British?'

'The British?'

'Well, America cannot expand to the east unless American statesmen can build on water as well as walk on it. The same applies to the south, the Caribbean is just as wet as the Atlantic. That leaves north and that is British? Strange, I am usually so well informed and yet I have heard nothing of your negotiations with the British whereby you will move into their territories and they will move out.'

'West, sir, west. America will expand across the Mississippi and into the Louisiana Territories. You know very well that is our intention because I have told you often enough that I am empowered by President Jefferson to negotiate for the purchase of those Territories.'

'Ah, the American dream of going west, of course. How very remiss of me to have let it slip from my mind. But if your Government wishes to push west with its borders, surely you should be in Madrid? The Louisiana Territories, as everyone knows, are Spanish.'

2

'The Louisiana Territories, as everyone knows, were negotiated back into French hands two years ago under the Treaty of San Ildefonso.'

'But my dear sir, I know of no such treaty.'

'The Secret Treaty of Ildefonso then, if you still prefer to play games.'

'Ah, the Secret Treaty of Ildefonso, of course.'

'Then if we both know that the Territories are French, we can discuss an American purchase and put these games to one side.'

'I assure you, my dear Monsieur Ambassador, this is no game. It is deadly serious. If I discuss the sale of these Territories with you, I acknowledge the Treaty of San Ildefonso to a third party and it becomes no longer secret. I would have broken the terms of the treaty and Spain would have the right to re-claim the Territories.'

The French Republic's Foreign Secretary spread his hands in that universal Gallic gesture which signifies, alas, what can one do?

Robert Livingston stood up angrily and paced the large and elegant room bringing his temper under control while Talleyrand sat back and watched him. Not for the first time the American Ambassador felt that the frustrations inherent in negotiating with this man were wearing him down to the point of despair. After a pause the gentle but almost mocking voice of Talleyrand resumed.

'Perhaps there might be a way.' Livingston turned. Could this be the first hint of negotiations actually beginning? He returned and stood at the desk. 'If America were prepared to leave the matter secret. You would, of course, pay France the full purchase price on the signing of a Secret Treaty, but then do nothing until Spain was satisfied that any publication of the new nationality of the Louisiana Territories did not adversely affect Spanish interests. If and when Spain was satisfied, France would then be free to judge how French interests should be protected. Of course if, while Spain and France considered their positions, America did anything to prejudice the terms of the Treaty, perhaps negotiate with some other government and thereby give them knowledge of the Secret Treaty, the Territories would revert to France. More accurately, because of the Secret Treaty of San Ildefonso, they would appear to revert to Spain because France would, of course, keep the terms of the Secret Treaty of San Ildefonso and not make the true nationality of the Territories known to any other party. For if France did that the Territories would revert to Spain whose Territories they appear to be to all those not party to …'

But Robert Livingston was no longer present to appreciate the culmination of the Foreign Minister's erudite exposition on the nature of Secret Treaties. The sound of his angry boots on the marble floor of the corridor rang out as he stormed away. A door in the corner of the fine office opened, Talleyrand's secretary entered and waited until the sound of boots on marble died away. He then crossed the room and stood by the large elaborate desk.

'It sounds as if it went well, Your Excellency?'

'Well enough for the time being.'

'You are too much for them, they lack flair, élan, subtlety …'

'You have studied our American friends closely?'

The secretary made a contemptuous gesture.

'Enough to know they are a country with thirty-two religions and only one sauce.'

Talleyrand laughed loudly.

'Very drôle. But eventually I will have to deal with our Americans friends and, one way or another, I think they will force my hand. Livingston is no great diplomat but neither is he a fool however much I make him feel like one. One day America will send someone who will make me listen,' he paused, 'unless of course the plan of our very clever Minister of Police, Monsieur Fouché, is successful. If that happens then they will find they have other, far more important things to worry them and perhaps forget for a time their dream of going west.'

Chapter Two

That Lawyer Macleod was a man full of hate did not make him exceptional. What did make him exceptional was the completeness of his hate, and its great depth.

Macleod raised his eyes from the article in *The Boston Commercial Gazette* which lay over the contract papers on which he had been working. A man of middling age, he wore a linen neck-cloth and a close-buttoned black coat. A man who despised display, his manner of dress was severely plain as was his view on the European war. If Europe was bent on self-destruction, then good luck to it. As far as he was concerned they could all go to hell in a wheelbarrow, led there by the strutting Little Corsican or Mad Farmer George. They could all dance to their graves to the music of musket-shot and cannon-fire. The French, the Prussians, the Austrians, the whole damned lot, men, women and children. Especially the damned British. In fact most of all the damned British.

He got up from his desk and went to the office window which was shut tight, his only concession to the late February weather. Down in the busy, wet street carriages and carts jostled and splashed. Crowds, wrapped in cloaks against the weather, hurried through the rain that carried with it flecks of snow with the promise of more to come. He looked at them for a moment. These were the people for whom he had fought in the late war, fought that they might be free and America independent. He had shed his blood for them. They were Americans, fellow citizens of the great new Republic. He would fight again for them if called on, yes, and die for them if necessary. But he could not feel for them. He did not wish to know their ambitions or aspirations, their sorrows, griefs or joys. To Lawyer Macleod they were a charge on his duty, a duty he owed to his country. They could never be an object for any personal emotion, because the only emotion left to Lawyer Macleod was hate. And that, of course, brought him back to the

British.

Macleod left the window and returned to his desk where he put thoughts of the late war from him. That was ancient history, something gone with youth and joy. As for foreign wars and the politics of war, they were nothing to him unless they threatened his country. But the soldier in Lawyer Macleod, though dormant, was not dead. He began to muse for a moment on Napoleon, his military achievements and his likely ambitions.

He had sometimes said to clients that in his opinion Napoleon would prove to be more interested in France as a kingdom, his own kingdom, than in spreading the ideals of Revolution and Republic across Europe.

'Mark my words,' he would say when business was concluded, 'Louis won't be the last king of France. The Corsican will be given the Crown when he asks for it. And he will ask for it when there is no one left with the courage or power to deny it to him.' And the client would nod and listen, and Lawyer Macleod would continue. 'America is the only proper home for a republic. The true Free Man exists only in America and can exist only in America. Everywhere else it is master and slave, aristocrat and serf, ruler and ruled. Europe can no more cope with the idea of republican liberty than it could with religious liberty. That's why Europe is dying while America is being born.'

It was an amazingly long speech by Lawyer Macleod's standards and his clients, somewhat surprised at such loquacity, were happy to agree with him when he had said his piece. He was deep, was Lawyer Macleod, and he knew his business better than most. If, once in a while, he chose to speak on some subject outside the law, well it was probably best to listen and, having listened, take your leave.

Lawyer Macleod gave up his thoughts and pulled out his watch. It was time for lunch. He went to the door of his office, opened it and called out, 'Lunch if you please, and make it now.'

There was the sound of someone jumping off a high stool in the outer office as the lawyer returned to his desk. An elderly clerk came in with a plain wooden tray bearing a coffee pot, cup and saucer, and a few dry biscuits. The clerk pushed the papers to one side, put the tray on the desk, then left closing the door behind him. As the coffee was steaming hot it was clear that the lunch had been ready to the minute, and that the clerk could have brought it in at the correct time without any command from the lawyer. But both lawyer and clerk were men of fixed habits, and men of fixed habits dislike change. For some years now the lawyer had opened the door at the same time each day and made the same peremptory command, at which the clerk had brought in the same lunch. No comment had ever passed nor was it likely that any comment ever would. The world of Lawyer Macleod's office had little or no variety and was universally regarded by his clients as dull as the eye of a dead fish – and the elderly clerk honoured him for it.

Chapter Three

If the lawyer's idea of luncheon was to read his paper, drink coffee and eat dry biscuits, there were those among his clients who took luncheon more seriously. They repaired, with others, to the select and popular Gallows Tree Club. The club's grim name belied its grandeur both outside and inside, but referred to Boston Common which stood opposite across Beacon Street. It was on that Common that in 1656 Ann Hibbins, a wealthy widow, had been hanged on an oak tree for witchcraft, one of three women executed for the same crime. The club's name was a tribute to the fact that the Boston witch trials pre-dated those of Salem by more than thirty years, a reminder if one was needed, that in all things of consequence Boston should regard itself as leader and guide.

In a well-appointed assembly room, after an excellent meal, a group of Boston's best and brightest gathered for coffee, cigars and serious conversation.

Here the talk could not be of fashion or the other frivolous matters more suited to the mixed company of the dinner table. Here the talk could be only of business, the state of America and the state of the world.

Macleod's last client of the morning was one of those who lunched at the club and was now sitting comfortably with coffee at his elbow and pulling on a good cigar. His fellow members listened as he told them that, while Macleod was an excellent Business and Contract lawyer, none better indeed, unfortunately he knew as much about politics as a dog knew about salvation. Heads nodded wisely in agreement. One of the older men commented that Lawyer Macleod took after his late father, a good man of business but a poor judge of life where its larger considerations were concerned. Another agreed. Yes, he most surely took after his father in that respect.

'Euan Macleod. Now there was a dour Scot if ever there was one.'

'It may be he takes after Euan in some ways,' offered another, 'but he certainly got his looks from his mother. Old Macleod was no picture but his son is a fine handsome man. He could have married again a dozen times over since the war on his looks alone.'

'And picked up a tidy fortune with some of the young ladies who would have been pleased to have him as a husband. Many a mamma would have been happy for her daughter to become the second Mrs Macleod.'

'Yes sir,' remembered a stout, bald gentleman who had long since published a substantial second edition of his chin, 'his mother was a fine woman indeed. I remember when I first saw her just after they had arrived over from Edinburgh.' And he was once again, in his mind if no longer in reality, a dashing young buck twirling his killing, black mustachios. 'Dam'me, gentlemen, on my life she was the prettiest thing that ever set foot in Boston.'

The older heads nodded in agreement and there was a brief pause of pleasant thoughts among the senior men. The mood was rudely interrupted by a man too young to be able to share any memories of the beautiful young Mrs Macleod.

'Stap me, gentlemen, so it was the old story, eh, beauty and the beast? She had the looks and old Macleod had the tin? Blast my idleness, it'll have to be the other way about with me, that's for sure.'

The stout gentleman spoke coldly,

'Not at all, Rayburn. The money was on her side as well as the beauty. What he brought to the match was brains, and fine brains at that. Euan Macleod may have had a face like a hoof-print in a cow pat, but there was nothing wrong with his business head. That man could make money out of fresh air and floor sweepings. He could see a good prospect at night, in a fog with a bag over his head. He was a fine man of business and died rich enough for plenty of good Boston Protestants to attend a Papist funeral.'

'Aye, aye. True enough. A fine man, though, as you say, a Papist through and through.'

Heads nodded and the talk threatened to turn to religion when a new voice cut in with a lazy drawl which was almost a sneer.

'So, Macleod's got his father's brains, his mother's looks, plenty of family brass and is now in a good way of business in his own right. Pity he doesn't seem to know how to enjoy any of it.

For all the fun he seems to get out of life he might as well be a backwoods parson. God knows he seems satisfied to dress like one.' And several of the younger men there grinned and sniggered in agreement.

Darcy was a young lawyer, in Boston only a year but well-to-do and dressed as near to the height of fashion as was possible. He spoke too loudly and too often for some of the older men but the younger set seemed to think something of him.

'True enough, Darcy,' agreed the self-confessed idler, Rayburn, 'he's a dull dog and dresses no better than his clerk, but I wish I had half the damned fellow's luck.'

'Some may choose to think Macleod a lucky man,' drawled the young lawyer, 'although I'd say you judge the luck of a man by the number and quality of his friends rather than the size of his house or the money in his pocket. Lawyer Macleod, it seems to me, has precious few friends of any sort. Does anyone see him in society? Does he dine? God's teeth, gentlemen, look at yourselves. You never refer to him by any of his given names. In fact, I've been a year in Boston and I still don't know what his given names are. No one uses them. He's either Lawyer Macleod or plain Macleod.' He paused, looked around, then smiled nastily. 'But I do confess I have heard he is the possessor of a very unusual nickname, although with such a dry stick as Macleod I can't imagine how he came by it. I was told he used to be called …'

One of the older men cut sharply across his words.

'You would do well to keep any tittle-tattle of that sort to yourself, Darcy.'

The atmosphere in the room suddenly became charged.

'What's so damn serious about a nickname, and such a funny one at that? I didn't make it up, although I must say it made me laugh,' and indeed he did laugh. 'How anyone like Macleod could pick up such a name as …'

But Darcy was again cut short.

'I know of only two men who thought that nickname suitable for public laughter at Macleod's expense. I'll introduce them to you if you like, they're not so far away. After meeting Macleod they decided to take up permanent residence very near here. I can take you to them both if you wish, they're not far, just across the Common in the Burying Ground, and for all I know they're still grinning at his nickname. But each one has a pistol ball in his head to remind him of what he's grinning at.'

Another drove the point home.

'In the head mind you, Darcy, not in the body.'

The older men, a few of whom had served with Macleod, nodded.

'Macleod was one of the best pistol shots in the army in his day. If his eyes haven't gone I still wouldn't want to be on the business end of any pistol he was holding.'

The atmosphere changed again, still charged, but for another reason. The gathering listened as a new topic opened up.

'But are his eyes still sharp, that's the question? It's some time since Macleod called anyone out.'

The gentleman with the chins smiled and looked around the assembly.

'You know, it would be a fine thing to see if Macleod can still shoot straight. Yes, sir, a fine thing.'

There was a pause before another voice added,

'And a finer thing to wager on.'

An excited stir ran through the gathering.

'By God, that would surely be something.'

'I guess plenty of money would get put down on whether or not Macleod can still put a ball in a man's head clean as a whistle. It would be a neat judgement either way.'

Murmurs of agreement met this profound sporting observation.

'Yes sir, a fine thing.'

There was another pause while the best business brains of Boston began to consider if such an event might be brought off. Their deliberations were interrupted by a thoughtful sportsman who put his finger on the one weak spot in the proposed entertainment.

'Except for the man Macleod called out, I guess.'

The room filled with laughter at this all too true observation, and suddenly all eyes were looking at Darcy. The young lawyer shifted uneasily and remained silent. He tried, without success, to look defiant. Before this afternoon he had merely disliked and despised lawyer Macleod. Now he found he hated him. After a short pause it became clear Darcy was unwilling to consider providing his friends with their entertainment or the prospect of making serious wagers. Someone cleared his throat and noisily took up a newspaper as a sign of change of subject.

'More trouble down in New Orleans, I see. Those roughneck frontiersmen are making a nuisance of themselves again. Mark my words, that Spanish Governor Salcedo will do something about it soon. He won't put up with it much longer.' Heads nodded. 'And when he does do something I can guess who he'll do it to.'

A senior member of the post-luncheon gathering who had sat silent during the gay repartee, not being of a frivolous nature, harrumphed loudly. This signal being given, a polite silence fell. They acknowledged that the time had come for the serious-minded member to hold forth on his favourite topic, the failure of the Government to support, promote, or protect the interests of business and businessmen. Businessmen were, when all was said and done, at the heart of the economy and therefore the backbone of the nation.

'Gentlemen.' He paused to look about him to be sure he had the floor free of any possible interruption. 'We all know the Mississippi is our main highway.' Nods and murmurs of agreement. 'And we also know that if Governor Salcedo squeezes us in New Orleans then we're in trouble, gentlemen, big trouble.' Hmms, ahs, and yes indeeds. The serious-minded member, feeling he had sufficiently conquered his audience with his opening salvo, settled down for a long occupation. 'Without tax-free warehousing in New Orleans how is the South to get its exports on to Europe-bound merchantmen at a price that would turn a profit? Once forced to pay taxes for warehousing in New Orleans, gentlemen, what we get is not profit but loss. Yes sir, loss.' Suppressed murmurs of agreement with at least two stifled yawns as the serious-minded member began to hit his stride. 'Why, if that damned Spaniard taxes our storage facilities we might as well shut up shop. And mark my words, it's our tax privileges Salcedo will have his eyes on. He'll use these roughnecks, real or imaginary, to get them. Yes, gentlemen, I think I speak for all of us, indeed for all honest businessmen up and down the Mississippi, when I say …'

Sadly the gathering was denied the wisdom of what he, on behalf of all honest businessmen up and down the Mississippi, was about to say because his throat, drying from sudden oratory, commenced a coughing fit. Port wine was poured and handed to him. But as he drank the tide of comment flowed away from his shores and conversation became general.

'Why don't the Government do something, damn them? What good are they sitting in their fine new capital, Washington? They talk a great deal, I dare say ...'

'And what they talk about is more of their new taxes ...'

'They push plenty of paper around but they do damn little.'

'And well paid to do that damn little by new taxes on our trade.'

'But when it comes to looking after that trade and protecting trade from foreigners, we hear little enough. As for action we see nothing, gentlemen, not a damn thing.'

'Haven't they got the wit to control a few roughnecks? Isn't trade bad enough with the war in Europe? But I guess you're right, trade isn't important to them, only taxes and politics, their eternal damn politics.'

'Gentlemen,' the serious-minded senior member had revived at last. Saved by an admittedly inferior port he now made a strong sally to regain the oratorical high ground. Silence settled, if somewhat sullenly.

'If we lose our rights in New Orleans we lose cotton. And if we lose cotton we lose half our economy. If we can't get the cotton out then, dammit, how are we to pay for the slaves to be got in? Already there's lily-livered abolitionists here in the North trying to hedge cotton around with dangerous and, yes I will say it, gentlemen, almost treasonous restrictions. Don't honest businessmen have to get the basic labour necessary for their trade? That's what we call economics, gentlemen, hard-headed economics. Not namby-pamby, addled clap-trap.'

Cotton-owning heads nodded, while others maintained a reserved silence.

'Slavery is as old as time, the black man was made for slavery. Why it's Biblical gentlemen, positively Biblical. I don't say this just because I'm in cotton. You all know I'm in cotton. I'm proud to be in cotton because what's good for cotton is good for America and what I always say is ...'

Alas, the indifference of the port told. What the serious-minded member always said was lost to another violent fit of coughing which turned his face a little more the colour of the port he was again offered.

'Gentlemen,' another voice quickly took the vacant floor, 'whether your business is here in the North or down South these are troubled times, war in Europe and divisions at home. I have no particular stand on slavery but facts are facts. No slaves means no cotton, and without cotton half an economy is what we'll be left with.'

'There's serious talk the British are finally turning against slavery altogether. Not just the trading, mind, but the owning of slaves.'

'Madness, sir, pure madness. It can't be done.'

'Madness perhaps, but ten years ago abolition lost in their House of Commons by eighty votes. Five years ago it lost by four. Don't tell me, gentlemen, that there's not a strong enough movement in the British Parliament to abolish the trade in slaves across their Empire. And if the trade goes then slavery itself soon follows.'

'Never, sir, never. Why a world without slaves, well it cannot be a civilised world ...'

But if business dominated these luncheon gatherings, scholarship was not altogether lacking. An educated cough brought a grudging but respectful pause. Learning wished to speak.

'The problem with slavery, gentlemen, is that it has become symbolic of what some are choosing to call "The Rights of Man". In doing so it sets business, or as our esteemed friend would have it, economics, against religion ...'

'Then damn all religion ...'

'Oh no, sir, not all religion. Just those misguided few who believe that this fallen state of ours can be made perfect on this earth by our own efforts. They're idealists and of course one admires their ideals. But here on earth, gentlemen, history teaches we must deal with life as we find it. That means allowing that the Devil will always be somewhere at work in men's affairs. And when that particular gentlemen gets involved then certain niceties, which we may all admire, must be foregone. As for the rights and wrongs of slavery, I can do no better than quote The Declaration of Independence, on which this great new country first took its stand as a nation. We all know and love those words, "that all men are created equal, that they are endowed, by their Creator, with certain unalienable Rights, that among these are Life, Liberty, and the pursuit of Happiness" ...'

'If you have a point, sir, damn well make it. This isn't a school room nor yet a lecture hall.'

'I will, sir, I will.' But, having observed the fate of business, scholarship paused to take a drink of wine before continuing. 'If we are to deal with the question of slavery ...'

'No question to deal with, sir. Always have been slaves, always will. Stands to reason.'

'Quite, but as I was saying, let us look at the Declaration. Are slaves, black men and women, who are traded like cattle, to be considered as endowed by God, like you and I, with unalienable rights?'

'Good point sir. Well made point.'

'Biblical, gentlemen, positively Biblical.'

'And mark the words that follow. "That to secure these rights, Governments are instituted among Men, deriving their just powers from ..." pause for emphasis, "... the consent of the governed". Gentlemen I ask you, as men of business and of sense, are slaves among the governed? Do they vote? Are they free citizens like you or I? Or are they property?'

'Well taken, sir.'

'Might as well give a cow the vote and call it free.'

Laughter.

'Good point, sound reasoning.'

'Do they participate in and contribute to the political life of the country, gentlemen, as we all do? I think not, gentlemen, I think not.'

A dissenting voice intruded.

'Clever words, perhaps, but what the hell has it to do with the matter in hand, sir?'

'Only this. Businessmen may talk economics and governments write declarations but the cloven hoof will be there, gentlemen. Anyone who thinks otherwise need look no further than Santo Domingo.'

A silence fell and a hushed voice murmured.

'Aye, Toussaint L'Ouverture.'

This brought a short, worried pause as heads nodded.

The scholar continued.

'Toussaint L'Ouverture indeed. No slavery has been his cry one way or another for many a year. He pushed the British out and he's pushed the French out and what we now have in our own backyard is no less than a Black Republic with him at its head.'

'I heard he's declared himself Dictator for life.'

'Aye, that's what I heard.'

'What isn't perhaps so well known, gentlemen, is that for some years he has been hand in glove with Hamilton and the Federalists. He has signed trade treaties as an independent ruler with both America and Britain, secret treaties giving him recognition and power.'

'But if blacks can have a Republic, why then, dammit, what next?'

'Just so, gentlemen, and as I said, hand in glove with the Federalists as well as the British. Fine bedfellows are they not?'

With the subject finally back to politics the mood changed once again and the scholar sat back, well pleased with the reaction his words had produced.

'So what are you saying? Hamilton and the Federalists have been in league with the British against American interests?'

'What about Adams? Is he in this as well?'

'Is it treason we're talking here?'

At this bold and dangerous question the scholar's enthusiasm for the subject promptly expired with a gasp of fear, alarmed at the forces his oratory had unleashed.

'Oh, no. I don't think, gentlemen, my observations and deductions should bear quite that interpretation. No, no, I could not go quite so far as that.'

'And it would be a black lie if anyone said it was true of any of them.' One of their number had stood up and looked around fiercely. 'They disagree, as politicians do. But they're true Americans and patriots, and I'll back that opinion with pistols or swords any time anyone cares to question it.'

Passions rose at this challenge. Tempers were ready to flare and sides were on the brink of being taken. For a moment violence threatened. Then a calm voice asked, 'What about that place the Sierra Leone Company set up in West Africa? Freetown wasn't it? A settlement for freed slaves who fought for the British in the war.

That means something, I venture. If the British have paid someone to make provision for some of their freed slaves it certainly looks like they've turned against slavery.'

Another equally calm voice took up the question and poured more oil on the troubled waters.

'Aye, sir, but they've put them back on the slave coast, where they came from in the first place. Putting them there is just putting them back into someone else's slave boats.'

'Seems to me a damned funny way to deal with men who've fought your wars for you.'

'Not so, sir. Twice sold goods means twice gained profits. Damn clever the British, and good at business. I've always said so.'

The general laughter at these sallies broke the danger. The fierce man looked round defiantly but, encountering no opposition, sat down and the talk resumed.

'I guess one way or another slavery's going to be an issue whether we like it or not.'

The minds of the men in the room concentrated on the awful implications of a world where the free transport of slaves no longer existed. With an almost superhuman effort and a long pull at his port the serious-minded member harrumphed himself to the floor again. This time, considering the vast import of the topic under discussion, he was determined to hold it.

'Half an economy, gentlemen, as I was saying, is no damned economy at all. What we need to consider is this war. France looks strong, I admit, but France won't save cotton. They've lost out in the Caribbean and won't be in a hurry to return. If it wasn't for their incomprehensible stance on the slavery issue I might be inclined to say we should consider some sort of agreement with the British.'

But a sudden flank movement caught him unawares.

'Aye, but will they win this war or lose it? Last year when the Austrians pulled out I thought we were getting somewhere.'

'Gentlemen, what I say is …' But it was too late. Let your flank once be turned and, as every strategist knows, you quickly lose the battle. The talk turned to Europe, the war and the politics of war. Slavery and cotton had been dealt with and were now finished. The general feeling emerged that it was good to see England on its own

17

at last. Now, if Napoleon really put his mind to it, the whole thing could be finished off and trade could resume. They had lunched well and the port and Madeira wine had circulated freely, sharpening further their already finely honed minds. The conversation became optimistic. Admittedly the British had done better than expected. But they couldn't go on alone.

'I give them six months, a year at the outside. Then the Mad German and his foppish prince of a son will be back home in Hanover happy to have their heads still on their shoulders.'

'And then things can get back to normal.'

'And Napoleon will be in London telling their damned Parliament what to do and how to do it.'

There was laughter, then a pause as each of them looked at the brighter future they had at last talked themselves into. Finally a voice observed,

'The British Republic. Now there's a thing I'd like to see, gentlemen. That Union Flag of theirs flying over the Republican Union of Great Britain.'

And the room was again full of laughter.

Chapter Four

Euan Macleod had been an astute man of business but also a man careful of his social position so, when the part of Boston Common bounded by Tremont Street and surrounding the old Granary burying ground was sold off, Euan bought and built. The result was a fine town house, a befitting monument to a man at the forefront of Boston commerce.

The house now stood, shuttered and silent, day and night, to all intents and purposes closed up and empty. What few rooms were occupied looked out over the Burying Ground and had been chosen by Macleod for that very reason.

That night, as he did every night, Lawyer Macleod sat in the library reading. The heavy curtains were drawn but could only muffle the sound of wind and rain hammering on the windows. Inside the room a tallcase clock ticked solemnly in the gloom, its hands nearing eleven. A lamp stood on a table by the side of his high-backed chair. It was turned low and its weak light struggled against the pervading gloom. Beside it was a heavy glass tumbler and a decanter, both of which held a dark golden liquid. Macleod was wearing a thick dressing gown with a woollen night-cap pulled down over his ears. On his hands were woollen fingerless gloves. His chair and the chair opposite him were positioned to take advantage of the large, elegant fireplace, designed for a fire the warmth and light from which would have touched even the remotest corners of such a large room. The seating arrangement was left over from his father's days when the main rooms in the house were often full of warmth and laughter and Euan and his wife would sit of an evening talking together or reading.

Macleod had changed nothing in the big house but had closed up most of the rooms, the furniture dust-sheeted and the windows permanently shuttered. No fires ever burned now in the elegant fireplaces. In the library the dusty books mouldered on their shelves. A fine set of brass fire-irons kept a useless vigil in the fireplace and a well-worked fire-screen stood in a permanent melancholy of disuse at their side.

Macleod read on grimly, an old blanket over his legs and his shabbily slippered feet kept from the cold floor by a small, threadbare footstool. He paused his reading only to take a drink or to refresh his glass. To an observer, had there been one, the scene could have passed for that of a more than usually close-fisted miser with a weakness for books and whisky. He was forty-four years old but his face looked older and carried the marks of suffering.

His book was *A Defence of the Constitutions of Government of the United States of America Against The Attack of M. Turgot in his Letter to Dr. Price, dated the Twenty Second of March 1778* written by John Adams. When that was done there would be others of a similar stamp, for Macleod's choice of reading was governed by a simple rule. The work should be dry, difficult and complex so that his mind, while struggling with abstruse arguments, constructed around complex political ideas, had its hands full and therefore had no time to slip into any thoughtfulness or memory.

He paused in his reading. The doorbell had been rung. He waited. It rang again – a persistent visitor. He waited again, and eventually the bell rang a third time. A very persistent visitor, and one who chose to call at such a late hour and in such weather. But he dismissed the matter from his mind. The cook-housekeeper would answer the door, although she wouldn't be in any hurry to do so. If the visitor cared to wait he would find out soon enough what it was all about. Macleod returned to his book.

Lawyer Macleod's French cook-housekeeper was the only servant now and was slow from necessity of age and from inclination of temperament. She had been with his family many years, brought from Paris as maid to his mother on her marriage. Macleod didn't know how old she was and he was sure that she herself had stopped counting a long time ago. However, it was not because of her age alone that she never hurried to answer the door. It was because she nursed a deep and rooted dislike of everyone. Amélie took pleasure now in only two things, making herself disagreeable to the few visitors who came to see the lawyer, and cooking badly for her master, neither of which bothered Macleod. He hardly noticed what he ate and, as far as visitors were concerned, anyone who wanted to see him at home had to put up with waiting for Amélie to open the door. Everyone knew that if you didn't like waiting then Lawyer Macleod wouldn't give a tinker's curse whether you stayed or went. The office was the place for business, home was the place for family and friends and, as Lawyer Macleod had no family and didn't want any friends, he expected and got very few visitors. After some time the cook walked unhurriedly into the library carrying a lamp, she crossed the room and threw a visiting card on the table.

'Un homme. Il attend dans la rue.'

'Mais il pleut. Pourquoi dans la rue?'

Amélie shrugged.

'Pourquoi pas?'

Macleod didn't really care if his visitor was waiting in the street and it was raining. It was just a response made from habit. He knew from experience any discussion of anything with Amélie ended up in some maddeningly inconsequential way. Amélie stood waiting. Macleod knew she could speak English well enough if she wanted to. But he also knew she never wanted to, so he picked up the thick, gold-edged card and read the name. Cedric Bentley. He knew Bentley well. They had served together several times in the army. Now Macleod acted as his business lawyer. Bentley had large holdings in cotton, interests in one or two of the newer newspapers in Massachusetts and fingers in numerous other lucrative pies. He was an important man who had powerful business and political connections. He had hinted to the lawyer that he and some friends were preparing something new and big, very big indeed. Knowing Bentley and knowing that cotton money was having to find new investments because of the European war, Lawyer Macleod had guessed it would be armaments. There was good money in mass destruction and there was going to be a lot more. More than in cotton, even when the European business was finished and trade picked up. Bentley was a good client and soon he would be a better one. Macleod spoke to the old cook in fluent French with the Paris accent he had picked up from her and his mother.

'Send him in and then stay out of the way.'

Amélie left the study muttering. Macleod only caught the words she fully intended he should catch, 'cochon', 'idiot', and 'merde'. He looked at the card and thought about the visit. On

21

those very rare occasions when Bentley chose to call at his home rather than his office it was to give him instructions which were of such a private nature that any office, even Macleod's, could not be considered sufficiently secure. But such visits were not usually conducted at night. Why the lateness of the hour and, just as strange, why an unarranged meeting? Macleod was intrigued.

Bentley came into the library and crossed the room into the light of Macleod's lamp. He was a man of similar age to the lawyer but, unlike him, his bearing and clothes announced his wealth and position. He was not only a successful man of business, he was a man of fashion which, in Boston society, was much the more important of the two. Macleod stood up and they shook hands. He offered no apology for the wait in the rain his guest had suffered. This was his home and here he did things entirely to suit himself, even if it was business.

'Sit down, Bentley,' he gestured to the chair on the other side of the fireplace on the edge of the light. Bentley sat down and rubbed his gloved hands at the cold in the library. He put his hat on the floor by his chair but he kept his wet top-coat on and buttoned up. He looked at the whisky on the table at Macleod's elbow. He would have preferred brandy but on such a cold, wet night even a glass of Macleod's whisky would be welcome. He waited, still rubbing his hands to emphasise his need for a glass of something warming. Macleod replaced the blanket round his legs, put his feet onto his footstool and looked impassively at his unbidden guest. Giving up on any hospitality, Bentley took off his gloves, dropped them onto his hat and gestured at the lamp.

'Turn that up, Macleod, there's no need for us to peer at each other through such gloom is there?' Macleod reached out and turned up the lamp. Why not? A few cents for extra oil would go on Bentley's regular bill. 'Damn me, man, why no fire in here? It's cold enough for Valley Forge.'

'As I remember you were never at Valley Forge and neither was I, so I can't say one way or another. You chose to call, Bentley, you weren't invited, so you must take me as you find me.' Macleod took out a large handkerchief and blew his nose long and loudly. Having made his point, that it was Bentley who wanted to speak to Macleod and not the other way round, he continued. 'It's you and your friends' new business I suppose?'

'No, not the new business, at least not in any way you might think.'

'You and your friends not ready then?'

'Not yet, not quite yet, but soon I think, perhaps quite soon. No this is something local, not what you'd call business at all.'

'Well then, if it's not business it can be nothing to me. Outside of business our lives don't touch and I don't care that they should. I'm not a social man as you well know and I don't care to have friends, old or new.'

Bentley was never comfortable talking to Macleod and especially so if it wasn't straight business talk, but he composed himself as best he could and began.

'You know young Darcy?'

'I know him well enough to know he's a third-rate lawyer and a first-rate fool. There's no point in knowing any more because he'll soon be hightailing it back to the Carolinas or wherever it is down South the nincompoop hails from.'

'Savannah. He's from Savannah.'

'The Carolinas, Savannah, the moon. What is it to me where he comes from?'

Bentley paused, then leaned forward and spoke slowly and deliberately.

'He's found out about the French Girl.' He saw Macleod stiffen slightly and allowed himself an inner smile. 'But you're not to kill him. Understand? You're not to kill him.'

Chapter Five

The French Girl was back again, back to haunt him, back to drive him, back to ruin what little peace of mind was left to him.

If Macleod's maternal grandfather had not been French, he might have lived a very different life, perhaps even a normal one.

Claude Vernier was a successful merchant who had moved from Paris to Edinburgh. Being an ambitious and clever man, he had looked across the Atlantic eager to enter the growing and lucrative markets of America. But he had two problems, a daughter, Françoise, and a wife, Clotilde. The daughter needed a husband and the wife insisted he should be Catholic. Finding a suitable son-in-law in Protestant Edinburgh had been a particular headache for Monsieur Vernier. It was not that he was at all devout. He was not. But, as his wife was devout enough for both of them, his own lack of piety was of no consequence. The problem was that his wife constantly nagged him to return to Paris so that Françoise should be found a Catholic husband, not some Protestant who would stand damned for all eternity at the altar even as he made his wedding vows.

The very last thing Vernier wanted was to go back to France for an extended stay. Thus it was that the pretty and pious Françoise was introduced to Monsieur Macleod, a young man Vernier had taken into his firm and watched carefully. Monsieur Macleod had a talent, perhaps even a genius, for business and, as his son-in-law, would be the perfect choice to launch the American development. As he was also a Catholic, Françoise was persuaded to overlook the drawback of his features and finally to concede, albeit reluctantly, to his proposal of marriage. Thus it came to pass that Euan Macleod acquired a bride, a partnership and a rich father-in-law.

And Euan Macleod fully lived up to his father-in-law's expectations and was indeed sent to establish offices in the American Colonies. And so it was that in 1758 the first, and as it transpired, the only child of Euan and Françoise Macleod was born in Boston and baptised Jean Marie Macleod. The naming of his son had been a gesture of thanks by Euan to his father-in-law for giving him a future in the New World so very different from that of the rest of his family in the Old. For Euan was a true-born Highlander who had rallied to the head of Loch Shiel in '45 and fought with the Bonnie Prince's army from Prestonpans to Falkirk. But after Falkirk, he had thrown away his claymore and shield and left the two of his five brothers who had survived that ill-fated campaign to die with what was left of the flower of the Highlands in the blood-soaked turf of Culloden Moor. He had walked to Protestant Edinburgh and there lived, thrived and married.

The birth of a son two years after their arrival in Boston crowned Euan's ambitions for success in business and society in his adopted country. It also allowed Françoise Macleod, for the first time in her marriage, to experience love, to feel a deep, warm affection rather than the cold satisfaction of a duty done. The baby was as lovingly tended as any baby could be both by his mother and her young French maid, Amélie. Amélie had been brought from Paris by Françoise's mother as soon as it had been arranged that the couple would sail for the Colonies. She had done this so that, even far away across the Atlantic, French would be spoken in the Macleod home and France, though far away, would not be forgotten.

Amélie, on arrival in Edinburgh, had at once proceeded to adore her mistress as an almost divine being while at the same time determining to detest Britain with an unrestrained loathing. Scottish Britain, English Britain, perfidious Britain, it mattered to Amélie not at all. Her lady was for France, for Paris, yes even for Versailles and the Court itself, and why not? Madame was not for this cold uncivilised place. She expressed her contempt by speaking nothing but French and it was a moot point, first in the Vernier household in Edinburgh and then in the Macleod household in Boston, whether Amélie wouldn't or couldn't speak English. If Amélie had loathed Edinburgh, she regarded Boston, indeed all America, as the innermost ring of hell itself. Britain at least was not so far from France, but America, mon Dieu, one might as well be on the moon. And where were the nobility in this wilderness? Where were the châteaux and grand houses fit for her

Madame to grace with visits? America was 'le barbarisme'. Only La France was for her Madame and, in France, only Paris and the best society. The truth was that Amélie had lived her day-dreams in a fantasy Paris, but when Jean Marie was born Amélie forgot her dreams and joined her mistress in a deep and unreserved love for the child, and as the baby became a boy he grew to be as happy as any child could be throughout his early years.

As he grew, it became clear that young Jean Marie was indeed a favoured child. He had inherited his father's cleverness and his mother's good looks. By the age of ten he had been given a thorough education in his family histories, French as well as Highland. He knew that all English, Lowland Scots, and German Protestants should be at least despised and at best hated and killed. He also knew that God spoke French and was a good Catholic.

All of this deep learning he took with him when he left his mother and Amélie in tears and went away to school where he found how quickly and completely the world can be made a living hell for any little boy unlucky enough to have, as his first two names, Jean and Mary. It was at school that he quickly and permanently became 'The French Girl', the name Darcy had now discovered and found funny. Found it so funny indeed, that it would very probably turn out to be the death of him.

Chapter Six

Bentley sat and waited for the lawyer's reaction. Macleod's mind turned over slowly while Bentley looked at him. For Bentley it was a pleasure to watch Macleod thinking, he could almost see the well-oiled cogs turning. There would be no rush. He wouldn't betray any surprise if he felt it. And he would squeeze the pips out of what had been said and the way it had been said. Bentley knew Macleod's response would be a good one, whatever he said would put him in an advantageous position to find out more without giving anything away. Oh, he was a joy to watch was Lawyer Macleod. But Bentley couldn't wait indefinitely.

'You understand, Macleod, that whatever happens, whatever he may say or whatever comes to your ears, you're not to kill him.'

And he waited once more but this time the wait was very short and when Macleod spoke, it was in a casual, matter-of-fact voice.

'Then I won't kill him.'

That was it. And Bentley knew Macleod had turned the tables on him. He couldn't leave it at that because that would leave him nowhere, and he couldn't afford to be left nowhere. Bentley almost permitted himself a wry smile. Macleod was certainly some piece of work, yes sir, Lawyer Macleod was some piece of work. Carefully Cedric Bentley proceeded.

'And you'll give me your word on that?'

'Yes, you can have my word.'

Too easy, much too easy. What next? Bentley waited.

'On your oath?'

'You can have my private word, Bentley, and on oath if you like. Without witnesses, completely deniable, given to you at a meeting which I would guess no one else even knows about considering the lateness of the hour. For whatever you think it may be worth to you, you may have my sacred word.'

'Well, say at least you will honour your word as a gentleman?'

Lawyer Macleod smiled and said nothing. Damn, thought

Bentley, that was a stupid mistake and he couldn't afford to look stupid. Macleod might or might not have some kind of honour tucked away somewhere, but he had none where being a lawyer was concerned, and tonight, even though this was Macleod's home, he was very much the lawyer. Bentley knew that all he had done so far was show the weakness of his hand. Well, leave it alone or go on? Lawyer Macleod watched Bentley carefully. But what he did not know and could not have guessed was that Cedric Bentley was deciding whether Macleod would live or die.

Bentley had decided that he had only two options, bring Macleod in or snuff Macleod out. Tell him or kill him. It was his turn to take his time and think. Macleod waited, he was good at waiting. Bentley thought about his choices. Killing would do the job in a way, but maybe telling would do the job better. A clock ticked in the darkness of the room as the two men looked at each other in silence. Finally Bentley decided. The lawyer would live. Telling him it would be, and if tomorrow morning or any morning, having slept on it, he changed his mind, well, he could arrange for the lawyer to be dead quickly enough. But only if that would be the better course to get the job done.

'Darcy's somehow found out about the French Girl. He was laughing about it in the club this afternoon. This evening he was drinking heavily and started in on it among his friends, making sport of you. I thought he had been made to see sense after luncheon. He was told about how you dealt with it on your last two outings, but I guess he may have got bottle brave. He doesn't like you Macleod and it seems he couldn't resist the chance to do you a bad turn. I thought I'd tell you about it before someone else did and,' he paused, 'before you decided to do anything about it yourself.'

There was no reaction. Bentley had hoped for one, but nothing came. Inside, Lawyer Macleod was raging. Darcy laughing at him and making others laugh, the little shit. Well, others had thought he could be made the butt of their laughter so perhaps Darcy should join them and not go back down South after all. Perhaps he should be persuaded to become another permanent resident of Boston Common's Burying Ground.

But Macleod made sure that nothing of his thoughts showed and when he spoke it was as if Bentley had said that it had been a nice day.

'Thank you for telling me.'

'Not at all. My concern was not for you and not particularly for Darcy. My concern springs from something more important than any duel or any death, yours or Darcy's. I will not allow you to kill Darcy because it is my duty, duty to my country, duty to America.'

At last, thought Bentley, the man had been reached. Macleod had looked almost surprised. It had only flashed across his face, maybe his eyebrows had risen, maybe his eyes had widened, maybe his lips had moved. But however small and however fleeting, it had been there. Bentley had reached into the man and knew he had scored a hit. They were back on level terms now. No, he was on top. With men like Macleod it was all or nothing. Let there be only one tiny crack in their fine façade and they would break wide open.

'For America?'

The calm voice was there, the set face was there, the unconcerned body was there. But it was all no good now. Macleod might look the same but he wasn't thinking the same. Now he wanted to know, he needed to know. It wasn't business any more. Maybe, thought Bentley, just maybe I've found a place where honour might mean something to this man, and honour in any man meant weakness, and weakness could always be used.

'Before I tell you anything of that, I need to be sure that you won't kill Darcy, no matter what he knows or says.'

Lawyer Macleod thought for a moment. He knew Bentley now had the upper hand.

'If Darcy has a slack mouth he must expect to pay for it. Business is business. If the Darcys of this world try to make fools of their betters they must be stepped on, and stepped on hard. Who could say what it might lead to if the likes of Darcy were allowed to play fast and loose with men of standing and be seen to get away with it? Would you still want to be seen doing business with me, Bentley, if I didn't stop Darcy's mouth? If I let people see he could walk all over me?'

Bentley knew that the lawyer was now his. Macleod wasn't talking, he was negotiating because he knew he was beaten. All that was left was to try and get the best terms he could. Well, thought Bentley, no harm in that, and maybe it was all for the best. After all, he wanted Macleod in one piece and working well. Yes, maybe it was better that way. If he made it too hard for him, perhaps even broke him, what use would he be? Bentley took his time. He knew now that he could afford to.

Bentley reflected. Macleod was right about Darcy in one way. Darcy was no good as a lawyer. But that was all right because within six months, a year at the most, he could stop playing at being one. Bentley was pleased that his little bit of theatre had so completely taken in someone as sharp as Lawyer Macleod. Bentley's mind turned to another matter. Darcy alive, yes, but what about Darcy with a neat hole in him? Nothing fatal of course, just a neat hole. That might be no bad thing, no bad thing at all, and it could kill two birds with one stone. If Macleod could be made to wound Darcy to order, in a duel say, it would prove that he had Macleod just where he wanted him. Secondly it would make a point to Darcy. Bentley knew that Darcy had been jockeying for a better position in the matter of the new business venture, and Darcy might indeed be the fool Macleod rated him if he had thought he could keep his little intrigue a secret. Yes, that would all fit together nicely. Macleod would put a hole in Darcy and afterwards Bentley would visit him and make it quite clear that his little scheme was known and if he tried anything like it again the next pistol ball he took would be straight in the back of his head.

Macleod waited patiently. He knew Bentley was working out what he would demand and he was prepared to let him take his time. Negotiation, even on such an unimportant matter as the killing of a coxcomb, never benefited from being hurried. Bentley was nearly ready. He was considering the one final detail. A wounded Darcy was one thing, a dead Darcy was quite another. A dead Darcy would need to be replaced and that would take time and there wasn't time. Bentley's problem was, how good a shot was Macleod these days? Could he be relied upon to put a hole in Darcy in the right place, the shoulder say, or the lung? Stomach wounds were unpredictable, anything might happen with a stomach wound. Could Macleod be relied upon to put a ball in Darcy without killing him? It was a tricky proposition.

'A wound perhaps? What if you just wounded him?'

'Shoot a man in the body and he can die just as surely as shooting him in the head. It may take longer and be more painful that's all. You saw that as much as I in the war. Men brought in with wounds that looked nothing at all and they were screaming in days and dead in a week. Others came in with their legs blown off and finished up with stumps, but alive. If I kill him I'll make it clean.'

'What about a chest shot? A ball in the lung can be dealt with,' he paused, 'especially if the doctor's ready for it.' He continued in a matter of fact way. 'It's amazing what doctors can do these days compared with twenty years ago. Why, Professor McDonald told me only the other day that he is quite sure that one day they will find a way of controlling even things like smallpox. It's just theory of course and, between you and me, it'll never happen. He was just talking things up and trying to get a donation out of me for his research. But he's right in one way. They can do things now that would have seemed miracles when you and I were soldiering.' Bentley thought for a moment and then an idea struck him. Oh my, he loved it when things came together. Yes sir, he just loved it. 'In fact, if McDonald was persuaded to be the doctor at the duel and he was told that the likely outcome was a chest or shoulder wound, I do believe he'd be just the man to make sure no lasting damage was done. If McDonald could have a wounded man up and about before too long, not fully mended of course, but maybe able to travel, why I might believe he was just the sort of medical man I should be making a fair-sized donation to. When I have confidence in a man I'm prepared to back that confidence with cold cash. Yes indeed, a donation and a handsome one.'

Macleod became impatient of Bentley's rambling and broke into his visitor's monologue.

'Well, man, what's it to be?'

Bentley's voice was flat and firm. He leant forward.

'A chest shot.'

It was his final offer and Macleod knew it. It was Bentley's turn to sit back and wait now. He, like Macleod, fully accepted that negotiations needed time to reach a conclusion satisfactory to both parties. The lawyer's brain turned. If Darcy really was important to the American Government he couldn't kill him. But was he important? He knew Bentley had powerful friends and not a few connections in or close to the Government. So far as he knew, Bentley had no personal or business reasons for protecting Darcy. But Darcy had to be stamped on. Perhaps Bentley's suggestion had merit. Duels were frowned on now, and a killing, even an honour killing, could become a messy business if it became too public.

'It'll only work if he shoots face on. It's no good if he stands sideways to fire.'

'Why?'

'Because if he's standing face on when my ball goes into his chest it will either go through him or lodge and if he's lucky it won't cause any real problem. But if he's side on it could go through the lung and maybe go on to hit his heart or some vital artery. I couldn't say where it might finish nor that it wouldn't be fatal.'

Bentley considered.

'And there's no way round that? Couldn't you reduce the charge, lessen the penetration?'

Macleod laughed dismissively.

'Have you forgotten everything you were ever taught in the army, man? If I reduce the charge enough to do that it would mean loss of accuracy, and if the ball strayed it might go anywhere. Hell, it might hit him on that thick head of his and bounce off and then the fool might even get a shot at me. No, the only sure way is for him to stand face on. Do you know if he has fought a duel with pistols before?'

Bentley shook his head.

'No, but I would doubt very strongly that he has.'

'Then he'll almost certainly stand side on, it's the natural stance for shooting. Only duellists stand front on. If they get hit they want the ball to lodge or go through.'

'And if he stood face on you could do it, for sure?'

Macleod threw the blanket off his legs and kicked the footstool to one side. He pulled off his night-cap, threw it down onto the blanket and stood up.

'Come, I'll let you judge for yourself.'

Macleod picked up the lamp from the table and led the way out of the library. They went through a door under the main staircase and down some stone steps. Below the house was a large cellar that had once been, among other things, the wine store, but now had been converted into a shooting gallery. Macleod put the lamp on a table, took off his dressing gown and hung it on a hook in the wall, lit a taper, then walked around the cellar lighting lamps set on the walls. He returned to the table and began to prepare a pistol. He nodded to a box on the table amongst the bits and pieces. It was about six inches by four and two inches deep. It contained flints.

'Empty that box and take it down to the other end of the gallery.'

Bentley looked at the box then at Macleod.

'What for?'

'This is business, Bentley, so think like a businessman. If I tell you I can hit Darcy in the chest and not kill him, are you just going to take my unsupported word for it?'

Bentley understood Macleod's point.

'I guess not.'

They both knew there was only one way to be sure.

'Then take the box.'

Bentley picked up the box, emptied out the flints, then walked slowly down the gallery. When he turned, the distance between them was about the same as in a duel and Lawyer Macleod was already pointing his pistol at him. Bentley felt a cold sweat form on his brow. No one knew of his visit to Macleod's house and Macleod had already guessed that was the case. There was no one in the house except that idle old French cook and even if she wasn't deaf he was sure she would be loyal. Darcy may have been a fool to think he could outmanoeuvre me, thought Bentley, but I must be a bigger fool to put myself so easily at the wrong end of Macleod's pistol. Macleod was pointing the pistol and waiting. On the other hand, thought Bentley, if Macleod was going to kill me I would be dead already. He was sure Macleod wouldn't have had any scruple about shooting him in the back. He called out.

'What now?'

'Put the box somewhere, on your shoulder or on your head.' Macleod smiled. Bentley thought it a nasty smile. 'Why not hold it between your legs, just under your crotch?' The smile widened to a grin, 'Anywhere you feel comfortable.'

This is a damn fine time to find out that the bastard has a sense of humour, thought Bentley, and placed the box carefully on his left shoulder leaning slightly over to his right so that it balanced. It wasn't an easy thing to do under the circumstances. And if Macleod isn't still the shot he was in the army it wasn't supposed to be me who would suffer any consequences.

Bentley looked back down the gallery and called out. 'I hope you haven't lost …'

But the sound of the pistol firing exploded through the cellar and pounded into Bentley's ears. The box was gone and he could see Macleod's mouth moving but, whatever he was saying, Bentley could only hear a loud ringing inside his head. He saw the lawyer removing two small pieces of wadding from his ears. Then Macleod pointed with the pistol at something behind Bentley on the floor. Bentley turned and looked down. On the floor behind him at the bottom of the cellar wall was the box. There was a neat hole in it, almost in the middle. He couldn't hear himself as he said, 'Damn and blast the Scottish bastard, that surely was some shot.' As he walked back down the gallery the ringing began to subside and by the time he was at the table where the lawyer was cleaning his pistol his hearing had almost returned to normal.

'I guess you could call it a hobby. I pistol shoot targets down here.' Macleod looked around the cellar. 'Sometimes I buy a caged bird and let it out to see if I can hit it on the wing. It's something to pass the time.' Macleod took his dressing gown off its hook and put it on. 'Now, shall we go back to the library and you can tell me what all this is about?'

Bentley nodded and waited while Macleod snuffed out the lights, picked up his lamp and left the shooting gallery.

Bentley followed well pleased with the evening. Yes, he would tell Macleod. He would tell him just enough to get the job done, but he certainly wouldn't tell him what this was all about.

Chapter Seven

Macleod once more sat alone in the library with the blanket back round his legs but the night-cap ignored on the floor and the footstool still where he had kicked it. He was looking blindly into the empty fireplace thinking of what Bentley had told him, trying to make some sense of it. Amélie came in, went to the table and picked up the empty decanter. She turned to leave. Macleod stopped her.

'No more tonight.' He wanted another decanter very much, but he also wanted a head clear enough to think about what Bentley had told him. Unfortunately he knew he couldn't have both. Amélie shrugged. She was well used to his late-night drinking. Lawyer Macleod hadn't gone to bed stone cold sober above a dozen times since his return to Boston at the end of the war. 'Did you hear me and M'sieur Bentley shooting in the gallery, Amélie?'

'I never hear anything. Perhaps I am deaf.'

Macleod smiled as Amélie left, then drank the whisky that was still in the glass.

To the world at large Lawyer Macleod must have seemed the embodiment of temperance. He had never been known to partake of any alcohol, no wine, no spirits, nor even ale. But in his own home at night, however, he felt free to seek some peace through fiery Scottish Highland malt whisky. But tonight's visit would make little sense if reflected upon through a haze of whisky fumes.

So, Bentley *was* connected to the Government in some secret way and Darcy was connected to Bentley. Now he was connected to both of them, though what that connection might mean for him he wasn't sure. And to make things worse it looked like the French Girl was back in his life. Well, he had never really believed he would remain free of her for ever. At least now she was out in the open where he could deal with her. He held out his hands, extending the fingers. They were shaking.

Chapter Eight

Bentley stood by the fireplace resting his arm on the mantelpiece, looking with disdain at the young man slumped in the chair.

'Macleod was right, Darcy. You're a fool as well as a bad lawyer.'

Darcy sat in his chair feeling unwell. He felt sure it was the previous evening's dressed crab which had provided him with the nightmares, but it was the claret which had left him so very fragile. The way he felt, the last thing he wanted was Bentley haranguing him in his own rooms, especially at such an ungodly hour of the morning. It couldn't be more than ten at the most.

'Well, Bentley, blame my family, not me, for being in the law. They're so damned Puritan. They would insist on my making a choice so that they could put me to something and, as I couldn't possibly be a military man, the law seemed a preferable choice to medicine. God, if I hadn't accepted being a lawyer, the only thing left was to end up as a damned parson.' He pulled petulantly at his robe and looked miserably at his expensively slippered feet. 'As for being a fool, you wrote that part for me. If the actor's a fool, it's only because the writer chose to make him one.' When he looked up he saw that Bentley, sitting opposite him, was regarding him in a most unpleasant manner. Darcy decided he wasn't up to being defiant in his present condition. The dressed crab was still preying on his mind and his stomach was still protesting about the claret. 'Look here, Bentley, we both know that my lawyering is only a sham and will be over in a year at the most. So long as I have a few clients the charade will hold good. I'm not supposed to be doing it for the income, am I? I have my own money. I'm supposed to be playing the lawyer so as to have a reason to be here and move in Boston society. Isn't that what we agreed? I thought antagonizing Macleod would be all of a piece with the part I've been given. He's as sharp as I am shallow and it's well known that he thinks me a jumped-up nincompoop. It's good sense that I make him the butt of my humour among the younger set. That or something like it is just what they'd expect. Mind you it's so easy to dislike the dull block that I have to say it certainly isn't a hard part to play.' And Darcy surprised himself by managing a smile. Bentley shared the smile as he delivered the message which had been the reason for his early morning call.

'Well the dull block, as you call him, is going to come to the club this evening and call you out. And in two days' time he's going to put a pistol ball in you.'

Darcy's smile vanished.

'Call me out? For a mere nothing, a little laughter among friends at a silly name? Good God, Bentley, nobody duels any more and certainly not over a little private laughter. If he's mad enough to try it why, you can tell the authorities and have it stopped.'

'And ruin my reputation alongside yours?'

Bentley watched Darcy as his words sank in. He had not been a party to selecting Darcy for the role of courier between Boston, New Orleans and Washington. Darcy, he had been told, was New Orleans' choice, but he knew the decision had, in reality, been made by the men in Philadelphia. It had been a choice made by the political side of things rather than the business side. So much for the judgement of politicians. Well, things would be different when the dust finally settled, and politics and politicians could be firmly put in their place. Bentley had already quietly sounded out two or three from the business side and knew the direction things would take when the whole affair was satisfactorily completed. From the responses he had already received, he felt sure that some of the politicians who were currently so necessary would rapidly become redundant once things levelled out.

'You have two choices, Darcy. You can stay or you can run. If you stay Macleod will put a ball in you. If you refuse to fight you'll be dead in Boston in everything but name, and as useless to us as if you were dead in fact. If you run I promise you you'll have a ball in the back of your head before you're halfway to wherever it is you might be headed for. And you know I can make it happen. You know I've made it happen before.'

Darcy now looked really worried. He knew Bentley had made it happen before. He smiled weakly.

'Great heavens, Bentley, we're on the same side aren't we?'

'Are we? It all depends on whether you think having Macleod wound you is more of a consideration than the smooth running of our little bit of business.'

Darcy paused.

'Wound me?'

'Aye, wound you. Nothing fatal, nor even very dangerous. Macleod's an excellent shot and let's just say I feel I can persuade him to put a ball in you where it won't do any lasting harm.'

Darcy scented a resolution to his dilemma.

'But what if he doesn't just wound me? What if he drops me, or what if he puts me in hospital for months? I don't say I'm all that important in the grand scheme, but just at the moment I don't think I can be dispensed with altogether, or immobilised even for a few months. Bringing in someone new could jeopardise things, Bentley, even cause a fatal delay. If you allowed that to happen who's to say how far you would get before the ball was in the back of your own head? I may not be as familiar with our partners in this as you are but from what I've heard and seen they don't seem a particularly forgiving lot. And they make their feelings known in the most direct manner.'

Bentley smiled. Darcy was playing his hand too strongly. Trying to threaten showed the weakness of his position. What to do? He wanted Darcy frightened enough to go through with the duel and take the wound, but not so frightened, that he might cut and run at the last minute. He knew too little about Darcy to be sure about him. Was he just weak, or was he fatally weak? Bentley looked at him lounging in his chair looking half frightened, half insolent, his left hand in his robe pocket, his right arm resting on the arm of his chair and his fingers playing with a crystal goblet on a side table. Bentley turned over the question in his mind.

Darcy would never stand at the wrong end of Macleod's pistol. He would say that he would, but in the end he would run. Unfortunately, as he had pointed out, just at this particular time he was needed. Bentley leaned forward putting his right hand casually into his pocket.

'You're right-handed, are you not, Darcy?'

'What if I am? What's that got ...' but the enquiry was cut short. Bentley leaned forward and gripped Darcy's right wrist forcing his hand to the table. The glass Darcy had been holding smashed on the floor and the room filled with a scream as Bentley slammed down an open clasp knife pinning Darcy's hand to the table.

That first scream of pain was nothing, however, to the one which followed. Bentley's eyes held Darcy's as he slowly dragged Darcy's hand against the blade so that it cut through the flesh and came clear of the hand between the fingers.

Bentley released the screaming lawyer's wrist, pulled the clasp knife out of the table and casually lifted up the edge of Darcy's robe and cleaned the bloody blade before closing the knife and putting it back in his pocket. Then he sat back in his chair. Darcy was still screaming and looking in horror at Bentley, nursing his wounded hand with his sound one. The blood was flowing freely, staining his robe and dripping onto the carpet. There was a confused noise outside the room, then the door burst open and Darcy's manservant dashed in. He stopped dead when he looked at Darcy.

'My God, sir, what's happened?'

Bentley looked at the man calmly.

'Is this how you normally enter your master's room, all noise and shouting, without so much as knocking?'

Bentley's reproof, his calmness and his superior manner stopped the servant dead.

'But Mr Darcy, sir. He's wounded.'

'A slight graze. I'm sure it looks worse than it is. Just a lot of blood, making it look serious. It's nothing, not much more than a scratch really.' Darcy was still nursing his right hand in his left but whimpering now and giving an occasional terrified look at Bentley. 'He's just cut himself on a broken wine glass. Go and get some towels and hot water to clean him up and bring some bandages to bind the wound.' The man looked at Darcy then at Bentley. On the floor by the table there was indeed a broken glass but there was no sign of blood on it. 'Well, what are you waiting for, do you want the carpet totally ruined, man?'

The servant looked at the bloodstain on the carpet then turned and ran out. There was a pause while Bentley patiently waited until Darcy could finally manage speech.

'God, Bentley, what have you done to me?'

'I may just have saved your wretched life, Darcy, that's what I have done to you.' Bentley smiled a nasty smile. 'But you needn't thank me now. I see you're upset, although why you should make such a fuss over a mere scratch ...' Bentley stood up and walked to the fire where he put his hands behind him and pulled the tails of his coat apart and warmed himself. His manner when he spoke was as if he and Darcy were chatting to each other in the club. 'Dammit, Darcy, you're behaving as if you would have preferred to have a pistol ball in you. I assure you it would have been considerably more painful. I know. I've had more than one musket ball taken out of me. Damned painful, very damned painful indeed.' Darcy began whimpering again so Bentley returned to his chair, reached across and caught hold of the lapel of Darcy's robe. His voice now was hard, the voice of command. 'This is what has happened. We were laughing about something and you brought your hand down on a glass. It broke and you gave yourself a nasty cut. If anyone asks how it happened that's what I shall say, and it's what you shall also say.' Bentley let go of the robe and sat back. Darcy looked at him and slowly nodded. Bentley's club manner returned. He laughed. 'And if our fine duelling friend Macleod wants to call you out he can. But he can't expect satisfaction until your hand is fully mended and by that time I shall have arranged for lawyer Macleod to be elsewhere.'

The pain of the wound had not diminished and Darcy was still very frightened, but the point Bentley was making did not escape him. One day he would revenge himself on Bentley but he would never again underestimate him. When he spoke, his voice had in it nothing but subservience.

'I dare say you're right and I ought to thank you, but need you have been so extreme? Wouldn't a nick have served just as well?'

Bentley permitted himself a laugh.

'Perhaps, perhaps, but a nick would have had you fit to fight too quickly. It may take me some weeks to get Macleod far enough out of the way. Anyway, I must be allowed my own little bit of fun. I don't get to use my knife much these days and I wanted to see if the old skill still lingered.' Bentley leaned forward, there was still a smile on his lips but his eyes told another story. 'I was quick wasn't I, and you didn't see it coming?' The laughter died out of Bentley's eyes and suddenly there was no smile on his face. 'Just remember that, Darcy, for that's how it will be, quick, and you won't see it coming. I don't want anything from you except your total obedience, and if I don't get it, well, I'm sure I've made my point.'

The manservant returned and came into the room with a bowl of warm water and some towels and bandages. Bentley got up and went to the chaise-longue where he had thrown his coat, hat and gloves on his arrival.

'I'll take my leave now and let your man tidy you up.' He gave a short laugh. 'I daresay you won't be playing a great deal of cards with that hand. In fact you won't be doing much of anything with it for some weeks. Damn lucky for you you're a lawyer and do all your work with your head, eh, and have a clerk to do your scribbling? Yes, I think you could say you were damn lucky, Darcy, damn lucky indeed.'

Chapter Nine

The night following Bentley's violent visit to his friend Darcy found Macleod sitting in his library, complete with blanket and night-cap. He was not reading. No book was needed tonight to occupy his mind. He was drinking and steadily cursing the events of earlier that evening when he had been betrayed by Bentley and made to look a fool by Darcy. In a muttered but intense undertone he cursed them both until he found he could curse them no more. Moving on he cursed life in general but, feeling his choice of mark too impersonal for any real satisfaction, he changed to cursing the God he didn't believe in. However, he soon found a non-existent God as unsatisfactory as life in general and finally settled to cursing just about anything he could bring to mind. At last, having run out of things to curse, he drank his whisky and reviewed his life in silent fury.

Reviewing his life was a thing of last resort which he did when the hate inside him had swelled up and threatened to engulf his very sanity. On such occasions he knew that madness and even self-destruction were very near. It was as if they were in the shadows of the room waiting their chance in the darkness, looking at him, knowing his strength to hold them off was fading. His only hope at such times was to slowly confront his life, beginning with childhood and youth, passing on to manhood with its war and loss, and then his coming home to Boston and what, over the years, had passed for living. Such remembrances served a single vital purpose, they reminded him how the hate had been born, why it had thrived and blossomed, and at whom it must always be directed. In this way he was still just about able to force the hatred back into the black and terrible centre of his being.

He picked up his glass, took a long drink, gazed into the blackness of the fireplace and began in the same place that he always began, with the 'French Girl'.

It was that name, and all that he had endured because of it, which had turned the hate that the child Jean Marie had been taught by his father into a hate which was all his own. A hate that he felt burned into his very soul.

By the time Jean Marie's schooling was complete and he returned home for good, he was a solitary young man with few social graces and no social ambitions. He had learned much at school and been an able scholar but he held two things as the most valuable lessons of his education. First, that there were much worse things than physical pain. This lesson he had been taught as he fought with, and was at first badly beaten by, older, bigger pupils when he refused to submit to the name which they had given him, and with which they enjoyed taunting him. The lesson had stood him in good stead when he was older, stronger and with long experience of school brawling behind him. Very few times in his last two years at school did 'The French Girl' raise her head and when she did it was never Jean Mary Macleod who regretted it most.

The second lesson was that the only certain thing about friendship was that it would, sooner or later, be betrayed. How was the young Macleod to know that school friendships, the friendships of children, were no more a pattern for life than were the lessons in the classrooms? The school Macleod attended was considered to be one of the better sort and it showed itself deserving of its reputation. The Jean Marie Macleod who left school was thoroughly and singularly marked by his experiences there. The school could rightly claim to have had no small part in making Jean Marie Macleod into the man he would become.

Macleod's mind returned with a hazy jolt to the present, he wanted a drink and his glass was empty. He looked at the table. The empty decanter was gone and a full second decanter stood beside the lamp. Amélie had come and gone unnoticed. Macleod poured whisky into his glass, took a drink and slowly recited in his mind the formula he had laid out for himself.

'There is yourself, and there is your immediate family who can be trusted. Outside that there can be no trust worthy of the name. And as their most loving and merciful God has kindly chosen that I should no longer have any living family it seems divinely ordained that I shall be utterly alone in seeking out the path of my life.' And he made a fist and held it up and shook it and shouted in French.

'Thank you, oh most kind, loving and merciful God.'

He lowered his hand. He would trust in himself and, beyond that, only in his country, America.

But although railing at a God whose existence you doubted might give some temporary satisfaction, it was no more than a gesture. Any satisfaction it brought was at best fleeting. However it did serve one purpose. The explosion of sound into the gloom finally brought Macleod's anger under some sort of control. Now, with a cold calmness, he could reflect on what had happened earlier that evening.

He had promised Bentley he would wound Darcy in a duel and the deal had been struck. He had gone to the club to seek out his opponent and challenge him in public. Done before those men who mattered most in Boston, Darcy could not have wormed his way out of accepting. But he had been made to look a fool and it was all deliberately done, all planned by Bentley to humiliate him.

Darcy had carefully stood with his wounded hand behind his back when Macleod had come into the club room where he and his friends were drinking. Darcy had been expecting him, had known he was coming and what it was he was coming for. Darcy had only brought his hand from behind his back after Macleod had slapped his face in front of his friends and said he was ready to give satisfaction as and when Darcy cared to meet him. Darcy had then raised his bandaged hand and showed it to the room and finally held it in front of Macleod.

'Dam'me, Macleod, I dare say you feel very brave calling out a man who can't shoot you dead as you deserve. Would you have hurried here so quickly, I wonder, if someone hadn't told you that with this confounded hand I won't be able to put a ball in your wretched hide for at least a month?'

And Macleod remembered how he and his braying friends had laughed, stood there and laughed at him, as Darcy had gone on to warn him not to run off when he saw the bandage was ready to be removed and the day of satisfaction near at hand.

As Macleod had stormed out of the club the laughter had rung in his ears and he heard, as was no doubt it was intended, what Darcy had loudly declaimed. That he normally wouldn't dream of putting a ball into a nice French girl, but as soon as his hand was better he would, in this special case, make an exception.

Chapter Ten

'Well, Bentley, I hope you can be sure to get Macleod away from here within the month. After this evening's little play I wouldn't want him around when this bandage comes off and I can hold a pistol.'

Darcy held up his bandaged hand and Bentley laughed.

'I heard all about it and the whole town will know tomorrow. You certainly carried it off well enough. I congratulate you. For a coward you certainly seem to have cut a dashing figure.'

'More careful than coward I would say but I did the thing well enough. In fact I did it so damn well that Macleod won't cool down on it. He'll want his satisfaction the moment my hand is well, and if he gets it I guarantee that I'll be as dead as mutton whether he shoots me through the head or the body. There'll be no wounding now.'

'He'll be gone, don't worry about that, and as soon as he has gone you will leave for Washington to deliver this.' Bentley pulled a sealed letter from an inside pocket and held it out. Darcy put down his cup and took the letter. There was no name: only the address of a government department. 'You will go to that address and ask for an official named Jones, Jeremiah Jones. They will tell you no person of that name is employed there. You will then return to your hotel and wait to be contacted. When Jones contacts you, you are to say that you have been sent by his friend in Boston with a private letter. Don't say who you are and, even if there's not another soul present when you meet Jones, you must mention no names at all.'

'And if Jones asks?'

'If Jones asks for names then get out if you can and run as fast and as far as you can because you will have been discovered and the man asking you for names will most certainly not be Jeremiah Jones. Although I have to say that if you do get discovered I wouldn't give a bent pin for your chances of living very long, never mind getting out and running.'

There was alarm on Darcy's face.

'But surely we're safe aren't we? Everything is going to plan, why should any of us be discovered?'

'Because, you simpleton, we're playing for very high stakes and no one is going to hand us the winnings on a plate. I think we're secure, I believe we're secure, but out there somewhere are those who are playing against us and they are as careful, determined and as well organised as we are. We have the advantage because we were playing for a long time before they even became aware there was a game up and running. But they're not fools, not by any means, they'll catch up as they go along, oh yes, they're catching up already. They won't catch up in time, that's all. The game will be over and they will have lost before they have discovered all the rules or even, perhaps, what the true prize is.' Bentley put his cup and saucer on a table. 'When you've shown Jones the letter and he's read it, take it back and destroy it there and then by whatever method comes to hand. Do you understand? You must destroy the letter and he must see it totally destroyed.'

Darcy nodded. He hated Bentley, but he had complete trust in his organising abilities. If Bentley said it was safe then it was as safe as it could be made. One day he would settle with Bentley, but that day was still a long way off and, until it came, Bentley must think of him as obedient, reliable and thoroughly to be trusted. He raised his bandaged hand and looked at it. Then he looked at Bentley and smiled.

'I must admit you caused me no small pain and fright when you stuck my hand this morning, but I can see now that it was the only way. When I showed it to the doctor he no more believed the glass story than my man did. But as it was the story I chose to tell, he chose to accept it. After he sewed me up he told me I was lucky to have got away with such a very clean cut, missing anything that might have done permanent damage.' Darcy examined the bandaged hand. 'It'll be out of action for a month at least and it will be at least another month before I get any real use of it back.' Then he looked at Bentley and smiled. 'However, being the kind of wound it is, shall we say an interesting wound, I trust the doctor's confidentiality enough to believe an accurate description of it could be had from at least a couple of dozen people by tomorrow. No one can doubt that I couldn't fight even if I wanted to and it gives you two months to get rid of Macleod.' He paused. 'Just as a matter of interest, why couldn't you have just arranged for Macleod to have been the one to have an accident? Boston isn't exactly free of ruffians and footpads. If a couple of them set about Macleod one night who's to say they might not hit him on the head a little too hard or stick a knife in some vital spot?'

Bentley laughed out loud. Darcy had let his feelings for Macleod show through.

'By God, Darcy, you take all this too personally. Why kill Macleod when I can use him?'

'Use him?'

'Aye, use him. Macleod is going to play a very pretty part in our little game. He won't know it of course, he may very well think he is playing against us rather than for us, but it doesn't much matter what Macleod thinks because he will be thinking exactly what we want him to think. Kill Macleod!' And again he laughed, 'Why waste him? With all the hate that man carries he's too powerful just to scrap. We're going to fuel up our precious lawyer Macleod 'til he blazes and then we're going to sit back and watch him roar. Oh yes, lawyer Macleod is in for some ride I reckon, some considerable ride.'

Chapter Eleven

In America's new capital, Washington, a young man sat at his desk and asked himself, and did his best to answer, many of the same questions about the little game that Bentley and Darcy had discussed in Boston. Although it was past midnight he was busy reading reports which had been heavily annotated. It was the young man's task to consider these annotations and compile a list of suggestions for actions he thought should be taken. Through a door of an adjoining office an older man, the author of the annotations, was also busy.

The young man was unexceptional, certainly not a man of fashion nor at all striking in features or bearing. He was a government clerk and fully looked the part. The same could not be said for the man in the adjoining office. Though plainly dressed he had a distinctly military air and his manner, as he read, conveyed intense concentration. He came to something in the report he was reading which made him pause, look up and stare sightlessly ahead in thought. Had you been able, at this moment, to look into his face you would have seen that his eyes ill-fitted his years. They were the hard eyes of an alert and vigorous mind, of a man used to command, who had many times made difficult decisions knowing that others would live and die as a result. And his eyes were not deceptive, he had not flinched from making life–and-death decisions in the past and would not flinch from making similar decisions again.

His thinking came to an end and he looked through the open door into the next office.

'Jeremiah, come here for a moment.'

The young man took hold of a stick which leaned against his chair, got up and walked as quickly as his limp would allow through the doorway into the office. The older man gave him the page of the report he was reading.

'Halfway down, the line begins "and will certainly mean …"'

The young man took the page, turned it to catch the light, found the line and read. After a minute he handed it back.

'Well, General, you wanted corroboration and this gives it.'

'Not completely, but with all the rest it is enough, I think, to justify some definite action.'

'What action will you take, sir? Assassination?'

The General gave a small laugh. 'Good God, man, nothing so drastic. What a bloodthirsty young devil you've become, Jones, always looking to kill people. A few sudden arrests and some deportations might be in order.

'This, Jones, is one of those cases which shows how right I was to have Adams put the Alien Act through Congress.'

'Yes, but it's Jefferson who's President now and I don't think he'd be pleased to see the Alien and Sedition Laws used.'

'Jefferson is fully aware of what's going on and knows well enough what needs to be done. This trouble isn't any part of some domestic squabble between Jefferson's Republicans and Hamilton's Federalists, although it has been very cleverly framed to look that way. This is aimed at the very liberty of America, and I didn't serve in the late War just to hand my country over to the English crown nor the French Republic. We've got to stop whoever's organising all this.'

'If that's your assessment, sir, then I would have thought a little blood-letting was entirely appropriate.'

The General was pleased.

'I think you're coming on in this business, Jeremiah, still a bit too keen on bloodshed, but maybe that's no bad thing as matters stand at the moment. Perhaps you're right and just arresting a few citizens and sending a few foreigners packing back to where they came from won't do all that's needed. So, before we pick up our foreign friends we'll make the arrests and have a couple of quiet executions. That way the right kind of message will get taken back.' The General pulled open a desk and took out a sheet of embossed paper. He signed the bottom of the sheet and held it out. 'Fill in the details and arrange for two of those we know about in Philadelphia to be arrested. Have them tried by a closed military court and then executed. Something for you to enjoy, eh, Jeremiah? A bit of your blood-letting.' Jones smiled but didn't speak. 'Losing the Philadelphia men should put a little sand in their axle-grease. They're not at the centre of things nor probably even near it, of that I'm sure, but they're important enough in their way. More important to me is that it will take time for them to be replaced and that's what I need more than anything else, Jones, I need time.'

'Have we heard something new, sir?'

'New?'

'Well it's not like you to agree so readily to any suggestion of mine. I just thought that perhaps ....'

The General nodded.

'Yes, we've heard something. Some time this year, and probably sooner than later, the French and the British will make peace.'

The young man showed surprise.

'Are you sure of that?'

'It's already agreed. The preliminaries for arranging a treaty are under way. I even know where it will happen. Amiens.'

'I see.'

'Do you, Jeremiah? This peace will not be any kind of real peace, just a mutually agreed pause for breath so both sides can re-equip and re-organise. They'll be at war again when either side thinks it's strong enough. Once the peace is in place they'll push to finish what they're up to here before the war resumes. That's the cause for our hurry on this side. So, Jeremiah, let's get the Philadelphia business done.'

Jeremiah Jones went back to his office and took the Philadelphia file out of a desk drawer. He selected two pages on which were five names, each with a brief biography. When he had made his choice, he prepared the official papers for the arrests. He then prepared the orders for the closed court military trial. In a separate, sealed envelope addressed as 'personal and secret', he added the necessary instructions for the verdict and execution of the two Philadelphia men he had chosen, a businessman and a local politician.

As he worked, he thought about the man in the next office who could arrange for such things to happen. He knew that George Washington had chosen him personally for the role he now performed, and that when he was required to answer to anyone, he answered to the President in person, to Jefferson now, as he had so recently done to Adams.

Jeremiah's work was reports, endless reports. But from those reports and many sessions with the General, Jones had developed a firm grasp of the political landscape.

Washington had seen that powers outside America could use internal divisions to undermine not only the government but the very independence of the new country. He never doubted the loyalty of men like Adams or Hamilton, who so vigorously opposed each other over the way the new country should develop, a strong central government or strong state governments. But it was an argument which could be used to worsen the already growing North-South divide and Washington was only too aware that certain interests, even certain American interests, would want to manipulate America's growing pains so that power fell into their own hands. And he knew such interests wouldn't be too scrupulous about how it was done. It was to guard against any conspiracy which might grow out of legitimate dissent that Washington had established an agency, within the government but separate from it. Not secret but not official, it was given powers to gather information, interpret that information and, when necessary, advise and act upon it. The man he had chosen to lead the agency was a man who had commanded under him in the War of Independence. That man had finished the war with the rank of General. Now somewhat elderly, the General still had a mind like a steel trap and a loyalty to his country which was absolute and unshakeable. It was this man, the General, who now sat in his office while Jeremiah Jones finished his papers. Jeremiah went to the door and called out loudly into the darkness of the corridor, 'Courier.'

He waited and after a minute the sound of boots could be heard approaching hurriedly towards the doorway. A man with a lantern and dressed for riding came out of the dark. He took the papers, looked at the address and put them into a satchel slung across his shoulder.

'They're urgent.'

'When are they not?'

The man disappeared down the corridor and Jeremiah Jones turned back and went to the doorway connecting the two offices.

'I'll go now, sir, if you don't need me further.'

'Not yet. There's a question I need to take your mind on.'

Jeremiah went to the desk and waited. He knew the General's methods. If the question was of importance he would marshal his words as he had once marshalled men. 'We know the game is being played for no less a prize than America itself and the strings are being pulled from Paris by their Minister of Police, Fouché.'

'Agreed, and if Fouché is pulling the strings it means he has found some powerful and highly placed puppets.'

'Just so. But what about the British? They're in this somewhere, but where and how deep? They wouldn't just sit back and let Fouché have a clear run.'

'No, sir, they most definitely would not.'

'How am I running in this race do you think, Jeremiah? Am I still up with the hounds or left behind while they're closing on the kill?'

It was now Jeremiah's turn to carefully marshal his words. Much, he knew, depended on his answer.

'To answer that, sir, I think we must find out all we can about what is happening in New Orleans. From what we know that's where I should say the next move must be made. If I'm right the British will have someone there already or damn soon will have. It's time, I think, to send someone down there and see if we can't put some sand in *that* axle grease.'

The General nodded.

'I think you may very well be right. Let me have your thoughts on who and how, a written outline on it tomorrow morning.'

'Yes, sir.'

Left alone a chilling thought crept into the General's mind. Fouché might have the best secret service in Europe but who had the best in America? He forced such thoughts away from him. The game's not done 'til it's done. Jones was right. New Orleans, that was what mattered now. Get someone there and get the job done. But just as important, done by someone he could trust.

Chapter Twelve

In a government building in London there was another man who, like the General in Washington, kept late hours reading reports by lamplight. He too had an assistant sitting at a desk in an adjacent office. The man reading the reports was a thick-set, rather ugly man in his thirties with short, grizzled hair. His manner of dress was careless, chosen for comfort rather than fashion. His coat could only be described as an unfortunate accident, being too black, too long and too loose, and on his feet, in what must have been a deliberate affront to fashionable sensibilities, were buckled shoes rather than polished riding boots.

His assistant differed from his superior in a variety of ways. Firstly, he was most definitely a man of fashion. Everything, from his high neck-cloth down to his skin-tight breeches tucked into glossy, riding boots spoke of up to the minute elegance. Next, he was young and handsome, although with a fullness of face and figure which spoke of easy living. And finally, his desk was bare and the young man was lounging back in his chair gazing at the ceiling. All ceilings, however, even the best of them, cannot grip the mind indefinitely and the young man, having lost interest in his particular ceiling, sat up, took a gold watch from his waistcoat pocket and looked at the time. He put the watch away in an annoyed manner, thought for a moment then stood up and went to the door between the two offices which he pushed fully open.

'God's teeth, Trent, do you know what the time is?' The man at the desk ignored him and kept on reading. 'Trent, it's damn well past eleven. You've no right to keep me here at this hour of the evening. I'm not some lackey to hang about on a whim of yours.'

The man put down the report and frowned at his young assistant in the doorway. His coarse features were further marred by a nose which at some point in his career had been badly broken. His small, dark eyes, set in such an unattractive setting, were unnerving and before their steady gaze the young man's temper wilted, but survived sufficiently to carry him into the office where he continued petulantly.

'What is it you want of me, anyway? I've nothing to do except sit out there. Dammit, Trent, if there's nothing for me to do why keep me?'

The man at the desk suddenly brightened as if he had been given a novel idea to consider.

'What a good question, Melford, why indeed should I keep you?'

Then he sat back, folded his arms and looked at his assistant with a smile on his face. The smile was not pleasant and his young assistant became nervous and, when nervous, he did what he always did, he blustered.

'Blast you, Trent, give me a civil answer or none at all. Why should I sit out there at this time of night waiting on your beck and call?' Finding himself not checked in his outburst he continued. 'What are you after all? You're nothing but a common thief-taker who's pushed his way up to being a glorified government clerk, but you're still a damn nobody. Why, you wouldn't get past the door of any decent house in London. Who do you know, and who knows you?'

The man sat, as if reflecting on what had just been said.

'Whom surely?'

The young man blinked at the unexpected question.

Hume? The name meant nothing to him.

'Who the hell is Hume?'

'Well there's John Hume, the Edinburgh philosopher, but I don't see …' and he paused for a second as Melford's confusion obviously increased. 'Ah, I think I see our error. I said whom not Hume. I was pointing out that you should have said, *whom* do you know? Not, who do you know? How very amusing.'

Trent's laugh was as loud as it was false and Melford's face whitened with anger.

'Are you trying to be funny at my expense, Trent?'

The man answered very slowly.

'My word, Melford, what a night it is for questions, but as you can see I'm rather busy. So many reports.' And he indicated the papers across his desk. The tone unsettled the young man and he remained silent. When the man spoke again his manner and tone

54

were calm and businesslike. 'However, concerning the lateness of the hour which originally brought you in here, if you want to leave before I dismiss you then by all means do so.' He picked up the report and resumed his reading then added as if an afterthought. 'But if you do, just pen a brief letter of resignation before you leave, would you?'

This simple request totally defeated the young man and his manner at once changed.

'Good lord, Trent,' he said trying his best to put a friendly smile on his face and into his voice, 'there's no need to take on so. I only meant it's damned irksome sitting out there with nothing to do. No need to cut up rough just because I got a little carried away. It's only the boredom getting to me. Isn't there anything I can do?'

'Another good question,' said the man as he picked up his pen, dipped it, and made a brief note in the margin of the page he was reading. Then he looked up at the young man, put the pen down again and sat back and put his finger tips together, assuming the air of someone faced with a more than usually difficult question.

'Is there anything you can do? And from that one might ask, are you capable of doing anything even half way well? Which leads one, of course, to the question of whether you have even the smallest of talents?' Suddenly the man leaned forward and put his elbows on the desk and looked at his assistant over his clasped hands. 'All good questions, Melford, very good questions. But before I answer those questions, may I share something with you? You labour under the illusion that your father, the Earl of Glentrool, made me take you on as my assistant so you wouldn't have to join the army and go to war as your elder brother has done. You're wrong, he didn't. He tried to, but, powerful though your father is, he hasn't the power to coerce me, and certainly not while we're at war. I took you on as my assistant because, when they shoved you in front of me and we spoke, I saw that you do indeed have talent.'

Trent relaxed back into his chair and the young man looked puzzled but pleased.

'Talent? Well, it's damn good of you to say so, Trent.'

'Although when I say talent I should of course say one single but very valuable talent. Being thoroughly false yourself you seem to have developed an almost uncanny ability to recognise falseness in others.' Seeing that his assistant took this badly and was about to speak, the man went on in a voice in which authority and anger were nicely blended. 'Understand this, Melford, if you can't understand anything else. I'm good at what I do, very good, and one of the things that makes me so good is recognising talent in others, especially in the people I choose to use. I knew you almost at once for the thoroughly false man you are, and when I knew that, I knew that I could use you. You won't be killed or maimed in this war, not because of your father's influence, but because I can make use of you.'

Lord Melford, younger son of the Earl of Glentrool, thought for a moment as Trent sat silently reading.

He was a young man who was vain about his looks, naturally idle, totally selfish and thoroughly arrogant. All of which he considered the natural and correct attitudes of a gentleman. He also knew that Jasper Trent's assessment of him was, regrettably, dead on the mark. He was quite without honour and he recognised that any man of good breeding who was without honour, whatever else his many merits, was indeed thoroughly and irretrievably false. He smiled a little smugly.

'Well, I dare say you're right, Trent. But as you think it's a useful talent in the work I do for you, and as your work is thought of as so dashed important, I don't think I need to be ashamed to own up to it. In war it is surely the first duty of a gentleman to look to his best parts when he chooses how to serve his country and you'd be the first to admit I'm not cut out for soldiering. As to my father's wanting me away from shot and sabre, well, if brother Hector dies my father will want one son left to be his heir and as there's only the two of us born on the right side of the blanket that he'll acknowledge, I call it damnably sensible of him to try and find me a safe haven.'

Trent looked up, smiled and put a question in an innocent and enquiring voice.

'You wouldn't say, then, that you're a coward?'

'God's blood, sir, I'd damn well call out any man who dared to say that of me.'

'Well, I rather think that I just did, didn't I?'

Lord Melford turned a rather bright shade of pink but said nothing. He had no intention of jeopardising his safe place in any way at all, and certainly not by calling out Jasper Trent. There was a brief pause then the manner of the man at the desk changed to one of brisk business. 'No matter, coward or hero means nothing so long as you're not a fool and can be useful to me. I have kept you here tonight because I think I have a use for that talent of yours. This report has come in from Jamaica and it's causing me some concern. In whose camp would you say Cardinal Henry Stuart was at the moment?'

'What's the Cardinal got to do with that part of the world?'

'My point exactly. Why should the Cardinal's name crop up in a section of the report on New Orleans? So, once again, who, if anyone, has the Cardinal's current loyalty?'

'He's ours of course.'

'Why so?'

'Because he's been taking a royal pension from us for over a year now, ever since the affair of the Papal Conclave in Venice.'

'True, he accepts our money.'

'More than accepts I'd say. Ambassador Minto bought and paid for him. If he's taking a pension from King George he's got to be ours.'

'Perhaps, perhaps not. But what concerns me is the visit those two Boston men made to our royal and religious friend. When they met with the Cardinal in Rome last year I'm sure they came to some sort of arrangement with him. But what, I ask myself, could the Americans have wanted with a Cardinal Bishop, even one whose name is Henry Stuart.'

'I suppose they knew he'd lost all his French benefices and had to give what little money he had left to the Pope to buy off Napoleon. A man like that, suddenly without money, would be in a particularly receptive frame of mind if somebody turned up with an offer.'

'Quite so. But an offer to do what?'

'Does it matter? Those Americans were so damned obvious, making a grand tour of Europe during a war for God's sake. And when they'd finished in Rome tried to arrange fast travel to Paris even though it meant passing through the middle of Suvorov's Austrians. Who in their right mind does that sort of thing? What else could they be but agents? And agents as obvious as that surely don't …'

'Maybe we were meant to notice them. As you say, they certainly drew attention to themselves. Don't underestimate the Americans, Melford. In fact never underestimate anyone. Our obvious Americans could have been acting on their own or they could as easily have been part of some scheme of Fouché's.'

'Yes, I remember you said that at the time. Though why Fouché would have felt it worth putting a Papist prelate in his pocket defeats me. The Jacobite cause is dead and buried and a Cardinal calling himself King Henry IX won't change that. He can mint all the medals he wants and make his high-flown declarations, but his feet will never touch English soil, never mind get his backside on a throne.'

'That was the thing that concerned me then and concerns me now. If Fouché wanted to hatch something with Henry Stuart, self-declared successor to his brother the Bonnie Prince, it wouldn't be to revive the Jacobite claim. But what else is our Cardinal good for and why would America get involved?'

'Perhaps Fouché used them as errand boys because they were neutral. Anyway, does it matter? We offered him a handsome pension which he accepted so, as I say, that puts him squarely in our camp doesn't it?'

'Do you think so, Melford? Our Cardinal is a clever man, he never formally relinquished his claim you know?'

'But surely, accepting a royal pension from King George means he acknowledges George as rightful King?'

'I'm afraid not. He's got an answer to that. He now claims the money is simply England repaying the dowry of his grandmother, Mary of Modena, which the government promised but, sadly, never quite got round to actually doing.'

'Is he? Then he's a confounded cunning devil. He takes the money, still claims the crown, and can play all ends of this damn game against each other.'

'Yes, a clever man. Offer him money and he'll surely take it. But never believe you've bought him up. He'll find a way out if way out there is, and he's found one out of our royal pension.'

'Why not just kill the Popish bastard? That way he's out of any game for good.'

'What a violent young man you are, Melford, and just a moment ago you were saying how you weren't cut out for soldiering. Thank you for the suggestion but, no, I think I want Henry Stuart alive. Alive he can tell us things, whether he means to or not. It was through watching him, remember, that we caught the Americans' visit and that eventually gave us some sort of start on all of this. No, we certainly won't kill him, not yet at any rate. What you will do for me, however, is go to Italy.'

'Italy?'

'Rome. I want some reports collected and I want some letters delivered by safe hand, your safe hand. And while you're there you can see to it that we become a bit more organised. Look around and find me a man who can become our eyes and ears in Rome.'

'What sort of man?'

'Ah, what sort indeed? If Fouché were to want such a man here in London what sort would he look for?'

Melford bent his mind to the question.

'A man who was already well placed.'

'Good, go on.'

Encouraged, Melford warmed to the task.

'A man of position, with connections and access, but a man who could be bribed, bought or blackmailed. A man who could be persuaded to treason, clever enough to do the job well but weak enough to be controlled.'

'Well done, Melford, well done indeed. You have described to his buttons the man you're to look for. But of course it was easy for you, wasn't it?'

Melford bridled at the careless dismissal of his efforts.

'Easy, why easy?'

'Because the man you described so well is you, my Lord Melford. Look for a twin brother in Rome and you'll have your man.'

'That's a damnable lie, Trent. I would never accept a bribe or act against …'

Trent leaned forward dangerously.

'No, Melford, you wouldn't. And we both know why you wouldn't, don't we? We both know what I would do to you if you even tried.' Trent leaned back and Melford subsided. 'You might as well see if you can talk to our Cardinal Bishop while you're there.'

'And ask him what?' asked Melford sullenly.

'Anything, anything at all. But remember, Henry Stuart is clever and was raised on Jacobite intrigue. He sucked it in with his mother's milk. It's in his blood and bones, and what he didn't learn among his family he'll certainly have learned at the Vatican. He'll probably tie you in knots, but that doesn't matter because you have your unique talent. Go to Italy, Melford, and see what you can find out about our Cardinal. Be judge and jury for me. If, when you return, you say he's going to play us false, maybe I will decide that it is better to snuff him out after all. Whatever else you do, arrange to keep him watched. In fact get your new man to organise a visit to our Cardinal as his first task. It would be a nice trial-run for him. It would give you a chance to see the man of your choice perform over a distance of ground, as it were.'

'A visit to do what?'

'Just let him ruffle through some of the Cardinal's papers, bring a few away, it doesn't matter what. Nothing of value need be taken but clear evidence of an uninvited visit.'

'Which will do what?'

'Let him know we are watching him, that his involvement is suspected?'

'His involvement in what?'

'It doesn't matter. If there is no involvement then no real harm is done. But if there is, we give him the illusion that he is discovered. It might do nothing or it might persuade him he is better off staying as a royal pensioner. If nothing else it will give our new organisation a chance to do something. Go and do this well for me, Melford, and there may be better things for you to do when you come back.' He paused for a second. 'If you come back.'

'If?'

'If our friend Fouché finds that we've got a Recruiting Sergeant offering the King's shilling on the sly in Rome, which Napoleon regards as his own private garden, then your dear father the Earl will once more have to drop his breeches, raise his standard and busy himself getting another spare heir.' Melford looked uneasy. Trent had made his point. 'But let's not dwell on that. If I didn't think you up to it I wouldn't send you.'

Melford revived like a watered flower.

'When do you want me to go?'

'As soon as you can, but not until you've done one other little job for me. I want you to find Madame de Metz and tell to her to come here and come quick as I need to have a few words with that most interesting lady. There, now I'm finished with you and you may go. But take care in Rome, Melford.' Lord Melford gave a grateful smile at Trent's concern. 'It would be a damn nuisance to have to break in a new man to replace you just at the moment.'

Chapter Thirteen

The next day Madame de Metz duly arrived in Jasper Trent's office. The dark February day was throwing rain against the office windows but there was little evidence of the foul weather on her rich, full-length hooded cape. Wherever she had come from she had made the journey by carriage. Trent, who was busy writing with the light of a lamp, ignored her. After a few seconds of waiting she sat down, pulled back her hood, undid the clasp of her cape and let it fall behind her over the back of her chair.

She was young and very beautiful, and what had been given her by nature, art of a high order had improved on. The curls of her black hair were gathered up in the style of a Greek goddess, her white dress was tightly waisted under her breasts then fell loosely to her ankles and on her feet were the tiniest of brocade pumps each decorated with a small, pretty bow. The wide, low neckline of the dress showed off her fair shoulders. She wore no jewellery, and her face was a picture of fresh innocence. Such an abundance of simplicity marked her out as one of the very wealthy. When it became clear to her that Trent would ignore her until she said something, she spoke in fluent French and with a clear edge in her voice.

'Eh bien, here I am and I hope you're going to make it worth my while. I have more important things to do than come running just because you call me.' Trent looked up from his writing and smiled his false smile and, as with his assistant, it unnerved her. 'Don't try to play your games with me, as I said I have more important things to do than ...'

Trent cut across her rapid French in slow deliberate English.

'My dear Madame de Metz, it's no good you talking French at me. It won't do you any good. And as for those more important things you have to do, I know exactly what they are. For my part I think you were wise to run to me when I called, and if I choose to play a game, any game, I expect your willing, nay enthusiastic, participation.'

Madame de Metz was ready for the smile this time.

'Cochon.' But although she said the word in French her tone of voice showed that Trent's words had hit their mark. When she went on it was in sullen English with no trace of a French accent, but rather a hint of Irish brogue. 'I'm doing nothing illegal, not at the minute.'

'Perhaps you're not, Molly, but with your help Jack and his friends are about to do something very illegal. This time they'll be taken, and when they're taken, my guess is that they'll find some way to pull you into it. You'll become just another counter on the bargaining table.' Trent stood up, went round the desk and sat on the edge of it, folded his arms and looked down at her. 'Sir Patrick Conover, estates in Mayo and Donegal, recently seen quite often in the company of Madame Eloise de Metz. Madame is welcome in all the best houses as the very intimate friend of the Duke of Dorset's eldest son, Sir Giles Landry. She is considered everywhere to be a lady above reproach. Society may have opened its doors to Sir Patrick Conover, but you and I, Molly, both know that he is, in reality, an old friend of ours, Jack Doran, born and raised in Dublin's worst slums, a dangerous man who goes in for robbery, murder and God knows what else. When I found out that Jack had suddenly become Sir Patrick, I asked myself, what is his purpose in getting into society, who is his target?'

Molly avoided Trent's eyes and shifted in her seat.

'I know nothing about any targets.'

'But I do, Molly, and I say the Duke of Dorset is his mark. What's more I say you've already persuaded Sir Giles to invite Jack to Dorset's place when he goes there in two weeks. One night Jack will let his friends in, a few heads will get cracked or maybe worse, Jack and his friends will scoop up what they can carry and off they'll go. When it turns out that Sir Patrick Conover had taken everyone in and was no more than a common thief you'll be as surprised and shocked as all the rest of them. You, of course, would have lost enough jewellery to cover yourself although, once it was re-set, Jack would have seen you got it back. It was a nice enough little scheme, Molly, and a considerable compliment to your skill in digging yourself in deep among the high and mighty.' Trent unfolded his arms and returned to his seat. 'Or perhaps a fitting monument to their stupidity. Either way it was a nice enough ramp. Nice enough that is, if I didn't know all about it. As it is, Jack and his friends will be taken tomorrow at Sly Joe's and then, after a brief rest in the Fleet prison, they'll swing.'

Trent sat back and gave Molly time to think. She didn't need long.

'What's all this to you, Mr Trent? You're not usually interested in a bit of honest thievery? Why are you pulling Jack?'

'Because I've been told to look after Sir Giles Landry. He sits at the tables of the powerful and deals in affairs of state and war. He's not a clever man, nor even a good man, but at the moment he's an important man. He will be there when negotiations for a pause in this present war start and they'll start very soon. So I was told to look after him, and that's how I came upon Jack and upon your little plot.'

'Can't I just warn Jack off?'

'No, Jack's time has come. My advice to you would be to get as far away from London as you can and do it quickly. Jack and his friends are gallows-meat this time and it would be a pity to get that pretty neck of yours stretched for no good reason.'

'If Jack knows he'll swing and can't bargain his way out of a noose, why would he drag me into things?'

'Because some naughty person such as myself might tell him it was you who peached on him. That would give him a good enough reason, don't you think?' The young woman said nothing, because she knew there was nothing to say. He had her exactly where he wanted her and she waited to see what the price of her neck would be. But Trent seemed in no particular hurry. 'Tell me, Molly, how old would you say you were?'

'I couldn't say, Mr Trent, we never kept birthdays in our family. I know I was just a little girl when my pa sold me to the Frenchies and they put me into a house in Paris. That was two years before the Bastille and that was what, thirteen years ago?'

'Dammit, that means if you're about twenty now, you began your whoring at around the age of seven.'

'That sounds about right. Those aristocrats were always asking for something new, and a pretty little Irish seven-year-old virgin would have been just up their alley. Pa would have got a fair price for me.'

'And now here you are in English society, admired by all. You've come a long way, Molly and, like I said, it would be a pity for that journey to end with you swinging from a gibbet among a set of cut-throats, especially when I've got work for you.'

She leaned slightly forward, interested. The bargaining was about to begin.

'What work?'

Trent sat back, pleased.

'That's my girl. I want you to go to New Orleans for me.'

'Good God, that's a bloody long way from London all right. It's the other side of the ocean.'

'Maybe it is, but I need a beautiful French lady of good family to go there. Someone who knows the ropes and can look after herself.'

A sly note crept into Molly's voice.

'If I need to know the ropes and be able to look after myself it sounds as if it might be dangerous.'

'Don't tell me you're frightened of a little danger?'

Now it was her turn to smile.

'I've been in danger of the gallows all my life. Danger don't bother me, just so long as it don't get out of hand. But danger puts the price up. You know that as well as I do, Mr Trent. Business is business.'

'Come now, Molly, I wouldn't have said you're too well placed to bargain.'

'Oh I don't know, Mr Trent. You can make it so I swing, but then again, how many girls do you know who could pass for French, and well-born French at that? I suppose it all depends on how important this work is to you.'

Trent laughed.

'Well done, my lovely girl, you're a shrewd piece of work and that's the truth. You're quite right of course, this is important to me and what's more it's urgent. Your time as a whore in the grandest bawdy houses in Paris has made you just right for this little job. You met the right sort there, didn't you?'

'Never you mind what I did in Paris nor who I did it with. The point is you need me and you need me quick.'

'Of course it is, Molly, of course it is. So I'll tell you what I want and you can tell me your price and then we can argue and then we'll settle on the figure I dare say we both had in our heads all along. How's that?'

Molly relaxed and sat back in her chair.

'Suits me, Mr Trent. I've always found you a fair man to work for. Cruel sometimes, but mostly fair.'

Trent laughed and Molly grinned. They were a well-matched pair and both knew it.

'Now, Molly, to the nub eh?'

'Aye, Mr Trent, the nub.'

'I need a lady who can pass for French among the French in New Orleans and I need her there as soon as she can be got there. When you're there I want you to look out a man named St Clair. He's up to something.'

'It'll be political I suppose?'

'Correct. Let's say he's in the importing line, takes things in and passes them on. See if you can find out what his connections are, who he passes his goods on to. And while you're there keep a sharp lookout for any other newcomer who might be mixing among the Frenchie swells. Somebody who has not long arrived and is interested in getting to know the nobs of the French community. Whoever it is won't be French. It will probably be a man, but it might just be a woman. Do you still cater for all tastes, Molly?'

'I do what the money wants me to do, Mr Trent. Will it be just sex and information or will I have to croak somebody? Croaking abroad might be tricky if you want it done in a hurry. I don't know the ways of the New Orleans French.'

'No, there's no blood to be shed until you find what I want. All I want is for you to put yourself alongside St Clair and any man or woman who's doing the same as you, worming their way into the French upper crust looking for information. If there is somebody and they get what I want before you do, then take it off them. If you get it first, well, once you have the information that will be the time for a little blood-letting if it's called for.'

'And if I get what you want how do I get in touch?'

'I'll see that a ship puts into New Orleans every two weeks. They'll be different ones but all small and fast and all will be captained by a Royal Navy officer although there'll be no uniform. The captains will have orders to carry anything given to them by

Madame de Metz. By your hand only, Molly, no messengers and don't contact any captain unless you have something to send me.'

'And how do I recognise these ships?'

Trent pulled open a drawer, took out a folded piece of material and pushed it across.

'Take a good look, you'll need to remember it.'

Molly picked it up and unfolded it. It was a blue pennant with three white stars on it.'

'What's it mean? Flags mean something don't they?'

'Not this one, not to anyone else. All it means is that the ship flying it is your ship.'

Molly threw the flag back onto the desk.

'So, what am I looking to find out?'

'There's things going on in New Orleans, things I need to know about.'

'What sort of things.'

'What interests me is that there's been put-up trouble. Frontiersmen breaking up the town and doing enough of a job of it to cause problems for the new Governor, Salcedo. He's started huffing and puffing and looking to come the heavy hand and deny warehousing to all American trade coming down the Mississippi. Something's afoot, we've known that for some time, but we don't know what. I think it started in Rome but now it's surfaced in New Orleans. The place is still run by the Spanish but it's the French who are calling the tune.'

'Oh yes, how does that work?'

'That whole part of the country is French again but they're keeping it looking Spanish for the time being which makes me think that whatever's going on is being organised from France, from Paris. And you can guess who it is in Paris that's doing the organising can't you, Molly?'

'Oh Christ, you're talking about Fouché. I'm fucked if I'm going up against him, Mr Trent, not for any amount of money.'

'If you go to America for me you may well be fucked and more than once, perhaps many times. But if you refuse me in this, I guarantee you'll be hanged alongside Jack before the month's out. It's your choice, I told you it would be dangerous, but it's a doubt against a certainty. Don't go stupid on me, Molly.' But Molly wasn't going stupid, she was just wondering whether going up against Fouché wasn't as sure a way to die as the gallows. 'What's to think about, girl? You've been rogered so many times by so many men that repeating the experience can't bother you. But the experience of a short drop with a good strong rope round your neck is different. It's not one that anyone gets to repeat. It's a once in a lifetime thing, Molly. A unique experience.' And he sat back. 'But as I say, it's your free choice, take your time. This or the gallows.'

'Why did you tell me about Fouché and all the rest? Normally you don't tell me nothing. What I don't know I can't spill.'

'Because this time you need to know. You need to know how good the enemy will be. I tell you frankly, I don't fancy your chances in this. It all turns on whether they accept you as Madame de Metz, on whether or not you can fit in. Trust no one and be more careful than you ever have in what I know has been a very careful life.' Trent leaned forward. For the first time in the meeting there was real animation in his face. 'Find me what I want, Molly, and I promise you I'll set you up as a real lady and you'll have enough money to go free and clear and live in comfort for the rest of your life.'

'And if I can't?'

'You're Irish aren't you? Would that make you a Catholic?'

'So what?'

'If you fail I'll have one of your priests say some masses for your soul. I dare say a soul like yours will need quite a few masses. It's win or die in this one. There's no third way for it to go.'

'Well, you've made it clear, I'll give you that, Mr Trent, so let's get down to terms. I'll need to take a maid, a good one, and good ones cost money. I'll need someone alongside of me who I can trust and who'll be useful to me, someone who knows the ropes. But she'll have to pass as a maid to a fine lady among maids who are the real thing, and that's not going to be easy.'

'Anyone in mind?'

'Kitty Mullen. We've worked together before. She's here in London and ready to work.'

'Whereabouts?'

'Sitting in a kip with her lover-boy.'

'Her lover-boy?'

'Jack Doran. So after tomorrow morning she'll be a free agent, won't she?'

'How very convenient.'

'She's a clever girl as a rule but Jack wormed his way under her skirts and she became his doxy. She was going to be the inside stand when they pulled the Duke of Dorset job. Jack knew he'd need someone with him, someone below stairs, so he worked on Kitty because she was just right for the job. Maybe he even married her, I wouldn't put it past him. He's done it before. Anyway, she's about to see Jack taken and be in line to have his neck stretched. Could you arrange it so she gets pulled with Jack and that I'm allowed to visit her?' Trent nodded. 'I'll make it clear to her that if she stays put she and Jack can go to hell together but if she comes with me she goes free. What choice would she have?'

'Not much I would say.'

'Do I get her?' Trent didn't answer. 'Come on, Mr Trent, you need me and I need Kitty and I need her willing and keen to slip London. This has to be a two-hander at the very least and you know it.'

'All right, you get Kitty.'

'I'll need clothes and I'll need plenty of working money.'

'And, within reason, you shall have them all. What about payment for you and Kitty?'

'I'll take care of Kitty out of my end, no need for her to hear any figures, is there, not if she's getting her life back as part of the payment? I'll want plenty up front. If there's a good chance of my not coming out of this I want something for ma and my kid that she looks after.'

'Not unreasonable.'

'And I want my brother sprung.'

'Another one off the hook? What's he in for?'

'He ain't in for nothing. He's in the army. I want him home safe so he can look after ma and the kid if he's needed.'

'Hmm, getting involved with the army. I don't like that. You're asking a lot, Molly.'

'No I ain't and you know it.'

'All right. I could probably bring your brother back if he's not dead already.' Trent pulled a drawer open, took out a folded piece of thick paper and pushed it across to Molly who picked it up, unfolded it and read it. She gave a low whistle.

'Jesus, Mr Trent, with that name at the bottom and that seal, it could be me putting you at the end of a rope.'

Trent was not amused because he knew she was right. He didn't like her having such a letter, but without it her chances dwindled to almost nothing and sending her became a waste of time and money.

'Don't use it unless you have to and never let it leave your person. And think hard where it will be if someone's bumping bellies with you. That letter gets you access to the fastest couriers we have, military or diplomatic.' Trent pushed the drawer shut. The business side of the meeting was over and they moved on to the last item to be settled between them. 'So, now to payment. What about you? What's to be in it for you if you get me what I want?'

And by the light of the lamp Jasper Trent and Molly O'Hara haggled about the price of her life as the February weather hammered against the windows.

Chapter Fourteen

A week had passed since Macleod's humiliation by Darcy, a week in which Macleod had suffered much. It was not that Darcy had in any way compounded his actions, rather the reverse. On the two occasions their paths had crossed he had been scrupulously polite which, if anything, made Macleod feel worse rather than better. Boston, or more accurately those in Boston who cared, had been briefly amused by the incident and then forgotten it. But in Macleod's imagination he was the constant focus of sly looks and hidden smirks.

But this day something unusual had occurred to take Macleod's mind off his morbid preoccupation with Darcy. A private letter had been delivered to his house.

Even sullen Amélie had not been able to conceal her curiosity when she had put the letter beside his plate as she served his dinner. Letters were business, they were for the office. A letter to the house was something incredible and surely must contain bad news. Amélie's curiosity had kept her fussing around the dining table, but Macleod had ignored her and the epistle and left it unopened while he ate.

Amélie knew that he must be as curious about it as she was but, seeing he would not give her the satisfaction of opening it in her presence, she finally left the room muttering.

Macleod had at once picked up the letter and examined the seal and the writing. The seal meant nothing to him but the writing seemed familiar. He broke the seal and pulled a single sheet of paper from the envelope.

The first thing he looked at was the signature and at once remembered where he had seen the writing before. It had been on military orders. The man whose name was signed at the foot of the letter had been one of his commanding officers during the war, a man he had respected and trusted as a soldier and almost as a friend. The message was short and to the point. Macleod was to put aside whatever he was doing and come to Washington. He was to make his excuses for his sudden departure but he was to tell no one where he was going nor who had summoned him. He was to use all possible haste.

Having read the letter once, Macleod put it in his pocket and went out for a walk. He needed to think and it was to be the kind of thinking he hadn't done for many years. He required motion. He needed to feel his body in action. This wasn't to be dry law-business thinking. This was to be call-of-duty thinking.

Macleod went into the Burying Ground adjacent to his house. There he could walk undisturbed. And, walking among the dead, he felt like a corpse recalled to life. He was wanted, needed. He would go. He would do as he had been ordered and make some excuse, then go with all speed. The General was in Washington and wanted him there and Washington meant that it was army or government business. As Macleod strode among the headstones he found himself wondering what might be the nature of the duty he was called to. But his was a limited imagination and after a short while he gave the speculation up as pointless. He turned and headed back to the house. Whatever it was, it was American business and as such was a call on his duty.

That night, in his library, Macleod sat by the empty fireplace wearing his night-cap and fingerless gloves with the same blanket on his legs. A tumbler of whisky stood on the table beside him but it stood untasted. He was busy reading, but this had become a night unlike any other because the lamp was turned up and he was reading with genuine interest.

A call to the new capital, Washington. A call to return to duty. A call back to life. Macleod put the letter down. He was ordered to give some reason to cover his sudden departure. Slowly an idea formed. An officer with whom he had served was seriously ill and needed him as both friend and lawyer. He was going, immediately, to Richmond to offer whatever support and service he might give. He smiled. It would serve, it would serve very well. His clerk would be given the necessary instructions the next day.

He picked up his glass and looked at it, then put it down again, threw off the rug, got up and went to the doorway. He shouted into the dark for Amélie then went back to the table, put the letter in the pocket of his dressing gown then stood with his back to the fireplace and waited. Eventually a light showed in the corridor and Amélie came in with the tray on which was the second decanter of whisky. She stopped dead when she saw Macleod standing in front of the fire. Then she looked at the still full decanter on the table.

'You can take both of them away, Amélie, I'll not need them any more tonight.'

Amélie shrugged and walked to the table and put the decanter onto the tray and went to the door where she stopped and looked back.

'When you call next time make sure the decanter is empty. I'm getting too old to carry a tray as heavy as this for any lazy pig.'

And muttering to herself she left.

Macleod smiled and let his thoughts drift where they would for a moment. Amélie had adored him as a child. Did she now hate the man he had become? Not that it mattered. He required no one's love and he cared nothing for anyone's hate. He took up the lamp. Tomorrow he would begin his arrangements.

In his bedroom a strange feeling came to him as he prepared to retire, a feeling he could not at first recognise. Then, suddenly, he understood what it was. His memory had stirred. He was not exactly happy, but he was contented. He had been summoned to serve. His country had called on him. Perhaps his life might yet have a purpose. He got into his long nightshirt and went to bed and, for the first time in many, many years, he fell asleep looking forward to the next day.

Chapter Fifteen

Two days later, at the end of the day, Bentley sat with Darcy in his rooms. They were drinking tea.

'Hell's teeth, Bentley, I knew you were efficient but I would call it a piece of damned magic. Just over a week after you say you'll get Macleod out of the way he's going round telling people he's off to Virginia to see an old army friend. How did you do it?'

Bentley smiled, he saw no harm in Darcy thinking he had arranged Macleod's departure. In fact he saw considerable advantage in it, so he was quite happy to take the credit.

'I have my methods.'

'How long will he be gone?'

'That depends,'

'On what?'

'On where he goes.'

'Curse you, Bentley, there's no need to be coy with me, is there? If you got him to go you must know where he's going and for how long.'

'True, I must, mustn't I? But there's no need for you to know. It's enough for you to know he's going. As for how long, we only need him away until you can travel.'

They drank in silence for a time, each thinking.

'He's still a damn fool though.'

Bentley looked at him.

'Why so?'

'His story, of course. Visiting a sick old friend in Richmond.'

'And why does that make him a fool?'

'Because everyone knows Macleod has no friends nor wants any friends, that's what makes him a fool. It's just the sort of shallow story a log like Macleod would come up with. He has as much subtlety as a …'

'Perhaps Macleod had friends once. You've only known him as a Boston lawyer, and you've not known him as that for very long.

You never knew Macleod the soldier nor Macleod the husband and father.'

'He was married?'

'Oh yes and had a pretty little daughter.'

'They died?'

Bentley nodded.

'And I think Macleod died with them. He just never got round to lying down that's all.'

'Fever was it?'

'No, not fever.'

'Then what?'

Bentley put down his empty cup, got up and stood before the fire pulling his coat tails up over his arms, warming himself.

'They died, Darcy, like all who die, because they could no longer live. They died because it was their time to die, as it will be for you and I one day. They died, and that's enough for you to know except that it was, perhaps, their death that put Lawyer Macleod, late soldier Macleod, into our hands.'

Darcy became nervous of the way Bentley was speaking. When Bentley spoke in this fashion there was usually a reason and the reason was usually bad news.

'More tea?'

'No, it's been a long day and I'm tiring. I'll take a spot of brandy to revive me.' Darcy got up. 'Tell me, Darcy, seeing as how you're not the fool Macleod is, what would you guess would make him drop everything and run off somewhere? And you're right, wherever it is, it won't be Richmond.'

Darcy thought, as he poured the drink. He didn't want to rise to Bentley's bait but, having called Macleod a fool, he didn't want to appear dull himself. He thought for a moment then smiled.

'Soldier Macleod you said.' He brought Bentley his drink and handed it to him. 'You've got the army to call him?' Bentley looked into his glass and said nothing. 'No. Not the army. Not even you could control the army or even a part of it, but it's something like.'

'Go on, Darcy, think it out. You're no fool remember?' And Bentley took a sip of his brandy. Darcy's brain turned rapidly, something like the army, but not the army. A light broke through.

'Duty. Somehow you've called on his damned sense of duty.

You've got someone high up in an office of government, someone in with us, to summon him. That's it, isn't it?'

A reluctant smile crossed Bentley's face.

'Well done, Darcy, you don't lack for cleverness I'll give you that.' Bentley took another sip of brandy. 'Very poor brandy this, Darcy.'

Darcy returned to his table, sat down and took up the teapot.

'I only keep it for visitors. I don't use it myself.'

Darcy poured himself half a cup of tea, filled the cup with hot water and sat back. Bentley stood in front of the fire in silence. Darcy sipped his tea and left him to his thoughts, happy enough to have shown how clever he was.

Bentley was pleased and annoyed. He was pleased that Darcy was clever enough to have found a satisfactory answer as to why Macleod was suddenly on the move. The organisation needed clever men, men who could read and interpret the intentions of others. But he was also annoyed that Darcy had shown himself to be so very clever and so quick. It didn't always do to have subordinates who were, or might grow to be, cleverer than their masters. Long ago Bentley had known Macleod as a young husband and father, then he had known him as a soldier and then as a widower. Now he knew him as a lawyer. He had laid all these in front of Darcy and Darcy had spotted the right track almost immediately. Bentley looked at Darcy and smiled. Darcy smiled back thinking Bentley's smile was one of approval of his quickness. But behind the smile Bentley was thinking that perhaps Darcy was too clever to live a long life. Someone as clever as Darcy might indeed come to pose a threat. When that happened, if it was allowed to happen, he must not be in a position to do any serious damage. Sometime soon Darcy's time would come, but not too soon. It would come when Darcy found that he had to die, because he could no longer live. Bentley put his glass on the mantelpiece.

'And now duty calls me. I have much to do, Darcy, letters to send before Macleod leaves Boston.'

Darcy also got up.

'And me?'

'Be ready to travel as soon as Macleod leaves.'

'And if my hand's not healed?'

'God damn and blast your wretched hand to hell, Darcy. You'll go when I say.'

Darcy was taken aback by this sudden outburst.

'As you say, Bentley, just as you say. I'll go as soon as Macleod has taken ship for Richmond.'

Bentley looked at him then grabbed up his overcoat, hat and gloves and left the room without another word leaving Darcy puzzled and, as always when Bentley flared up, a little afraid.

Chapter Sixteen

Away from the large centres of population, overland travel in America remained a primitive and uncertain business. The surest route was the coastal highway where vessels of all sizes plied the busy shipping lanes. Up and down the coast the main rivers were also busy providing access inland from the seaboard ports. Macleod took ship from Boston, travelled south to Norfolk, Virginia and from there took ship up the Potomac and finally arrived at Georgetown.

He took a room at the City Tavern, recommended to him by the captain of the vessel on which he had arrived.

'Fine place, Mr Macleod, only built five years ago and considered as good as anything you'd find in New York or even Boston. Why, only a year or so ago they gave a banquet to President Adams himself there.'

'You are a native of Georgetown, Captain?'

'Proud to have been born here, sir.'

'Hmm.'

And Macleod felt sure that the Captain's eulogy to this City Tavern was based more on civic pride than any wide experience of fine buildings.

But Macleod was forced to revise his opinion of the City Tavern when he got there. It was indeed a fine, three-storey brick building with large, regular sash windows and, he was forced to admit, would not have been out of place in Boston, no, not even on Tremont Street itself.

After unpacking and settling into his room he ate an excellent dinner in the spacious, well-appointed dining room then retired. A comfortable fire burned brightly in the small fireplace and as the wine had been as excellent as the food Macleod found that he felt positively cheerful. He retired and slept soundly until he was called at seven the next morning to find his fire refreshed and a plentiful supply of hot water together with warm towels and shaving materials laid out ready for use.

After a breakfast as good as the previous evening's dinner, Macleod enquired from his waiter directions to get to the new capital.

'Well, sir, it's not a long ride. You head east over Rock Creek Bridge and then follow the trail through Foggy Bottom.'

'A strange name.'

'On account of it being low-lying near the river. There's a settlement there, Funkstown, German-speaking mostly but it's not what anyone would call a thriving place.'

'And beyond Foggy Bottom?'

'Oh the trail's clear enough, sir, you can't miss it. There's plenty of hauling goes along it taking men and goods to the new capital.'

'And can you recommend a place where I might hire a good saddle-horse?'

The waiter could, of course, oblige and Macleod, armed with that information, went out at once to begin the final leg of what he had almost come to regard as his great adventure.

Macleod found the livery stable, negotiated a good price for the hire of a horse and was grudgingly given free directions. Soon after, and in a good temper, he rode over Rock Creek Bridge and followed the trail to Foggy Bottom.

The trail was as the waiter had said. The trees had been cleared well back and it was rutted with use. It was not long before Macleod passed two lumbering carts, each pulled by a team of four horses and both loaded with rough-cut timbers. Soon after passing the carts he came to the straggling settlement of Funkstown, as unprepossessing in looks as its name. Even if his journey had been considerably more advanced he would not have been tempted to stop at the settlement. The low-lying land was not far from the river and the air had an unwholesomeness to it which made Macleod spur on his mount and quickly leave the settlement behind him.

As he rode on he dredged from his mind memories of the man who had summoned him.

Many of his fellow officers had thought him a hard man, some even that he was careless of the casualties his orders incurred. But Macleod knew that his hardness was that of a man who would not allow any emotion to cloud his military judgement. He also knew that he cared passionately. He cared that the men he commanded should do their job. He cared that they should make America free.

He passed several more wagons going his way and as many empty ones returning and, as the horse seemed willing and able to stay on the trail without guidance, he was free to let his thoughts wander through his past, which he did, paying scant regard to the country he travelled through.

The trail breasted a rise and his mental wanderings came to an abrupt end as he reined his horse to a halt. Before him lay America's new capital. He sat and looked. This, he felt, should be a moment savoured, his first sight of the new home of the President and the American government. He tried to fill his breast with an appropriate pride but found only an impatience to be on his way, so he rode on.

Quite what he had expected he did not know, but it was certainly not what he rode into. The trail widened and tracks branched off to both sides where the wagons unloaded their timber, stone and equipment into chaotic piles of building materials. From this apparent chaos an endless stream of men and horses carted and dragged their loads towards more organised piles, out of which recognisable buildings were rising. The wide dirt track took him onwards up a hill which became bordered by open land with a tended, park-like quality. Reaching the top of the hill Macleod stopped and his breast did indeed fill with pride. There, to his right, built of pale white stone, stood a handsome, square, three-storey building topped all round with a balustrade. The new Capitol, the home of Congress.

Macleod turned in his saddle to take in the view from this hilltop. Behind him, over a small copse of trees, he could look down on the Potomac river. Turning back he looked further along the dirt road. Somewhere out there, among this fine new city that was arising, was the home of the President.

If Macleod had closed his eyes and used his imagination then he might have looked into the future and tried to envisage what Washington would one day become. But Macleod had a very limited imagination and with his eyes open was only able to see what was there.

He put a hand inside his greatcoat and pulled out the letter. The address at the top meant nothing to him just as it hadn't meant anything to anyone at the City Tavern when he had enquired the previous evening. He looked at the letter again.

It was headed *The Office of Internal and International Information, Washington*. No more. In the open space in front of the Capitol were several coaches with coachmen and grooms standing about. Macleod rode across and hailed one of the coachmen and asked him if he knew his way about the new Capital.

'As well as any man, sir, although as yet there's not so very much to know.'

'I'm looking for "The Office of Internal and International Information".'

The coachman shook his head and called to another.

'Office of what?'

'Internal and International Information.'

The new arrival proceeded to shake his head. At that moment a man came from the Capitol building and called. The first coachman turned to the voice.

'My Congressman, sir. I'll ask him.'

The coachman ran across to the man and they exchanged words. The Congressman looked across at Macleod then got into his carriage. The coachman got up into the driver's seat and brought the coach to where Macleod waited. The Congressman lowered the window.

'I don't know who gave you that address, my friend, but I fear they were pulling your leg. There is no Office of Internal and International Information, nor any like it.'

'Are you sure, sir?'

'Friend, I'm a Congressman. My job is government and I know all the offices of government both here in Washington and back in Philadelphia. Fine sort of Congressman I'd be if I didn't. No, friend, I don't know where you've come from but you're on a fool's errand.'

And the window shot up. The Congressman rattled the roof with the knob of his stick and the carriage moved off, turned on to the track and disappeared down the hill leaving Macleod alone and puzzled.

Chapter Seventeen

Macleod pressed on with his inquiries but it soon proved to be exactly as the Congressman had said. If there was an Office of Internal and International Information it belied its own name by not having told a living soul in Washington where it might be found and by mid-afternoon Macleod had to admit total defeat.

His was a dogged nature but even the most dogged of men must finally give in to hard facts. There was no office of the name he was looking for. Wearily he turned his horse and headed back through what there was of the new capital. He left behind the fine buildings, those finished, unfinished and as yet unstarted and took the trail on which he had come that morning with such high hopes and expectations.

He had been ordered to come, and he had done as ordered. He had tried his best to report his arrival, but how was that to be done if no one knew of the place he had been ordered to? As he rode away and left the Great New Federal Building Site behind him a stranger on a horse came down a track from a wooded hill and pulled alongside him.

'Headed for Georgetown, friend?' Macleod didn't answer or look at the new arrival. He didn't want company, he wanted to think, but his attitude did not deter the young man now riding at his side. 'A silly question really. Heading this way you must be for Georgetown as indeed I am myself. Perhaps we could bear each other company?'

Macleod responded by spurring on his horse and pulling away from the stranger who continued to let his horse walk but called out to Macleod's back.

'If that's the way you want it, Mr Macleod. But if you insist on travelling alone and ignorant in these parts I doubt very much you'll ever get where you're going or meet the man who sent for you.'

Macleod reined in his horse. The young man came alongside.

'You seem to know my name, sir.'

A big grin split the face of the young man as he looked at Macleod.

'I do, sir, and I know more than that. I know that inside your coat somewhere you carry a letter and that letter is what brought you here.' The grin settled to a smile and he held out his hand. 'I'll thank you for that letter, sir. It has served its purpose and can now be returned and disposed of.'

'And what makes you think I'll hand it over to you, even supposing it exists?'

The young man withdrew his hand.

'Because, sir, I have asked for it graciously and with such charm of manner. Surely graciousness and charm of manner are worth something even in these wicked times,' he paused, 'even to a hard-headed lawyer who's come all the way from Boston.'

Macleod had the overwhelming feeling that he was being mocked. His natural instincts were to spur on his horse and leave this young jackanapes behind him. But he knew that instincts were best trusted only as a matter of last resort and he was a long way yet from last resort.

'I'll need more than that, sir, a lot more before we can talk further on any subject.'

'No, Lawyer Macleod.' The smile had gone and the voice had changed. For all his youth he had the voice of command and Macleod recognised it. 'Not a lot. Just one thing more. A direct order to hand over that letter. But if you've forgotten how to obey a direct order then you're no good to me,' and here he paused, 'or to anyone I serve.' He held out his hand again. 'Come man, the letter or we part company here, now and for good.'

Macleod looked carefully at the stranger. He was young, but that was nothing. He himself had been as young when he was soldiering and handing out orders.

He sits there now, thought Macleod, with the look and manner of command. But is he someone I can trust?

Unfortunately there was only one way Macleod could think of to find out. He slowly put his hand inside his coat and handed over the letter. The other man opened it and read it carefully. He seemed satisfied and tucked it away inside his own coat. They resumed the journey at a walk. It was Macleod who broke the silence.

'How do you know I didn't make a copy?'

'Why would you, and even if you had what good would it do you? The Department you were referred to, as you found out, doesn't exist. It was there just to make sure that when you arrived and began to enquire we would get to hear about it. No, now the original is safe I don't think we need worry about anything like copies.'

'But what if I showed the original to someone?'

'Yes, now there's a big, "what if?". But you see you didn't show it to anyone, so it's a "what if?" that doesn't arise.'

'How can you be sure?'

'Because if you had shown it to anyone you would now be dead and as you are so palpably alive it means that your eyes alone have seen it, other than mine and those of the writer of course.' The young man kicked his horse into a canter. 'Come now, Mr Macleod, this won't do. We must move faster than this if I am to be your guest and dine with you tonight at the City Tavern.'

Chapter Eighteen

Macleod and his guest had eaten, but the dining room of the City Tavern, being deservedly popular, was crowded, making any confidential talk impossible, so when the meal was over they had gone to Macleod's room. The young man had a limp and walked with the aid of a stick but Macleod had not felt the necessity of waiting for him and was standing in his room when the young man finally entered.

'I'm sorry to be so slow but this damn leg of mine has an awkward way with stairs.'

Macleod watched him as he limped across the room to a chair and sat down.

Macleod crossed to the fire and stood before it taking all the benefit of the warmth.

'Well, sir, you've had your food and you've had your wine and all at my expense. Now do I get something?'

But the young man seemed in no hurry to get down to the purpose of the meeting. His voice, when he spoke, was casual and conversational.

'You know they say that Jefferson was mightily pleased that our new Federal Capital was to be in the South.' He waited, but Macleod stayed silent. 'They say that he felt that the North was so commercially minded that it degraded any man of honour. Well, now he's President he can move in when Adams moves out and breathe clean Southern air to his heart's content.' He looked up at Macleod with a half-smile on his lips. Then he made a gesture with his stick as if impatient of idle chatter. 'But enough of that, Mr Macleod, we're not here to discuss the relative merits of the air, North or South, are we? We're here to attend to business.'

Macleod knew he was being mocked but again he let it pass.

'Yes, sir, and the business is, why was I summoned here?'

'Ordered is a better word I think. Yes, ordered would be the right word. You recognised the name on the letter, so I think we can both agree that you may now consider yourself a man under orders. I hope you agree, Mr Macleod, otherwise I see no way of proceeding further in the matter.'

'Ordered if you will, but as I have no knowledge of what the matter is, ordered or summoned are much the same to me.'

'Ordered it is then. Now for your next orders. I was told you speak fluent French. Is that so?'

'It is.'

'Could you pass for French?'

'No.'

'Colonial French, perhaps from north of the border, Quebec, somewhere like that?'

'Perhaps I could get by as far as the language is concerned but as I know nothing of the country it would be easy for anyone to find out I was playing a part.'

'Then you will have to be as you are, an American who speaks French. You are to go to New Orleans. Once there you are to tell people that you are a wealthy lawyer from Boston who has decided to go into business. You are not decided yet between tobacco or cotton or whether to get into sugar-cane planting.'

'What rubbish. What would I know of any of that? What *do* I know? I'll be made to look a fool at once.'

Jones smiled.

'That will make you all the more welcome. A fool with money who's looking to invest in something he knows nothing about? Why they'll fall over themselves to befriend and advise you.'

Macleod was enough of a man of business to see the soundness of Jones's reasoning.

'And while I'm in New Orleans?'

'You will enter into society. You must change your way of life to become a man of fashion and manners.'

But this time Jones had gone too far to carry Macleod with him. Macleod snorted a derisive laugh.

'That's too much of a change for me. I know nothing of fashion and don't want to, and my only manner is plain-speaking.'

The young man's voice took on a hard edge.

'Then you must learn, Macleod, you must study how to be fashionable and put a restraint on the directness of your speech. There is trouble brewing in New Orleans, French trouble, and it is aimed at America. You are to find out what it is and who is involved. That means you will have to go where society goes, talk as society talks and do as society does. In short, you will do whatever is necessary to find out what we want.' The young man looked Macleod up and down. 'I will help you do as well as can be done in the way of clothes here in Georgetown. It won't be much, but anything will be an improvement on what you look like now. You will have to fit yourself out more properly once you're in New Orleans.'

'Assuming I can play the dandy, which I doubt, and assuming I can get invited into society, which I also doubt, what sort of thing am I looking for?'

'It will be political, well-financed and in some way in contact with Paris. The person or persons you will be looking for will be highly placed and influential and there won't be many of them, four at most. They probably won't travel much but they will have contact with others who travel both in America and abroad. Whoever they are they will spend a lot of time in each other's company, they will be close and exclusive.'

'In which case how will mixing with society help me?'

'New Orleans isn't such a big place yet, though growing fast of late. For the most part it's like any other port and garrison town, something of a rough house. Most of the best society is made up of old-established families, what I believe they call Creoles. Stiff-necked and exclusive so I'm told. That should make your task easier.'

'How easier?'

'The people you'll be looking for will be comparative newcomers, certainly not born or even brought up there but come over from France and come over not so very long ago. They'll be rich and influential and for that sort to stay too much out of society would cause comment and raise questions, and that would be the last thing they'd want, so they'll be found where society meets. It's not a large number of people you'll be watching and not spread over too wide an area. When the city first got built they laid it out as if was a chess board, all straight streets criss-crossing each other, and although it's growing at a pace these days it'll be in the older part of the city you'll find what you're looking for. So sharp eyes and ears should be able to narrow the field pretty quickly. But take care, Macleod, one sniff that you're looking for them and you'll be dead. They don't take chances and they don't play games. Never doubt the importance of what you are doing and don't be fooled by appearances. Your quarry may look a fop in public or even a fool, but underneath they will be hard and sharp.'

'And if I find anything?'

'Then you report it to me.'

'And where will you be?'

'I will arrive in New Orleans three weeks after you. I will be on government business, to negotiate certain concessions on warehousing and harbour facilities. The negotiations will be difficult and therefore prolonged. I will be asking for too much but not so much as to provoke an immediate rebuttal. If you find out anything you come directly to me. Otherwise you don't know me and I don't know you.'

'And what name will you use if I have to ask for you?'

'Jones, Jeremiah Jones. And, as for names, we shall need one for you.'

'If I'm to be a Boston lawyer what's wrong with Macleod?'

'We'll keep Boston and we'll keep you a lawyer but the name must be changed. If anyone takes the time and trouble to check they must find what we want them to find. How about Darcy?'

'Darcy!'

'He's a Boston lawyer, a man about town and well-off. Any enquiry that doesn't go too deep would be satisfied. What do you say to Darcy?'

'I say damn Darcy and damn …'

'Good, that's settled then. Darcy it will be.'

Having swallowed so much Macleod found himself gagging on this final humiliation. The young man took his stick in his hand and pushed himself into a standing position.

But Macleod's contract-lawyer brain came gloriously to his aid.

'And who will arrange to replace the name on the letters of credit that I carry?'

'What?'

'I have letters of credit good at any bank in New Orleans or anywhere else, but all in the name of Macleod. If I am to be a man of fashion it will take money, plenty of it, and if I'm to be Darcy as you say then it can't be money in the name of Macleod.'

For the first time since their meeting the young man looked a little less than certain of himself.

'How much do you have?'

Macleod named a sum, a very considerable sum.

'I see. You realise of course that going to New Orleans in your own name increases the risk you take, the risk to you personally and to the task you have been given?'

'And you realise I cannot operate as you ask without adequate funds?'

The young man stood silent for a moment, then realised he had been bested.

'Very well, be Macleod. But play your part damn well, well enough so no one will want to ask in Boston what sort of man is Lawyer Macleod. Now, on to other things,' and he looked at Macleod from head to foot. 'I'll call for you tomorrow morning. Be ready at nine and make sure your wallet is full. I'll do the best that dollars and Georgetown tailors can manage but I doubt it will do more than dent the surface. If I'm to transform you from a fashion bumpkin into a thing of beauty we will have a heavy day ahead of us,' he shook his head slowly, 'a very heavy day indeed.'

Chapter Nineteen

New Orleans greeted Macleod as it greeted all who came to it from the sea, with clamour, noise and bustle. Under a clear blue sky and an already hot sun Macleod stood looking at the waterfront where ships were tied to massive piles driven into the river bed at the edge of an expanse of heavy wooden decking which stood barely a few feet above the river, and under which the dark waters lapped and gurgled. The dark, heavy timbers of the decking were covered with bales and barrels, sacks and chests, boxes and bags, constantly on the move, carried and dragged, loaded and thrown, manhandled somehow, anyhow, by an army of toiling, sweating workers. Here sea-going ships exchanged cargoes with the Mississippi boats which moored further upriver. The bounty of the interior, once so small but now grown prodigious, the cotton and the tobacco, the hides and the furs, all that the world wanted, was piled up ready to begin its journey. And the manufactured goods from the great world were piled up waiting to be taken up the Mississippi to make the life of those who lived alongside that great river highway, and relied on it, almost civilised.

What could not be laden, or was not ready, was carted off to be stored in the great, new, stone-built warehouses which stood behind the docks and hid the city from its new arrivals.

Beyond the warehouses the streets began. As Jones had said, they were straight and at right angles to one another, and those nearest to the docks were no more than a jostle of people, carts, horses and mules, all blurring into one another in the smog of dust thrown up from the dry dirt of the roads which lay between the buildings lining either side. At first these buildings were not so different from the warehouses, drab, functional places of business. But as Macleod walked on holding a handkerchief over his mouth and nose against the dust, the furious activity of a city learning how to get and gain gave way to a more relaxed atmosphere. Small houses stood on either side of the streets and the pavements were clear of caked mud. For the most part they were single-storey terraces with pitched roofs and comfortable verandas behind whitewashed fencing.

Jeremiah Jones had been right, that part of New Orleans which serviced the docks was indeed much of a rough-house. But beyond the warehousing, the taverns, the whorehouses, above the river on a gentle hill there was another New Orleans, a place of refinement and beauty, of elegant houses with bright stucco frontages with upper-storey French windows which opened on to elaborate wrought-iron balconies and verandas. Here the aristocracy of the city, plantation money, slave money and most honoured of all, old money, maintained a luxurious and cultured idleness. And it was among these lordly ones that Macleod was ordered to introduce himself, to become accepted by them and mix with them on terms of easy intimacy, the better to learn their secrets.

Macleod, when he had first walked through their streets, didn't know whether to laugh or cry. His new Georgetown wardrobe might be a vast improvement on his severe, practical Boston attire but, in contrast to what he saw in New Orleans, he felt like a country clod and knew that here he looked like one. His overwhelming impression was that he might stay in New Orleans till hell froze over before finding any acquaintance who might introduce him into the houses where he needed access. But he had been sent to this city on duty, so he spent his days in reconnoitre, and by the end of his first week felt he had made progress. Strangely enough it was his lack of fashionable attire that gave him his idea for breaching the defences of the formidable fortress to which he secretly laid siege.

He found the most suitable bank, one favoured with much business from the best of society. Here he deposited letters of credit, opened an account and announced his business intentions. The manager was impressed not only by the size of the deposit and the promise of more funds but also by the spaciousness of Macleod's plans. The way Macleod described them it seemed either he was going into tobacco by buying up Virginia or going into cotton by buying up one or other of the Carolinas and, if the market was favourable, perhaps both.

Through the good offices of his new bank manager he found and rented some rooms on the Faubourg Ste Marie side of Rampart

Street, not actually within the French citadel but close enough to serve his purposes. He found where he could eat, where he could drink and where he could idle part of the day and, in doing all three, achieve the most publicity and be noticed. He knew he was not sufficiently practised to play the easy socialite so he had decided his part would be something to which he was, for the moment, better suited – a man of mystery. Someone who bought himself the best, didn't count the cost and kept himself very much to himself. Most importantly of all he finally spied out on Bourbon Street his first point of engagement, the best tailor the city had to offer.

He had been in New Orleans about three weeks before he made his way to this tailor. The shop contained only two dandies who gave him a look and turned away, their expressions eloquent commentary on what they thought of his manner of dress. An elderly man came out of a back room, saw Macleod and came across to him.

'Good day, sir. Can I be of service?'

His accent told Macleod the man was French so it was in French that he responded.

'M'sieur, if you can be of service it will be in one of two ways.'

The elderly man raised his eyebrows questioningly.

'I beg your pardon?'

'Either you can dress me so that I'm fit to be seen, sir, or you can put a pistol ball in my head and put me out of my misery.'

For a second the tailor paused looking at Macleod's serious face. Then he laughed and Macleod smiled.

'Eh bien, M'sieur, as I would rather not kill a new client I must see what I can do for you in the other way.'

Macleod stood back and opened his arms wide.

'I urge you to look well, mon ami, before you commit yourself and see what you're up against.' He turned round once and dropped his arms. 'If you admit defeat I shall attach no blame. London or Paris might take on such a challenge but I doubt, sir, yes I very much doubt that anywhere *but* London or Paris can effect a cure for such an extreme case as mine.'

The tailor continued to laugh, but more from good manners than anything else. He was somewhat stung by Macleod's assessment of what he could do.

'Well, if M'sieur cannot go to Paris …'

'No, alas, I cannot. Business prevents it, more's the pity.'

'Then you are fortunate that Paris has come to you.'

Now it was Macleod's turn to affect emotion. He registered surprise.

'Paris come to me? In what way come to me, sir?'

'In me, sir. I trained in Paris and was, some were kind enough to say, perhaps the foremost tailor in that fair city. Fair, I say, until the arrival of that infamous lady, Madame La Guillotine. Too many of my clients died under that lady's blade, so I decided that the safest thing for me would be to put the deep Atlantic between myself and their revolution.'

'Sensible fellow. No sense in losing your head over something as paltry as politics, eh?'

'C'est vrai, M'sieur. My thoughts entirely.'

'Yes, but are you in touch, that's the question? I don't want to look like something on its way to the court of the late King Louis. I want to wear what Paris and London are wearing today, not what they were wearing ten years ago.'

The shop wasn't a large one and Macleod had been speaking loudly enough to ensure that the two exquisites busy examining handkerchiefs by the window couldn't fail to hear his every word. One of them crossed to Macleod and the tailor.

'M'sieur, I can assure you that if Philippe dresses you,' and here he paused to take in the full horror of Macleod's garments, 'you will be, in the deepest sense of the word, dressed.'

Macleod made a slight bow of acknowledgement.

'If you and your friend are examples of his handiwork then I take you at your word, sir.'

The man smirked at the compliment, then addressed the tailor.

'Look after him, Philippe, I see he needs all your skill. Do not spare yourself.'

'I will do my best, Your Excellency.'

His Excellency was about to turn back to his friend when Macleod spoke.

'Thank you. Perhaps when I'm fit to be seen in public I can return your kindness by inviting you to take some refreshment with me.' His Excellency paused. He did not know the man. He was not at all sure he wanted to know him. Macleod read the doubt in his face. 'If you will permit me to say so, even dressed by Philippe I doubt I would believe I was fit for company until I had achieved your complete endorsement.'

This raised a self-satisfied smile. Macleod had guessed he would be an easy man to flatter. He also guessed that it would not be the same way with the man still by the window who stood scowling at Macleod with unconcealed dislike.

'Well, let me know when Philippe has finished with you and I might cast an eye upon you. I make no promises you understand. You may, as you say, be beyond even Philippe's help, but I may cast an eye over you.'

Macleod gave a bow and pulled out a small rectangle of thick pasteboard and held it out.

'My card.'

His Excellency looked down at it with disdain.

'I'm sure it is,' and turned away, 'come, St Clair, there's nothing here for us today.'

St Clair dropped the handkerchiefs he had been holding on to a small table.

The tailor made a dash for the door and got it open just in time for the two exquisites to sail out into the street where an open carriage with a black, liveried driver waited and a black, liveried page-boy held the carriage door open. The sight caused Macleod to stand stock still and stare. For, sitting erect in the carriage and dressed in the height of fashion, staring straight ahead, was the most stunningly beautiful young woman Macleod had ever seen.

The carriage had certainly not been there when Macleod had arrived because if it had been he would have felt the blow then which he suddenly felt now. He stood, staring, almost gaping, as the two dandies got into the carriage. The boy closed its door, jumped up onto the back and the driver with a flick of his whip urged the pair of jet-black horses into a walk and the carriage moved slowly off taking the object of Macleod's gaze with it. Macleod and the tailor stood in the shop doorway watching, and, after what seemed like an age but in reality was only a second, Macleod, by an overwhelming force of will, hauled his consciousness back to the business in hand.

'And the two gentlemen were?'

The tailor turned.

'The one to whom you spoke was Etienne Henri de Valois, the youngest son of the Duke of Toulouse who, as the Duke and all his immediate family went to the guillotine, should now by rights hold the title, if there was still a dukedom or indeed if there was any sanity left in France.' They moved back into the shop. 'His companion was Louis Antoine St Clair, they are said to be inseparable.'

Macleod steadied himself to make his next question as casual as possible.

'And the lady in the carriage?'

He knew at once he had failed miserably when it drew a knowing smile from the tailor.

'His Excellency's wife, Madame Marie Christine de Valois, and, as I see you have already noted for yourself, probably the most beautiful woman in New Orleans, and that is always bearing in mind that New Orleans is famous for its beautiful women. She turns many a head I assure you. You are by no means alone in admiring her.'

With an effort Macleod got his manner and voice back under control.

'Yes, a fine woman to be sure. Admirable. But not the reason I'm here.'

'No, of course.' The tailor took a thick, leather-bound book from under his counter and opened it out. From a glance at the number of pages used and the appointments already on the open pages Macleod could see that business was good. 'Now, sir, when can I put you down to be measured? Shall we say Thursday morning at ten?'

'Yes. I shall look forward to it.' Macleod went to the shop door, opened it and turned. 'You'll have some designs to show me?'

'Mais certainement.'

'And they will be of the latest style?'

The tailor smirked.

'You will see, I assure you M'sieur, nothing that would not grace the best houses in London or Paris.'

'Good. Tell me, how do you manage to stay so up to date with your fashions?'

The smirk dropped away and a look of caution came into the tailor's eyes.

'Ah, that is my little secret, and if I told anyone my secret, how long would I keep my clients? Not long I think. Goodbye, M'sieur.'

Macleod accepted his dismissal, left the shop and took out his watch. He was pleased with himself, very pleased. Now it was time to visit his rooms and begin to make a record of things. His first little campaign had been a total success. He had marked down his quarry and manufactured a meeting. The first skirmish had taken place and contact with the enemy had been made. Also he had picked up an extra cherry by finding out that the tailor, Philippe, had some secret way of keeping up with Paris fashions which meant a carefully guarded but effective line of communication. Also, if Philippe was right, he had found two men who were rich and influential, one of whom played the foppish imbecile. Could he have been so lucky so quickly? Macleod, with the memory of Madame de Valois undoubtedly colouring his vision, decided that the day had been a great success. He felt elated. He seemed to himself a changed man, a man who felt that life might offer something considerably more rewarding than merely a nightly path to oblivion.

Chapter Twenty

'I miss the gin, I do, Molly. I know brandy's what the nobs all drink but I still miss the gin. It's what I'm used to.'

Kitty Mullen took another good pull at her glass and put it back empty on the table in front of her.

Molly O'Hara pushed the bottle across.

'Well there is no gin, only brandy, so you'll have to suffer.'

And took a drink from her own glass.

They sat either side of a small table in the neat living room of the apartment which, to New Orleans society, was that of Molly O'Hara's alter ego, Madame de Metz.

The apartment was not large but situated in a quiet yet convenient corner of fashionable New Orleans just off the Rue de Chartres. It had taken the newly arrived Madame de Metz a remarkably short time to find a kind gentleman friend who took her needs to his own heart. He was touched by her plight, a young widow of noble birth whom the wicked Revolution had cast adrift in a cold and indifferent world, left to survive as best she could on the kindness of strangers. He had held her hand to show his sympathy, she had allowed it to show her gratitude. She had nothing, absolutely nothing. The monsters had taken everything. She had but one maid, a few trunks of simple dresses and gowns, barely enough jewels to be seen in public and, as for money, less than nothing. His hand gently rested on her knee, "Please, dear lady, do not think of money, do not worry your pretty head." She smiled at him and did not remove his hand or blush that it was not on her pretty head that his eyes rested but slightly lower down.

She found that he also had his cross to bear. He was a widower of some years, he lived alone. He was wealthy, but what was money when one had no one to share life's little pleasures? Some might consider him too elderly to consider ... "No, no, sir, not elderly." "Well then, perhaps not elderly ..."

And so it had continued. Madame de Metz got a neat little

apartment, an introduction into society, new friends, new clothes, new jewels, in short, everything she had set out to get. And her very good friend and benefactor got what he deserved, the gratitude of a very pretty young woman and the envy of handsome, younger men as she bestowed her smiles and caresses on him in public, and in private, coffee, touches, kisses and a hint of more tomorrow, if tomorrow ever came.

It was neatly done, the quarry marked down with the skill of an expert hunter, the kill quick and clean. Madame de Metz was now not only established in society but welcome in all the best houses. The husbands might ogle her, but what of it, so long as the wives didn't fear or resent her. And she was careful that they had no cause. She had a friend, a very generous and jealous friend, she neither needed nor wanted any other male interest. She was no threat to any lady whose husband might, given the slightest encouragement, stray.

Madame de Metz and her maid had both had a full day. They had visited, watched, listened and gossiped, Madame in drawing rooms, the maid in kitchens. Now a lamp burned between them on the table. Now the roles of Madame de Metz and her devoted maid had been put off for the day so they could sit in comfort and review their progress in the company of the bottle of brandy. They had let their hair down, taken off all their day clothes and were loosely wrapped in robes.

'How did it go for you, Kitty? Anything?'

'Nothing to speak of above the usual. For all their fine airs and graces they don't seem so very different here from London. Mostly they're so busy with their clothes and manners and la-di-da that none of them would have the time to be at anything else even if they had the brains for it. If any ramp is coming off among this lot, political or any other sort, it's too bloody well hidden for anyone back stairs to have got wind of it. God knows I've tried but I haven't had a sniff.' They both took a drink. 'What about giving our Boston lawyer a closer look?'

Molly gave a snort of derision at the suggestion.

'Boston? The mysterious Mr Macleod? That has to be a joke, Kitty.'

'Well, who else have we got? Trent told you to watch out for someone at the same game and the only one I've seen who might fit the ticket is Boston.'

Molly threw her head back and laughed.

'Good God, girl. What do you think we're looking for? A Drury Lane comic villain?'

'Laugh if you like but as I say, who else is there? We've been here nearly a month, you've got yourself dug in, visit the best houses and go everywhere the nobs go, and up to now we've seen nothing of interest except Boston. So why not him?'

'Because if he was here for the same reason as us, he'd behave like us. He'd dig himself in, he'd fade in among them and he'd do just as I've done. But no, not our Mr Macleod from Boston. He makes a great show of keeping himself to himself but while he's at it he goes everywhere and makes sure everybody sees him. If he wanted to attract any more attention he'd have to dance naked through the street.'

'All right, so tell me what his game is then? He has to be up to something behaving like he does.'

'I've thought about it and I reckon he's looking to try for a tumble with pretty young Marie de Valois.'

'What! Madame de V.? She'd not give him a second glance. What makes you say it?'

'Oh I've watched him, Kitty. He doesn't concern our little game but I've watched him just the same. He makes sure he goes where she's likely to turn up and then moons at her from a safe distance.'

'Looking don't mean much. Plenty of the men would like to get under her skirts. Looks don't mean anything.'

'Maybe not, but for all his keeping himself to himself he's trying damn hard to get on the right side of the husband and I'll give him his due, he's not making a bad fist of it. He's got the ninny tutoring him on what to wear. De Valois may have nothing but vacant rooms upstairs but he thinks he knows everything that's anything when it comes to fashion and he may not be far wrong. If I gave Mr Macleod credit for any brains I'd say he'd made a clever move.'

'Except for one thing.'

'What's that?'

'If he ever gets into a bed in that household I hope he knows what he's in for, because chances are it'll end up being Mr de V.

he'll be cuddling not Mrs.' And they both threw their heads back and laughed. 'And if he scores a hit then he'll have St Clair chasing him.' They laughed again. 'Does Boston know do you think?'

Molly gave the question a moment's thought.

'No, I doubt it. De Valois and St Clair keep themselves pretty much clear of too much gossip. It's like you say, Kitty, no different to anywhere else, so long as no one pokes you in the eye with it no one gives a cuss.'

Molly picked up the bottle and refilled their glasses.

'What do you think about St Clair and de Valois, Kitty? Them being so careful, like. What if it wasn't just the bum-pumping, what if they were keeping things close for another reason?'

'It's a thought. It would be a clever way of keeping any nosey-parkers satisfied and out of their hair. Do you rate it, Molly? It's damn well done if it's an act.'

'Oh they're at it all right, the question is, what else might they be at or, more to the point, what might St Clair be at? De Valois's the donkey he looks but St Clair, now there's a man I think it might be worth knowing better. What about his household, anything?'

'No loose gossip from that quarter. You may be right about him. Maybe you should try to give him a closer look.'

'Well, if I can't get at him direct …'

'And you can't through your usual channels.'

'… then I shall have to go the roundabout way.'

'Which is?'

'The wife of his lover boy.'

'That's roundabout enough but as we've nowhere else to go at the moment, why not?'

They sat in silence for a moment, each thinking and drinking. Then Molly pushed her glass a little way from her.

'I don't know whether it's me or the brandy but I've just had a thought, Kitty. What if you're not off the mark and our Mr Macleod is doing a sweet job of pulling the wool over our eyes?'

'He hasn't the brains. You said yourself …'

'No, listen. I was told some sort of political shenanigans were being cooked up here and Trent wouldn't be wrong about that even though we've not tumbled anything yet. He also told me to look out in case anyone else came looking.'

'So?'

'What if Macleod is here for the same as we are but somehow got wind of us before we saw him?'

Kitty considered it.

'You mean he nailed us and decided to put on an act that would take him out of our reckoning.' They both took another drink and considered the mysterious Mr Macleod. 'No, that's the brandy talking. All he wants is to get into her pants, it can't be anything else.'

'I'm not so sure. I find I want to get into de Valois's house and cosey up to the wife, so does he, and he's already started. Makes you think, don't it?'

They both took another thoughtful drink. Kitty reached for the bottle and tipped it up. It was empty.

Kitty gave a quiet belch and finished what was left in her glass.

'Let's sleep on it.'

Molly nodded and finished her glass.

'Good idea.'

They stood up and let their robes drop to the floor. Molly picked up the lamp from the table and they made their way across the living room towards the bedroom door.

'We'll think about it again in the morning.'

'Good idea.'

Kitty's hand held on to Molly's free arm to steady herself indicating she had managed to overcome her earlier prejudice against the brandy. They left the living room and the bedroom door closed behind them. There was a brief silence which was broken by Molly's voice.

'Hurry up, girl, don't be all night with that chamber pot, there's others waiting.'

'Hold on to yourself, nature can't be rushed.'

'Nor held back too long so get a move on.'

There was loud, coarse laughter followed by sounds of movement until silence fell once more and the light under the bedroom door went out. The agents of His Gracious Majesty, King George, had taken to their deserved rest.

Chapter Twenty-one

Madame de Metz sat with her new friend, Marie de Valois. It was late morning and they were drinking chocolate in Marie's boudoir. The windows were open to provide some comfort to the room but beyond the balcony the rain storm, combining with the heat, made everywhere dark and oppressive. Marie was looking bored and idly fanned herself but Madame de Metz was lively and animated. She seemed to be enjoying herself.

'But who is he, your husband's new friend, the mysterious Mr Macleod? Everyone is asking the same question, who is he? Is he anyone?'

Madame de Valois ceased her futile work with her fan.

'How should I know and why should I care? He is someone who has attached himself to my husband. Other than that I know nothing and care less.'

'I have heard he is a fabulously rich lawyer from the North down here looking to invest in cotton or tobacco. I'm told he seems to talk about business well enough, but as far as actually doing any he seems to prefer spending his time making his way in society. The question I ask myself is, does society want him?'

'Society can do as it wishes. *I* don't want him, not even as a topic of discussion. Find something else, for heaven's sake, or I'll start to get a headache.'

'Of course it might be a clever ploy. There's plenty looking to get money invested. Business is not being well served by this war. Saying you have plenty to invest and then dilly-dallying while people come to you with propositions might be …'

'Oh for pity's sake! Don't go on so about business. Leave that to the men. It seems to interest them and keeps them out of the way, thank God.'

Madame de Metz changed tack.

'Do you think him handsome?'

'I don't think him anything.'

'No, not handsome perhaps, but attractive in a clumsy, innocent sort of way. He makes me laugh.'

'Ah, an amusing man. Now that is different. I might take an interest in an amusing man.'

'It's as if he was a child playing a part in household theatricals. He takes himself terribly seriously and tries so hard, but is so hopelessly bad at his act that one ends up finding him rather sweet and encouraging him in his efforts, just as one would with a child.'

'Playing a part?'

'Oh, yes. He is acting the gay cavalier and the successful man of business at the same time. Now he might be the man of business but as a cavalier he has about as much understanding of manners and fashion as ...' and she cast about in her mind for a telling simile but before she could finish the door of the boudoir opened and Marie's husband entered. He stopped dead when he saw Madame de Metz. He didn't like her, in fact he was a little afraid of her but, since she seemed to be everywhere and know everyone, he could not avoid her. But he definitely didn't like her. It was something about the way she looked at you, he thought, like some sort of dangerous animal marking down its prey. He spoke pointedly at his wife.

'I am sorry, Madame, I didn't know you were entertaining company.'

'Yes, sir, I do have company. May I introduce Eloise de Metz?'

Madame de Metz looked at him and smiled. It almost made him step back.

'If you wish to speak to your wife alone, sir, I will, of course, withdraw.'

But she sat there looking immovable as a rock. De Valois read the eyes rather than the words, "try to move me if you dare, sir, and see what happens".

'Ladies, I will leave you. I just wished to let you know, Madame, that I lunch today with St Clair.'

Madame de Metz put a mocking surprise into her voice.

'What, not your new friend from the North?'

'Madame, the man to whom I think you refer is the merest acquaintance. I hardly know him and he is certainly not a friend.'

'Indeed. But I hear he is your constant companion.'

'I cast an eye over him, he values my opinion in fashion.

Rightly or wrongly he relies on my judgement so I cast an eye over him, Madame. No more, no less.'

'You are too good, sir, you are a saint to do as you do for a stranger, a nobody. You are too good for this world.'

De Valois finally managed to get his hand on the door knob and opened the door. He gave a quick bow.

'Ladies, your servant.'

And he left hearing the laughter coming from the room as he walked furiously away.

'I know I shouldn't do it but I can't help myself. He makes it so easy.'

Marie resumed the fan.

'Pray don't apologise. I get little enough to laugh at so I take whatever comes my way with gratitude and, as you say, he does make it so easy. But tell me, why do you bother with the man?'

'Macleod or your husband?'

'Is that his name, Macleod?'

'Yes. His father was Scottish but his mother was French. He is a lawyer and he is from Boston, although whether he is as rich as he acts I'm not so sure. My interest is that he plays the fool but is clever enough to have wormed his way into society through your husband. Perhaps our Mr Macleod is not at all what he seems.'

'My goodness, Eloise, what a lot you know about him. You do make it your business to find things out about people, don't you?'

Not for the first time in their acquaintance Eloise de Metz wondered if this beautiful young woman was truly as innocent of worldly ways as she appeared. She was sure the indifference for the opinion of others was real enough but what lay behind that indifference? She would need to be more careful about the beautiful Marie Christine.

'I'm insatiably curious, Marie, and there's precious little in New Orleans to be curious about so I have to settle for what I find around me. For instance, I'm fascinated by you. You're such an enigma.'

'Me! I would have thought my life is an open book and certainly as dull as most books.'

'You're the best-looking woman in the city yet you seem to have no lovers. Don't tell me you are faithful to your husband out of love. I won't believe that.'

'Then I won't tell you it's for love.'

'Duty?'

'No, not duty nor loyalty either before you ask.'

'Then what?'

Marie laid down the fan once more.

'Tell me, Eloise, by what right do you question me about my most intimate affairs?'

There was a tone in her voice that Madame de Metz had not heard there before. It told her that her little game was up. She knew at once that she had gone too far too fast and the door to friendship had been slammed well and truly shut. Oh well, it would have happened sooner or later and she was fairly sure that neither of the de Valois's was involved in what she was looking for. She rose.

'I must be going, my dear.' Marie sat in stony silence and did not offer her hand to her departing visitor. 'I hope I haven't given you a headache with my chatter. If I were to have inflicted pain on such a dear friend I would be desolate, I assure you, absolutely desolate. Pain can be such a nuisance. Adieu.'

Marie sat staring ahead as Madame de Metz left the room. She had never liked the woman, but then again, whom did she like, man or woman? Her thoughts turned, unwillingly, to the topic she had so recently dismissed, Macleod.

Perhaps he was indeed different. But, if so, what could that mean to her? Nothing. Yet having been placed in her mind by Madame de Metz, he somehow lingered and this annoyed her. Dismissing men from her thoughts had long ago become the simplest of all simple tasks. They meant nothing to her and so they were gone. But Macleod would not be dismissed and this annoyed her. In raising even that small emotion she had to admit he was indeed different. She began again to fan herself and, reflecting on the empty day she would face, it occurred to her that M Macleod, absent and unknowing, might do her a favour. He might provide some small diversion in the unending procession of empty days which constituted her empty and meaningless existence.

Chapter Twenty-two

Macleod sat in his rooms staring moodily out of the window at the afternoon rain. After a good start to his campaign he was bogged down and getting nowhere. True, he was now as well-dressed as any man of fashion in New Orleans and he was accepted into society as the minor protégé of de Valois. He was carrying off the part of the fashion dandy as well as he could and, it seemed to him, being successful at it. But although his plan had worked it had actually got him nowhere, he had entered the citadel only to find no enemy within. Nor had he got anywhere with the tailor, despite cajoling, flattery, veiled threats and hints of money. He was no nearer knowing how he got his up-to-date designs from Paris than when he had first met him. In fact the tailor now regarded him with a deep suspicion which he did little to hide. And, as to his high hopes that de Valois and St Clair might be the men he was looking for, they were soon dashed. He had spent enough time in their company to be quite sure that de Valois really was indeed a semi-imbecile and his friend, St Clair, was no more than what he seemed, de Valois's close friend. If there was any kind of intrigue going on it was too cleverly hidden for him to spy it out.

So here he was, with his story of great business ventures worn as thin as tissue paper and nothing more urgent to do than sit in his rooms staring out of the window with no more idea of what was going on than an onion in a stew. He freely admitted to himself that he had no strategy to move the situation on from its present position so that he might make some kind of report.

Jeremiah Jones had arrived three weeks after Macleod, just as he had said. Now, nearly one month on, Macleod guessed that Jones would be getting impatient, and if he wasn't, then he should be. A good officer gets results and the only result Macleod could report was that he was now a man of fashion who could drivel and prance with the best of them. Not a battle honour he cared to point to with any pride.

However, Macleod was not being completely honest with himself in putting down his feelings of anger and frustration to the lack of progress in his investigations. The truth was, it was his lack of progress in getting noticed by Marie Christine de Valois which so unsettled him. Perhaps if Macleod had applied the same effort to his duty as he had to attracting that lady's attention he might have had more than the improved cut of his clothes to report. But a man smitten for the first time by great passion, especially when well past youth, does not see the world as others do. Self-delusion is the greatest delusion of all and Macleod honestly believed he was doing his best to watch and listen and, in a way, it was true. But it was Madame de Valois that he watched and listened for.

The truth is Macleod had, for too long, brutally repressed in himself all joy in living, and tried to live on hate alone. In Boston he had almost managed that grisly feat. But the human psyche will not be ridden over roughshod by simple force of will. In taking on the part of the gay socialite Macleod had unwittingly opened the flood-gates for long suppressed, but very necessary, human urges, and Nature was busy restoring the balance with a vengeance.

To himself, Macleod was as in control as ever, playing a part to gain an end. To anyone who knew him, Macleod would have appeared to be undergoing a metamorphosis, a sort of re-birth.

His thoughts, as he looked absently at the rain, should have been about trying to work out some way of furthering his objective. But it was another objective that, as usual, his thoughts slid to and the beautiful face of Madame Marie de Valois rose once more into his brain.

A gentle knocking broke into Macleod's reverie. Annoyed at any intrusion into his thoughts he got up and went to the door. If his visitor had bounced a cannonball off his head she could not have stunned Macleod more effectively as he stood, struck dumb, staring.

Marie Christine de Valois had been stared at too many times to take offence and, in any case, she wanted something from this man so she smiled at him.

She shouldn't have done that. Her smile hit Macleod between the eyes at a moment of weakest resistance, and any small sense of what was fitting between a gentleman, receiving a visit from an unaccompanied married lady, expired.

'It is Mr Macleod, is it not?'

Macleod snapped out of his trance. He had stood staring at her like a common lout. He was in no more than his shirt, practically naked! And he was forcing her to look at him in this state. Beast!

'Madame, a thousand apologies.'

He turned, went to where his robe lay over the back of a chair, hastily pulled it on and returned to the door.

She smiled again but Macleod, with difficulty, this time managed to hold his ground.

'Please, Madame, forgive me. I never expected this pleasure, this honour.' Macleod knew he was close to babbling but he was on fire with delight and humiliated with confusion. 'Please, come in. Madame, I apologise for …'

Marie interrupted.

'No, thank *you*, sir.'

Macleod was at a loss. She was refusing to accept his apology. Why?

'You do not …'

'For a lady alone, sir, a married lady, to enter the apartments of a man who is not her husband …'

Macleod at once recognised the enormity of his blunder.

'Madame, what a fool you must think me, but …'

But what indeed? Why was she there? Why had she come? It was wonderful that she had. But why?

'I thought I might find my husband here, that he may have called on you. But I see I must have been mistaken.'

Macleod's mind raced for a response, a witty reply, a subtle compliment, something charming or perhaps tender.

'No, he is not here.'

Desolation!

Madame de Valois turned as if to leave but stopped.

'Perhaps you would be so good as to escort me home. The lady who accompanied me here has gone on elsewhere and I have no carriage.'

Delight!

'But of course, Madame, it would be my pleasure and an honour. If you would …'

He stuttered to a halt. He couldn't leave her at the door and he couldn't ask her in. What could he do? Confusion!

It was too much for him, he gave up.

Fortunately women are better constituted than men to deal with such situations. Marie Christine had not felt real passion for many years, not since she was thirteen and had fallen hopelessly in love with the young woman her family had hired to teach her to dance. But she could still recognise passion in others. She had seen it many times in the looks and manners of young men who had been captivated by her beauty and desired something more than just her looks. She was rather charmed to see such feelings at work in as mature a man as Macleod. Madame de Metz had been right, she decided, he was indeed sweet. If it turned out he was also amusing something might be made of him.

'I will wait downstairs.'

Of course, only a clod would not have seen it.

Buffoon!

She left and Macleod quickly threw off his robe and found his most dashing coat and best hat and, snatching up his silver-topped stick, hurried after her. Almost as if by some miracle the rain had stopped by the time they stepped out into the street together. Macleod's mind desperately searched for some suitable topic of conversation to captivate her with his wit and fluency.

'How fortunate that the rain has stopped, Madame.'

'Yes, it is fortunate.'

'Rain is always so, so …'

Words again failed.

'Wet?'

'Precisely.'

Clod! Imbecile!

His mind redoubled its efforts.

But his mind didn't get a second chance. Marie had manoeuvred this meeting for a purpose, the purpose of her entertainment, and she didn't propose to waste any time in polite chit-chat. The sun now shone brightly so she put up her parasol and began to walk with Macleod, who was thinking furiously, at her side.

'Tell me, Mr Macleod, why are you really in New Orleans?'

Macleod stopped dead and Marie, looking for all the world as if she had merely remarked that it was now a warm day, waited. Macleod's mind reeled from the suddenness of the question.

'I don't understand, Madame.'

Marie moved off again and Macleod fell once more into step.

'Really? I would have thought it quite clear. I asked you what was your real reason for coming to New Orleans? My husband tells me that you say you are going into business but he also tells me that you don't go. You don't seem to do anything except be seen.' She looked at him, the question now in her eyes rather than her voice. But Macleod had no answer. 'Of course, if your reasons are secret then you cannot tell me, I understand that.'

'Madame, just to have seen you is justification enough for coming to New Orleans.'

Macleod was delighted with the remark. It was almost gallant. He was disappointed and confused that Marie's response was to laugh.

'Sir, I appreciate the compliment but pray don't evade the question. Either tell me your reason or tell me I am not to know. Either way you will end my unforgivable intrusion into your private affairs.'

Macleod thought about it. There was no question of allowing her to know why he had come, that was impossible. But for some reason which he could not fathom she had taken an interest in him. If he repulsed her now, any chance of getting to know her would almost certainly be gone. He had to tell her something.

'Madame, if it were possible for me to tell anyone my reasons for being here there is no one I would rather confide in than yourself.'

He paused and Marie waited until it was clear to her that nothing more was immediately forthcoming.

'But you are not going to.'

'Not going to?'

'Confide in me. I must assume then that your reasons are secret. How intriguing. What a man of mystery you are. You come here from Boston, deposit a large amount at the bank used by the best people in society and put out some story through the bank that you are looking to go into business. Very cleverly you engage the attention of my husband and use him to introduce you into society. But nobody really knows anything about you, and as far as going into business is concerned you take considerably less interest in that than you do in me. As I say, a man of mystery.'

Macleod couldn't believe his ears. This woman, this stranger, had just thoroughly and comprehensively described to him what he thought was his cleverly concealed plan. Had his actions been as obvious to everyone, even down to his fascination with the woman who now walked at his side?

'Really, Madame, I don't know what to say.'

And he really didn't.

'May we cross the street? The sun has become tiresome and there is shade on the other side.'

'Of course.'

He offered her his arm on which she rested her hand ever so lightly, and he led her across the street into the shade.

'Shall I tell you what I think, M'sieur Macleod? I think you are a very clever villain who marked down my husband as a simpleton and used him to get into society so that one night you can choose the easiest and richest victims, cut their throats and make off with your loot.' And she laughed. 'Yes, I think you are a dangerous cut-throat and I'm terribly afraid of you.'

Macleod was not so smitten by passion as not to recognise that he was being made a fool of.

'Madame, make jest of me if you wish but I assure you that ...'

But of what could he assure her? Nothing. Then he had a flash of inspiration. He remembered seeing a lurid poster in Boston for a play. At the time he had treated it with utter contempt. Now he thanked God it had made enough of an impression to rest in the recesses of his memory.

'Oh very well, Madame, since you have found me out I will confess. I am Black Jake, the Philadelphia cut-throat, come to plunder all that is rich and fair in New Orleans. Except you, of course. Not even Black Jake could bring himself to harm such a pretty neck. I will not plunder you, not unless you ask it.'

Now it was Marie's turn to stop for a moment. She had not expected such a sally and she did not like the way he now looked at her. There was something about him, something that might indeed be dangerous. He was no longer sweet, no longer a source of innocent entertainment.

Then Macleod tried to give her a knowing smile and Marie found she could laugh, genuinely laugh. He was a sweet and innocent fool after all. They moved on again, Marie now sure of

111

herself, Macleod confused.

Up to now Macleod had, of necessity, worshipped from afar. As a result, the object of his desire existed more in his head than anything else. But this Marie at his side was no image and had an existence quite outside his head, and Macleod was finding that of the two he preferred the former to the latter. Lust can easily overcome laughter, but love will not so easily survive and Macleod did not try to hide the bitterness of his feelings at her treatment of him.

'I'm glad I amuse you, Madame.'

'Oh, don't be offended. If only you knew how tired one can get of clever, witty men who always know what to say, just how to say it and never mean any of what they say. You are like a breath of spring air for me. But I ask myself, what brings this breath of spring to New Orleans? Everyday I watch shallow and vain fools playing their parts and I play mine alongside them. What else can one do? Now, sir, you play your part with great diligence, but I'm afraid that to anyone who cares to look at all closely it is obvious that it is an ill-fitting part. You wear the right clothes, know the right people and visit the right houses, but you are not one of us. You move among us to watch us. You want something from us, but what is it you want, I ask myself? And all of that makes you different and, being different, interesting. If I seem hard and callous it is because I am surrounded by hard and callous people. Innocence, honesty and simplicity are rare things indeed in my world and, when found, usually die young.'

They walked on for a while in silence.

'Why did you call, Madame? Your husband, as you say, has been kind enough to introduce me into society but he would never call on me, and of that I'm sure you're well aware.'

'I called to see whether we might be friends. There, now you know my secret. I would like a friend.'

Macleod was cautious. Was this genuine or merely a ploy to lead him on so as to make an even bigger fool of him?

'You do not seem to lack friends. I see you always in company.'

'In company, yes. With friends, no.' Marie stopped and drew down her parasol. They were at the door of her house. Her manner, as she looked at him, somehow seemed to change. 'I fear I have been too forward, sir. I hope you will forget my visit and my too bold enquiries into your private affairs.'

Whatever she had wanted from their meeting, it was now over. She was dismissing him.

'If that is your wish, then consider it done. It is forgotten.'

'Thank you, sir. And thank you for accompanying me home. The rain is returning, I fear you will get wet on my account.'

'Think nothing of it, Madame. Good day.'

Macleod turned and set off back towards his rooms. If his somewhat ungracious departure surprised her, she didn't show it. She was satisfied. She had enjoyed her little entertainment. In addition she had confirmed what Madame de Metz had told her of him. Mr Macleod was not what he appeared. It was enough. Her escapade was over. She erased him from her thoughts and entered her house.

Macleod almost marched back along the way he had so recently come. She had not made a fool of him, he had made a fool of himself. He had allowed the part he played to take hold of him, let a pretty face deflect him from his duty like some callow youth. He would go to Jeremiah Jones and tell him he had failed, that he had discovered nothing, never would discover anything and that he should be replaced.

When he got to his rooms he began preparing for his departure. That very afternoon he would go to the bank and wind things up. Tomorrow he would see Jones and then book passage on the first ship heading north. He would get out of this foul place and stop playing the fool. He was not a society fop, but now he knew he was also no longer any kind of soldier. If he had truly been under orders he'd be in irons by now and awaiting a court-martial for dereliction of duty.

And so Macleod prepared for his retreat from New Orleans, an angry and beaten man with a little more to add to his private store of hate. Nature might have tried to restore the balance, but for all its hard work nothing had really changed.

Chapter Twenty-three

The de Valois residence, like that of its neighbours, was in darkness. A church clock struck two as an uninvited visitor quietly entered at the rear of the house and, with a shaded light, passed through the kitchen, made his way to the hall and began to climb the stairs.

On the first floor the visitor moved along the corridor, stopped, silently opened a door, entered the room and crossed to a bed. The dim light from the lamp showed two figures lying still under the thin white sheet.

The light was placed carefully on a table at the bedside and soft sounds of movement were followed by two clear metallic clicks. A hand moved into the narrow light thrown by the shaded lamp, gripped the sheet and pulled it sharply back to reveal two naked bodies.

The oath which sprang to the lips of one was instantly drowned by the crash of a pistol shot and his body was thrown back onto the bed. The other man gave a high-pitched scream of terror and pulled up the sheet as if it might afford some protection.

Another shot filled the room with sound and the note of the scream changed from terror to pain. There was a clunk as the hand put the double-barrelled pistol on the table and took up the lamp.

One man lay dead, his unseeing eyes looking upwards to the ceiling, blood oozing from a hole in his chest. Beside him another figure squirmed and screamed in a frenzy of agony under the sheet which was rapidly acquiring a dark, spreading stain. The hand pulled away the sheet to reveal a man holding his stomach with both hands as blood came freely through the fingers.

It had been a clumsy shot for such a close range, even though made through a sheet.

The shooter picked up the light, crossed to the bedroom door and waited. There was silence.

Two pistol shots in such an enclosed space would certainly

raise the house, but no sounds came.

The light waited at the door, the screaming from the bed continued but the rest of the house remained silent.

The light returned to the bed and the lamp was set once more onto the table, this time positioned to show the leather satchel which the intruder carried. Hands picked up the pistol and carefully re-loaded one of the barrels. Once done, the hammer was cocked and the light turned back to the bed. The hand made no mistake this time. It put the barrel to the head of the screaming man, pulled the trigger and, after the roar of the shot, there was silence.

The pistol was put back into the satchel and after a cursory cast across the bed, the light went to the bedroom door, out into the corridor, then stopped. Somewhere not too far away a door had been pulled open. The light waited. From further away, only just audible, another door slammed shut. The shots had caused somebody to leave in a hurry but no one, it seemed, was coming to investigate. The servants were showing excellent good sense, no doubt waiting until they were sure the armed intruder had finished and left before venturing to render assistance.

The light moved on along the corridor, went back down the stairs and slipped out the back door as silently as it had slipped in.

In the bedroom the two naked bodies lay sprawled in the awkward attitudes of violent death. Their blood flowed onto the sheets and mingled. Etienne Henri de Valois and Louis Antoine St Clair lay together, united in death as they had been in life.

Chapter Twenty-four

The night following Marie de Valois's visit to his rooms found Macleod unable to sleep, his mind filled with anger and despair. He realised that any hope of regaining a life with some sort of purpose was over. He had behaved like a lovesick ninny which was bad enough, but he had also failed utterly in the duty laid on him. The night passed slowly but at last dawn crept into the sky and Macleod began packing. He would leave this vile city as soon as he had visited Jeremiah Jones, told him of his failure and the reason he had failed. He would leave no room for doubt that the failure was complete and the responsibility for it entirely his own.

Jones's reaction to the news was not at all what Macleod had expected.

'I've seen the lady whom you say turned your head and blinded you to your duty, and I find it quite easy to believe she might have that effect on any man except, of course, her husband.'

Quite what Jones's cryptic reference to de Valois meant Macleod didn't know or care to know.

'As I can be of no further use to you here I'll leave as soon as I can find a ship bound for Charleston. From there I'll get a berth back to Boston. I'm running away, deserting. There was a time when I would have been shot for doing as much.'

There was a hint of nostalgia in Macleod's voice which Jones was quick to pick up.

'Well I'm sorry to disappoint you, Macleod, but I'm not a regular officer and you're not in uniform and we certainly don't draw attention to ourselves by shooting people because they want to go home, not unless we have to, of course. Come, Macleod, I shouldn't worry too much about things if I were you. You were asked to find something and failed. And maybe you're right, maybe it was because you were briefly ensnared by a pretty face. But there'd be precious few men left alive if either or both were capital offences. Now if you will excuse me I have had a busy night myself and I still have work to do. I also leave New Orleans and, if it's any comfort, my negotiations also failed. Of course in my case that was the intended outcome so it's of no consequence. But against that I didn't have the pleasure of an encounter with anyone like Madame de Valois, so I'd say we were about even.'

Macleod stood for a moment and then realised that he was being dismissed. The meeting was over and nothing had come of it.

'Is that it? I leave, you leave and it's all finished here?'

Jones's voice became severe.

'As far as you're concerned it is. Go back to Boston and your lawyering. You did your best, now go home, and if you'll take my advice, forget New Orleans, forget Marie de Valois and everything to do with the place. Now, as I have already said, I have work to do. Good day.'

Macleod left as angry and frustrated as he had been after his meeting with Madame de Valois. If the failure of the mission could be so easily dismissed, why had he been sent?

Back at his rooms he spent the rest of the morning picking at that question. Why had he been sent? What was he supposed to have done? And why, when he told Jones he was leaving, did he speed him on his way? But, as the morning passed, he came no closer to making any sense of it. He went out and took lunch. After lunch he walked the streets. Finally he bought a bottle of brandy in a tavern and returned to his rooms.

His recent abstinence from strong drink and lack of sleep the previous night meant that, after half the bottle was gone, he fell asleep in his chair and woke up hot and uncomfortable in the late afternoon. He went out and walked for a while to clear his head then went down to the docks to enquire about ships to Charleston.

He was fortunate, one was due in the next day and would leave two days later. If he came back the following day he would be able to arrange passage. After his visit to the docks he went to his bank and explained to the manager that he was leaving, that he had urgent business to return to in Boston and would need to withdraw his balance in letters of credit. The manager mouthed the usual regrets at losing such a good customer but told him that his letters would be available if he returned in one hour. Early in the evening, having obtained his letters of credit and packed his trunk, he went out, took a small meal then returned to his rooms to finish his brandy.

Sitting, the bottle now empty, the same question shared his mind with the brandy fumes. If his failure was of so little consequence why had he been sent with such urgency?

He couldn't bring himself to believe that his old commander would have summoned him as he had done and then sent him on a fool's errand. The only solution he could find to fit the facts as he knew them was that the letter had been a forgery and he was being used by Jones and others as some sort of pawn in a game he was too stupid to see, let alone understand. Tiredness overwhelmed him and he closed his eyes and thought with regret that it would have been better to buy two bottles. But alas, it was too late.

Chapter Twenty-five

The night was oppressively hot and Macleod, open-shirted and sweating in the heat, sat and stared at the darkness beyond the open window. The brandy and the wine he had taken with his meal had left him fuddled, but any real sleep, he knew, would not come so he had not retired to bed. Outside, the sky was suddenly split by a streak of jagged light and a loud peal of thunder cracked across the city and seemed to rattle on in the very street below.

Suddenly Macleod realised that the rattle was, in fact, a loud knocking on the street door below. He roused himself from his confused thoughts and noticed in a detached sort of way that the storm which had threatened all evening had broken and there was rain splashing into the room through the open window soaking the carpet. Someone, he thought, should close the window. The late caller knocked again. Who would call at such a late hour on such a night? He looked at his watch which lay on the table. It was past midnight. Once more the knocking returned, if anything louder. Macleod dismissed the matter from his mind. Whatever it was it could be nothing to do with him, and tomorrow, thank God, he would book his berth and in two days New Orleans and all who lived there could go to hell.

From somewhere below there was the sound of raised voices, then what sounded like someone hurrying up the stairs followed by a loud knocking at his door. Macleod looked at the door but didn't speak or move. The knocking resumed even more loudly and this time there was a voice, a woman's voice, pleading.

'M'sieur Macleod, please open the door. I know you're there. I can see the light under the door. Please, M'sieur, for the love of God.'

It was a voice he recognised. But still he didn't move. The knocking and the voice resumed.

'M'sieur Macleod, if ever a woman's distress touched your heart let mine touch it now. In the name of mercy please let me in.'

Macleod felt stiff and awkward and not a little confused but he managed to push himself upright and stand. He was drunk, but not falling-down drunk. He crossed to the door, unlocked it and pulled it open. Madame de Valois didn't wait for any invitation. She pushed past him and Macleod felt the rain on her cloak as it brushed his hand. He stood holding the door handle looking at her. She turned. All pleading had fallen away. Now, for some reason, she seemed angry.

'Mon Dieu, don't just stand there, close the door.' Macleod came to life and closed the door. 'And lock it. Make it secure.'

Macleod did as he was bid then turned to his visitor.

'Madame, I ... Madame, to what do I ...'

His words came out thickly so he paused.

'Are you drunk?'

It was a genuine enquiry with no hint of disapproval. Its frankness caught Macleod unready and he answered without thinking.

'Yes. I think I am, a little.'

She looked at him for a second as he stood, stupidly, allowing her to scrutinise him. Once again her tone changed. Now she became business-like.

'I hope to God you're not too drunk. I'll get you coffee.' Macleod watched her as, holding her cloak tight about her, she went to the door, unlocked and opened it, then stood outside shouting into the darkness. 'Down there, black coffee and quickly.' It was the voice of a woman used to being obeyed and obeyed promptly and a voice, whose reply Macleod couldn't quite catch, answered. Madame de Valois came back into the room, closed the door, walked to the table and looked first at the empty brandy bottle beside a half full glass, then at him. 'You look a poor specimen at the moment, M'sieur, but I am in dire need of help and I pray you might be the one to see it given.'

Macleod made an effort to clear his brain. He didn't try to grasp what was going on. That would have been too much, but he managed at last to speak.

'Would you care to take off your wet cloak, Madame?'

It was only politeness, the merest good manners, but it was a start, the best he could manage.

Madame de Valois responded by, if anything, holding her cloak even tighter.

'Thank you, but no. Apart from my shoes and my cloak I have nothing else on.'

Macleod swayed slightly. Her revelation had been delivered in a tone much like her question about his condition, simple and direct. But the information she conveyed, her lack of clothing other than shoes and cloak, had an almost miraculous effect on Macleod. The idea of there being nothing between him and her naked body but the heavy cloak she held about her sobered him instantly. Sudden and unexpected lust can, in some people, be a wonderfully powerful corrective.

However, sober though he might be, he was still utterly confused. This was the same woman who only yesterday had, quite rightly, refused to enter his rooms unaccompanied, and on that occasion she had been fully dressed. Now here she was not only alone with him, but, if she was speaking the truth, in a state which no one except her husband had any right to expect.

'While we're waiting for the coffee perhaps you might get me one of your shirts and a pair of trousers. They will at least offer me some covering.'

'Of course, Madame, but most of my belongings are packed. It will take me a few minutes.'

'I would appreciate it, M'sieur, if you could be as quick as you can, sir.'

Macleod left the room and went into his bedroom where his trunk stood against the wall but stopped when he caught a glimpse of himself in the dressing mirror. His sweat-soaked shirt was wide open. He had been in that condition since she had arrived. He saw his robe on the bed, grabbed it up and put it on then went to the trunk. He was about to unstrap it when his brain finally managed to function. He returned to the other room.

'In my bedroom, Madame, you will find plenty of clothes in the drawers and wardrobes. Please feel free to help yourself.'

'But I thought you said you were packed?'

'I am only taking those things in which I originally travelled from Boston. I find I have no need nor desire to take anything else I have acquired here or elsewhere on my journey.'

'In that case I will see what I can find.'

And, holding her cloak securely closed, she went into

Macleod's bedroom and closed the door behind her.

Macleod tried to make his brain function. Something had happened, something which had driven her from her home, almost naked, into a night of wind and rain. She had come, at night in a storm, to his rooms. She had beaten on his door in a panic of pleading. What catastrophe could have driven her out and why choose him for help?

There was a knock and the voice of his landlady came through the door.

'Your coffee, sir.'

Macleod went and opened the door. His landlady in nightcap and shawl stood holding a tray. Macleod took it.

'Thank you, Madame.'

She stood looking past him into his room. She was obviously intrigued as to what was going on.

'Can I be of any further service? Does Madame de Valois require anything? Should I send for someone?'

'No, thank you. Nothing further.'

Macleod stepped back and pushed the door shut with his foot. He took the tray to the table, put it down, poured himself a coffee and resumed his thoughts. What sort of catastrophe was so complete, so overwhelming that it left you no time to even clothe yourself? And whatever the calamity, why him? She barely knew him and when they had last met she had treated him as a fool. No, it was a mystery and utterly beyond him.

The bedroom door opened and Madame de Valois came back into the room. She wore a white shirt of light silk with a lace-frilled front. Macleod had never liked it. He had been recommended to buy half a dozen by de Valois who said he wore them himself. Macleod had despised their style as overblown and effeminate. But on Madame de Valois he saw at once that he had been mistaken. It was an excellent shirt, the very best sort of shirt. She had rolled up the sleeves to her wrists and tucked the excess into the waist of a pair of his trousers which were held tight by a belt and had the legs rolled up. She still wore her own dainty pumps.

The general effect of her long, black hair cascading unchecked over her shoulders and her beautiful face surmounting such a comic outfit was unsettling. It took Macleod even deeper into the strange world of unreality into which her sudden appearance had plunged him. He didn't know what to say, what to do or even what to think. Perhaps he had drunk more than he had thought and passed out and this was all some alcohol-fuelled hallucination.

'Mr Macleod, I know you must be alarmed by my sudden and altogether unexpected arrival ...'

Macleod gave up any hopes he was dreaming. She was all too real.

'Madame, I assure you ...' But of what could he assure her? The trite formula of polite exchange expired on his lips. This was no occasion for society manners. 'Madame, I am at a loss, but if you are indeed in need of help and if I may be of service then please tell me what I can do.'

At last, he had said something that was not utter drivel. It was plain and straightforward and Madame de Valois's response was to cover her face with her hands and burst into tears. Her uncontrolled weeping removed the last, lingering sense of unreality in Macleod. He went quickly to her side, put an arm round her and led her to his chair where she sat down and sobbed. Macleod picked up his unfinished glass of brandy. He took hold of her wrist and gently eased her hand away from her face and put the glass in it.

'Take a drink. Just a sip.'

Madame de Valois put the glass to her lips, tilted it and handed it back to him empty. The drink brought relief, the tears stopped and she looked at Macleod with an unnerving brightness in her eyes and her voice took on an almost theatrical tone.

'What must you think of me? To arrive as I did. You must have thought me insane.'

Macleod watched her carefully.

'Not at all. A little odd perhaps, somewhat ...'

Marie smiled, but it did nothing to reassure Macleod. Her smile was as theatrical as her tone.

'M'sieur, I was afraid, terrified, and when I came into these rooms I did not know what to say.'

'Of course. Perhaps now you can ...'

Suddenly her mood changed once more.

'Each day I, like all the others, pretend and pretence becomes a way of life and ...' She paused and looked around the room as if only now noticing where she was. Then looked back at Macleod with almost a frenzy in her eyes and her voice. 'Let us pretend now, M'sieur Macleod. Oh, let's pretend we're lovers, all alone ...'

Macleod leaned forward and slapped her hard across the face. This was no longer uncharted territory to him. He had seen such a look and heard such a voice before, from young officers new to the horrors of war and meeting violent death on a grand scale for the first time.

He looked again at her eyes. At first there was hurt surprise, then fear, then anger, until at last gratitude took its place among the tears and her whole body seemed to relax.

'I'm sorry but it was necessary. Are you all right?'

A genuine smile came to her lips.

'M'sieur, I am indebted to you, more than you can imagine. I did not know who to turn to, where to go. I was alone, afraid ...'

And once again her face was in her hands and her shoulders heaved with sobs.

After a few minutes the sobs subsided and the hands came down and Macleod saw that her eyes were clear and focussed.

'Do you feel well enough to talk? I do not press you, Madame, but I ...'

'Please, my name is Marie. Don't you think that under the circumstances we can dispense with the normal rules of social convention?'

'Yes, Marie, I think that tonight the normal rules of convention have completely flown out of the window.'

The rain, though somewhat diminished from its height, was still coming in through the open window.

Macleod closed it, drew the curtains and returned to her.

'The rules of convention may have gone but I think perhaps the rules of necessity remain and I think they advocate urgency. What brought you to my door at this hour?'

'A name. Before I tell you at least give me a name I might call you by other than Macleod. M'sieur, I am going to trust my life to you and I would prefer to do it with someone whose given name I at least know.'

'Marie.'

'Marie!'

'Jean Marie Macleod. In honour of my French grandfather. So

you see you will be trusting your life to one with whom you share a name. Think of it as a good omen.'

And for the first time since entering his school he blessed the day that he had been christened Jean Mary. Marie seemed to be reassured, not so much by his words perhaps, but by his manner, confident, gentle but also somehow strong.

'Jean Marie, a terrible thing has happened. My husband is dead.'

'Dead? How?'

'Shot. I fled the house without dressing and covered only by my cloak. I came to you because there was no one else I could turn to in safety. When we last met I said I thought you were here in New Orleans playing a part. I hope to God I was right. I'm afraid I was a little cruel when I last talked to you, but at that time I didn't think I would so soon have to call on your services. I humbly ask your forgiveness just as I humbly ask your help for I know I am entitled to neither.'

'Marie,' he felt uncomfortable using her name, but also he felt pleasure, 'what is past is past. You need my help. Enough, you have it for what it's worth. You say your husband is dead?'

'Yes, I am sure he lies dead in bed at this moment.'

'Yet you are here!'

'Yes.'

A sudden, terrible thought came to him.

'My God, you killed him?'

'Me?'

Her amazement at the question was again quite genuine.

'Well, he is dead in your bed, you flee naked. Something horrible has been done and you can go to no one except a stranger. What else can I think?'

Indignation replaced amazement.

'Sir, I came to you ...' then the indignation evaporated. 'Of course, why not? You do not know me. Perhaps I am capable of murdering my husband. God knows I wanted rid of him. But, Jean, it was not I that shot him and the one he lay with.'

It took a second for her words to sink in.

'The one he lay with? He had another woman in his bed, in your own home? The monster.'

'No, not a woman.'

125

'But if not a woman then …'

Suddenly Macleod understood. The thought stunned him into silence.

'He and St Clair were lovers. We have not shared a bed for some years.'

Macleod was appalled. Marie's words had dragged him suddenly and starkly into a world he knew almost nothing about except that he was revolted to his very soul.

'My God, you should have killed the swine long before now.'

Her voice took on a slight edge.

'I told you, I did not kill them.'

'No, of course, I'm sorry. But if not you, then who?'

'I don't know who, but I know why they were killed and I knew that when the assassins pulled away the sheets to make sure of their work and saw two men in the bed they would come looking for me. I sleep alone so I wear no night dress when the nights are hot and close. The shots and the screaming woke me and I guessed what was being done so I put on my shoes pulled on a cloak and left by the back stairs as quickly as I could. I came to you because I don't think anyone will look for me here. But the woman who let me in certainly recognised me so I won't be safe for long. I need to leave New Orleans as soon as possible. I need to go far way and travel quickly. I need to go to the British, they are the only ones who can make me safe.'

'The British?'

'Yes, and please don't ask why.'

'But I must ask.'

She considered for a moment.

'Of course you must, and I must tell you. If it becomes known that I have been with you then whoever killed my husband will kill you anyway, whether you know my secret or not. My husband was a vain fool, but he was a well-born fool who had money and position. His father sent him over here from France supposedly to look after the family plantations, but I think it was more a question of getting rid of an embarrassment. As it turned out he was lucky. The Revolution sent the rest of his family to the guillotine. Not surprisingly he chose not to return to France. He met St Clair and decided to settle in New Orleans. To fit into society he felt he needed a home and a wife so he looked about him and chose me. I was young and unschooled in the ways of the world. But my family were all too aware of what was being done to me.'

'And they still allowed the marriage?'

'Oh yes. They were happy to sell me and they got a good price. I was just the sort of decoration de Valois was looking for.'

'But did you and de Valois never ...'

'Come together as man and wife? On those few occasions early in our marriage when we thought that despite everything we might still produce a child he had to have St Clair in the bed to rouse him enough to achieve his duty with me.'

Both were ashamed, Marie for having to say what she had said and Macleod for having listened.

'But once you knew what he was like, why didn't you leave him?'

'And become what? Someone's mistress, a courtesan, a common prostitute? What was there I could do other than sell my looks, my body?'

'There must have been something.'

'A convent? Throw myself on the mercy of the Sisters and dedicate my life to God? Or perhaps starve in the gutter, poor but honest?'

'What about your family?'

'My family had struck a bargain. They would honour that bargain whatever I told them about de Valois and St Clair. You must understand, Mr Macleod ...'

'Jean.'

'Yes, sorry, Jean. When a woman marries all she has becomes the property of her husband. She herself becomes his property. It is not only society that wills it to be so, it is the law. If I took money or jewels and left him, even my own money or my own jewels, it would have been theft and although de Valois was rich, he was also mean. To St Clair he was lavish, to me he was a miser.'

'But the dresses and the jewels. You are probably the best dressed woman in New Orleans.'

'For display. He couldn't very well let his wife appear in public in rags, could he? Inside the house it was he or St Clair who wore the jewels when they pranced around together naked. I became invisible in that house and that is how I learned their secret. As far as they were concerned I was not there and they became careless.

127

My husband was a fool, but not St Clair, except where his infatuation with my husband was concerned.' She looked down at the front of the shirt and absently brushed the lace. Macleod waited while she readied herself to tell him what she knew. She looked up at him. 'St Clair was part of a conspiracy.'

'A conspiracy?'

'Yes, conceived by France to overthrow the government of your country.'

'Overthrow the government of America? How could anyone …'

'The French want America as an ally. But America wants no part of their war with England. Very well, America must change its mind. Money is spent, men of influence are persuaded, plans are put in place, arrangements are made. A man is found who can lead a new government, one who will do exactly as Paris tells him and, voilà, America has a new government and France a new ally. Why not? It is politics. I do not understand it, but, believe me, it is as I say.'

Macleod didn't want to believe her, couldn't believe her. It was too fantastic. But he had been sent to New Orleans because there was a plot, a plot which threatened his country. But overthrow the government? No, that was too much.

'You must be wrong.'

Marie gave a small cry of exasperation.

'I am not wrong I tell you. I listened, I know what I heard. I know what I saw with my own eyes. St Clair received orders from Paris, they came to him through his tailor. St Clair sometimes brought them to the house in a small leather satchel when he and my husband returned together. While he and my husband were busy I managed to see some of them. That is how I knew what they were. There were letters, sealed letters, addressed to places in America.'

'But letters, sealed letters. They may have been anything, business letters.'

'There were instructions with the letters, instructions to St Clair. To send money to this place, to collect reports from that place. Once to meet a courier who would arrive on a certain ship, to meet him himself and receive by hand what he carried. What is that if not part of a conspiracy?'

Macleod was fighting to make some kind of sense of what he was hearing. Was what she was saying proof?

'And he had money, plenty of money. He was by birth a common little man. I knew, I could tell. But he had money. Where, I asked myself, did this money come from? He had no plantation, no business, he had nothing. Yet all the time he had money.' She waited but Macleod said nothing. 'Oh, Jean, please, you must believe me. I cannot tell you everything now. This is not the time. But there is a plot to steal America, Jean, to steal it and use it in the European wars. That is why St Clair is dead and also my husband.'

Macleod was stunned, but he no longer doubted what she said. In a few words she had given him what he had been sent to New Orleans to discover.

'But why didn't you do anything, tell someone?'

'Because I was clever, I made it my business to listen. Once I had enough, I intended to blackmail St Clair so he would make my husband release me or, if that did not work, sell what I knew and start a new life somewhere else.'

'But it was America. If there was a plot you should have ...'

'Pah! What was America to me? It was nothing. Why should I care if America had some French puppet to govern it? All I knew was that I was trapped in a life of misery and at last I saw a way to free myself.' If anything Macleod was more appalled by this show of indifference to the fate of his country than by the revelations of de Valois's behaviour as a husband. 'Jean, understand. Please understand. I am talking about my life. Knowing St Clair's secret was my only chance to break away from New Orleans and de Valois. But tonight all those hopes ended. Now, to save my life, I must sell what I have quickly and the only people who can save me are the British. They will pay me for what I know. They will pay me and protect me. You must take me to them somehow. You must get me on a ship for Jamaica.'

Macleod was thinking, thinking hard. She was right, she needed to get away from New Orleans and she needed protection. But not from the British. He had to get her into safe American hands. Then his reason for being in New Orleans flooded back. He was here to discover a plot. He had done it. He was here to get information. He must get it. He needed to know more about this enemy. Who had killed de Valois and St Clair and might even now be looking for

129

Marie?

'Who do you think killed your husband and St Clair?'

'I'm not sure, it could have been St Clair's enemies to try and stop the plan going forward or his friends because they knew he was becoming careless.'

Macleod knew something was wrong, but he couldn't think what it was. It was staring him in the face and he couldn't see it.

'There's something wrong.'

Marie stood up.

'My God, is that all you can say? My husband and his lover lie dead in my house and my life is in danger and you say something is wrong. Everything is wrong. You must get me away from here, quickly. We must go to the British.'

Macleod saw she was once again in danger of becoming hysterical. He couldn't very well slap her again but somehow he had to calm her. He stood up, took her in his arms, pulled her to him and roughly aimed a kiss at her mouth. It was a clumsy attempt but he managed to make contact with the side of her nose as she averted her face. He let her push him away and they stood looking at each other. Had it worked? Her eyes were full of fury. Neither spoke for a second and it was left to Macleod to break the silence.

'I'm sorry. I had to do something, I thought you might begin to scream. I couldn't bring myself to slap you again. Please forgive me.'

The fury left her eyes as she looked at him.

'No, Jean, it is I who should apologise.' She sat down again. 'We must talk, you must tell me what we can do. Please, sit down, I am calm now. We must make a plan, one that will keep us both safe.' Macleod sat down. 'Now, Jean, tell me how you can get me to Jamaica where I can sell what I know to the British and then get far away from this cursed place and start a new life.'

Macleod's mind was a welter of confusion. Yet strangely the thought uppermost in his mind was that he had kissed her. She was sitting there, asking him to sell the details of a secret plot to overthrow his beloved Republic to his hated enemy the British, and she was doing it calmly, with a gentle smile, as if they were planning a picnic in the country.

Macleod forced his faculties, such as they were, to function again in something like a normal fashion. He would save her, but not at the expense of selling his country.

He stood up. He felt more in control if able to move about.

'On this floor there are only these rooms that I rent. The landlady and her family occupy downstairs. There is no one else. They must remain silent about your presence here.'

'How many servants are there?'

'Three, the landlady who let you in, her husband and a grown daughter who helps.'

'Could you kill them?'

She was still calm and smiling sweetly.

'No, Marie, I could not kill them.'

She shrugged.

'What then? Threaten them, take the daughter, beat her and demand their silence?'

'I will pay them.' He didn't want her to offer any more suggestions. The memory of the kiss lingered, but her words, and the manner of saying them, dimmed its power more than a little. 'I will buy their silence until we can get a ship out of here. Also I will need the woman to give you some clothes.'

'Clothes? Her clothes?'

'Yes. We will travel as husband and wife and we must not attract attention. I dress as I started out in this, plain and honest. You must do the same. However, people here know I have no wife so we cannot go to the ship together. If you are to walk to the docks ...'

'Walk! But I cannot walk. And certainly I cannot go dressed as a washer woman among the scum of the docks.'

Her manner shocked him into speaking more plainly than he perhaps intended.

'Good God, woman, try to think straight or we'll both end up dead. You're not a lady of fashion now, you're a target, either for a pistol ball or for a blade to slice your pretty white neck. We need to ship out of here and that means going to the docks without getting noticed. Do you suggest we use your husband's damn carriage to get us there?'

Macleod was surprised to find that he was thoroughly angry and his manner, he realised, had become that of a bully. But he didn't care and was not about to apologise. And Marie saw that it was so.

'Of course, I see you are right. I must forget for a time the woman I have been and resign myself to the woman I must become.' She looked up at him. 'But you will do your best, Jean, promise me you will do your best to protect me, to take me away.'

But in his present mood Macleod was not so easily softened by a look. He would save this woman if he could, but now he was again a man under orders. He had information vital to the safety of his country and he must at all costs deliver it. He had to get in touch with Jeremiah Jones and let him know how things stood. But first, and most importantly, he had to make Marie believe he was going to take her to the British. She had to believe in him and believe in him completely.

'I will go and arrange with those below and then I must go out.'

'Go out?'

'Your husband has been shot, you have disappeared. I must go and see what is happening. You must stay in this room. Do not answer the door to anyone but me or the woman from below. I will get you clothes and today book a passage for us. As soon as possible we shall leave this place, but until we do, stay here. If they have any brandy or wine downstairs I will ask them to send it up. Try to sleep if you can.' He took off his robe and threw it over the back of the chair, adjusted his shirt then put on his coat and picked up his hat. I will be back as soon as I can.'

'Thank you, Jean, and be careful.'

Macleod left the room without looking back. At the bottom of the stairs he found the woman waiting with a candle.

'I heard you coming down, sir, so I brought a light. Strange doings, sir, very strange, especially for a respectable house.'

'Madame, something terrible has happened. Madame de Valois's husband has been murdered by intruders. She escaped with her life and has come here for shelter.'

A sly look came into the woman's eyes.

'How terrible, M'sieur. How very terrible.'

'Terrible indeed. What do you think we should do?'

She wasn't ready for that.

'Do, sir? We?'

'I think I should go and tell somebody. I think we should bring the authorities here.'

'Oh no, sir. If she has come to us for help ...'

Macleod waited but the woman had nothing more to offer. Hers was a limited imagination and didn't extend beyond spotting a chance to make a little money. As to how it might be made, she had to leave to others.

'Perhaps you're right. Perhaps we should offer her shelter, a time to rest, to feel safe after her ordeal until she is ready to talk to someone in authority.'

'Oh yes, sir, I think that would be the kindest thing to do. It would be hardly any trouble to look after the lady, hardly any trouble at all.'

Macleod pressed home his advantage.

'No, you must get someone to help you.'

'Help, sir, but I have time on my hands as it is. Bless you, sir, we'll need no extra help.'

'Then it will be just ourselves who know she's here?'

'Just us, sir, until she's better and able to talk to people.'

'Then take this,' Macleod pulled a small purse out of his pocket, 'it's not much but I'm sure there'll be more, plenty more, if Madame finds she is being well cared for and not bothered.' The woman handed him the candle and took the purse. She opened it then tucked it away. 'Of course if even so much as a breath of a word was to let anyone know she was here, then her husband's murderers might come looking for her and, if that happened, I'm afraid we'd all end up with our throats cut.'

The woman's eyes grew large with fright.

'Oh don't say so, sir.'

Macleod inclined his head down to her.

'But I *do* say so, Madame. If a word of her presence is breathed abroad throats will be cut. I know it, in fact I'm sure of it.' He saw that she understood exactly what he was saying. 'Now I must go out. There are things to do. Have you any brandy?'

'A little, sir.'

He handed her back the candle.

'Then after I'm gone take it up to Madame and then find her some clothes, yours or your daughter's, whichever fit best. Now get me a lantern: I must go out and see how things stand.'

The woman left him and a few minutes later came back with a lantern.

'Thank you. I'm sure we have both done the right thing and both understand how we stand in this.'

'Oh yes, M'sieur. You may rely on me.'

'As you may rely on me that things will be just as I say they will be.'

Macleod left the house and set out on his way to rouse Jeremiah Jones and report that his mission, after all, had turned out to be a success.

Chapter Twenty-six

Jeremiah Jones was not best pleased to be roused so very early in the morning and listened with ill-concealed annoyance until Macleod had finished making his report.

'Well, it's good news I suppose, but I wish you had brought it at some more reasonable hour.'

Macleod did nothing to hide the sarcasm from his voice.

'I'm sorry, Jones, but I had the silly idea that what I was doing here was of some importance. I have the information I was sent to get and I have ...'

'But you haven't, have you? You haven't got the information. Madame de Valois has the information, or so she says.'

'But I have Marie, that is I have Madame de Valois, and can deliver her to you.'

'Good God, man, what would I do with her? I'm the representative of the government of America, a very minor one to be sure, but a representative nonetheless. What would I want with a woman who may have just murdered her husband and his lover?'

'She did not kill them. They were killed by assassins.'

Jeremiah Jones pulled his robe more tightly round him and leaned forward.

'A woman you hardly know comes alone after midnight to your rooms and tells you that her husband and his lover have been killed in their bed, while she has managed to walk away unharmed, and you believe her when she tells you that they were the victims of assassination?'

Macleod took his point.

'But she told me she knew about the plot.'

'And what, exactly did she tell you?'

'That there is a plan to overthrow the government. That she has the names of the men involved, American names.'

'I see.'

'Men of the highest position.'

'Yes, hmm, highest position.'

'She says they're planning to steal America.'

'Steal America? I see. Tell me Macleod, had you been drinking?'

Macleod didn't like saying it but it needed to be said.

'Wine with my meal.' Jones leaned back and waited. 'And a glass or two of brandy later.' Jones waited. 'Then more brandy. Perhaps a little too much brandy.'

Jones seemed satisfied.

'Yes, I think I do see. Well, you're the one who's got her, so you're the one who will have to keep her and find out one way or another if there's anything more to her story than the ramblings you've brought me tonight. See to that first, Macleod, and after that you may do as you see fit.'

'What do you mean, do as I see fit?'

'Macleod, you've been a booby once tonight, don't be one a second time or you will try my patience too high. If she knows something, get it out of her and, if you get it then she has no further value to us and can be disposed of. Do I make myself clear?'

Unfortunately he had made himself abundantly clear.

'You do.'

'Good.' Jones stood up. 'Now, if you have no objection I will return to my bed.' Macleod stood and turned to leave. 'One moment.' Macleod stopped. 'Give me your papers.' Jones held out his hand. Macleod looked at him.

'My papers?'

'Yes, give them to me.'

'What papers?'

'Great heavens, man, are you sure it was only half a bottle? Your identification, any papers you carry that prove who you are.' Jones shook his waiting, outstretched hand impatiently. 'You do carry papers?'

'Yes, I have several letters of credit and ...'

'A letter of credit will do.'

Reluctantly Macleod pulled out some papers, sorted through them and handed one over to Jones who quickly glanced at it, then folded it and put it in his robe pocket.

'Don't worry, I'm not going to steal from you. I will use this as identification for a man I will send to Washington. It will ensure he gets access to the General as quickly as possible. He will report that, according to the wife, de Valois and St Clair, an intimate of her husband, were involved with others in a plot to overthrow the government. He will say that you are interrogating Madame de Valois and will report as soon as the interrogation is complete.'

Macleod ignored Jones's error in including de Valois in the plot.

'You say you are returning to Washington. Why can't you make the report yourself?'

Jones paused before answering.

'The army must have been different in your day, Macleod.'

'Different?'

'When it was obviously common practice to ask your seniors to explain their actions to you?'

Macleod accepted the rebuke.

'Shall I go now?'

'Do, and by the time you get back let's hope Madame de Valois hasn't thought better of running to a stranger with a story a five-year-old would find hard to swallow and gone on her way looking for some other booby to gull.'

Walking back to his rooms he thought things over. He was sure Marie had told the truth, but why did he think so? Was it a pretty face, a clever act, or was it that he wanted to believe? No, he had met de Valois and St Clair, and he could believe that what she said of them was too palpably true. And if she was putting on an act then she was indeed a great actress. He had seen hysteria before and he had seen it tonight. Something had happened which had terrified her. His thoughts turned to Jones. Why had he been so dismissive of the whole thing? De Valois might have been a popinjay but St Clair fitted perfectly the description of the man he had been sent to look out for. And why take the letter of credit? Why not just send someone or, as he was leaving anyway, why not go himself? And there was something else, something Jones had said, but it wouldn't come back. Macleod walked on deep in thought asking himself questions for which he had no answers. Outside the front door the words of Jones came back, *she has probably gone on her way*. Macleod opened the front door and ran up the stairs to the door of his rooms. It was open. He hurried in. The landlady turned and looked at him. No one else was in the room.

'Where is Madame de Valois?'

Before the landlady could answer the door of the bedroom opened and Marie came out dressed in a mop cap with a shawl over a dress of coarse, thick, off-white material. She smiled at Macleod, came into the room and spun round.

'Well, Jean, will it do? Do I still look like that grand lady Marie Christine de Valois, the best-dressed lady in New Orleans?'

Macleod, relieved, turned to the landlady and held out his lantern.

'Thank you, you may go now. Look out some more clothes and bring them up packed as if you yourself were going on a journey.'

The woman took the lantern.

'As I would do it for myself?'

'Yes.'

'Very good, sir. If you say so.'

She left the room closing the door behind her.

Marie stood and looked at Macleod.

'You did not go to my house, did you?'

'No.'

'Did you go somewhere to find out what to do with me?'

'Yes.'

'I see.' She sat down. 'And what is it you have been instructed to do?'

'Find out what you know, if anything.'

'Then.'

'Dispose of you.'

'Kill me?'

'Killing you would be one way of disposing of you.'

'I see.'

'No, you don't see. And neither do I see, I wish to God I did but I don't.'

She looked up at him.

'Can you tell me anything about who you are or why you came to New Orleans?'

'No.'

'Not even who sent you? The French, the British, the

Americans?'

'No.'

'And will you do what you have been told to do?'

'Yes. I have no choice.'

She looked down at her hands in her lap.

'No, we never have any choice, do we? We are told, and we do what we are told. My Church tells me that we are free because we have been given the greatest of all gifts by an all-merciful God, the gift of free will. And because we have that great gift we are always free, free to do exactly as we are told.'

'Marie, you must tell me what you know. After that I will dispose of you, that is to say, you will disappear. Madame de Valois will cease to exist. She will be disposed of.'

She raised her head.

'You would disobey?'

'No, never disobey. Obey in my own way perhaps, but never disobey.'

She smiled.

'Were you educated by the Jesuits perhaps?'

'No, not by the Jesuits. Why do you ask?'

'Oh, it's just that you what you said sounded a little like a Jesuit, *obey in my own way but never disobey*. My mother had a Jesuit Confessor. I liked to talk with him when I was a girl. Life was never simple the way he described it, more of a puzzle, but a puzzle always capable of manipulation. The secret was to know the right words, no, not the right words, the right way to use the words. There is always sin but, if you know the right way to use the words, there can also be forgiveness. My mother said ...'

Macleod broke through her rambling.

'Marie, you must tell me what you know and then we must get away from here.'

'To the British? It has to be someone I can trust to keep me safe. It has to be the British.'

'If it has to be the British then so be it.'

'To Jamaica?'

Macleod had thought about that and had his lie ready.

'No, it cannot be Jamaica or any other place in the Caribbean.'

'But why, they are so close?'

'That is the very reason why. Marie, by now your husband will have been found dead in bed beside his dead lover. You have fled the house and disappeared. What will people think?' And he saw that Marie had indeed begun to realise what they would think. Her mind was now working rationally and he need make no further explanation. 'They will be looking for you, and when they don't find you they will watch the docks. If we ship out as man and wife heading back to Boston we may get past them.'

'Boston?'

'As far as anyone at the docks is concerned we will be going home to Boston. Once there I'm sure you will be safe and from there you can go north and tell what you know to the British.'

She was thinking about it.

'But Boston is far away. It will take so long.'

'It is the only safe way, and it is best that you are far away from here. Trust me, Marie.'

'I want to trust you, Jean, and as you are the only one who can help me, perhaps I must trust you, but if I tell you what I know, how can I be sure what you will do? After I come here for help you go to someone who tells you to dispose of me, really dispose of me. You must see how difficult it is for me.'

Macleod did indeed see it. What he didn't see was what more he could do.

'Marie, we do not have much time, even as we speak this thing moves on. Either you will trust me or you will not. The choice is yours.'

It wasn't much, but as she had no other choice in the matter, it was enough.

'I will try to trust you. You must decide what to do. I am in your hands.'

She lowered her head and looked again at her hands folded in her lap.

God's teeth, thought Macleod, either she's the most wonderful actress in the world or the most wonderful woman and damn me if I can tell which it is.

'All that matters at the moment is that we get out of New Orleans. If we get on a ship headed north we can talk about trusting me or whatever you know about this conspiracy then. First try to get some sleep. I'll book passage for us on any boat headed north to any port where we can get a ship to Boston. In Boston, when you are sure that you are safe, you can make up your mind what you want to do.'

Marie looked up.

'Thank you, Jean.'

She stood up.

'Now go to bed and try to sleep.'

'Yes, I will try.'

Marie went to the bedroom and Macleod watched the door close. Suddenly he felt infinitely weary, as if all energy had been drained from him. He fell into a chair. The brandy, the sudden action, the tension and excitement all combined so that, without even realising it, he closed his eyes and in a matter of minutes began to snore.

Chapter Twenty-seven

Molly O'Hara was angry and disappointed that the hangman standing beside the noose was handling her roughly, gripping her arm and shaking her. She was angry and disappointed because, despite the heavy beard and tricorn hat, she recognised the eyes as those of Jasper Trent.

Then she was wide awake.

Kitty was standing beside the bed shaking her and speaking. Sleep completely gone, she listened as Kitty broke her news.

'De Valois and St Clair are dead and our pretty bird has flown.' Molly pulled back the clothes and swung her feet to the floor. 'Looks to me like our pretty bird might have croaked them both.'

Molly looked around for her robe.

'Maybe, maybe not. When did it happen?'

'Last night, throats cut horribly was what I was told but all I know for sure is that they're dead. The story's running all over town.'

Molly gave up on the robe.

'Right, get me washed and dressed and let's get over there. Salcedo's Jacks will be stamping all over the place and I want you to get what you can from below stairs before the servants are scared so shitless they won't be able to see straight, never mind talk straight.'

Molly and Kitty went to work and soon that grand lady of fashion, Madame de Metz, accompanied by her faithful maid were under full sail and heading for the stricken house of de Valois.

There are times when even the most rigid barriers of convention must bend if not actually break and the crowd outside the front door of the de Valois house contained not only interested idlers and loafers but the better class of servants from neighbouring houses, all mixing for the moment as equals. The idlers and loafers claimed the moral high ground. They were there on their own account, the servants were there as servants, gathering what they could to take back to their masters and mistresses. All parted, however, to make way for Madame de Metz as she swept through them, mounted the few steps that led up to the front door and waited while her maid worked on the large brass knocker.

The door was opened by a man in uniform. Madame de Metz brushed him aside and entered, talking loudly to no one in particular.

'Where is my dear, adored friend? Will someone not tell me where is that unhappy, grief-stricken child?'

The uniformed man caught up with her and reached for her arm.

'Madame ...'

He stopped speaking and quickly withdrew his hand. The look she turned and gave him was as effective as a musket ball.

'Do you address me, my man?'

'I, I ...'

He gave up the unequal struggle and left, hurrying to find a superior.

Madame de Metz swept on through the hall.

'Marie, darling Marie,' she called announcing her presence to all and sundry. Then quickly and in a low voice, 'Hop to it, Kitty, wring their guts of all they've got and get back to the kip when you can.'

Kitty left and headed for the stairs beyond which she knew she would find the kitchen.

Madame de Metz went into the living room, sat down resting her hands on the handle of her parasol and waited. After a moment the uniformed man came in, stopped and side-stepped cleverly, putting the man who had been following him between himself and the formidable lady sitting looking at them from the chair.

'And you are, sir?'

'First I think I would like to establish who you are, Madame.'

'Madame de Metz, intimate friend and confidante of Madame Marie Christine de Valois.'

'And what is it you wish here, Madame?'

'And you are, sir?'

'I am the representative of His Excellency Governor Salcedo.'

'And your business in this house?'

'There has been an incident ...'

Madame de Metz rose like a rocketing pheasant and let out a wail which almost caused the uniformed man to raise his arm in defence.

'Ah, it's true. Oh pray tell me, sir, that it isn't true. I beg you by the blessed blood of our Saviour to tell me it isn't true.' She wailed again, dropped her parasol and threw her arm across her eyes while at the same time coming forward enough to fall on her knees at the feet of the representative of Governor Salcedo whose face was now a nice blend of horror and astonishment. She clasped her hands as if in prayer.

'By God's pity, sir, tell me the awful thing I have heard isn't true, that Monsieur de Valois and his dear friend Monsieur St Clair have been brutally slain.' She unclasped her hands and wrapped her arms round his legs. She knew she was overplaying it but she needed a result and quickly. 'Please, sir, by the tears of our Holy Mother, say that my beloved Marie is not harmed. Please, sir, I beg of you ...'

The Governor's representative capitulated unconditionally in the face of such an unstoppable onslaught.

'Madame, please, it is I who beg you.' Molly let him unwind her arms and raise her to her feet. 'Madame, I regret that Messieurs de Valois and St Clair *are* dead, as you say, brutally murdered. As to where Madame de Valois is I cannot at this time say, except she is not in the house.'

Madame de Metz changed again and was no longer either the great lady nor the distraught wailer but now only a humble petitioner.

'I apologise most humbly, sir. Despite what I had heard I had hoped that it might not be true. But now you have told me, I must go and pray beside the bodies of my two dear friends.' The Governor's representative was about to speak but she drove her humility roughshod over whatever it was he was going to say. 'Although I am sure they are both already in heaven I will add my poor prayers to all the many others which will be offered up for them this day. Please hand me my parasol.'

And she stood with downcast eyes and her hand out.

The Governor's representative made an impatient gesture to the uniformed man who darted forward, recovered the parasol and placed it in her hand.

'You may take me to them.'

Her voice sounded so much like a benediction that for a fleeting second he almost crossed himself. Instead he turned and led the cortège of two past the Governor's representative and on up the stairs to a bedroom where he opened a door guarded by two more uniformed men and led the way in. On the bed, covered by a sheet which had once been white but was now mostly blood stains, the two bodies lay in the positions the murderer had left them.

Madame de Metz crossed the room, knelt by the bed, joined her hands and spoke to the uniformed man as she bent her head.

'Thank you, you may leave me now to my prayers.'

The uniformed man paused awkwardly.

'I think, Madame ...'

Madame de Metz began a slow and elaborate crossing of herself slowly intoning.

'In nomine Patris, et Filii, et Spiritus Sancti.'

The uniformed man mumbled, 'Amen', turned and left the room closing the door quietly behind him.

Chapter Twenty-eight

An hour later Molly and Kitty were back in Madame de Metz's rooms sharing notes.

'Once the Jack had gone I had a good look at them and one thing is certain, it wasn't any pull that turned sour. It was a clean enough job, one shot each to the body then reload and one ball in de Valois's head. St Clair took it to the heart and died right off but the first shot didn't kill de Valois. It was low down and he would probably have screamed like a stuck pig. But that didn't bother our man. He reloaded and finished the job. A cool piece of work, bloody cool.'

'Ah, cool indeed, and he was lucky or he was wise. The servants were sensible. They stayed under their bedclothes when they heard the noise and kept out of it until they were sure all the fun was well and truly over before they raised the alarm.'

'Who did you talk to?'

'The cook. We used to talk when you visited. She's a gossipy old bag and makes up twice as much as she ever hears, but she puts herself about, I'll give her that. She reckons the wife did it, but she didn't give any reason except de Valois's bedroom antics.'

'No, Marie didn't do any shooting, first because her husband's bedroom antics couldn't be anything new to her and second because she isn't the killing type.'

'How do you reckon she got clear?'

'I don't think our man cared about her. His mark was in that bed.'

'Which one, St Clair or de Valois?'

'De Valois couldn't be important, he was a fop and a fool, but St Clair's always interested me. He was clever and, except for de Valois, he kept himself pretty much at a distance. And he wasn't a vain clothes-horse like de Valois, but that didn't stop him visiting one particular tailor more frequently than his wardrobe would account for.'

'Anything in it?'

Molly shrugged.

'Maybe. I went in to the shop and got him talking about Paris where he'd been in business before he came over here. I couldn't pump him too much without him smelling a rat, but all you have to do is use your eyes to know that somehow he's keeping up with the latest cut of Paris threads. That means someone is bringing in the fashion plates he needs.'

'And not just fashion plates maybe?'

'It begins to look that way. And if St Clair was mixed up in something, then he would have made sure his own home was secure. No chance to croak him there, but the home of de Valois, that was a different matter. That could be a weak point. Did the cook say anything about someone nosing about among the servants, asking questions, friendlying up to any of them?'

'Last time we visited she told me that she was sure that the wife's maid had a gentleman caller on the sly.'

'Did she, by God?'

'Very cagey about him the maid was apparently. Wouldn't say who it was but couldn't resist letting it drop that she reckoned she was going to become a lady and mix with the toffs. When she told me, I thought it was the same old story and all the maid would get was knocked up and left to whistle, but now it looks different.'

'A secret gentleman caller. Well, well. Someone's been planning this for a while.'

'Looks like it. Cook reckoned the maid sometimes let him in after the house had gone to bed.'

'A night-time caller who liked to stay invisible. Did the cook have any ideas?'

'Not what you could call anything solid but she was curious. She's been in houses where there's been quiet callers, but this one, well she didn't like it. This one was too careful for her peace of mind, so she watched out and one night caught a glimpse of him leaving. All she could see was that he walked with a limp.'

'A limp? Who do we know that walks with a limp?'

'No one, but if we're right then he could be our killer.'

'Did you speak to this maid?'

'No, the cook said no one had seen her since the previous night and her bed hadn't been slept in.'

'That pretty much settles it then.'

'Dead you think?'

'She has to be, she's the only one who could name the killer. He wouldn't have left her around to squeal to the Jacks once the job was done.'

'So what do we do now?'

'I'll do a round of the houses to see what I can pick up and you do the docks.'

'And I'm looking for what?'

'Let's say that when our bird heard the shots and the screaming she had the sense to run for it. The question would be, where would she run to? She hasn't gone to the authorities nor to any of her friends. If she had she'd have shown by now. So, let's assume pretty Marie knows something, or is involved in something, and she's bolted. She can't stay hid long in New Orleans, can she?'

'She'll try to ship out somewhere.'

'She will. See what's due to leave and where bound. She has family somewhere, Baton Rouge I think, maybe she'll try to get back to them.'

Kitty gave a short laugh.

'If that pretty bird goes anywhere near the docks, I'll do more than clip her bloody wings.'

'Maybe, but first we have to find her, so it's off to the docks with you and off into society with me.'

And Madame de Metz and her faithful maid set out, each on their own mission.

Chapter Twenty-nine

As Marie de Valois sat in Macleod's rooms waiting for his return from the docks, Madame de Metz made her round of the best houses in New Orleans and was freshly shocked in each one by the terrible news her friends so gloatingly poured out to her about the murder. She listened, fascinated by their various interpretations as to what the mysterious disappearance of Marie might mean. That she lay somewhere horribly murdered, was slight favourite ahead of that, suffering from a fit of madness, she had cut St Clair's and her husband's throats before drowning herself and, coming a respectable third, that she had run off with a secret lover after he had murdered the faithless husband and his lover. All of which told Madame de Metz that no one had any idea why de Valois and St Clair were dead nor where Marie was.

She was tired and hungry and awash with coffee when she finally returned to her rooms. She pulled off her cloak and threw it on the bed.

'Well, Kitty, I've drawn one blank after another and downed enough coffee to float a frigate. When I've relieved myself I hope you'll have news for me.'

She left the room and Kitty poured two glasses of brandy and water. When Molly returned she took up her glass and held it up.

'Here's to a capacious bladder, girl. It's sometimes more use than money.' And having taken a drink to her toast she sat down. 'Well, how did it go with you? Any news?'

'I've news all right. I saw that Boston lawyer, Macleod. I nearly missed him. He was dressed down like a Quaker going to Meeting House, plain black, not a sign of the fancy threads we've been used to seeing him in.'

'What was he doing?'

'He booked passage on a ship headed for Charleston in two days, and here's the best part, his wife is to travel with him.'

'A wife, eh? So that's who she ran to. The lawyer's got her, has

149

he? Damn his eyes, he's the one we should have been looking at, and under our noses all along. God's teeth! He's a smooth bastard. I had him down as just one more moon-calfing after Marie de Valois. I'd have staked ready money that it wasn't an act, but it seems he's been too much for us. Still, he's shown his hand now.'

'What do we do?'

'We take the pretty bird from him.'

'Do we want her?'

'We do if she knows what St Clair was up to.'

'If you think Macleod did the killing then what about our limping friend?'

'All that means is Macleod isn't working on his own. He's been working the same ramp as us. He works above stairs and his limping friend works below. If he's taken the trouble to snuff out St Clair and snare the pretty bird it's because she has the information he's been after. Well, if he's got her we shall have to set about taking her from him.'

'How do we do that?'

'When did you say they're due to sail?'

'Day after tomorrow at three in the afternoon. They'll board an hour before sailing.'

'Then we wait until they go to the ship and we lift her.'

'How?'

'We know they'll be on the docks headed for that ship at around two. You follow him, get close enough to knife him and grab her. I'll be there to stop them for you and when he goes down I'll start enough of a rumpus for you to put the snatch on. Just show her the knife and you won't have any trouble. The surprise of me popping out from nowhere will hold her attention while you stick him. She probably won't even notice that you've put Macleod down. I'll get down beside him and when I see the blood I'll go into an act long enough for you to get clear.'

'What if they're not together, if they go to the boat separately?'

'All the better, we lift her as soon as we see her. Either way you keep a sharp lookout for me when you get near the boat. Once you spot me, off we go.'

Kitty lifted her glass.

150

'Good. I like it plain and simple. Here's to blood and money.'
Molly returned the toast.
'Blood and money, and plenty of both my girl, plenty of both.'

Chapter Thirty

Kitty held her knife by the handle with the blade reversed against her forearm, her shoulders and arms covered by a light shawl. She sat by the door of the covered carriage looking out of the window. Molly sat next to her. Neither spoke.

The carriage waited down the street from Macleod's rooms, ignored by the servants, tradesmen and other pedestrians who passed it.

'How long since the carter came and took the trunk?'

Molly took out a small, gold watch.

'Fifteen minutes. He won't be long now.'

As she put away the watch, Macleod came out into the street and walked away in the opposite direction from where the carriage stood. After walking briskly for about thirty yards he suddenly stopped.

'We're off. I'll see you at the docks.'

Kitty opened the door and got out of the carriage and spoke to the driver.

'To the docks.'

The driver touched his hat with his whip and flicked the horse with the reins. The carriage moved slowly off and Kitty stepped up on to the pavement and waited.

The door out of which Macleod had come opened again and Marie de Valois emerged dressed like a serving woman and carrying a large bundle tied together and slung over one arm. Kitty could see she was looking thoroughly sorry for herself.

Marie walked slowly for a few yards then stopped, moved the bundle awkwardly to her other arm and then set off again. After walking a short distance Marie stopped once more and moved the bundle back. It occurred to Kitty that if Marie de Valois travelled at that speed all the way to the docks she'd probably miss the boat by some margin. Macleod had watched Marie come out of the house and waited while she adjusted and re-adjusted her bundle but, apparently satisfied that all was well, set off, not looking back at Marie who struggled on frequently glancing up at Macleod's back as the distance between them increased.

This caused a problem for Kitty. She wanted them both in her sight but if she held back from Marie there would be a chance she could soon lose Macleod. Kitty walked and watched. Was it a clever ploy by Macleod in case he was followed? If he was indeed as sharp as Molly now thought, he certainly wouldn't think he could walk away from New Orleans with his pretty prize and expect no one to care one way or the other.

Suddenly Macleod stopped, turned and looked behind him. Marie was still unhappily struggling on and he waited until the gap between them was almost closed, then turned and walked on again. Marie stopped and flung her bundle to the floor as Macleod walked off. Obviously she had thought he would wait and help her and, equally obviously, she had been disappointed. Kitty was taken completely by surprise and nearly stopped walking, but caught herself and, as she almost came up to Marie, crossed the street, turned a corner and waited. Marie picked up her bundle and once more began her slow progress but Kitty noticed that the look on her face had changed. Clearly Kitty was not the only one heading to the docks with murder in her heart.

What's the clever bastard up to, thought Kitty, as the procession reconvened. Don't look at all, then tell the world you're looking? Well, my sharp bastard, we're on to your game now, so act the simpleton all you want because I'll soon be bringing the curtain down for good on your little pantomime.

And she gripped the handle of her knife a little harder.

As Macleod walked, his thoughts were not of being followed, they were a confused jumble amidst which he kept trying to tell himself that all that mattered was doing his duty, keeping Marie safe so she could give her information to the General. But he couldn't shake from himself a thrill of anticipation about them sharing a small cabin all the way to Charleston. They would have to pass as man and wife during the journey and that surely meant she would have to put on some sort of display of fondness. Who knew what might be the outcome by the time they got to Charleston?

He awoke from his daydream when he reached the streets

leading on to the docks. There was no room for dreaming of any sort among the hustle and bustle, especially when he saw that the crowds soon became penned in among towering warehouses on one side and shops, taverns and counting houses on the other. Once the crowds had begun to thicken and the noise and jostling increased he decided there would now be no danger in them walking together. He waited until Marie came up to him. He smiled at her, oblivious of the look on her face.

'From here I think we are safe to become man and wife.'

Marie dumped her bundle at his feet.

'Animal! Cur! Pig!' Macleod almost recoiled in shock and surprise at her words and manner but Marie continued. 'You walk on with your nose in the air and leave me to carry that, that thing, that detestable burden. You stand here and grin at me while I suffer. And I am forced to do it,' she gesticulated with her hands at her dress and mob-cap, 'dressed like a common servant, a cook, worse, a washer-woman. I will carry the bundle no longer. I would rather die. Carry it yourself or leave me here. Either be a gentleman or get out of my sight.'

The crowd milling past them took no notice. Most had witnessed such a scene before. A husband and wife, the husband one of the weak sort and on the receiving end of a tongue lashing.

Only a pair of passing sailors who had lunched on a liquid diet stopped to offer comment.

'Black her eye, mate, in fact black them both or that missus of yours will have you squashed under her thumb. Mark my words.'

But his fellow took a contrary view.

'Too late, Tom. He's squashed already and I shouldn't wonder if maybe she's the one who's blacked an eye afore now.'

'I think you have the truth of it, Billy.'

And with sorrowful looks at Macleod they passed on their way.

In a doorway across the street, Kitty waited and watched. What the hell are they up to now? Standing and making a show of themselves. She watched as Macleod stooped and picked up the bundle and the two of them walked on.

Kitty came out of the doorway. She knew where the Charleston vessel was berthed so there was no need to get too close so long as she kept them in view. As they all approached the entrance to the quay where their ship waited, the crowds thinned out. Neither

Macleod nor Marie looked back and Kitty adjusted her fingers on the knife handle and moved the shawl slightly so it would be clear when the knife was needed. She saw Molly standing beyond the warehouse walls on the wooden quay with the moored ships beyond her. Kitty began to close rapidly, the knife turned now, blade out in her hand and just covered by the shawl. She was almost on them and had the knife clear when her head exploded, everything went black and she fell to the ground.

Marie and Macleod both heard the cry. They stopped and looked round. Behind them there was a slight commotion. A group of workers had gathered round a figure lying on the ground. Macleod dropped the bundle and made as if to go and give assistance, but Marie grabbed his arm.

'What are you doing? It is nothing to do with us. A woman has fainted or had a fit or dropped dead. It happens all the time. We must go on, we must get on board the ship. There I will be safe. Leave her, whoever she is. Someone will take care of her.'

Macleod hesitated, then bent down to pick up the bundle and as he did so Marie gave a small gasp. He looked up and saw Madame de Metz hurry past. Macleod straightened up, holding the bundle.

'My God, did you see who that was?'

'It was Madame de Metz. What is she doing ....'

But Macleod wasn't listening. He watched as Madame de Metz arrived at the group and fell to her knees beside the woman lying on the floor.

Macleod turned back to Marie.

'What in God's name is she doing here?'

But he didn't wait for an answer. He grabbed Marie's arm and hurried them forward. He had no idea why the de Metz woman should be on this particular quay at this particular time and he had no intention of waiting to find out. He had planned their departure as a carefully guarded secret and was sure he had left nothing to chance, yet here was someone who never set foot outside the best salons waiting almost beside the very ship which would get them out of New Orleans.

Once safely on the deck they looked back. In the small crowd that had gathered around the inert form, Madame de Metz was kneeling beside the body, but her head was turned to the ship and her eyes fixed on Marie.

155

Chapter Thirty-one

Molly had seen the knife almost under Kitty's body as soon as she had knelt down. She picked it up and slipped it away, then looked at the ring of dirty, curious faces looking down at them.

'Clear a space. She has fainted, she needs air. A space I say, get back.' The small crowd shuffled back at her words of command and she was able to look past them and watch Macleod and Marie hurry up the gangplank and Marie stop and look at her.

Well, nothing could be done there now, so she turned her attention once again to the crowd.

'You and you,' she pointed at two burly men, 'lift her carefully and take her to the nearest tavern.'

The two men moved forward and did as they were told. Molly followed and once they had Kitty in a chair in the tavern took her purse and gave each man a few coins. The men touched their foreheads with a knuckle, took the money and went off to the bar. Molly crouched down next to Kitty who had begun to come round. Molly looked across to the bar. The barman was staring at her, understandably curious that someone of such class should come into his tavern following two men carrying a woman's body.

Molly called to him.

'Brandy and quick about it.'

The barman busied himself for a moment and then came over carrying a tray. He put a glass and a flask on the table then stood back but didn't leave. Now he had a ringside seat, he was keen to see what would develop.

Molly turned and gave him the full blast of a Madame de Metz look. He took a step back, murmured something suitably apologetic, turned and went back behind the bar.

Molly gave her attention to Kitty.

'What happened? One minute you were right behind them then you were down.'

'You tell me. I saw you and was almost up close enough to

stick him when the sky fell in. Next thing I know I'm in here with you.'

Molly reached up and felt the back of Kitty's head. Kitty winced.

'Shit, that hurts.'

Molly looked at her fingers then showed them to Kitty. They were smeared with blood.

'Christ, Kitty, he had someone on you all the time. As soon as whoever it was saw you make your move, he laid you out cold.'

'The bastard, we should have known he wouldn't let us take her so easily. Now I see why he was playing the fool all the way to the docks. It was so I wouldn't notice he'd got someone behind me.'

'He's good, Kitty, up to now too bleedin' good and I don't mind admitting it. He took me in with everyone else about Marie de Valois and now he's done us down again. They're on the ship now and no way we can get at them.' Molly sat down and poured a brandy which she lifted to her mouth and drank off. She put the empty glass on the table. 'Help yourself, girl, we'll need to do some thinking about this.'

Kitty needed no second invitation. She also poured a glass and swallowed it off.

'You saw no one, Molly?'

'I caught a glimpse maybe, just the back of a man walking away from where you were lying as I got down beside you. Just a glimpse before he was away but I noticed one thing. He limped.'

'The pistol who did for de Valois and St Clair?'

'It has to be.'

'And we should have been ready for it. We knew his man did the killing and we left him out of the picture. We should have been ready.'

'Well we weren't and there's no point in crying into our brandy about it. What's done is done. The point is we'll make no more mistakes. Next time we'll be ready for him.'

'Next time?'

'Oh yes. He's bested us today but there'll be a next time. And when there is we'll settle accounts with our clever Mr Macleod. Settle and close them.'

'Well, Kitty, Mr Macleod has our pretty bird safe on a ship bound for Charleston. If he's gone to all this trouble to take her along my guess would be that he hasn't been able to pump her for the information. She hasn't told him what he wants yet.'

'How do you figure that?'

'If she had told him then why take her along?'

Kitty thought of the late Jack Doran.

'Because now she's his doxy. He's snared the bird, got under her skirts and she likes it. He's got a journey ahead so he takes her along as company. Plenty of time to slit her throat and ditch her once he's in Charleston.'

'No. I told you, no more mistakes. We know to our cost he's thorough and doesn't take chances. If he'd got the information he'd have got shot of her the same way they got shot of the maid. Travel alone, travel fast and leave no traces.'

'All right, then why hasn't he beaten it out of her?'

'Because, like you say, he's got under her skirts and he wants her to trust him. That way he has a better chance to get it all. Beat it out of her and he couldn't be sure, not in the time that was available to him. With St Clair dead we wouldn't be the only ones who might come looking. He had to run and he had to take her with him. I think he plans to ship her somewhere he can park her safely until he sells her on. It's what I'd do. Either he'll sell her to whoever sent him or, if someone makes him a better offer ...'

Kitty saw where Molly was going.

'And you want that bid to come from us?'

'Got it in one.'

'So where do you think he'll go?'

'My guess would be that from Charleston he'll take her to Boston.'

'He's a homing bird you think?'

'Like I said, he's got her and he wants to sell her on or get her information. Either way he needs a safe haven to hold her. If she trusts him then why not take her to his home?'

Kitty felt the back of her head and Molly poured another brandy, took a drink and passed the glass to Kitty.

'What if he holds on at Charleston or heads elsewhere?'

'Then we're beaten and I might give thought to taking what's left of Trent's money and running.' Her words, however, carried little conviction, running to where Jasper Trent might not be able to reach her to exact his vengeance was not a happy thought.

'We've got to play a better game than we have up to now if we're to come alongside him and lift the bird from him.'

'Well, he's made no mistakes yet, so I don't fancy him for making one any time soon and Boston seems too obvious to me.'

'Ah, but there you're wrong. They ship out for Charleston today. From Charleston they'll go further north pretty quick I imagine. He thinks he'll be home safe and get his business done before anyone can come after him from New Orleans.'

'And he's right, isn't he? It could be days before we could get on something that would take us north and then we'd still have to get to Boston.'

'Not so, girl. I've been given a trump card that might get us there sooner than he thinks. With good luck and a fair wind we may even get there before him.'

'How, sprout wings and fly?'

'Not quite. I find us a friendly sailor and wave a bit of paper at him and tell him to get us to Boston as fast as he can.'

'You're making no sense.'

'Oh yes I am. If we can find a certain ship in the next two or three days we'll beat the clever bastard and be ready and waiting when he gets there. This time they won't see us coming and there'll be no one to cover his back.' Molly pulled the knife out of the recesses of her costume. 'Here, I picked this up outside. Take it.'

Kitty took the knife and slipped it away and managed a small smile.

'If he won't do as we want the easy way it'll be a pleasure to get another chance to use it and if I do I won't miss.'

Molly poured another drink which she held up.

'To our Gracious Majesty's Royal Navy, may they be there when you need them.' And she drank the glass off and handed it to Kitty. 'Drink up, girl, we've work to do.'

Kitty poured a glass and swallowed it.

'I don't know what I just drank to, but whatever it is I hope it works.'

Molly took out her purse and handed it to Kitty.

'Go and pay for the brandy then let's get out of here.'

Kitty stood up and went to the bar and paid. The barman and the two men who had carried Kitty in, and who were enjoying the

159

fruits of their labour, watched them leave.

'Queer doings, mates.'

The sailors nodded.

'Ah, very rum.'

'And they didn't behave like a fine lady and her maid. More like shipmates on shore-leave.'

The men nodded once more.

'True, friend. Very strange.'

'I'll tell you another queer thing as happened. They fished a body out of the docks only the other morning. Young woman, dressed like a fine lady's maid. Probably from one of the big houses.'

'Ah, got herself into trouble no doubt?'

'In a manner of speaking. Her throat was cut. Murdered and dumped in the river somewhere, and fetched up among the boats. Nasty business.'

'True, friend, very nasty business.'

Chapter Thirty-two

The General sat looking up at Jeremiah Jones who was standing in front of the desk leaning heavily on his stick. His leg was hurting but, as the General hadn't asked him to sit down, he stood and tried to ignore the pain as he delivered his report.

'St Clair was almost certainly the initial disburser of incoming funds as well as orders and information from Paris. But I couldn't find a way to get close to him or of getting anything out of him. Then someone put a pistol ball in him and that was that.'

'I see. Any idea who might have done it?'

'Well, as it wasn't us, I imagine either the British or the French.'

'The French? Why would the French kill their own man?'

'Why do any of us do anything? In some way they thought they would gain an advantage by his death. If I had found out about him others could or already had. If so, Paris may have decided he had become a liability. But my money is on the British, there was a woman down there calling herself Madame de Metz. She was good, she passed herself off as the real article easily enough.'

'But you think she was working for London?'

'We wanted someone in New Orleans, I assume London would have seen the same signs and drawn the same conclusions. She came from nowhere and despite all her fine talk and lofty manners no one really knew anything about her except what she herself told them.'

'Could she have killed St Clair?'

'Very possibly. Once she'd got herself well established she made it her business to cosy up to the wife of St Clair's friend and lover, a wet dandy of a man called de Valois. It was probably her best way of trying to get close.'

The General finally motioned for Jones to take a chair.

'And Macleod?'

Jones sat down grateful for the respite from his leg.

'Ah, now there it is a different story. I take my hat off to Mr Macleod and to you, sir, a clever and very effective choice. I congratulate you.'

'Damn your congratulations. Tell me how he did?'

'Moved in amongst them smooth as you like. He got close to de Valois, don't ask me how as it was something I could never do, and through de Valois got to St Clair. It's my opinion he knows pretty much all there is to know of St Clair's part in all of this. He may well know most of his contacts here in America.'

'So where is his report?'

Surprise filed Jeremiah Jones's face.

'His report?'

'I assume, if he did so well, he made a report of it to you?'

'Has he not reported to you directly?'

'Would I be asking for his damn report if he had?'

'I see, that is to say I don't see.'

'Stop gibbering, man, and tell me what happened.'

'He came to me on the night of St Clair's murder. With St Clair dead he reckoned his work in New Orleans was finished. I asked him to make a report which I could bring to you but he refused. He said he wouldn't commit the information he had to paper. He said the plot went to the highest level, even into the government. He was only prepared to name names to someone he trusted absolutely. I tried to reason with him but he was adamant, so I told him to come to you as fast as he could. I couldn't leave for several days. I had to tie up what was left of my supposed negotiations. I thought he would have been in contact by now.'

The General sat in silence for a moment.

'Well, you thought wrong. Macleod is dead.'

'Dead!'

'They found his body down some alley near the docks. His head had been smashed in.'

'You're sure it was Macleod?'

'He was carrying a letter of credit that identified him. It was Macleod all right. Whatever information he'd managed to get never left New Orleans. The mission has been a total failure.'

Jones stood up with difficulty.

'I will have my resignation on your desk immediately, sir.'

'Sit down you fool, what would I want your resignation for? If I decide any of this *is* your fault I won't want your damned resignation, it'll be your hide I take.'

Jones slowly sat down and waited.

'Either the French were on to him or the British, that Madame de Metz woman. Either way he's dead, and what he knew died with him. But St Clair is also dead and their operation in New Orleans shut down for a time. How did St Clair cover what came in?'

'His tailor was Fouché's man. It was a clever piece of work. The tailor made sure that everyone knew he was getting Paris fashion plates brought into him secretly so no one thought to ask what else might be coming in. And having the latest designs from Paris meant he could be the tailor of choice to money and fashion so St Clair could visit him as often as he liked and no one suspected anything.'

'You left him in place?'

'Why not? If they think it's safe to use that route again we know about it and it's watched.'

'How did that side of things go?'

'Well enough. We've a small group recruited who'll keep an eye on things and make reports but my guess is that what matters will move on now. From what we already knew I'd say that St Clair's work in New Orleans was pretty much done. He'll be no real loss to them.'

'You said his lover, de Valois, had a wife. Could she know anything?'

'I doubt it, and even if she did she's too busy running back to her family to matter to us or anyone else.'

'Running?'

'St Clair and de Valois were killed while they were in a compromising position together. The wife must have heard the shots and run, but nobody knows where. As far as Governor Salcedo is concerned the matter is closed. The wife killed them both either from rage, jealousy or in a fit of madness, then either took her own life by throwing herself in the Mississippi or the sea. One way or another she's gone and I don't think we need bother with her any more.'

'Are you sure?'

'De Valois was a vain fool who lived for social position,

fashion and St Clair. St Clair may have been his bedfellow but he was certainly no fool, he wouldn't have told de Valois anything and I can't imagine his relations with the lady of the house were ever of a nature which would encourage him to intimacy, so I doubt he confided in her.'

'Well, a mixed result but, on the whole, progress.'

'You don't think it a considerable loss not having Macleod's report? He said he could name names.'

'People say a lot of things. Remember, Macleod was an ex-officer with no experience in our kind of work. He wanted to do well, but enthusiasm without experience can be a lethal combination. And if there are people high up who are involved in this I doubt St Clair would have known their names. He was a provisioner and a source of orders and information. His knowledge of who was involved would be very limited. If Macleod got names they would probably be the ones that led us to New Orleans in the first place. No, I regret losing Macleod. In his day he was a decent enough officer, if of limited imagination and resource. I'm sorry he's dead, but it was a chance he took. Suffice to say that he fell in the service of his country. No true American can ask for more. Well, nothing stopped while you dallied in New Orleans so you've a considerable back-log so it's back to burning the midnight oil, Jeremiah, after all that gallivanting among the fleshpots.'

Jones stood up.

'It's a pleasure to be back, sir.'

Jones closed the door the General sat with his thoughts. A body found with Macleod's papers but features possibly unrecognisable. Does that make the body Macleod's? And if not, who put the papers there? And a wife who can't possibly know anything, but nonetheless has conveniently disappeared. He looked at the closed connecting door. Deep games, Jeremiah. It begins to look like someone's playing deep games. But it doesn't do to get out of your depth unless you're a strong swimmer. I wonder, Jeremiah, with that game leg of yours how strong a swimmer you might be. Maybe the time has come to find if you're as strong as the others in the water. Yes, I think that time might very well have come.

Chapter Thirty-three

Charleston Harbour was a crowded mass of shipping. To any landsman it seemed incredible that the forest of masts, furled sails and rigging that grew skywards from the cram of vessels could ever be sufficiently unravelled for these ships to put back to sea. But the miracle was daily performed by the vast army of slaves who toiled on these docks to get them ready.

Endless lines of cotton bales led from the great stone warehouses to the ships awaiting them. On other quays lines of tea-chests were disgorged from holds to be manhandled into other warehouses awaiting sale at the Exchange. On yet another quay another valuable cargo was led, staggering and in chains, also to be stored in warehouses until it too, like the tea, could be taken to its own Exchange and there auctioned off.

Macleod stood watching two of the crew bringing his trunk ashore down the gangplank. Marie stood next to him, and beside her stood the bundle which another of the crew had carried down minutes previously. A kind of frozen silence surrounded the pair amidst the noise and confusion of the busy quay.

Macleod was glad the passage was over. From the moment they boarded Marie had assumed an air of silent hostility which generated in him a mood of impotent anger. This had communicated itself at once to the crew and the other passengers, three merchants' representatives who shared the one other cabin. Macleod found both himself and his supposed wife politely isolated for the entire journey. After a few uncomfortable and almost totally silent attempts at communal meals with the other passengers Macleod and Marie, to everyone's relief, chose to eat in their small cabin. When they walked on deck the three representatives found they had business to attend to and, as far as the crew were concerned as they went about their business, Macleod and Marie, walking in stony silence, were invisible.

If some great actor had taken on the task of coaching the pair so that they might convince the crew and fellow travellers that they were indeed man and wife no better result could have been achieved. Marie, for all her dowdy clothes and the mob cap, which she insisted on wearing almost as a proud badge of her humiliation, was still a woman of outstanding beauty. Yet to the man who was at her side and supposedly sharing her bed she seemed to mean no more to him than his own shadow.

When they were forced to exchange words they did so in such a cold and formal way that even though the days were warm and the breezes balmy anyone near could have sworn there was a sudden chill in the air.

Not a soul on board ever doubted for one second that this frosty couple were indeed man and wife, from the moment the ship had got underway at New Orleans until it docked in Charleston and they stood frigidly together on the quay.

Macleod turned to Marie.

'Wait here by our luggage while I go and find a carter.'

Marie didn't answer but slightly raised her chin and gazed sadly into the distance in a way that Macleod had come to recognise as meaning, "See how I am made to suffer, see what indignity is heaped on me, yet I do not complain nor repine. It is my lot, I am only a woman. See, I obey."

Macleod ground his teeth, clenched his fists and pressed his lips firmly together as, many times before, words crashed unspoken about his mind.

He turned and walked away. The three representatives were now disembarking. A large woman was waiting by the gangplank and, as the first of them stepped ashore, came forward, firmly took his arm and passed hers through it and stood holding him.

He accepted his capture and meekly pecked at the woman's cheek before looking at the ground in beaten subjection.

The woman looked across at Marie who had been watching. The woman's eyes sent the message, "I know, my dear. They're all brutes, every one, if they're not kept in their place."

And with a tilt of the head she turned and led her captive away.

The other two representatives came down the gangplank. Perhaps they had seen the prisoner taken before and had allowed the painful scene to close before they themselves came back to dry land. They lifted their hats to Marie with formality and when past

166

her broke into happy conversation and headed away from the toiling docks to the streets beyond and the nearest tavern.

They were not married men.

Macleod returned in a matter of minutes and called up to a sailor on the deck coiling ropes.

'The carter will be here to collect this trunk and bundle shortly. Keep an eye on it, will you?'

The sailor made the universal acknowledgement to his betters by touching his forehead with a knuckle. Macleod took out a coin and flipped it to him. The sailor deftly caught it, gave it a look, touched his forehead again and returned to his business with the ropes.

'Come, we must find somewhere to stay.'

He offered his arm to Marie who took it and the couple set off away from the ship with the sailor watching them. He turned to a fellow who had arrived and begun to stow the coils.

'They say the strongest poisons often comes in the prettiest bottles.'

His colleague nodded.

'My missus has one eye, a small moustache and gets violent when in liquor but you wouldn't catch me wanting to swap wives with *that* poor sod.'

'Ah, poor sod indeed.'

And both returned to their business.

Macleod thought hard as they walked away from the docks. He didn't want to spend any more time sharing a room with Marie in the humiliating farce of man and wife. The recent voyage had stripped away any illusions he may have entertained for that situation. The only solution he could come up with was that they came from New Orleans and she was his sister.

'When we take rooms, you shall be my sister and we shall have come from New Orleans.'

'If you say so.'

'I shall be a lawyer heading to Boston on business. You can be accompanying me because you have a friend in Boston whom you wish to visit.'

'Does this friend have a name?'

Macleod wondered whether a name would be needed. He decided that it was highly unlikely but would do no harm.

'Bentley, your friend is Mrs Bentley.'

Eventually they arrived at the tavern which the captain had recommended and Macleod took two adjacent rooms. Macleod was eager to sail as soon as possible but first had to find a bank and cash one of his letters of credit to cover their stay in Charleston and pay passage to Boston. He went to Marie's room where he knocked and waited.

Marie eventually opened the door.

'I must go out on business. I would suggest you stay to your room until I return. I doubt you are in any danger here, but the less we show ourselves the better.'

Marie had been thinking of her situation ever since the ship had begun to approach Charleston. The terror brought about by what had happened in her house in New Orleans had diminished early in their journey, as had any inclination to trust the man she had chosen as her saviour. Macleod, when she had fled to him in panic, had seemed a veritable white knight, but too soon she realised that she had been sadly duped by what, in calmer judgement, she saw was nothing more than a mean-spirited bully. Was a man who could positively revel in humiliating her be deserving of her trust? Assuredly not. True, Macleod had got her away from New Orleans, but what were his motives? Once she had told him of her secret he had quickly spirited her away to Charleston where, as she was utterly alone, he could do exactly as he wished with her.

As she sat in her room contemplating the vile bundle that was her wardrobe she wondered whether, if she could get her hands on enough money, she might not give him the slip somehow and get away. She had accepted that the authorities might be watching for her at the docks in New Orleans but no one would be interested in her in Charleston. However, the only access to money would be from Macleod and she had decided that any hope of getting her fingers into his wallet would depend on how close she could get to him when he was off his guard.

It was, therefore, quite a different Marie who had opened the door and now looked at Macleod.

'Jean, please come in. I must speak to you.'

Macleod had been ready for the cold look and the acid word. The soft tone and the gentle manner caused him to pause.

'You wish me to come in?'

'Please, Jean, don't be cruel. If only you knew what agonies I have suffered while on that awful boat, you would pity me, not blame me. I assure you that if the Holy Mother of God had shared a cabin with me on that journey I would have treated her no better than I treated you.' Her eyes took on a pleading look. 'I am a weak woman whom you have saved from a terrible fate and I have repaid you like a common scold, a washer-woman. I would not blame you if you could not find it in your heart to forgive me.'

Macleod was now quite well aware of how unschooled he was in the ways of women, especially women like Marie de Valois, but he was no poltroon. She had made a fool of him often enough in their short acquaintance for him to realise she wanted something and had changed her manner only to assist her in getting it. But his job was to get her alive to Boston and keep her there until he could deliver her and her information to the General or to his deputed agent. That being so he entered Marie's room.

'Jean, in Charleston if I am to play the part of your sister I must have more suitable clothes.'

The request was not, Macleod knew, unreasonable. Even on board the ship he had felt she was hardly dressed as he would have wished any real wife to be. But he couldn't help feeling somewhat frustrated and annoyed that Marie's first consideration, now they were safe, was that she be given nicer dresses to wear. It was not what he looked for from one who shared such a situation of adversity.

'I shall send someone to you with a selection of dresses and cloaks. Once you deem yourself fit to be seen in public I will provide you with sufficient money to buy what you consider a suitable wardrobe.'

'Jean, you are so kind. After the way ...'

'Suitable, I should remind you, to the unmarried sister of a simple lawyer in a modest way of business.'

Marie took the rebuke humbly.

To escape this impossible brute she felt she would have taken a physical blow humbly. She had thrown herself on his mercy and he had taken cruel advantage of her and now, she had become sure, he would betray her. He would sell her because of the secret knowledge she possessed.

'You are kind, Jean, too kind. I will do as you say and wait here until the clothes come. But you must choose. I have only ever dressed as a lady of fashion is expected to dress and I don't think I have ever met an unmarried sister of a Boston lawyer, and certainly not one in a modest way of business. You must decide what I shall wear.'

Macleod was now impervious to her mockery or her play-acting. He welcomed it. Had he been able, he would have thanked her for it. It helped him thrust from his mind the knowledge that once, in a distant past, he had felt something for this woman.

'You may choose whatever you think would suit a woman of simple and honest disposition who would be indifferent to any manners of fashion. If you can do that, Madame, you will fit the part very well. Good day.'

Macleod left, Marie's eyes fixed on his back. Once the door was closed a phrase shot from her lips. It was one she had heard as a girl when a pony on which she had been riding had stood on the foot of the groom who was trying to help her dismount. Its vividness had struck her forcefully, although its meaning was, at that time, obscure. But now, feeling exactly as the groom must have felt, it seemed entirely appropriate.

Chapter Thirty-four

On making enquiries from the owner of the tavern Macleod was directed to the Citizens and Southern National Bank of South Carolina.

'There's branches of the First and Second Banks of the United States, sir, but if you'll excuse me saying so, you being a northern gentleman, I'd prefer to recommend one of our own institutions, sir.'

As Macleod had no financial preferences, northern nor southern, he followed the advice and at the recommended local institution exchanged a letter of credit for cash. He then found a dress-shop and gave the lady there instructions to take a small selection of smart but simple dresses and cloaks to his sister's room at the tavern. Then he went down to the docks to find when they could take ship for Boston. He was glad to be busy and glad that he was edging closer now to ending this business. He told himself that all feelings for Marie de Valois, and certainly any attraction, were totally dead. He told himself that all that mattered now was his duty to his country, nothing more. That was what he told himself, and that is what he chose to believe.

'Excuse me, sir.'

Macleod looked at the ill-dressed, greasy individual who had addressed him. His appearance suggested someone who was about to tell a sad story and ask for money. Macleod didn't stop walking and the man wheezed along beside him.

'Would you be a Mr Macleod, sir?'

Macleod stopped. He knew no one in Charleston and certainly no one like the individual who stood beside him.

'Who wishes to know?'

'If you are Mr Macleod then I have a message for you.'

The man waited with an air of false servility.

'A message from whom?'

'Ah, now there, sir, I'm afraid I can't say. She didn't give no name but she's a French lady and not the sort who can run around after a gentleman and certainly not the sort who could wander about in rough surroundings like these. If you're Mr Macleod …'

The greasy man paused.

'Well then, I'm Macleod.'

'Ah, good, sir. Then this lady would like to meet you to …, and she was most particular about the words, to discuss a matter of importance to both of you, a matter that requires discretion.'

'And what does that mean?'

'Now there, sir, you have me. She described you to me, told me where you were staying and said I was to watch out for you, wait until I was sure you were not followed then give you her message. As to what it means I know no more than the words I was told to speak.'

'And what am I to do with these words?'

'The lady said that if you was willing, only if you was quite willing, I was to take you to her.'

Macleod looked at the man. He was small, flabby and his breath spoke of cheap tobacco and cheaper liquor. Macleod felt that he, himself, was no threat.

'Tell me about this lady.'

'There's nothing to tell. She's French or at least sounds French, dresses very fine, pays handsomely for small service, and for those who take an interest in such things I would call her a beauty. Oh, and she's newly arrived from New Orleans. I took the precaution of asking at her lodgings. As you can doubtless see for yourself, sir, I ain't the sort of man who can afford to get mixed up in dubious business as might draw the attention of the authorities, if you take my meaning.'

Macleod took his meaning.

'Very well, take me to this lady.'

'At once, sir. Be so good as to follow me.'

The greasy man turned and headed off further into the docks.

It may have been Macleod's imagination but as they walked the man's breathing wheezed less and his legs gathered speed. They turned from the docks between two blank warehouse walls which then led into a system of alleys. Macleod caught hold of the man's arm and pulled him to a stop.

'Where are you taking me?'

172

The man smiled a greasy, apologetic smile.

'I was told to bring you a back way, sir. Not to be seen, sir. Come, not far now.' They moved on a short way when suddenly at a dingy intersection of dark alleys the man stopped. 'Here we are, sir.'

Macleod turned a second too late. The cudgel caught him on the temple as he lifted his arm in self defence while a foot hit him hard behind the knee. He fell as another blow to his head finished the matter and two sets of feet ran off down the cobbled alley.

Chapter Thirty-five

The voice inside Macleod's head was gentle but insistent.

'Come along now, Mr Macleod, can't have you lying about in the street like this. Come along, sir.' And Macleod felt someone trying to lift him by his arm. 'Now, now, sir, this won't do, why you're hardly scratched, not what I'd call even knocked about really. Why I've seen men up and down the rigging like monkeys with worse than you've got.'

Macleod allowed himself to be helped into a sitting position.

'What happened?'

The man helping him picked up Macleod's hat and pushed his fist into it to straighten out a deep dent.

'Look, sir, the first strike was only a glancing blow and this fine hat of yours took enough of the killer one to make sure it didn't do any lasting harm. God love us, who hasn't had a bit of a knock about the head and laughed over it, aye and laughed heartily?'

The man put the repaired hat back on Macleod's head and helped him to stand.

Macleod's brain cleared. The man looked familiar.

'You saw it, you saw the men who attacked me?'

'I did, sir.'

'Then why in God's name did you do nothing?'

'I did do something, sir. I watched. I was too far away to do much else. They were quick and it was all over in a second. Anyway, there were two of them. If I'd have tried to mix it, well, I ain't got a nice strong hat like you, and him what used the bludgeon wasn't any novice. Now, sir, you can walk I think, and we need to get you back to your tavern.'

Macleod looked at the man as they set off and finally placed him.

'You're from the ship, the ship we came on from New Orleans.'

174

'That's right, sir.'

'What on earth were you doing following me?'

'Captain's orders. Keep an eye on that gentleman, he told us. Keep a sharp eye on him and the lady and see nothing untoward befalls either of them. Those were his very words, nothing untoward befalls either of them.'

'You wouldn't call being lured down an alley and having my head cracked came under the heading something untoward?'

'Ah, now there, sir, I must say things were what you might call out of my hands. When I saw you stop to talk to your greasy friend I wasn't too worried. The gentleman's no fool, I said to myself, to be taken in by the likes of him. Then, blow me, off you go with him calm as a lamb with a shepherd. Why did you do it, sir? You should have known no good would come of it.'

'Yes, I can see that now.'

'Well, no real harm done is there, except to the hat, so no need for tears.'

'No harm done! If I have been attacked then what of ...'

'Ay yes, sir, the lady.'

'Yes, damn you, the lady.'

'Well, sir, as to the lady ...'

But Macleod wasn't interested. Marie was in danger.

'Quickly, get me out of these alleys and back to the tavern.'

The sailor knuckled his forehead.

'Just as you say, sir. Follow me.'

And together the sailor led them back to Macleod's tavern where the first thing Macleod did was to hurry up the stairs to Marie's room and knock on the door. There was no answer. He knocked again and called out her name but there was still no answer. He threw open the door. The room was empty, but a chair was lying on its side and a lamp had been knocked to the floor. On the carpet was a dark stain. Macleod hurried to it and knelt down and touched it then looked at his fingers. It was blood, fresh blood.

Chapter Thirty-six

Macleod stood up and turned. The sailor was standing in the doorway of the room watching him.

'I'm a damned, cursed fool. I left her undefended and now she is dead or taken.'

'Would that be the lady that on the journey you said was your wife, would it, sir?'

Macleod was amazed that the sailor should take it so calmly.

'Yes, damn you, that lady.'

'Shouldn't we have a look for her, sir, before settling on the worst?'

'What?'

'Well, if you say it's blood then I'm sure it is, but that doesn't mean it's hers. Maybe she's next door.'

Macleod rushed to the door, pushed past the sailor and burst into his own room. Marie was sitting on the bed looking with terrified eyes at a grim and dangerous-looking fellow who stood opposite her with his arms folded across a barrel-like chest.

On Macleod's entrance she jumped up, ran to him and threw herself into his arms.

'Oh, Jean, thank God. This man has come to kill me. He has already killed another and now he wants to kill me.'

Macleod looked at the man. It was the other sailor from the boat who had watched them disembark. The sailor unfolded his arms and touched his forehead with his knuckle.

'I'm glad you've arrived, sir. The young lady was taking on so that I had to shake her a bit to quieten her down. Me not speaking French and her not speaking English, I couldn't see any other way. No offence intended, I'm sure, but as I'd pushed the body under the bed ...'

'Body!'

'Yes, sir, and that being the way of it I couldn't have her calling out so I shook her a bit then brought her in here where I thought she might be a bit calmer. I'd appreciate it if you'd explain that there was no offence intended.'

Macleod's head felt tight. It hurt from the blows it had received and it hurt from trying to make sense of what was going on.

Marie held him and regarded the sailor with continued terror.

'See, Jean, see how he threatens us.'

Macleod looked down at Marie and suddenly realised that he was holding her very close. He released her and then tried to explain.

'He is not threatening us, Marie. He is apologising for shaking you. He says he meant no harm.'

'Jean, he is lying. He killed a man who came to my door.'

'What man?'

Marie stamped her foot.

'What man? I don't know what man. How should I know what man? A man came to my door and knocked.'

'You didn't open it?'

'No, not at first, but he spoke French and he said that he came from you, that you had sent him to bring me to you urgently. He said he had a note from you. So I opened the door.'

The grim sailor interrupted.

'Is the young lady explaining, sir? Have you told her I meant no harm?'

'Yes, I have explained, she knows. She says a man came and said he had a note from me and that she was to come with him. Did you see any of this?'

'I did, sir, I was down a few doors in the shadows watching. As to what he said, sir, I couldn't answer because he spoke French, but it wasn't no note he had behind his back. It was a knife. As soon as the young lady was, if I might be so bold, so foolish as to open the door I knew he would be in and the job done, so I came up quick and hit him hard on his head with this.' The man looked a little sheepish and pulled a short but serviceable bludgeon from the back waistband of his trousers. Marie gave a little gasp as she saw the weapon and clung tighter to Macleod who thought it best to place a protective arm around her. The sailor replaced the bludgeon. 'Too hard as it turns out. I'm afraid I croaked him. Well, as I said, I took him into the lady's room and pushed him under the bed. I'm afraid the young lady took it all a bit strong, saying things in French what meant nothing to me, so I gave her a bit of a shake like and when she choked off the noise I brought her in here and sat her on the bed. I didn't like a young lady, as I sensed was of quality, sitting on top of a dead body. It didn't seem proper. Then I waited.'

He then touched his forehead again, folded his arms across his chest and lapsed into silence.

'What is he saying, Jean? Do they want money? Give them money, Jean. Give them anything they ask.'

'No, Marie, they don't want money. The man who came to your room had a knife. I'm afraid he was sent to kill you and this man saved your life. Unfortunately in doing so he had to kill the villain but as he has explained it, he had no choice.'

'They watch over us?' All her alarm returned. 'But who knows we are here? Who sent them?' Then she seemed to come to life and her eyes widened. 'But, Jean, we know them. Are they not from the ship, the ship that brought us from New Orleans?'

'Yes, they are. Their captain sent them to see we came to no harm. As it turned out if they hadn't been following us we would have come to considerable harm. I was,' he paused and decided that the whole story of the incident at the docks need not be too fully explained, 'attacked by some men at the docks and left unconscious. No doubt that was to ensure that I was out of the way so that the villain who attacked me could come here and ...'

Macleod left the sentence unfinished.

'But I thought we were safe now? You said we were safe.'

'I was wrong. We must have been followed.'

'But how, how could anyone follow us so quickly?'

Macleod thought about it, found he could provide no answer, so finally put the question to the sailor who had acted as his preserver.

'Could anyone on the ship have been following us from New Orleans?'

'The man who attacked you and came here to do in the lady was on the ship. He boarded at New Orleans and travelled alongside of you.'

'Came with us?'

'Yes, sir. He took passage very late and that in itself seemed odd. He said he was a traveller, a whiskey drummer, but we spotted straight away that travelling in whiskey or anything else wasn't his real game. There were two proper travellers on the ship and he cosied up to them both and made himself very friendly from the stock he carried, the more to hide himself is my bet. When we made harbour the captain asked us to keep an eye on you both while we were in port. It's just as well our whiskey friend made his move today because we'll be on our way tomorrow.'

'But why did the captain ask you to look after us? I don't complain you understand, I'm more than grateful, but I am at a loss as to why he took such care.'

The sailor lost his friendly, rather easy-going manner and became somewhat formal.

'As to that, sir, you would have to ask him yourself. All Jake and me do is carry out orders. We're no more than poor sailors, poor men of the sea, sir, getting by on little pay and hard graft.'

And he stood silent as if waiting for something.

Macleod put his hand into his coat pocket, pulled out his wallet and handed the sailor two silver coins.

'Of course, I quite understand and I hope you and your friend will accept this as a token of my,' he looked at Marie then back at the sailor, 'our gratitude.'

Marie saw that money was about to change hands and, although she knew nothing of what had been said, understood enough to know to smile her most winning smile at the sailor.

The sailor took the coins, looked at them then stuffed them into his trouser pocket.

'Most gratefully accepted, sir, as it is by Jake I'm sure. And, seeing how you've been so friendly, I can see no harm in telling you that just before we sailed the captain had a visitor and it's my opinion that money changed hands and it was this visitor as asked the captain to look out for you both.'

'Who was the visitor? What did he look like?'

'A very careful man he was, came all wrapped up in a cloak and muffler round his face. I couldn't give you a name nor say what he looked like but I can tell you one thing. He walked with a stick.'

'A stick?'

'Aye, sir, not a fashion stick neither, not some light fancy cane but a proper stick to aid walking. I heard it tap-tapping on the deck and as he walked down the gangplank. Gentleman had a limp.'

'I see.'

'And now, sir, we must bid you farewell. Our friend under the bed next door won't trouble either you or the young lady no more so I think our task is completed and I shall go and report to the captain. Come on, Jake.'

Jake came to life and joined his shipmate at the door of the room.

Macleod watched for a second then also came to life.

'Wait, what about the body?'

'What about it, sir?'

'But you can't leave it there, under the bed. You must take it.'

'God bless you, sir, what would we want it for?'

'You must dispose of it.'

The sailors looked at each other then at Macleod.

'I'm sorry, sir, but we cannot oblige. Carrying a body through the streets in broad daylight would cause comment and attract the wrong sort of interest, if you take my meaning. Normally we might accommodate you but we sail tomorrow and we'll be needed on board to make ready. I'm sorry, sir, it can't be done, not even for ready money.'

'Then ask your captain what's to be done. You say you think he was paid to see that nothing untoward befell us. Well, finding a dead body in this lady's room is, I would say, considerably untoward.'

The talkative sailor rubbed his chin thoughtfully.

'You have a point. I can't deny but that you have a point.'

Macleod produced his wallet once more.

'Return after dark, remove the corpse and you shall have two more coins.'

'I'll have to ask the captain.'

'Of course.'

'And that would make three.'

'Three?'

'Three as knows and must be taken care of.'

Macleod felt now was not the time to haggle.

'Then three it shall be.' The sailor smiled and stepped forward with his hand out. Macleod put away the wallet. 'When our friend next door is gone.'

The sailor's hand dropped and he returned to the door. He was not one to press his luck too far.

'We'll be back at nightfall, sir, with all that's necessary to do the removal. Now good-day to you both.'

The two sailors touched their foreheads and left. Marie looked at Macleod obviously expecting him to explain to her what had passed and what was to be done. He led her to a chair and sat her down. It wasn't clear in his head what exactly had happened, nor how it had happened and certainly not why it had happened, but she was looking at him so expectantly and so obviously thankful that such an awful experience had finished with them both alive and unharmed that he felt he should at least try to find some sort of explanation. So he tried.

'I think it's like this ...'

Chapter Thirty-seven

Lord Melford looked and felt self-satisfied and relaxed. He stood by the desk in his office and regarded Jasper Trent through the open door. Trent, having suddenly demanded his urgent attendance, now kept him waiting while he read yet another report. But Melford was proof against any small annoyance Trent might choose to inflict on him.

The sun was shining, London was looking its best, and that evening he proposed to meet a fascinating creature in one of the Dark Walks of the Vauxhall Gardens. He had high hopes of where the assignation might eventually lead. All in all, since his return from Rome two days earlier, he thought of himself as a very devil of a fellow.

Trent put down the report and sat back.

'And now, Melford, come and give me your news. I am, as you can see, all agog to receive it.'

Melford ignored the obvious sarcasm. He didn't let either Trent's tone or manner dent his feelings about himself. He knew he had done well and intended to say so. He walked into Trent's office, sat down with a flourish and dropped the satchel he had been carrying beside his chair.

'If I say so myself, everything went well. Rome may be the court of the Popish Antichrist, an abomination to all true Christian gentlemen, but by God they do themselves well and have some fine women around them, damn fine. Accommodating too, damned accommodating.'

'I'm so glad you had the time to find plenty of diversions suited to your taste.'

'Oh I did what you asked, of course. I delivered your letters and collected your reports.'

Trent leaned forward and held out a hand.

Melford reached down beside his chair, pulled up the flat leather satchel and handed it across to Trent. Trent took it and put it down beside his chair.

'So much for letters and reports. Next.'

'I managed to arrange a meeting with our friend the Cardinal-who-would-be-king.'

'And your thoughts on that royal and holy gentleman?'

'Royal Stuart and Cardinal he may be, but he's without doubt a villain in his dealings with us.'

'False then you think?'

'I do.'

'So do I. Now, on to other business. How did your role as Recruiting Sergeant go?'

Melford became flustered.

'I don't understand.'

'No? I would have thought the question simple enough. Did you recruit anyone to be our eyes and ears in Rome?'

'No, I mean about the Cardinal. I said he's playing us false, I'm sure of it.'

'Yes, I know that's what you said, and I said I agreed with you. Then I asked you how ...'

'But you said that if that was the case then you might have to snuff him out.'

'Did I say that?'

'Look here, Trent, what's going on?'

'What's going on is that I'm trying to get a report out of you and finding it, as you might put it, damned difficult. Did you or did you not recruit anyone? Come, sir, out with it.'

Melford answered sullenly.

'Yes I did.'

'Good, that wasn't so hard was it? Who did you recruit?'

Melford perked up.

'Ah, now there I think I scored a palpable hit. His name is Brutti, Count Silviano Brutti. And through him I picked four stout fellows who'll serve us damn well. Capable fellows and with Brutti over them I think ...'

'Yes, I thought so. Well done, Melford, you have managed to confirm what I already suspected. Things are clearing nicely.'

'How do you mean, already suspected. I thought I was ...'

'You see, there you go again, thinking. I don't pay you to think, I pay you to do just as you're told.'

Melford, despite Trent's strictures on using his mental processes, thought about the way Trent had dismissed his assessment of the Cardinal.

'Are you telling me that you knew about the Cardinal's treachery?'

'Hardly treachery, he's only looking out for his own best interests, or so it must seem to him.'

'I see.' Which was, of course, a black lie. 'But Brutti. I did well with Brutti, at least allow me that. He's a damn well-placed fellow, knows all the best people, mixes with politicos and everyone of any moment.'

'I know. If he wasn't so well-placed, Fouché wouldn't use him.'

'Fouché!'

'Oh yes, Brutti is Fouché's man, has been for some time. Fouché knew you were coming so he arranged to palm him off on to you. The eyes and ears you collected for me in Rome report to Paris before they report to us, and when they report to us what they say will be dictated by Paris.'

Melford didn't doubt for one second what Trent was telling him because, now he knew the truth of it, he could see that it had all been far too easy. Brutti had indeed been palmed on to him, smoothly palmed by one of the damned attractive and very accommodating ladies he had so much admired and whose conversation and company, among other things, he had enjoyed.

'Dammit, Trent, you might have told me. A little trust? It's not too much to ask I think, a little trust and confidence.'

'But Melford I *do* trust you, I trust you to do exactly as I expect. Brutti had himself palmed off on to you and is now wholly convinced he has fooled us because you played your part so excellently well, and you played it so well because you believed in it completely. Knowing that you believed in it, I had every confidence in you, my dear fellow, every confidence.'

It wasn't a compliment, Melford could see that quite clearly. But it was spoken so like a compliment that Melford decided his best course was to accept it as such.

'Well then, it seems things turned out as you expected, so I suppose my visit to Rome must be counted a success although I can't say I see it myself.'

'But it's clear enough, surely?'

'Not to me. It doesn't seem at all clear to me.'

'Tell me, Melford, do you play chess?'

'I *can* play but I find it damnably dull. I prefer cricket.'

'In chess one must see the whole board. If a player concentrates only on the pieces that are in play he will not see the threat on some other part of the board and when that threat materialises he will, in consequence, not have any suitable defence. Let me ask you a question, where does the greater danger lie would you say, in the idea or the man?'

'What the hell are you talking about, Trent?'

'Boney wants the world and he wants it for himself. Fouché wants the world but he wants it for Republicanism. If the idea defeats the man, no power on earth will be able to put that genie back in its bottle. If the man defeats the idea, well, any man, even the great Napoleon, might be stopped.'

'Are you saying you'd prefer we fight Napoleon rather than the Republic?'

'I'm saying I'd rather fight someone I know can be defeated. Try to see the whole board, Melford, not just any one part of it, nor even all parts looked at separately, but the whole board.'

Melford bent his mind to what Trent had said.

'I think I see what you mean. Yes, I think I do. Damned clever point, Trent, damned important point.'

'Well done, Melford, we'll make something of you yet. Ours is an age of information. It is no longer enough to know who your enemies are, where they are, nor even how strong they are. It is not even enough to know what they know, you need to know *more* than they know. My job, and yours, is to provide our masters with the information they require and it must be accurate information. I suspected that Cardinal Henry had been approached by the French, to what purpose is still not entirely clear, but we can safely assume it will be damaging to His Majesty's Government. I sent you to Rome and Brutti attached himself to you. That, together with your assessment of the Cardinal shows me that my suspicions were correct. We now know that Fouché is keeping a close eye on the Cardinal which means he's important to him and if he's important to Monsieur Fouché he is twice as important to us.'

'Seems a damned roundabout way of finding out something as

simple as that Fouché is keeping an eye on the Cardinal.'

'Do you think so? Well perhaps you're right. But if we are to keep what we know to ourselves then deception and subterfuge must be our bread and butter. Fouché is satisfied that, through Brutti, he will know exactly what we get up to in Rome especially concerning Cardinal Henry. Very good. Let's keep him thinking that. Now, to the whole board. We must put some serious effort into finding out exactly what it is Fouché intends to do with our Cardinal Henry. I've had a report from Madame de Metz. She's found what I sent her for. Unfortunately she hasn't got it. Some lawyer has.'

'What lawyer?'

But Trent ignored the question.

'Fouché's clever music box is set to play its tune in America and we found out that he had established a main point of supply for his agents through New Orleans. The operation was co-ordinated there through a man named St Clair. I had to assume that as we had this information, others might also get it.'

'Others? What others? The French organised it and we know about it. Who else is there?'

'The Americans. I hardly think they would be indifferent to what the French have been up to, and by now they will be thoroughly mixed up in whatever it is. I sent Madame de Metz to find out what lay behind St Clair's operation, and while she was doing that keep an eye open for anyone else who might be doing the same. Well, things finally moved quickly. She found her man but not until he had killed St Clair and run off taking another man's wife with him.'

'The swine.'

'Melford, he killed St Clair to put the block on his operation and took the woman because she must know something. Her husband was a close friend of St Clair, an intimate friend, very intimate. The sort of intimate friend that meant Madame de Metz, even with all her charms, couldn't get near to him.' But Trent saw that Melford still didn't fully understand. 'They died in the same bed.'

And Melford understood.

'My God, the beasts.'

'The man we want is called Macleod. He's a Boston lawyer, almost certainly working for Washington and, far from being a hound, he sounds a most capable and resourceful agent. I wish I had agents about me half as capable and resourceful.'

'I see.'

'I doubt it but tell me what you see.'

'If he killed St Clair and this other fellow he'd have to run, and run quickly, which meant he had to take her with him.'

'Yes, go on.'

'And to do that with any chance of success she would have to travel willingly. It would seem then that your resourceful Macleod not only killed St Clair but also persuaded the lady to go with him willingly.'

'You're the ladies' man, Melford, how clever would you say was that little trick?'

'Damn clever, damn clever indeed.'

'I'm glad you realise it because that's why Madame de Metz needs you. She's after him and will try to get the woman from him, but if our assessment of Macleod is accurate it will be no easy matter and she'll need help. She thinks he's headed for Boston so you also must be for Boston and I have something for you that you might find helpful, a manservant.'

'I already have a manservant.'

'Not like the one I'm giving you.'

'What's special about your man?'

'Let's just say that what he lacks in charm of manner he makes up for in other ways.'

'Well if I must have him I suppose I must. When do I leave?'

Trent took out his watch.

'Now, you're already late. Your man's name is Gregory and he's gone ahead of you with your trunk. He'll meet you at Liverpool. There's a carriage outside to get you to the coach. They'll hold it for a short while but I suggest you get a move on.'

'But dammit, Trent, I can't just drop everything and dash off.' But as he looked at Jasper Trent he found that Trent was right after all, he could drop everything and dash off. He stood up. 'What do I do in Boston?'

'Anything and everything Madame de Metz tells you to get this Macleod business resolved. After that, do whatever in your judgement I would want done. And remember, no pretty faces, not on this one. Now off with you. Your carriage awaits.'

Chapter Thirty-eight

The merchantman ploughed south-west, one day out from Halifax, Nova Scotia, driven by a fresh summer wind. The crew went about their business and took no notice of the two women passengers walking the deck, talking.

'So Molly, have you decided who you are now?'

'Yes, and it's nothing like Madame de Metz. I want nothing fancy when we get to Boston.'

'English or French?'

'What would you say to Irish?'

Kitty grinned.

'Why not?'

'How about Mary Conover.'

The grin left Kitty's face and was replaced by a dark scowl.

'Why that name? Jack Doran's exactly where he deserves to be, burning in hell fire, God rot the bastard's black soul.'

'Amen to that, but you brought it on yourself, girl, falling for his lying Irish charm.'

'Maybe I did but he said he'd marry me and we'd go back to Ireland and settle down proper after the Dorset job.'

Molly gave a short laugh.

'And you believed the lying shite.'

'Forget Jack Doran and let's get back to business. Who will you be?'

'Mrs Fanny Dashwood, a well-off widow-woman. I'm in Boston because my late husband talked about opening an establishment there, said there were good prospects and the competition would be light compared to what he was used to. After his death, and I still haven't quite made up my mind how he died, I decided to come over and look around for myself.'

'I like Fanny Dashwood. It has a nice ring to it, a bit racy but nothing common about it. And what line of business is Fanny in?'

'It needs to be something not altogether honest but not altogether criminal.'

'Whorehouses?'

'No, that wouldn't serve, not if what I've heard about Boston is near the mark.'

'What then?'

'What would you say to gaming clubs? Let's say my late husband owned two gaming houses, one in London and one in, where do you think? Somewhere fancy to give it a bit of class.'

'Bath.'

'Good, I like it. Bath it is. And now I've come over to see if Boston is ready for a bit of London-style fast living. I thought it through on our navy boat coming up and I think it fits well enough.'

'If you'd sorted it out on the boat why did we go to Nova Scotia? Why not straight to Boston? When we left New Orleans you were all for haste. Why go to Halifax?'

'When you get thrown a slice of luck, use it to your best advantage. Trent arranged for a ship to be there to pick up my report if I made one. It was our luck that it was in when we needed it. Once out of New Orleans I could see she was a fast craft and well-handled so it gave us time to do our arrival in Boston right.'

'Right?'

'A ship docking in Boston unannounced and for no reason other than dropping off a lady and her maid would cause tongues to wag and notice to be taken. We need to arrive without any fuss which is why I told our tame sailor to take us to Halifax. He wasn't wearing any uniform but he was a Royal Navy captain so he could deal with the authorities there and we could keep everything neatly wrapped up. From Halifax I could send my report to Trent and we could travel to Boston without arousing any interest.'

'What about Trent? When we get to Boston do we wait to hear from him or crack on as soon as Macleod turns up?'

'When Trent gets my report my guess is he'll send out help. We're on our own and a long way from home. What we're involved in is something put together by Fouché, so trying anything by ourselves is too risky. As for Macleod, either he's acting for himself, which doesn't seem likely, or the Americans have dealt themselves into the game. The question is, will he listen to a sensible offer or will we have to do it the hard way?'

'If he comes back. All this is based on your guess that he'll bring his prize back to Boston.'

'He will, I've seen his handiwork up close and I know how his mind will work. That outing in New Orleans wasn't his first, nor his second neither. He's no novice when it comes to villainy, aye, and villainy on a grand scale. They don't teach his tricks in any schoolroom. He may front as a lawyer but his real business is no different to you, me or our late friend Jack Doran. He came well prepared, played a clever game and got clean away. But he's travelling with baggage now and I doubt he planned for that. He played that bird on the wing, I'm sure, which means he'll need a ready bolt-hole to keep her snug until he's ready to broker the best deal he can. Remember, Kitty, it's all about money with the likes of us and so it will be with him.'

'So what do we do? Make him an offer when he turns up and, if he won't play, take her whatever way we can?'

'No, we sit on them and hope Trent sends someone quick.'

'And if he doesn't?'

'If it looks like we might lose her then we'll go for a quick lift. How we do it I'll work on when we get there and I've had a chance to see what the lay of the land is.'

The ship rolled gently and they both paused to steady themselves.

'I almost hope he turns down any offer. I owe that bastard for a crack on the head.'

Molly laughed.

'Well then, let's take the doll first by whatever means we can, and then maybe we'll finish Macleod just for the fun of it.'

And Kitty joined in the laughter.

Chapter Thirty-nine

In his comfortable rooms Darcy drank tea with Bentley. To the outsider, had one been present, they would have presented the perfect picture of Boston, rich, relaxed, confident and without any care to trouble their days.

Bentley held a letter out to Darcy.

'It came today.'

Darcy took it, read it, then handed it back.

'What the hell was he doing there?'

'A good question and one to which I wish I had an equally good answer.' He put away the letter. 'All I know is that our lawyer friend is murdered in New Orleans and that St Clair is also dead, perhaps even at Macleod's hands.'

Darcy looked up from his cup in surprise.

'What makes you say that?'

'Macleod runs off from Boston leaving some cock-and-bull story behind. Now we find he turns up dead in New Orleans just after St Clair is murdered. Wouldn't you say that was all a little bit too much to be coincidence?'

'You mean Macleod was sent to kill St Clair?'

'It's possible. He spoke fluent French, could handle a firearm, was brave enough and knew how to obey orders. At least he did when I knew him as a soldier. One way or the other it looks like he became yet another expendable unit in our dirty game. I shall miss him, Darcy, indeed I shall.'

'Well I can't say I will.'

'No, I dare say you won't. Still, we can't let these things trouble us too much. St Clair's death is a nuisance but nothing more. His main usefulness was past, he had become little more than a posting stage now that the operation is pretty much in place. What we must concentrate on now is what you brought back from Washington.'

'Ah, so I'm finally to be told what was in that mysterious

sealed parcel I was sent to Washington to collect and run all the way to Philadelphia to pass on. Seeing you rushed me off with a wounded hand I hope it was worth it.'

'Your hand survived so that's no matter. What you were given was the first part in the finalé of our enterprise.'

Darcy put down his cup.

'Really? We're ready at last?'

'We are and the first step is already in train. A few years ago a journalist called Callender published a pamphlet. It was a virulent but populist attack on Jefferson's opponent, John Adams, claiming he was a monarchist and deeply involved in political corruption. Jefferson used his secretary, Lewis, to put Callender up to it and Callender expected to be well paid if and when Jefferson got to be President. Once Jefferson got the Presidency, Callender thought he'd get to be Postmaster of Richmond as his reward. But Jefferson gave him nothing. Callender had money troubles and his political enemies, of which there were plenty, were making things hot for him so he went to Jefferson, but Jefferson sent him packing. As you may imagine, it wasn't hard for friends of ours to persuade him to publish, in the Richmond Recorder, that Jefferson has for many years kept as his concubine one of his own slaves, a woman named Sally Hemmings. She masquerades as his housekeeper but does her best work on her back apparently.'

'That's a bit tame surely? Jefferson's a widower and any slave owner might do much the same even with their wives alive.'

'True. But Jefferson isn't any slave owner and Sally Hemmings isn't just any slave. He's President and she's his late wife's half-sister.'

'The Devil she is! Has there been any issue?'

'I don't know and don't much care. Slavery's a powder keg waiting to be ignited and Sally Hemmings will be the match we shall use.'

'It'll split the country, North against South. Ohio has already come out against it.'

'They have, but made damn sure they won't find themselves becoming home to black runaways from Kentucky across the river. They'd line the banks with men carrying muskets first. Without slavery cotton is finished and, if cotton is finished, so is the South. If this is properly handled, and believe me it will be, North and

South will soon be at each other's throats. When that happens the country will welcome with open arms any strong man who can step in and save us all from civil war. Can't you see, Darcy, it's not the fact of Sally Hemmings, it's the timing.'

'I see. One more thing, not in itself so very important, but among so many others.'

'Exactly. We don't want actual war, we want the threat of war. From now on your job will be to see that the pot keeps boiling. The Federalists will take up the story but you must see that they take it up with a vengeance.'

'And our strong man?'

'Not yet, Darcy, not yet. He must be seen as the one with clean hands, not for the South nor yet for the North. Neither a die-hard Republican nor die-hard Federalist. An honourable outsider with a proven record of service to his country. Most importantly one who seems to seek nothing for himself, one reluctant to put himself forward for high office. A man all true Americans can trust because he offers the nation peace and security and asks nothing for himself.'

'Well, tea hardly seems appropriate to this occasion, Bentley. I think brandy is called for.' Darcy went to the table where the brandy and glasses stood and returned with two glasses. 'When will I get to know the name of our nation's glorious saviour?'

'In time, Darcy, all in good time. Come, Darcy, these are your rooms so you must choose the toast. What shall it be?'

'How about, to the beginning of the end?'

'Yes, I like it. I'll drink to that, sir.'

And they raised their glasses.

'To the beginning of the end.'

'The beginning of the end indeed.'

Chapter Forty

Macleod was considerably alarmed by the attack on him and the attempt on Marie's life. He had taken passage at once on the first ship travelling north, a slow coaster that made several stops and ended its journey at Wilmington, Virginia. From Wilmington they had gained passage after three days on a ship headed directly for New York. From there, Macleod knew they would have no difficulty in completing their journey.

Marie had remained calm and seemingly untroubled by the delays and discomforts of the long, slow journey. Macleod put the change down to the attempt on her life in Charleston. He assumed that it had made her realise, at last, the true gravity of their position. Whatever had caused the change he accepted it gladly because his mind was fully occupied trying to work out how to get her to agree to go to Washington instead of trying to take what she knew to the British.

Macleod's assessment of Marie's manner was somewhat wide of the mark. Once into the sea voyage from Charleston, Marie had had time to reflect on her situation and how she had dealt with it, and she was not happy about either. She was penniless and a fugitive who had survived one attempt on her life and might expect others to follow unless she could reach safety. As for her actions since the murder of her husband, she had behaved throughout like a child. Since leaving New Orleans she had been by turns petulant, pouting, cajoling and shrewish as the mood had taken her, and she had cast Macleod in whatever role best suited her mood. It was the behaviour of a child and a spoilt child at that.

At sea, and not having to share a cabin under the pretence of being married she had been grateful for time to think, not only about what had already happened to her and what might yet come to pass but also about herself, who she was and what she wanted to become.

She had grown up a happy and indulged child and her

happiness lasted until she was sixteen. At seventeen she had become a wife and at eighteen had achieved the status of a pretty caged bird, called on to do nothing, think nothing and say nothing. The happy child had gone but it was not a real woman who had taken its place. It was a half-child, a crippled child, a pretty doll, but a broken one.

From Wilmington to New York she felt lost in her reflections and time seemed suspended. She was lost on an inner journey that should have begun years before.

That gentle, dreaming half-world ceased abruptly when the ship docked at New York. New York stunned her. She didn't have time to see much. They changed ship and were on their way within two days, but what she saw was enough to make her revise her views from top to bottom. She was shocked by the size of its buildings, by its abundant dirt and the incessant noise and clamour. Its activity and energy confused her. Most of all she was frightened by the city's obvious and overwhelming contempt for the individual. The New York Marie encountered, albeit briefly, was a buzzing hive packed with frantic, faceless hordes always on the move. Marie de Valois, the society beauty, the lady of fashion, the epitome of Southern grace had finally come face to face with – Industry. The Southern Belle beheld that almost mythical beast, the North.

On setting sail once again her thoughts had ceased to be detached and reflective. In only two days New York had changed her. The city had opened her eyes to a horizon of possibilities she had never even guessed could exist.

The women of New York were not delicate, refined creatures to be cared for and pampered and in return be gracious and amusing. She had seen women, well-dressed women, moving almost as equals in the thronging hordes, jostled and jostling, women busy making a place for themselves, women with minds of their own and spirits to match. No matter that she had seen little and understood less, no matter that hers was merely a glimpse round a curtain. As New York receded she finally knew that what she would become was hers to make for herself. She must be like those women in New York, she would be jostled by circumstance but she would respond in kind. Whatever she had been, she would now become a real woman and a capable woman at that. She needed to think and act independently, to make decisions and follow them through. She needed to embrace the spirit of the brutal, dirty, energetic, awful, marvellous North.

And Macleod saw none of this. Macleod saw her quiet and gave thanks that she was so, for he was as busy with his own thoughts for the future as she was with hers. So it was that they travelled for days on end together, miles apart.

The Marie de Valois who disembarked at Boston saw herself as a sort of Jeanne d'Arc figure, a woman who could not only survive in the world of men but succeed and excel. When Macleod stood next to her on Boston dry land he felt a great surge of relief. He beamed a smile at Marie as if to say, look, here we are at last and it is wonderful.

The new Marie accepted the smile with a mixture of nobility, suffering and a new strength of purpose.

Macleod thought she looked tired, and that possibly she was hungry.

'Boston at last, home and, I think, safe now. I'll arrange for our things to be taken to my house and then take you there so you may eat and rest. Wait here.'

Macleod strode off and Marie stood and watched him go.

Was she safe? Would this man whom, in truth, she hardly knew, help her to get to the British and real safety or would he betray her?

Then she realised that Macleod had been right. She was tired, no, not just tired, weary. And she *was* hungry, hungry for real food, a hot meal served at a dining table with wine in crystal glasses. She wanted quiet and rest and comfort. Well then, she would let him provide for her immediate needs and, once recovered, she would consider what was her best course of action.

Macleod soon returned.

'I've arranged for a carriage to come and take us and our things to my house.'

'I would be happy to walk if it is what you wish.'

Macleod grinned. Nothing, not even a liberal dose of Marie's humility could dampen his spirits now he was back in Boston.

'Walk! Why this is Boston, this is where I live. Your arrival here must be celebrated in style. There is no question of walking.' He looked down the quay. 'Ah, there it is.' An open carriage was making its way slowly down the busy quay. Marie watched until it stopped beside them.

She hesitated.

'But an open carriage?'

'Why not? The weather is warm. The drive will be pleasant.'

'We will be seen. No, more than that, we will on display. It is too dangerous. I beg you, find us something more discreet.'

Macleod was a little annoyed. He had deliberately asked for an open carriage. He wanted Marie to see his home city. He was proud of Boston and he wanted to display it to her. Now she had raised an objection and, worse, for her it was a perfectly reasonable objection. The carriage arrived and stopped beside them.

'Come. This is Boston, my home. We will be seen, yes, but by people who will be your friends and neighbours. There are no enemies here, I assure you.' But he could see that Marie was anything but reassured. 'Marie, I have not brought you here to be a prisoner in my house. I have brought you here to be safe, to be surrounded by friends who will protect you. Rely on me and trust my judgement. Boston will be safe.' Macleod opened a door and offered her his hand. Reluctantly, with no other choice but to accept, Marie got into the carriage and sat down.

Macleod, pleased with himself, joined her and pulled the door shut. The driver loaded their luggage behind, mounted his seat and slowly turned the carriage. Macleod sat back with a contented smile. He told the driver to take the route round the Common. As the carriage pulled out of the dock area and crossed Dock Square and began to move through the familiar city streets in the sunlight Macleod felt sure Marie had been wrong and he was right. This was Boston, his city. These people were his neighbours. What ill could befall them here? What ill indeed?

Chapter Forty-one

Darcy hurried along the street, took the club steps two at a time, went through the hall and looked into the large assembly room where a few men were drinking and talking. One of them looked at him standing in the doorway.

'Darcy, come and join us. We were just discussing ...'

'I'm looking for Bentley.'

'He was here, I saw him. Try the reading room.'

Darcy re-crossed the hall and went into another room, looked around and saw Bentley sitting reading a newspaper.

'Bentley, I need to speak to you.' Another gentleman reader, seated nearby, lowered his paper and looked angrily at Darcy. Darcy ignored him. 'I need to talk to you urgently. It's business and the kind of business I don't think should be kept waiting.'

Bentley folded his paper deliberately, stood up and dropped it onto his chair. They left the club reading room and walked out into the hall.

'Well, what's so urgent?'

Darcy looked around, the hall was empty.

'I've just seen Macleod.'

'What!'

'Riding in a carriage and looking precious pleased with himself.'

'It was definitely Macleod, you couldn't have been mistaken?'

'It was Macleod all right, still dressed like a country parson but with a damn pretty woman sitting next to him. Do you know what I think?'

'No. Tell me, Darcy, what do you think?'

Darcy ignored Bentley's tone.

'Dead or alive he was no more in New Orleans than you or I, it's my opinion he was away somewhere courting a new young wife.'

'A wife?'

'He was in an open carriage where everyone could see him and the young woman was alongside him. There's no mama, no chaperone and they have luggage at the back. They've obviously travelled together from wherever he found her and, as she doesn't look to me like some pretty bit of flotsam picked up in a port somewhere, I'd hazard a guess at a new wife, wouldn't you?' But Bentley was not interested in hazarding any guess so Darcy continued. 'Whatever she is, wife or no wife, one thing is certain, Macleod is not dead. That report you got was wide of the mark by some distance.'

Darcy waited while Bentley digested his news.

'Get on your way, Darcy, I need to think about this. When I've decided what we are to do, if anything, I'll come to your rooms.'

Darcy turned and left and Bentley turned to the reading room but decided he needed to think about Darcy's news and would prefer to do his thinking free from any possible interruption. He collected his coat and hat and left the club, crossed Beacon Street and walked out on to Boston Common.

What a damned unpredictable man Macleod was, gone from Boston one minute, dead in New Orleans the next and then back to life and in Boston again taking the air with a mysterious young lady. What would the erratic fellow do next? Whatever he was up to, he wasn't a man on the run from anyone, nor worried about who knew he was back.

Bentley walked on through the Park where a few cows still grazed and, with the trees, gave the place an air of countryside. His path took him well away from the few other strollers as he set himself to thinking about Macleod and his young lady and whether their sudden appearance might require him to take any action. His steps and thoughts finally brought him to the far side of the Common and the Burying Ground. He stopped and looked at the lines of headstones.

The sight of these memorials to mortality brought him to a conclusion. Yes, Macleod was proving nothing if not unpredictable and any loose cannon, even such a small one, was an unwanted complication at this time and might well require him to take some action to fix it. Fix it once and for all.

Chapter Forty-two

Away from the club rooms where Darcy had hurried with his news, in the not-so-fashionable district at the back of Faneuil Hall and off Dock Square, a young woman stood at a door in Ann Street listening to a pair of shabby boys. When they had finished whatever it was they were saying she handed them a few coins and closed the door. The boys pocketed the coins and then lounged against the wall waiting. Inside, the young woman went quickly upstairs.

'He's back, Molly, and our bird is with him. They arrived at his house no more than ten minutes ago.'

'You're sure it's them?'

'The boys said it was a pretty young lady and an older man in plain black with travel luggage and he had a key to the front door. It's them all right. What now?'

'Are the boys still at the door?'

'Yes, I told them to wait.'

'Tell them we want a sharp eye kept on our Mr Macleod, where he goes and what callers he gets.'

'And her?'

'I doubt she'll come out. She knows no one and speaks no English. How did they arrive?'

'In an open carriage, just breezed up to the front door large as life. What's he up to, Molly?'

'He's being clever, Kitty, sharp as a razor our Mr Macleod. Come home with a pretty young woman at your side. Bring her to your door in an open carriage and in she goes. What are people to think, would you say?'

'He's brought home a fancy bit from his travels to warm his bed and a bit more beside.'

Molly laughed.

'No, girl, this is Boston not London. This is his home town where he's a respected lawyer and well-thought-of man of business. Over here they don't bring their pretty young lady-friends to their front door in open carriages for all to see. These good puritan gentlemen have them tucked away quiet like, so they can go to church on Sunday with their wives on their arms and their heads held high.'

'What then?'

'Lawyer Macleod's gone and got himself a new wife is what they will all say, a lady of breeding from somewhere down South. Leave them alone for a while, they'll say. He'll bring her out to be introduced when they're settled and ready. And that's what he'll do, wait a while then walk her about a bit, show her off and let everyone know she speaks nothing but French. Everyone will lose interest and Macleod can get on with passing her on and getting his money. He thinks he's safe. He'll be in no hurry, why should he be? Take your time and do it right. He's smart all right, but this time I won't underestimate him and remember, he doesn't know we're here. The advantage lies with us this time and we're going to make it count.'

'How long do we wait?'

'I arranged with our Navy Captain to get my report to Trent on the next ship bound for London. If Trent got it around the time we made Halifax and shot a man on his way to us, then he should be here before too long. We'll wait three days. Macleod can't move her on in that time. We'll wait three days and watch. If no one has come by then I'll think again. You're sure there's no one else in the house except that old French bag of a housekeeper?'

'No one. It's well known she's his only servant.'

'Good. Then we wait. If Trent's man isn't here by then you may well get another chance to use your knife.'

Kitty gave a satisfied smile.

'And this time we won't miss.'

'No, this time clever Mr Macleod goes down and he goes down for good.'

Chapter Forty-three

Marie's arrival at Macleod's home was an unqualified success. Amélie, surprised by their sudden appearance, had been inclined to be crotchety and bad tempered but Marie had taken charge and with a few well-chosen words had won her over completely.

The truth is that Marie had captivated Amélie's shrunken old soul from the minute they had met, stirring fond and powerful memories of her first mistress, Macleod's long dead mother. It was, for Amélie, as if the clock had suddenly been turned back many years and she was young again.

Macleod told her that Marie was a lady in need of help and protection, help and protection that they must provide. He gave no further explanation and Amélie needed none. For her it was enough that here, at last, was another whom she knew instinctively was worth her love and service.

Marie was settled in the living room where the curtains were thrown open and the late afternoon sunshine allowed to stream in and Macleod, after seeing her luggage brought in, joined her. A few minutes later Amélie brought coffee then left to prepare rooms.

'Well, Marie, you are safe in my home now. You must rest and recover yourself after all that has happened. When you are ready, but only when you are ready, we will talk about what is to be done. Amélie will look after you, she seems already to be fond of you.'

'Yes. Has she been with you long?'

'Many, many years.'

'She is French. I had not expected anyone French here in Boston.'

'She came from Paris to be maid to my mother in Edinburgh before I was born. I think it must have been a comfort to my mother to have someone close who would talk to her in her native tongue.'

'She knew you as a child?'

'She has known me all my life.'

'She must be very old.'

Macleod laughed.

'Oh, very old, Marie, even older than me.'

After coffee, Marie disappeared with Amélie and Macleod sat, trying to force his mind away from the pleasure of being back in his own home, to the still unresolved problem of how to get Marie to go to Washington. But his mind seemed unwilling for the task. Whether it was the sunlight or Marie's presence or a combination of both, the house seemed to come alive. Marie brought a freshness to the place and Macleod welcomed it.

Marie finally reappeared just before dinner.

'Amélie has shown me everything and told me so much.'

Macleod received the news with considerable reservation.

'Alas, I fear, at her age, she has a poor and unreliable memory.'

'Indeed? To me her memory seems excellent.'

That evening the meal, even to Macleod's inexpert taste, was delicious, the wine excellent and Amélie, in what looked like a new dress, served them with something bordering on cheerfulness. After the meal they sat for a while together in the living room. Macleod had decided on their arrival that the first and most important thing was to make Marie feel safe and that could not be achieved among explanations or the making of plans. If Marie wished to talk then he would talk. As it was she seemed happy to remain silent wrapped in her own thoughts. Quite suddenly she stood up.

'I would like to retire now.'

Macleod stood.

'Certainly.'

He went to the door and was about to shout for Amélie as had been his usual custom but stopped himself, returned and pulled a bell-cord by the fireplace and offered a small silent prayer that the thing, after years of never being used, still worked. He stood and waited and finally Amélie entered.

'Ah, you heard me ringing for you?'

'No.'

'No?'

'I saw the bell jangling about like a demented thing and supposed you were trying to summon me. The clapper fell out of that bell last time it was used, more years ago than I can remember. You were lucky I was in the kitchen and saw it otherwise you might have waited a pretty time before I came. Why didn't you bellow like you usually do?'

Macleod realised quite well that the performance was for Marie's benefit and accepted it as such.

'Madame de Valois wishes to retire. Will you take her to her room and assist her?'

'Of course I will. You don't think I'd let her do it by herself do you? Some of us in this house aren't savages. Come with me, Madame.'

Marie wished Macleod good night and left with Amélie. Macleod, left alone, took up a lamp and went into the library where he sat down in his usual chair, fixed his gaze on the empty, cold fireplace and began again to think about how he was going to get Marie to go willingly to Washington. About an hour later Amélie entered with the whisky tray and a lamp.

'I'm leaving them here now so as to be ready in case Madame needs me at any time.'

'Not tonight, Amélie, I won't need the tray tonight, nor any night unless I ask for it.'

Amélie shrugged and turned away.

Macleod returned to his gazing and thinking. He closed his eyes and let his mind wander over the present situation. Marie was in his home. She was, at this very moment preparing to retire. Above, in her bedroom she would be …

He woke suddenly feeling cold and stiff. He had no idea what the time was but, whatever it was, he knew that his bed summoned him. Once in his room he prepared to retire. It may not be, he thought, the best of all possible worlds, but it was certainly a vast improvement on previous experience.

Chapter Forty-four

In Congress Square stood the latest monument to Boston's unstoppable progress, the Congress Coffee House and Hotel. It rose massively a full seven storeys, a miracle and a wonder and one of the tallest buildings in the whole of the country. It was built in the Classical style and its pillared and porticoed entrance which fronted on to the Square invited those who could afford it to see for themselves that its outside grandeur was more than matched by its interior.

Outside this entrance, standing on the cobble-stones of the Square beside two large trunks and a small bound box stood a short, stocky individual with a tall hat at a drunken angle over lank grey hair that reached down over his ears. His clothes, though doubtless clean, had a disordered air and he held his arms straight at his sides with his hands clenched into two large fists. Pedestrians passing by avoided him. His face was set in a scowl and while one eye watched the Square, the other seemed to roam madly here and there settling on nothing.

This was Gregory, the manservant pressed on Lord Melford by Jasper Trent.

Suddenly Gregory reached up, snatched off his hat and held it by his side. Lord Melford came out of the hotel entrance, walked to the trunks and nodded at them.

'This place will do, Gregory. It seems quite habitable, almost civilised.' Gregory nodded once. 'Get them taken up to my rooms. When all is ready come and fetch me from the Coffee Room.'

Gregory nodded once again, put his hat back at the usual angle, turned and walked off towards the entrance.

When Lord Melford had first seen Gregory standing waiting for him at the Liverpool coaching terminus he had, like most people who came on Gregory for the first time, to suppress a strong desire to be elsewhere. Gregory did not have a prepossessing appearance or manner. He looked slightly mad and possibly violent. Nor were his looks entirely deceiving. But on the journey Melford had, sensibly, made it his business to find out why Trent had forced Gregory's services on to him. And his efforts had been well rewarded, for he was now satisfied that Gregory was just the sort of man he needed at his side to help him in his task. As a valet to a man of feeling and sentiment where clothes were concerned, he might leave a great deal to be desired. But, Lord Melford had said to himself three days out from London, are clothes everything when all is said and done? And he had decided that, for an agent of Jasper Trent on foreign soil and likely to encounter danger, they were not.

Lord Melford looked around him. Congress Square was as busy as the rest of this busy, bustling city and Gregory had never before set foot in Boston. Yet their acquaintance on the voyage from London had left him in no doubt. Lord Melford allowed himself a smile.

If Gregory can't make contact with Molly O'Hara inside forty-eight hours I swear I'll eat that tall hat of his, yes dammit, positively eat his hat.

Chapter Forty-five

Macleod stood at the living room window looking out at the early sunshine. Amélie was busy laying the breakfast table.

'Well, Amélie? What do you think of Madame de Valois?'

Amélie pretended to think about it, but the pretence didn't fool Macleod and, when she saw that it hadn't, she shrugged and left the living room.

Macleod turned and looked out of the window once more. It was going to be a fine day and he felt happy. He was home and they were safe and Amélie had actually taken a liking to Marie.

'Good morning, Jean.'

Macleod turned. Marie had come into the room and was standing looking at him.

'Good morning, I trust you slept well. Amélie had very little time to prepare the beds.'

'I slept very well, thank you.' She looked at the breakfast table. 'I will only take coffee but if you wish to eat …'

'No, coffee will suit me. I will call Amélie.'

'There is no need, she came and helped me to dress, she is bringing the coffee now.' She went to the table and sat down. 'She looks after me as if I were a small child, she is very kind. I'm glad she likes me.'

They sat at the table and in a few minutes Amélie entered with the coffee, put it on the table and left. Marie reached out to the coffee pot and poured two cups.

'Last night Amélie and I talked again, we talked a great deal.'

She replaced the pot and held a cup out to Macleod.

'Thank you. What did you talk about?'

'You.'

'Me? Well, you mustn't let Amélie persuade you too much. Ours has been a long relationship but not without its, how shall I put it, not without …'

'I asked her if I could trust you.'

The cup stopped at Macleod's lips. He paused then put it down.

'And what did she say?'

'She said I could trust you totally and if necessary with my life.'

Macleod fingered his coffee cup for a second.

'And did you believe her?'

'At first, no. I thought she spoke as a loyal servant would speak to someone who was a stranger, I did not think she spoke from the heart. But I have thought about it a great deal through the night and now I am not sure. I need to trust someone. Alone I will ...,' Macleod waited as she looked down at her coffee cup, 'alone I know I will die,' she raised her eyes, 'and I do not want to die.' Then she looked down again as if she had said something shameful. For a moment Macleod feared she would cry. He had no idea what he would do if she did, so he waited. But when she looked up there were no tears. 'Do you think me a coward?'

'No, you're not a coward, far from it. You have behaved bravely, with great courage.'

'I have behaved like a child, thinking only of myself and never truly thinking of how much I have put you into danger for my sake.'

'Then think about it now and trust me, Marie.'

'I don't know, I want to trust you but I do not know. Coming here on the ship I thought a great deal. It was then that I realised that I am still in many ways a child, but a child who has been burned and still fears the fire. I thought my parents loved me but I was sold. I thought I would be loved by my husband but I was humiliated. I lived surrounded by friends who cared nothing for me. I was a pretty doll, nothing more.' She looked at him with a challenge in her eyes. 'I want to become a woman, a real woman.' She saw Macleod blink in surprise and his cheeks slightly colour. 'No, Jean, not a woman in that way. Although if that were to happen then I don't think it would sadden me, perhaps, if it were to happen with you.'

'Really, Marie, I assure you that not for one moment ...'

'But you have thought about it, Jean. Remember I have seen the way you looked at me so many times in New Orleans. I have seen that look in other men's eyes and I know well enough what it means.' Macleod wanted desperately to make a denial but, looking

209

at her, he found he couldn't. 'Jean, if I am to become a woman, a person with my own mind and spirit, you must help me. There is no one else.'

'Of course, I will do all I can, but I don't quite see what it is that you want me to do.'

'What you have been doing, helping me and guarding me and, most of all, trying to be my friend even when I am a spiteful, selfish child. Have patience with me, Jean, and be my friend.'

Macleod was struggling for some kind of response to this appeal when the front door-bell rang and Macleod stood up hurriedly, thankful for the interruption.

'Excuse me, Amélie is always so slow. I will see who that is.'

He left the room. Marie heard him open the door and then the sound of voices. After a moment Macleod came back into the room followed by another man. It was Bentley.

It took no great intuition on Marie's part to sense that the visitor was unwelcome. Neither of them had discussed how they would explain her presence in his home. Macleod spoke to her in French.

'This is Mr Bentley, a business associate.' He then changed to English as he turned to Bentley. 'May I introduce Madame Marie de Valois. I regret Madame speaks no English, only French.'

Bentley came forward, smiling and holding out his hand. Marie offered hers. He took it and touched it to his lips. He spoke slowly in French, as if finding difficulty with his words

'Enchanté, Madame. I regret I do not speak French well but if you will bear with me I will do my best.'

'Your French is better than my English which does not exist at all.'

There was a pause which Macleod hurried to fill.

'Madame de Valois is a relative of mine. She has come to visit me.'

Bentley reverted to English.

'A relative? I see. I heard that you had come back from wherever you've been with a new wife so I thought I'd come round and offer my congratulations. I apologise for my mistake.'

Macleod looked shocked and Marie, seeing it, became concerned.

'What is it, Jean? What does he say?'

'He says he thought you were my wife.'

'No! How could he think such a thing?'

Bentley looked at Marie and spoke again in French.

'A friend of mine saw you arrive together, Madame. He made an error. I apologise.'

'Madame de Valois is a cousin of mine, a distant cousin. On my mother's side. My mother was French.'

Bentley smiled.

'Well, Macleod, all I can say is I envy you your cousin no matter how distant and from whichever side. I hope we will see a great deal of you while you are visiting your cousin, Madame. It would be an honour to introduce you to my friends.'

Marie returned his smile.

'Thank you, M'sieur Bentley but I have not settled on how long I may stay in Boston.

'I see. And you have come from where, Madame, to visit your distant cousin on his mother's side?'

Macleod intercepted the question.

'Savannah. Marie is from Savannah.'

But Bentley brushed aside the intrusion and continued to direct his words to Marie.

'Ah, Savannah, I know it well. In fact I have business interests quite nearby. We must talk together about Savannah, Madame, perhaps we have mutual acquaintances. I know a great many people there and I find it distinctly odd that I have never even heard of Madame de Valois.'

Marie looked to Macleod for help who rallied as best he could.

'I meant we met in Savannah. We travelled here from Savannah. She was visiting friends and it was there I had arranged to meet her.'

'I see, visiting friends, of course.' Bentley turned back to Marie. 'And where is your home, Madame, if not Savannah?'

Asked the question bluntly and now in fluent French Marie looked for a suitable answer, found that she had none, so answered the truth.

'I come from New Orleans.'

'Ah, Madame de Valois lives in New Orleans. I regret it is a city I do not know.' Bentley turned back to Macleod. 'Presumably Madame lives in New Orleans with Monsieur de Valois. May one be so bold as to ask if there are any little de Valois's?'

Macleod answered tersely. His anxiety at Bentley's questioning had evaporated as he became increasingly angry at both the questions and the questioner.

'Madame is a widow. Her husband passed away some years ago. Now, if you will excuse us …'

But Bentley wasn't ready to leave now that his French had so noticeably improved.

'Madame, please accept my condolences on your husband's death.'

Marie forced out a sad smile and nodded.

'Yes, the fever, some years ago.'

'Well, Macleod, I will take my leave. I only called to pay my respects and welcome to Boston your,' he paused, 'distant cousin on your mother's side was it not? I will impose on you no longer.' He turned back to Marie and spoke in a French that had improved most remarkably since his arrival. 'I hope that you will not be a stranger among us, Madame de Valois, however short your stay. I admit that Boston isn't Paris or London nor even New Orleans but it has its points of interest, yes indeed, it does have its points of interest. Good day.'

Bentley left and Macleod could see that his visit had clearly disturbed Marie.

'Who was that man?'

'I told you, a business associate.'

'Why did he come?'

'As he said, someone saw us arrive and told him I had come home with a new wife.'

'He lied. He was spying on us I am sure. Did you notice that he said his French was poor but by the time he left he spoke it well enough? And he did not believe I was your cousin did he?'

'I doubt it.'

'But he did believe I came from New Orleans.'

'Probably because it was, unfortunately, the truth. Well, it can't be helped.'

'Should we fear him, Jean? Will he try to harm us?'

Macleod found himself in a difficult position. If Bentley *was* working for the Government, perhaps even for the General, then he could be an ally. But if he was an ally then he would certainly try to stop Marie going to the British. He might be Macleod's friend in this matter, but if so, would he then be Marie's enemy?

'I tell you truthfully, Marie, I don't know.'

He saw that she knew he had avoided answering her question. He damned himself for a blockhead who had no way with words when words were needed. She had been so close to trusting him and now once again she was unsure.

'If you will excuse me I think I will go to my room.'

'Of course, you must feel free to do as you wish while in this house. Think of it as your own home.'

'Thank you, you mean it kindly I know, but my homes have not been places I remember with joy. I will try to think of this house as a place of safety.'

'Do that, Marie, and I swear by all that I hold dear that while you are here I will be your true friend and guard you with my life.'

Marie hesitated, slightly taken aback by the force with which Macleod had spoken. Then she turned and left the room.

Macleod went back to the window and looked out. He found that he had been wrong earlier. The day was not fine and he was not happy and, as for safety, it was proving far more elusive than he had at first thought.

He turned his mind to Bentley. Friend or foe, Government or … Government or what?

And Macleod's mind set off down a new and even more troubling line of conjecture.

Chapter Forty-six

When friends meet pleasantries are exchanged, or so we are told by those who know about such things. Two figures had indeed met and were dimly visible in the light from a tavern window among the scraps, rubbish and other detritus that somehow grows and thrives around such establishments.

'What the hell do you want you bloody, wall-eyed bastard? Let me alone.'

From this mode of greeting we may safely assume that the man who had caught hold firmly of Kitty Mullen's wrist and held it tightly as she squirmed to free herself was not one of those she regarded as a friend.

'Hold still, Kitty, or I'll twist your blasted arm off altogether.'

Kitty gave up the struggle. The wall-eyed bastard, or Gregory as we know him, released her wrist.

'Try to run and I'll break your leg at the knee.'

Kitty looked at him, sullenly rubbing her wrist, and as running was not an option open to her, expressed her feelings only in words.

'What's brought you over here? Scarpered have you? Gone on the run? Paper out on you in London, is there? Some magistrate finally tumbled you? About time.'

The dingy street was not far from Ann Street, dark and ill-lit as befits a neighbourhood of taverns, jilt shops and brothels frequented by sailors from the nearby docks of Bendell's Cove. A small commotion in an alley beside a low tavern would have disturbed no one, had anyone been close enough to hear it. Kitty couldn't see Gregory's good eye on her, but she could imagine it as he spoke.

'I dare say you heard someone was about? Heard someone was asking around?'

'Maybe.'

'You did. I know it. I made it my business for you to know and to know quick. That's why you thought it best to slip out the back when you saw me in the tavern.'

'You were at the bar when I saw you. How did you get here before me?'

'Ah, quickness is a thing you learn early if you want to be a successful thief-taker. And I've been very successful, ain't I? Very successful indeed. So successful, in fact, that I've moved up in the world.'

'Oh, yes, what are you now, a public shit-house attendant? No, not you, nothing so fancy, how about a shit-house attendant's arse wiper?'

Gregory's face moved closer and what light the grimy window gave out fell on it. He grinned and his wandering eye became even more active as the other beamed on Kitty.

'Very drôle, Kitty. I always did think you a girl with a keen sense of fun.' Then the grin disappeared. 'But we can't stay here exchanging pleasantries like old friends, can we? You have an appointment with someone and it's my job to get you there.'

'You've no rights to pull people over here. You're a London tickler and outside London you ain't worth spit and this ain't even outside London, it's America. I could call for help and have you put in charge.'

'You could try to call for help, dearie. You could try, of course. But I doubt anyone would come to your aid. You see, you'd be dead with that pretty neck snapped if I saw you as much as try to open your mouth. Come now, be sensible, Kitty. You're taken. Let's go quietly shall we? No sense in any fuss.'

And Kitty saw the sense of his argument. England or America, she was indeed taken, so she went quietly.

Chapter Forty-seven

Lord Melford was at a solitary dinner in his rooms when the door opened and Gregory pushed Kitty into the room, followed, and closed the door. He then snatched off his tall hat and stood with his arms by his side.

'Kitty Mullen, sir. As asked for and now delivered.' Gregory turned to Kitty. 'This here is Lord Melford, a proper Lord, not the Jack Doran sort. So watch your tongue and your manners or you'll get my hand across you.'

Kitty looked at him with a scowl then turned her attention to the man sitting at the table. Melford smiled a greeting.

'Miss Mullen. Please come and sit down. I'm dining as you see and I hope you won't think it churlish if I carry on with my meal.' Melford gestured to Gregory. 'Come now, Gregory, let's be gentlemen. See to the lady's chair, sir, if you please.'

Gregory took a chair, pulled it out and motioned to it with his hat.

'Arse over here, dearie, and sharp about it.'

Kitty wasn't sure whether to be defiant or humble so she walked non-committally to the chair and sat down. Melford waved his knife at the bottle on the table.

'Come, Gregory, do the honours. Give the lady a glass of Hock, fill her glass.' Gregory leaned across, picked up the dark bottle and poured the light coloured wine into the glass on the table in front of Kitty. She looked at it suspiciously. Melford laughed. 'She doesn't trust us, Gregory. Well, nothing wrong in that. I like to see a little sensible caution. Take a sip, Gregory, show her there's nothing there but Hock.'

'No, you taste it, Mister. Poison would have no effect on him.'

Melford grinned.

'Sensible girl.' He picked up the glass and took a healthy drink, put the glass down, reached for the bottle, refilled her glass then refilled his own. 'There now, point proved, all friends together.'

Kitty looked at the wine, then picked up the glass and swallowed the contents at one go. Melford watched her and laughed. 'Damn me, I wouldn't want to match you glass for glass if that's how you drink. Another?' Kitty wiped her mouth with the back of her hand, nodded and held out her glass. Melford motioned once more with his knife to Gregory and carried on eating while Gregory poured, but half way up the glass the wine gave out.

'This one's dead.'

'Then get another, Gregory, we have a guest. We can't give a bad impression on first acquaintance, can we?'

'This ain't no first acquaintance, sir. Kitty and I have met before.'

'Old friends, how wonderful. Even more reason for another bottle.'

Gregory provided another bottle, finished refilling Kitty's glass then moved away and stood watching them. Kitty took another drink and waited. No doubt she would be told what it was all about when the man at the table was good and ready.

Melford finished his meal and Gregory cleared the table except for the bottle and glasses. Melford turned to Kitty, smiled and picked up his glass.

'To friends, old and new alike.' He drank. Kitty picked up her glass and took a drink without responding to his toast. 'You're a girl that doesn't waste words I see. Better and better. A slack mouth can be a very troublesome thing. But now, my dear, we must get down to issues. Issue one, why am I here? Issue two, what do I want? Issue three, where do you fit in? Very well. One, I am here on business, urgent business. Two, I want to meet with your mistress. Three, you must bring her to me. There, clear and simple.'

'It's neither clear nor simple to me. What business, what mistress and why me?'

'As to my business, that's my affair. As to what mistress, then let's call her Madame de Metz shall we?' Kitty remained silent. 'No? How about Fanny Dashwood?' Again no response. 'Oh dear, still nothing. Then how about Molly O'Hara?'

'All right, you know her. But that still don't mean I should bring her here.'

'Too true. She'll want a reason to come. How about you tell her that Lord Melford sends his compliments and begs her to attend on him in his rooms.'

'Does she know you?'

'I'll let her answer that, Kitty. Now, you know the reason Gregory brought you so your visit is finished, as I see is your wine, so you'd better be on your way. Would you like Gregory to escort you? No? I thought not. Well then, goodbye, Miss Mullen.'

Kitty got up and went to the door.

'If she agrees to come, and I only say if, mind you, when would you want it to be?'

'Well, it's too late now for a respectable lady to come to a gentleman's rooms, so it will have to be first thing tomorrow. Ask her to breakfast with me at nine.'

Kitty opened the door.

'I'll ask.'

'Good girl.'

The door closed and Melford looked across at Gregory.

'Should you follow?'

'No. I know their roost. Will she come do, you think?'

'Oh yes, she'll know Trent sent me. She'll come all right.'

And Lord Melford poured himself another glass of Hock.

'Decent Hock this, I feared for the wine over here but this Hock is quite acceptable, quite acceptable.'

Once out of the hotel and across Congress Square, Kitty hurried back to Fanny Dashwood's rooms in Ann Street and was out of breath when sat down at the table beside Molly.

Molly pushed her glass across.

'Take a pull and get your breath. I knew something was up when you were gone so long.'

Kitty took a drink of the gin.

'I told you someone was asking questions about us and when I was out, I heard he was nearby in a tavern.'

'Heard how?'

'It doesn't matter now. It was a fix. The bastard sucked me in like a babe. I went into the tavern, saw him at the bar and then slipped out through the back. That's where he took me. It was Gregory.'

'Gregory!'

218

'No other.'

'And he took you?' Kitty nodded. 'But this is Boston not London. Why should a London thief-taker pull anyone over here? What in hell's name is he doing over here anyway?'

'He's working for a man named Melford, styles himself Lord Melford. He took me to him. This Melford seems to know you, Molly, knows you were de Metz and now you're Dashwood. Even knows your true name, O'Hara. Who is he?'

Molly stood up, her concern gone.

'He's Trent's man, he's been sent by Jasper Trent and if that cunning bastard Gregory is working with him then, thank God, say I. Come on now, take me to Melford.'

'He said nine tomorrow, breakfast.'

'We go now, Kitty, sod and damn tomorrow and breakfast. We go now and I'll make Lord Melford jump. Sending for me and coming the high and bloody mighty. Come on, Kitty, we've work to do so let's be at it.'

Chapter Forty-eight

The next morning brought another early caller to Macleod's house. Macleod was, this time, in no hurry to leave the breakfast table and left Amélie to answer the door. As usual she took her time but the caller had patience and she eventually came into where Macleod and Marie were seated.

'There is a man who says he wishes to see you.'

'Does this man have a name?'

'He says he is an English m'lord and calls himself Melford.'

Macleod looked across at Marie who shook her head to indicate the name meant nothing to her.

'Does he say what his business is?'

'No. Just that he is m'lord Melford and wishes to speak with M Macleod.'

Macleod stood up.

'I will come.'

Amélie left the room to return to her duties and Macleod excused himself to Marie and went to the street door. Standing waiting was a well-dressed young man who wore an air of confidence and a false smile which he bestowed on Macleod as soon as he saw him.

'Mr Macleod?'

'I am.'

'I am Lord Melford. You don't know me but I have heard a great deal about you. May I come in?'

'State your business, sir.'

The false smile broadened.

'Ah, direct and to the point, the American way. Well, sir, I wish I could be as direct but I fear that here on the street that is not possible.'

'Your business, sir, or I close this door and you may go to hell.'

The smile disappeared.

'My business is of the New Orleans sort and, forgive me if I seem coy, it involves a lady whose name I refrain from using in so public a place. A lady, I may add, sadly recently widowed. That is my business, sir.'

Macleod stood to one side.

'Come in.'

Melford entered, waited while Macleod closed the door then followed him into the room where Marie was waiting. Marie stood up.

Melford turned on his smile.

'Madame, please do not get up on my account.'

'Madame de Valois speaks no English.'

Melford let his false smile play on her for a second then spoke in perfect French.

'Eh bien, Madame, we must of course speak French.'

'Come, sir, you said you had business with me. What business?'

'As Madame de Valois has risen, need we detain her? Business, especially our kind of business, is such a bore for the ladies. Perhaps she has other more interesting things that might occupy her?' Macleod looked at Marie who did not move. Melford waited a second then accepted the situation. 'The lady chooses to stay, very well. But I warn you, Madame, my business is of the very dullest sort, in short it is money business. Might we all sit down, do you think, Mr Macleod?' Macleod motioned to a chair and Melford waited until Marie had sat down then seated himself. Macleod remained standing. 'My business is delicate, Mr Macleod, so I ask again whether Madame de Valois might have other things to do rather than ...'

'Madame de Valois wishes to stay. Whatever you have to say will be said in front of her or not at all. Now, get to it or get out.'

'Very well, bluntness is to be the order of the day, I see. Good, that suits me well enough. You have a property,' here he looked meaningfully at Marie, 'I am charged with making you an offer for that property, a cash offer. Name your price, sir, and if it's within reason I'll be happy to accept. There, would you say that was sufficiently, getting to it?'

Shock and disbelief were nicely blended in Macleod's reply.

'Are you asking me to hand Madame de Valois over to you for money?'

'To be blunt, sir, I am. All we need to decide is how much money. And if you will be advised by me, make it a handsome amount. My principal expects to have to pay well for the property, so why disappoint him?'

Macleod returned to the door and pulled it open.

'Get out.'

Melford stayed seated.

'Come now, Mr Macleod, no histrionics, this isn't Drury Lane. You are a man of business and so am I. Let's behave as such.'

'Get out of my house, damn you, before I throw you out.'

For the first time since entering, Melford's self-confidence seemed shaken. He stood up unsure of what to do. There was a brief pause of indecision among the three of them until Marie spoke.

'Please sit down, Lord Melford.' She then looked at Macleod. 'Please, Jean, close the door.' Melford smiled a smile that was no longer quite so obviously false and sat down. They both looked at Macleod and waited. Macleod slowly closed the door, came back to the table where he remained standing while Marie continued. 'Now, Lord Melford, am I right in assuming that the property you refer to is myself?'

Melford's confidence had fully returned.

'Quite correct, Madame. I thought I would be dealing with this gentleman but I see now it is you I should be talking to. You have information which my principal is willing to pay for. It is of no concern to me or my principle which party is paid for this information so long as we get it.'

'Who is your principle?'

'Ah, now there I must decline to answer, but if you doubt the sincerity of the offer I can reassure you easily enough.' He put his hand into his coat, pulled out a folded paper and handed it across. Marie took and opened it. 'A banker's draft made out, as you see, to the bearer and the amount left blank.' He held out his hand and Marie passed the paper back to him. He put it back into his coat. 'Once I am satisfied that the information is indeed worth whatever price we agree, I will fill in the amount and hand over the draft.' Marie said nothing. 'If you are in any doubt about the genuineness of the document perhaps you would like Mr Macleod to look it over. He is, I understand, a lawyer.'

'That will not be necessary.'

Macleod could contain himself no longer.

'Who the hell sent you?'

Melford looked up at him.

'As I said, no names. Except perhaps one to show good faith, his Royal Majesty, King George. I do not mean that literally, of course, it was not him who sent me, I am but a humble cog in that wheel of State, a mere messenger, but ultimately my authority to act in this matter resides in the British crown. So, Madame, will you take His Majesty's money and share with me what you know?'

'No, damn you, she will not and you, sir, will get out. I've heard all I care to from you. Neither Madame de Valois nor any information she may have is for sale, not now, not ever.'

But Melford wasn't shaken this time. Marie, he was sure, was interested in his offer and it was she who had the information, not Macleod.

'I see. The lady must do as you wish not as her own inclinations might dictate. Am I to presume then that while she is a prisoner in your house she must obey your wishes?' Macleod didn't answer. Melford saw that the point had struck home and followed up his advantage. 'Well, sir, keeping a lady against her will would be frowned upon in London but I must assume that here in Boston it is merely another part of the American way.' The monstrousness of the charge momentarily confused Macleod. He wanted to take Melford by his collar and throw him out but he also wanted to refute totally the charge that Marie was being forced, against her will, to remain in his house, a prisoner. 'Unless, of course, I am mistaken and the lady is here of her own free will?'

He looked at Marie for an answer.

'I am here, sir, entirely of my own free will.'

Melford returned to Macleod.

'Then I think, Mr Macleod, that what it comes down to is, what does the lady wish in this matter? Does it not?'

Macleod realised that the moment for action had passed and also realised that what Melford had just said was, unfortunately, absolutely true. The choice was Marie's to make. He looked at her and waited.

She stood up.

'I regret that you have been misinformed, Lord Melford.'

'Misinformed, Madame?'

'I have no idea what information you are talking about. Certainly I have none that I could sell to you, even if you *are* acting on behalf of His Majesty King George. All the information I have is that I am a distant cousin of Mr Macleod's on his mother's side and I am paying him a visit. Not, I fear, information of any value but you may have it without charge. You must tell His Majesty King George that I regret any inconvenience or expense I may have unwittingly caused him. Good day, sir.'

Melford looked from Marie to Macleod, who was looking at her and smiling.

'I see.' Melford stood, bowed slightly to Marie and walked to the door where he stopped. 'I am sorry to have troubled you both. Please accept my humble apologies. Perhaps you would accompany me to the door, Mr Macleod, since my business here is quite finished for the time being.'

Lord Melford left the room followed by Macleod. Marie heard the street door open and close. No words, as far as she could tell, were exchanged.

Macleod returned to the living room, walked about for a moment, then came and stood in front of Marie.

'I don't understand.'

'What is it, Jean, that you do not understand?'

'You said you wanted to sell your information to the British.'

'Yes, that is what I said.'

'And Melford is from London. Why did you refuse to deal with him?'

'This Lord Melford *says* he is from London and he acts the English lord very well but tell me, Jean, have you ever met an English m'lord?'

'No.'

'Neither have I, so all we truly know about him is what he himself told us. Yesterday your business friend, Monsieur Bentley, comes to question you about me. First he does not speak French so well, then he speaks it very well. Also he mocks the story we tell him and he does not hide that he is mocking it. Today a stranger calls who says he represents the British Government and offers money for the information I have. Does it not seem to you that these two callers might be connected?'

And it suddenly seemed to Macleod that she was right. They might very well be connected.

'I hadn't thought of that.'

'Think of it now, Jean. You said we were safe now we were in Boston. It does not seem to me that we are safe. It seems to me that we might still be in great danger.'

Macleod reluctantly agreed with her but decided that if she thought herself in danger, now was the time to persuade her to place herself on the side of America.

'Marie, there is only one sure way for you to become safe. You must go with me to Washington. There is a man there, a man whom I trust completely. He was the one who sent me to New Orleans. He is a high official of the American Government. You must come with me and tell him all you know. Once that is done you will indeed be safe.'

'And then?'

Macleod didn't understand the question.

'And then, what?'

'I will be safe to do what? I have no home, no money. I am running away from the murder of my husband. If I tell what I know to this man you trust so completely, will he pay me, will he pay me enough to go away and start a new life in the safety you say he can give me?'

Macleod was painfully aware that all he could truthfully say fell far short of what he wished he could say.

'He is an honourable man, I'm sure you will be treated fairly.'

'Oh, Jean, I am trying to behave like a woman, to think like a grown person not a child. Do not become a too trusting child yourself when I need you most. We were followed from New Orleans, you were attacked and I nearly murdered. We arrive in Boston where you think I will be safe and your house is at once besieged by people who know who I am and why I am here. If I travel with you to Washington would you say I had a good chance of getting there alive if we are already watched, as we certainly are? I think not.'

Macleod saw her point.

'But what else can you do?'

'We can think. Are Bentley and Melford together and, if so, who do they represent? If they are not together, does Lord Melford really represent the British? Are St Clair's friends here yet and will they try to silence me once more? How much should I ask for the information I have? There is a lot to think about before I decide what I must do, Jean, would you not agree?'

Macleod's grasp of the situation, he was becoming aware, was considerably less than that of Marie.

'You may be right, you probably are right, but how do we go about answering any of your questions? These people come from a world of secrecy and intrigue that we neither of us know nor understand.'

Marie paused for a second as if Macleod had said something of importance.

'Jean, why were you chosen to go to New Orleans by this man in Washington that you say you trust?'

'I served as an officer under him in the late war.'

'And?'

'And he knew that I spoke fluent French.'

'And?'

Macleod thought for a second but nothing came.

'That's all, except that he trusts me.'

'You were a soldier and speak French and because of that he chooses you for a most secret and dangerous mission, a mission which requires you to be a skilled agent, to move among people who live, as you say, in a world of secrecy and intrigue?'

'He needed someone he could trust, someone unconnected with this business, someone from the outside.'

'Why? Did he not trust those who worked for him?'

'I suppose not, not all of them anyway.' Macleod found he was becoming increasingly confused and uncertain of himself. 'But I trust him and I know that if we could get to him we would be safe.'

Marie was obviously not convinced.

'You may be right, but the question is, I think, would we get to him? And my answer is that we would not. No, first, Jean, we must try to do what we can here in Boston.'

'But you said Boston was not safe.'

'No, not so long as we remain in ignorance of who these people represent. If we could only be sure that Lord Melford was indeed working for the British. If he is, then he is my best chance.'

Macleod knew that any further appeal to her would be futile

until somehow he had her full trust and the only way to regain her trust seemed to be to help her in the matter of Lord Melford. He didn't like it, but he could think of no other way.

'How do you think we can find out?'

'Oh, if only I knew that, Jean, all my troubles would be over.'

'If he is working for the British then he will return.'

'What makes you think so?'

'If he wants what you have, and has come all the way from England to get it, one refusal will not stop him. He will return and try again. When he does, we must think of some way to make him prove who he is.'

'Of course. How clever you are, Jean, and you must go to this man Bentley and find out in what way he is involved.'

'How do you suggest I do that?'

'Hurt him, hit him, use violence. You are strong. Make him tell you.'

Macleod was as much shocked by the calmness with which she spoke as by what it was she suggested.

'Even assuming he is involved, I cannot just beat something out of a prominent local business man. This is Boston, for God's sake. Besides Bentley is strong and fit and I'm not sure that if it came to violence it wouldn't be me who might end up getting thrashed.'

'Then we must think of some other way.'

But as it happened, very little actual thought proved necessary.

Chapter Forty-nine

Molly was on her feet and Melford was lounging in a chair. Both were furiously angry and both were trying not to show their anger. Kitty leaned against a wall with folded arms taking no part in the exchanges. She was all too used to these scenes of falling out after some plan that couldn't possibly fail had misfired.

'You're a fool, Melford, but what is worse you're an arrogant fool.'

'Ah, the delegation of blame, how very prompt and how very predictable. I only did what I was told to do, but the fault for failure must be mine. For, if not me, then who else but you?'

'Me? I wasn't the one who went to make the offer.'

'No, I did. But I was told I should not try and be too clever because I would be dealing with a sharp character, a thorough professional, someone who didn't make mistakes. Make a good enough offer and he'll drop, you said. He's after money so give it to him, you said. Keep it simple, you said. So I did exactly as you said. The trouble was that when I got there the only simple thing was Macleod. If that man's an agent of any sort then so is my left boot.'

Molly's problem was that, whatever she might have said, she didn't think for one second that Melford was either a fool or incompetent. She also believed in his version of the events at Macleod's house. Why would he lie? She didn't understand. Either she had made a serious error of judgement or Macleod had put on an act for Melford worthy of any stage in London. But why the need for any act? If he held Marie de Valois for money why turn down a good offer?

'Is he holding out for more, do you think?'

'As far as I can see he isn't holding out at all. When he knew what I was there for he was all shocked sentiment and bluster. I could do nothing with him. He was all for throwing me out on to the street. It was her I had to deal with and, because I'd gone off on the wrong tack from the first, not surprisingly I got nowhere with her. Dammit, how can I be expected to succeed if I don't have accurate information behind me?'

'Stow it, Melford, I want to think.'

'And now, thanks to you, they know I'm here and what it is I want.'

Molly gave him a look which made him decide that enough had been said. He had made his point so he left things as they stood. Molly turned to Gregory who stood stolidly with his tall hat, as always, in his hand and his arms at his sides.

'What about this Bentley?'

Gregory's good eye left off gazing at nothing and looked at her.

'The boys took me to his house. Fine house, rich gent. Got business interests here and there, well thought of. Solid citizen. But I'd say there's another side that he don't care that people should know of.'

'Another side?'

'Gets visitors at night sometimes, people shy of being seen. Has a man called Darcy on a string, uses this Darcy to go on errands for him, long errands. Meets with this Darcy quite a bit but does no actual business with him that anyone knows of.'

Molly wasn't convinced.

'Men in business can be secretive about their dealings and they can send people on errands rather than go themselves. Darcy could just be a particular friend. None of it may mean anything.'

Melford, however, wasn't so sure.

'What do you think, Gregory?'

Gregory touched the side of his nose with a long forefinger.

'I smell 'im as a wrong 'un, sir.'

'You think so?'

'I'd put money on it. In this present matter he was quick enough off the mark to look the young woman over and after he'd done that it was straight to this Darcy fellow for a long talk. As the lady here says, sir, each thing by itself may mean nothing but taken together I'd say he would bear watching.'

Melford agreed.

'Then see that he's watched. Well watched.'

Gregory nodded and winked his non-roving eye.

'Already done, sir.'

'Good. So, Moll, what do we do now?'

While Gregory was speaking Molly had made up her mind.

'I resurrect Madame de Metz and go to see Marie. She knows me from New Orleans so I'll tell her how things stand and then put my cards on the table. Kitty, you come and see if you can hook into the French hag in the kitchen. At all events spy out what you can of the house in case we need to crack it. You might as well come with me, Melford, and make your offer again if she decides to see sense. As far as Macleod or Marie are concerned you're the lead in this, you're the one with the money making the offer. Gregory, spy out the back of the house to see if there's a good way in.' Molly looked at each of them. 'If we're doing it, let's do it right this time, and let's get started.'

About half an hour after Lord Melford had left Macleod's house another visitor rang the bell. Macleod answered it himself. He had become nervous of the kind of visitors he was getting and didn't want to wait for Amélie. It was Bentley.

'Well, what is it this time?'

'We need to talk, Macleod, you and I, without Madame de Valois present.'

'About what?'

'About your death.'

'My death?'

'Yes, some days ago in New Orleans.'

Macleod looked at him. He was sober and he was serious.

'Explain yourself.'

'Not on the street and not in front of any third party.'

Macleod desired no further talk with Bentley, nor indeed anyone, but Marie had given him the task of finding out his involvement so he stood to one side.

'Come in. We'll go into the library.' Once in the room Macleod faced him. 'Now, my death in New Orleans, what do you mean by that?'

'A man was found there murdered, throat cut. Papers on him identified him definitely as you.'

'And how did you come by this nonsense?'

'Not nonsense, Macleod. If the person who sent me the message says a man identified as Macleod was murdered in New Orleans then it happened, believe me. How do you explain someone having your papers in New Orleans?'

'If what you say is true, what is it to you?'

'It is nothing to me, but it may be something to the Government.' Bentley waited but Macleod remained silent. 'It seems then that you have indeed been to New Orleans and it looks as if someone has gone to considerable pains to make it look as if you stayed there permanently. That in fact you died there. Yet here you are, alive and well and with a young lady who speaks nothing but French. That she is your cousin I don't believe for a minute but that she comes from New Orleans I believe completely. I'm afraid I must insist on an explanation, not for me, you understand, but for those I serve.'

Macleod had no idea what to do or say. Any wrong or ill-considered words or actions he knew could lead to disastrous consequences for Marie. But if Bentley was indeed in the service of the American Government then surely he was the best hope of getting Marie to the General. He was spared making any decision by a renewed assault on his front door as the front door bell rang once again.

'See who it is, Macleod, and send them on their way.'

Macleod went to the front door. Madame de Metz, Lord Melford and a maid stood there together. Madame de Metz beamed a smile at him and spoke in French.

'M'sieur Macleod, how charming to renew our acquaintance which was so suddenly interrupted in New Orleans. How is the lovely Madame de Valois? She travelled with you, did she not?' Macleod was astounded by this sudden appearance at his front door of Madame de Metz. Was there no one, he asked himself, who was unaware of his presence here with Marie? Madame de Metz took advantage of his confusion. 'Come now, sir, you cannot expect us to stand about here in the street.'

She pushed past him and entered the house before he could object with Lord Melford close behind who smiled and bowed slightly as he passed. Macleod at last regained enough possession of himself to speak.

'You can't come in. I'm in a very important meeting. You must leave at once.'

Kitty slipped in behind him gently and closed the door. Madame de Metz, in the hallway, turned.

'But as you see, we are already in, and I'm sure your visitor, M'sieur Bentley, will not mind our presence. It may well turn out that your business with him is identical to your business with us.' She stood in the hall and shouted. 'M'sieur Bentley, please show yourself, there is no need for shyness.'

Bentley came to the door of the library.

'Madame, I fear you have the advantage over me, you seem to know me but I do not know you.' He looked at Lord Melford. 'Either of you.'

'Then M'sieur Macleod, our host, will introduce us.'

They all stood looking at Macleod.

'Madame de Metz, Lord Melford, this is a Boston business associate of mine, M'sieur Bentley.'

Bentley made no response. Lord Melford gave him a cold look and the slightest of nods. Madame de Metz again took charge.

'Enchantée, M'sieur Bentley. Now, dear M'sieur Macleod, please lead us to Marie so that we can all sit down and discuss our business in a civilised manner.'

Macleod hesitated, but Marie herself appeared in the doorway of the living room and spoke to him from there.

'I have heard everything that was said. Please ask them to come in. I agree, we all need to talk.'

And she disappeared again into the living room.

Madame de Metz smiled and spoke to no one in particular.

'Listening at doorways, it is *not* ladylike. It is the habit of servants, but I think in this case dearest Marie has been wise to listen. Shall we go in, Messieurs?'

And without waiting for an answer, she led the way. Lord Melford followed her, and Bentley reluctantly fell in after them. Kitty alone remained. She curtsied nicely, smiled at Macleod and waited. Macleod gave up. It was his house but he felt anything but master of it. He left Kitty and joined the others in the living room.

Chapter Fifty

Bentley and Melford were standing either side of the large fire-place, the two ladies sitting, but not near each other. Each was in a position to see all the others. No one seemed anxious to begin. Macleod entered, closed the door and Madame de Metz broke the silence.

'I see no one wants to speak first. In that case I will begin. Marie, you know me, you were my friend in New Orleans.'

'Not your friend.'

'As you wish, but we moved together among the same people. Earlier today Lord Melford came to see you. He explained his business and you sent him away. No matter, perhaps you were wise not to make a decision so quickly. Now, I intend to lay my cards on the table. Lord Melford represents the British, his offer is quite genuine. You will ask how I know this and I will tell you. Because I also am employed by the British. I was sent to New Orleans by ... well no matter what the name is. I was sent to find out what I could about a plot organised by the French Government through one Monsieur Fouché, the French Republic's Chief of Police. I had my very strong suspicions of St Clair but my usual methods were of no avail. You, my dear Marie, know better than anyone else why that was so. While I was there I encountered dear Monsieur Macleod who, I freely admit, took me in completely. I watched him carefully. He was, like me, a new arrival who, also like me, wormed his way into the society where St Clair moved. I had been told to watch out for just such a one because he would almost certainly be an agent of the American Government. But as I say, he fooled me. I was convinced that his only interest was you, Marie, that you had captivated him. He made no attempt to get close to St Clair, only to your husband. That was his greatest cleverness. He appeared to avoid totally the man who was, of course, his main target.' She turned to Macleod. 'M'sieur. I salute you.' Macleod ignored her. 'Then St Clair and your husband were murdered and ...'

Macleod's voice cut in.

'Did you kill him?'

'Me, M'sieur Macleod! Why would I kill him? He had the information I needed, information that I had travelled far and worked hard to get. What good would he be to me dead? I assumed that having somehow won Marie's affections, and again I salute you, I naturally assumed that it was you who killed St Clair and de Valois, or had it done by your accomplice.'

'Me!'

Bentley interrupted.

'The matter of who killed who in New Orleans may interest the rest of you but it means nothing to me. In fact the whole of this nonsense can be left to another time, which can be never, as far as I'm concerned. I won't be present to have my time wasted.'

'Monsieur Bentley is right. To business.' Madame de Metz paused, making sure her next words had their full effect. 'I am an agent of the British Crown working against the interests of America.' She looked round at her listeners and saw she had their full and undivided attention. 'And I can vouch that Lord Melford also represents an agency of the British Government, an agency which is responsible for what we may call Britain's informal foreign policy.' Turning to Marie she continued. 'Knowing what you now know and understanding, I am sure, the very parlous position in which it places both myself and Lord Melford, you can believe me, Marie. The offer is quite genuine.'

It was this last part of Madame de Metz's little speech which seemed at last to catch Bentley's attention.

'What offer?'

'Ah, Monsieur Bentley, that at least interests you? That, you do not regard as nonsense. Good. Now, we all know who I am and who Lord Melford is. Perhaps Monsieur Bentley, who so hates his time being wasted, will tell us who he represents. If so, I think great progress will have been made.'

All eyes turned to Bentley but none more interested than Macleod's.

Bentley reluctantly spoke.

'I serve the American Government.'

Madame de Metz, clapped her hands.

'Wonderful, then how fortunate for you to be here when Lord Melford and I called.'

'Fortunate?'

'But of course. You serve the American Government and I have confessed before witnesses that I am an agent of a foreign power. I have identified Lord Melford as also being an agent of that same power. I have stated freely that I work against the interests of your country on its very soil.' Listening to Madame de Metz speaking so brightly of their role as agents, Melford began to look somewhat uneasy, but Madame de Metz continued. 'I confess freely that we are involved in a plot which threatens the American Government. It is not a British plot you understand, but a plot nonetheless. How it threatens America we do not yet know, but if Marie is sensible and accepts Lord Melford's offer, we soon shall. Now, dear Monsieur Bentley, would you be good enough to send out for officers to arrest us and we will all then be quite certain that you are what you say you are, a representative of the American Government.' But Bentley did not move and Melford visibly relaxed. He even went so far as to smile, this time a very genuine smile of relief. 'Alas, it is as I thought. Monsieur Bentley is not quite what he says he is. So, once more, pray enlighten us, Monsieur Bentley, as to who it is you really represent.'

But Bentley still remained silent. Madame de Metz looked at Melford, giving him his cue, which he now felt comfortable in taking.

'Then, Bentley, as you seem not to be entering into the spirit of our little gathering and seem to have nothing more to say, I think it might be time for you to withdraw, and let those of us who have business conclude that business.'

Before Bentley could reply Macleod stepped forward.

'This is my house and I say who stays and who leaves.'

He looked around angrily. He was confused and totally at a loss to know where he stood with any of these people. Bentley, he now felt sure, had lied to him about serving the Government. Madame de Metz he mistrusted from experience and from her own words. Lord Melford, as a British aristocrat, he was happy to mistrust on principle, and it was Lord Melford who spoke.

'You disagree that Bentley should leave, Macleod?'

'Lord Melford, if you are indeed a Lord, though I personally don't give a damn one way or the other, I do think M'sieur Bentley should leave. And I think that you are no more than a low scoundrel and that you also should leave. As for you, Madame, I think it is a very ungentlemanly thing to do to lay the hands of violence on a woman, but if you don't leave of your own accord I'll take the greatest of pleasure in damn well throwing you out. Now get out the lot of you. Get out and stay out. If any one of you so much as knocks on my door once more I swear I'll answer with a pistol in my hand and blow whoever it is to kingdom come.'

There was a shocked silence in the room at this outburst. Then Marie stood up, went to the door and opened it.

'I think Monsieur Macleod quite means what he says and I think, therefore, you should all leave.'

Bentley turned and strode out. Melford hesitated and looked at Madame de Metz for guidance but edged slightly closer to the door.

Madame de Metz rose slowly and gave a gracious smile to Macleod who glared at her.

'Thank you for a most interesting and informative visit, Monsieur.'

Lord Melford left the room followed by Madame de Metz who, when she reached the door, paused and leaned across as if to kiss Marie who drew her face away.

She turned to Macleod, smiled and shrugged, then followed Lord Melford.

Macleod didn't move, his outburst had left him almost shaking with anger. But after a second he came back to life and went into the hall to check that they had all gone. When he returned to the living room Marie was again seated. The sight of her sitting there, frail, defenceless, beautiful, reignited his anger.

'Damn and blast the lot of them, such a collection of lying, cheating, devious …'

'Yes, Jean, I agree with you and I thought you were magnificent,' she paused as Macleod let his anger subside.

'Well, the way they behaved …'

'Was exactly how they should have behaved. They are people from that secret world of intrigue which you and I must try very hard to understand. Now they have gone and we must decide what it is we are to do.'

'Do?'

'Yes, Jean, do. I have information. Obviously it is very valuable information, perhaps even more valuable than I at first thought but, if so, it is also more dangerous. We need help and those people might be the ones who can help us.'

Macleod stood for a second as her words sank in.

'I hadn't thought of that.'

Marie gave a small sigh.

'Think of it now, Jean.'

'Yes.'

'And tell me, who is this man Bentley? Who does he really represent? Is he dangerous or might he help us?'

'I don't know.'

'Do you think he might work for the Americans?'

'I don't know.'

'Do you think you could find out?'

'I don't know.' Marie gave another small sigh. 'I'm sorry, Marie, I lost my temper. It was seeing them all there like carrion crow waiting to peck over you. And when that damned British coxcomb of a lord started to behave as if this was his house, well, I just lost my temper.'

'Never mind, what has passed has passed, but we have learned a little more. I think Madame de Metz and Lord Melford really do represent the British and, if that is so, their offer is almost certainly genuine. The question we must ask ourselves is: who does the man Bentley represent and could we, perhaps, get a better offer from him?'

On hearing her mention money again Macleod went to a chair and sat down. He was out of his depth in almost every way he could think of and had no more idea of how to proceed than the chair on which he sat.

'I think, Jean, I must make contact again with Madame de Metz and you must make contact with your Monsieur Bentley. Do you not agree?'

No, he did not agree.

'Marie, I think today there has been more than enough contact. In fact I feel I have had enough contact to last a considerable time, probably the rest of my life.'

'Of course, I did not mean today. We must leave them for a

237

time. Keeping them uncertain about what we intend will, I think, improve the offers we can get.' Marie stood up. 'Shall I go and tell Amélie that she can start to prepare lunch now? She must be wondering what all the coming and going has been about.'

'Yes, Marie, tell her to prepare lunch, but before she does, ask her to bring me the tray.'

'The tray?'

'The whisky tray. She'll know.'

'Of course, Jean, it has been a busy morning, you deserve a little refreshment.'

Marie left and Macleod sat, staring into space, thinking. It had indeed been a busy morning, although what it had all achieved he had no idea. Was Marie safer or not? He didn't know. What should he do next? He didn't know. Was Bentley a friend or enemy? He didn't know. Was there anything he *did* know? He thought about it and finally came to a conclusion. He didn't know.

Chapter Fifty-one

The pistol shot that killed Amélie came at about two in the morning. The noise of the shot woke Macleod who lay on his bed fully dressed. He recognised it at once for what it was and that it had come from the direction of Marie's room.

Given the events of the day, he had taken the precaution of placing a loaded pistol on his bedside table next to a lamp that was turned down as low as possible. He picked up the pistol and the lamp and hurried from his room through the door which he had made sure was left open.

Along the corridor he caught a glimpse of a shaded moving light which he took to be someone about to descend the stairs. Without stopping he raised his pistol and fired. The crash of the pistol shot echoed about the corridor walls but beyond it Macleod could hear boots hurrying down the staircase. Marie's room door was wide open. He threw the discharged pistol to the floor, turned up the lamp and went in. There was a woman's body slumped across the bed with a large dark stain spreading over the back of her dress. Macleod at once recognised the body as that of Amélie. She was sprawled across Marie who was motionless below her. Macleod gently turned Amélie's head. Her dead eyes stared sightlessly at him. He brought the lamp closer and looked at Marie, her eyes were closed. As he looked they flickered and opened.

'Thank God. I thought you were dead.'

'Am I wounded? I feel no pain but a weight seems to …'

She looked away from Macleod's face, saw the dead eyes of Amélie staring at her and screamed.

Macleod put the lamp on the bedside table, lifted Amélie's body off Marie and laid it carefully on the floor. Marie was whimpering with fear. Macleod knelt beside her.

'Marie, it is all over. I am here.'

'Amélie is dead?'

'Yes. Can you remember what happened?'

'I was asleep, there was a noise. I opened my eyes and there was a light. Someone shouted, then an explosion and something hit me. The next thing I remember is you looking at me and then …'

She put her hands to her face.

Macleod stood up and looked at the body on the floor.

'I must leave you for a moment to reload my pistol. I do not think anyone will return but if they do I will be ready.'

Marie's voice was filled with shock and fear.

'No, you cannot leave me here. I must come with you. I cannot stay here alone.'

'Very well.'

Macleod turned his back as Marie got out of bed but instead of putting on her robe she immediately grabbed his arm. He picked up the lamp, and with Marie clinging to him they left the room and Amélie's body. In the corridor he picked up the pistol. Together they went to the stairs. Halfway down there was a landing where the stairs turned and on the landing a window. Macleod stopped and held up his lamp. One of the upper, right-hand panes was shattered, marking where his shot had gone.

Macleod made a silent prayer.

'Thank God Amélie was more watchful than I and managed to stay awake.'

'Why do you wait? What are you looking at? You must reload your pistol to protect me.'

They came to the bottom of the stairs, crossed the hall and went into the living room. Macleod went to a small table and lit the lamp that stood there. All he needed to recharge his pistol remained where he had laid it out before retiring on the previous evening.

'Here, hold this lamp for me.'

Marie took the lamp. There was no need for a second one, but Macleod wanted Marie to be occupied with something, anything. He began to reload his pistol and Marie watched. After a moment she spoke, her voice calmer.

'What has happened, Jean? Why is Amélie dead? Who was it who killed her?'

'Amélie must have heard or seen something.'

'Then why did she not call you, raise an alarm?'

'I don't know. She must have rushed into your room, got herself between you and the pistol and took the ball that was meant for you. The shot woke me and the assassin knew he had no time for another shot, or time to use a knife, so he ran. I got a shot off at him but missed.' He turned and showed her the loaded, cocked pistol. 'But now you are safe.'

'No. I am safe nowhere. I am afraid. I think I will be killed.'

Marie cast her eyes down and suddenly realised she was wearing nothing but her nightdress. Macleod had already noticed.

'Here, give me the lamp. Now take this pistol and wait. I will go to your room and get you your robe.'

Marie took the pistol and held it with two hands.

'You will be quick.'

'I will.'

Macleod left the room, hurried upstairs, found her robe then returned to the living room. He turned his back as Marie put it on.

'Thank you, Jean, you may turn now.' They stood in silence for a moment, neither sure what to do. Then Macleod picked up the pistol which Marie had put on the table.

'I will put a chair by the stairs and keep guard. You must go up and try as best you can to rest. This night has been an ordeal for you.'

'No Jean, I am calm now, and there is Amélie.'

'Yes, of course, there is Amélie.'

They both stood silent for a moment.

'Do you think she knew she was giving her life to save mine?'

'Perhaps, probably. She certainly stayed awake and watchful to see that you came to no harm, thank God.'

'Poor Amélie. Did she love me so much in so short a time? I think you should put her on my bed. I will sit with her until morning and pray for her soul.'

'I will watch at the foot of the stairs until daybreak. And this time I will not sleep.'

'No, Jean, neither of us will sleep any more tonight. Only Amélie. Come.'

And together they mounted the stairs to put Amélie to rest.

Chapter Fifty-two

Bentley arrived at Darcy's rooms, threw off his cloak and hat, snuffed his dark lantern and sat down heavily. Darcy brought him a brandy which he took gratefully and swallowed.

'By God I needed that.' He held out the glass. 'Macleod must have had a pistol by him. He got a shot at me and damn near took my head off.'

Darcy almost dropped the glass he'd taken.

'He saw you?'

'Don't be alarmed. He saw someone. He cannot know it was me.'

Darcy went and poured another brandy.

'If he had a pistol by him do you think he knew you were coming?'

Bentley took a drink.

'I don't see how he could. Maybe he was being cautious. That visit from Melford and the de Metz woman would have rattled him. It certainly rattled me.'

'But you got her?'

'I don't know.'

'Don't know!'

'I hit someone, but I fear it may have been that old French scold of a housekeeper.'

'My God, what did you do, rouse the house when you arrived?'

Bentley finished his drink.

'I got in through the back, went upstairs and found her room all right, but the old woman must have heard me.'

'The housekeeper, not Macleod?'

'No. If he was close he must have been asleep, but she was obviously sitting up listening somewhere.'

'But why? You say Macleod had a pistol by him. If so, why put an old crock of a woman on guard and go to sleep yourself? It makes no sense.'

'No, no sense at all but there she was. Before I could get a shot off she rushed in, cannoned into me and I dropped the damned lantern. I got my shot away but which one I hit, if either, I couldn't say and I didn't think it was wise to stay and find out. I got my lantern and ran. Macleod was up at once and nearly put a ball in my skull when I was on the stairs. In the dark it was a damn fine shot even to come close.'

Both men sat in silence.

'Well, Bentley, you're the brains in this. If you killed her, all well and good. But if you missed, if she's still alive, what do we do now?'

'The British seem to want her, so first and foremost we must make sure they don't take her.' Bentley held out the empty glass. 'Get me another, then set out writing materials. If she's still alive I must send at once for someone, someone who won't miss.'

Chapter Fifty-three

The night had passed. Marie had dressed and come downstairs soon after day-break and insisted on going into Amélie's kitchen to make coffee. They sat together at the table in the living room, Macleod's pistol by his cup.

'The question is, will they try again and, if so, when? You were right, Marie, and I see now that I was wrong. You are not safe here in Boston, not safe even here in my house. You are still in great danger and it seems that I alone cannot protect you. Fool that I am, I realise at last that you will remain in great danger wherever you are until this whole business is finished one way or the other. These people can reach across the Atlantic as if it was just the other side of some street in London or Paris.'

'But if that is so where can we go? There must be somewhere, somewhere I can be safe.'

'First you must tell me all you know. If I am to help you I must know what this is all about.'

'You are right, my danger has become your danger. I will tell you and then we will decide what it is best to do. There is a plot as you know and, as Madame de Metz said, it originates in Paris from the office of Monsieur Fouché, who is head of their police. It is aimed, of course, at the British, to weaken them in their war against France. It is aimed at the British but it is to be carried out here in America. Fouché plans to make America into a kingdom, but a kingdom controlled from Paris.'

Macleod couldn't believe what he was hearing.

'That's madness. How could anyone turn our Republic into a kingdom? It couldn't be done.'

'Oh, but it could. There are important people in America who have agreed to work with Fouché, people with money and people high in your Government. That his plan has gone so far should already show you how clever this Fouché is.'

'You mean there are traitors, traitors even in our own

Government?'

'How else could it be done? St Clair was a part of the plan and wanted to tell people what a great man he was, but of course that was impossible. So he talked of it to my husband. He boasted how clever Fouché was and how stupid the Americans. De Valois laughed when St Clair laughed but did not comprehend, he was too stupid to understand. That I might hear did not bother them. I was a woman, a doll, nobody. I was invisible. But I understood, and I understood that what I heard was my chance of freedom, so I listened. It was as if I was in the schoolroom again, learning my lessons. I sat in a corner, sewing, listening and remembering. There is a natural antagonism in your country, the North and the South. The North has factories, the South has plantations. The North is for barbarians, the South is for gentlemen. The South must have slaves, the North opposes slavery. There are other things which I didn't understand, things to do with your politics.

'The plan is simple but very clever. Fouché's agents are well placed to see that the North and the South can be brought to the point of civil war. When they are at each other's throats and know they cannot draw back, a group of men will step forward. They will talk of the horror of civil war, the certain disaster that awaits all unless a solution can be found, they will propose the one plan that could avert such a calamity. They will put forward a man who can be trusted by both sides. A man who has served his country, a man who has held high positions, positions of trust, untouched by loyalty to North or South, whose loyalty is to America alone. They will ask him to form a government, a temporary government to find a way forward and avoid civil war.'

'Which man?'

'I do not know.'

'But how will one man achieve what Fouché wants?'

'Because that man will say that a Republic has been tried and has failed, the only way forward is to establish a monarchy, to put on the throne a king, a ruler in name only but one who will be above all politics. A government which served such a king could lead the country back from the abyss. It will be a temporary kingdom only, he will say. When the time is right the king will be invited to step down and the Republic restored. Of course this king will choose a government of Fouché's agents and once in power they will keep power. They will establish an alliance with France and Fouché will have what he wanted, an ally across the Atlantic to threaten the British.'

Macleod thought for a moment then shook his head.

'No. It couldn't happen. America would never let things get to the point of civil war. To think so is sheer madness.'

'I think Monsieur Fouché would disagree with you. The Governor of New Orleans answers to Paris and allows Fouché's agents to provoke unrest. They stir up the slavery problem and do many other things. The plan is real, the plan is working and unless the British do something to stop it, the plan will succeed.'

'The British! Why the British? If you know who these traitors are we must go to the American Government. Once they know what is happening and who is involved they will stop this treason. We must go to the Government. You must give them the names.'

'I cannot.'

'Yes you can. Forget the British, forget the money. For your own safety and mine, for the safety of America you must.'

'I cannot.'

'Damn it, Marie, I have risked my life for you. How can you now …'

'But, Jean, you don't understand. I know of the plot, what it is, how it works, but I do not have the names of your traitors. I saw names on letters in the satchel but only briefly. How could I remember them? I have no names to give to the American Government, I have no names to give anyone, only what I know about the plot.'

The full meaning of Marie's words sank in.

'My God. But don't you understand, without names your information is useless to us.'

'No, Jean, I know the plot, I can tell them all …'

'Tell who? How would you know who to tell? If, as you say, Fouché has agents high up in Government, who could you trust?'

Suddenly it dawned on Macleod that what he was pointing out to Marie applied just as well to himself. Who could he trust? He had given his papers to Jeremiah Jones, and Bentley said they had been used to identify a murdered man as himself. If true what did that mean? Bentley said he worked for the Government, but which Government, the true one or the treasonable Government-in-waiting? As Macleod thought about it he became aware that there was now no one, literally no one, he could trust with Marie's information, not even the General. He and Marie were completely isolated in a world of secrets, lies, intrigue and murder and, if he believed in Marie's plot, helpless while his beloved Republic was being eaten away from within.

'Marie, if what you say is true, then we are on our own. There is no one we can trust but each other.'

'But the British, they will help us surely? If we go to Madame de Metz and Lord Melford they will listen and reward us. They will make us safe.'

'What do you really know of Madame de Metz?'

'She was accepted in New Orleans. I never thought to question who she was. I suppose it was the same with others.'

'What if Madame de Metz really works for Fouché? What if she was sent to spy on St Clair? Maybe Fouché was worried he might become careless. We know that he had become careless. What if she decided that St Clair had become a risk? What if she even found out that he had been careless in talk in front of you?'

'Well?'

'She would silence him and then try to silence you. We were followed from New Orleans and an attempt was made on your life at Charleston. We arrive here and she is waiting for us, and tonight there is another attempt on your life. Would you still say we can trust what Madame de Metz chooses to tell us about herself?'

'But this man Bentley, you say you know him. Can he help us?'

'No, I find I don't know Bentley at all.'

Marie sat silent for a moment, thinking.

'Then it is as you say, Jean, we are alone.'

'Alone unless we find the names and then we will know who we can go to. You are sure you have no names, not even one?'

'No, none. Except,' she paused, 'except perhaps one.'

'Thank God, what is it?'

'It will be no good to us.'

'Tell me anyway, anything is better than nothing.'

'I only heard it once.'

'And it was?'

'Cardinal Henry Stuart, Bishop of Frascati.'

Chapter Fifty-four

Macleod tried hard to retain control of himself. They needed names and even one name might be enough. But of all the names and titles she might have given him, this one made him despair.

'A bishop?'

'More than a bishop. A cardinal in Rome. St Clair said he would be the one who would become the new king. That it was a great joke on the British.'

'It seems more like a great joke on us.'

'No, no, I did not understand, but that is what he said.'

Something stirred in Macleod's memory.

'A cardinal as king? No, it makes no sense. Did he say anything else?'

'Only that the great joke on the British would be that he could finally succeed where his elder brother had failed.'

Suddenly, forgotten memories from Macleod's childhood came flooding back sharply into focus and he was once again a child at his father's knee listening to stories of the old hatreds. How his father had fought for the Catholic Prince Charles Edward Stuart.

'My God!'

'What is it, does the name help us?'

'I don't know but I think I might know why Fouché would choose a Catholic cardinal to be his king. If Cardinal Bishop Henry Stuart is the younger brother of Charles Edward Stuart then he is the last Jacobite claimant to the British crown. If Fouché could put him on a throne, any throne, it might re-ignite the Highlands. At the very least London would have to garrison Scotland again. A Jacobite king with his own kingdom looking at Farmer George's throne from across the Atlantic. The Stuart cause would live again. My God, it's not madness, Marie, it's genius.'

Marie misinterpreted what she saw as a burst of enthusiasm.

'It has helped? It will make us safe?'

'I don't see how.'

'Will this Cardinal Henry know the names we need, the important ones?'

'If he is involved ...'

'Yes, if he is?'

'Well, I doubt he would get involved with something like this without being sure there were men behind it whom he could trust to carry it through.'

Marie clapped her hands.

'Then we have a name, Cardinal Bishop Henry Stuart.'

'But he's in Rome and we're in Boston. I don't see how it helps us.'

'Then we must go to Rome. We must see this Cardinal and we must ask him for the other names.'

'Please, Marie, even if we could get to Rome and managed somehow to see him, why would he give us the names? You must be sensible.'

'No, Jean, it is you that must be sensible. Twice they have tried to kill me here in America. Amélie lies dead upstairs. Now we know that even here, in your home, I am not safe. To be sensible is to go away, to be sensible is to go to Rome. This Henry Stuart is a Bishop, a Catholic priest, he cannot refuse to help, to save my life.'

'But how could we get there?'

'You have money, you are rich. You live in this fine house and in New Orleans you had the best clothes and plenty of money.'

'Yes, but money isn't our problem. If it was Fouché's agents who tried to kill you then going to Europe makes it that much easier for them.'

'How could the danger be any greater than it is here? If we move quickly they might not be able to follow us. They would not know we go to Rome, and once there the Bishop will shelter us.'

'But ...'

But Macleod couldn't think of anything to offer in place of going to Rome. He could not trust his own Government, nor keep Marie safe even in his own house.

'Jean, we must go. Last night they failed but now there is no more Amélie to stay awake and be watchful over me.'

Macleod was stung by her words, but he could not deny their truth. He had slept while Amélie stayed awake and watched. It was Amélie who had kept her alive and was now dead. In Charleston it had been the sailors who had watched over her while he allowed himself to be stunned in an alley.

'Very well. But if we go, we must go at once. I will make the best arrangements I can.'

'We will see the Cardinal, Jean, and all will be well. Do you not think so?'

'Of course.'

It was a very small lie, considering their situation. For uppermost in Macleod's mind was not how to get to Rome, or how to see the Cardinal, but how to get them both out of Boston alive.

Chapter Fifty-five

'Two pistol shots!'

'Two.'

Molly and Melford looked at each other then back at Gregory who stood, hat in hand, with one eye roving and the other fixed on a point just above their heads. His manner of delivery strongly resembled someone giving evidence before a magistrate.

Molly's response, however, was not in the least like that of a magistrate.

'Damn and blast you, you wall-eyed monkey. Why did you let anyone get in? Didn't you realise he might be after her?'

'Ah, but I wasn't told to stop anyone, was I? I was told to spy out a soft point of entry if there was one. I did that and told you about it. You told me to go back and observe. Your very word, ma'am, observe. So I observed. I observed him going in, heard the shots and I observed him coming out. Then I came back, roused you both and now I'm making my report.'

As Molly seemed temporarily lost for words, Melford took up the questioning.

'Did you recognise him?'

'Yes, it was the man Bentley.'

'Are you sure?'

'Yes, sir.'

'Did he see you?'

'No, sir. I made sure I wasn't seen.'

Melford turned to Molly.

'Is she dead do you think?'

'How should I know?'

'So what do we do?'

Molly turned back to Gregory.

'Go back there, monkey, and see what you can find out.'

If Gregory resented being called a monkey he didn't show it.

'How do you want it done?'

251

'How the hell do I know? You're supposed to be the expert at that sort of thing. Use your judgement.'

Gregory lifted his hat carefully onto his head, turned and left.

'It wasn't his fault, Molly. He was told just to keep an eye on things.'

'Yes, and we both know which of his two blasted eyes he used.'

Melford shrugged. If she wanted to vent her spleen on Gregory, he didn't care much one way or the other. The door opened and Kitty came in.

'I saw Gregory leaving. What did he say?'

'Bentley went into Macleod's house, there were two pistol shots then Bentley came out again. The witless fool just let him walk in and then walk out.'

'Two shots together or a gap between them?' Kitty looked at Molly and Melford in turn, but neither answered. 'Stap me, did neither of you ask?'

Molly said nothing. Melford gave a small shrug of indifference.

'Does it matter?'

'Two shots together would both have come from Bentley. Two shots apart could mean someone must have heard Bentley's shot and taken a pop at him. It would be handy to know, I think, which it was.'

Molly and Melford remained silent. Both knew the question should have been asked.

'Did you think to ask if Bentley was moving normally when he came out?'

Melford tried to regain some little ground.

'Why do you ask that?'

'Because unless he was carrying something with two barrels or a pepper-pot he'd only get one shot. A double barrel is a heavy piece to cart about and a pepper-pot is fine if you're almost in touching range, but useless even from even a small distance. My guess is Bentley only got one shot off. If I'm right, ask yourselves who the second shot came from?'

Molly answered.

'Macleod.'

'Yes, Macleod. And if he hit Bentley it would likely show in the way he moved.'

'But why does it matter? If the first shot was Bentley's then Macleod was already too late.'

'If Macleod was ready with a pistol by him then it means he was expecting something like this to happen. Bentley got his shot off, but if they were ready for him who's to say what he was shooting at, maybe no more than a bolster stuffed under the sheets. He used a masked lantern I suppose? He couldn't have gone in blind, he'd need to see what he was doing.'

Molly was beginning to regret her outburst against Gregory. Kitty was asking the right questions, the ones she should have asked but hadn't, and now she had no answers.

'I don't know, I suppose he had a lantern.'

'Mother of mercy, Molly, what's got into you? Other than Bentley getting in and out and two shots being fired, do you know anything?'

The reply was surly but honest.

'No.'

Kitty stood up.

'Then I'll go and get Gregory, bring him back and we'll see what else he knows. You sent him back to find out what he could, you managed that much?' Molly nodded. 'Good. Now, we have two ways it can go. One, she's dead. If that's the way it is we have to take Macleod and hope she spilled what she knew to him. Two, she's not dead. If she's alive then Bentley's little outing has finished any chance of negotiating, so we'll have to croak Macleod. It's the only way we'll get her from him. While I'm out give your minds, such as they are, to working out what we do once we know the way things have gone.'

Having delivered her summary of the situation Kitty left them and went in pursuit of Gregory.

'Well, Molly, I think we've both just had a good telling off by your maid.'

'We have and we deserved it. I was a fool and you were a dummy. Well, forget that and let's do as she says and give some thought to what we do now.'

'Which is?'

'We make Macleod the mark. If she's alive we want him dead, if she's dead, we want him alive and somewhere we can put the squeeze on him. Either way we want him, and we'll have to look sharp and go careful. If he was ready for Bentley then I was right and he's not the booby you took him for.'

'No, it seems I was wrong, though God knows why he chose to play such a part. And I confess I hadn't anticipated any such move from Bentley.'

'No, nor I.'

'Why did Bentley go for her though? If he wants her dead then that makes him with the French doesn't it?'

'Perhaps. If the French think she knows anything they'll want her mouth stopped all right but I don't see how he could have been sent after her. He lives here. He's a respected citizen not somebody sent here to finish her off.'

'True. But he's in this, we know that.'

'Oh, he's involved all right, but I don't know how.'

'Well, whoever he's working for, he seems to want her dead.'

'Right, and if he missed tonight he might try again, so we have to move before he does. If she's not dead and Macleod put any kind of hole in Bentley we'll have had a mighty big slice of good fortune, and the way things are that's exactly what we need.'

Chapter Fifty-six

Macleod was furiously busy all morning making preparations for their departure. He left his house as soon as he knew the offices of his clients would be open. His first visit was to a feed and grain merchant. He stayed ten minutes, talked of nothing in particular, then left, leaving the feed and grain merchant extremely puzzled as to why he had called at all. His next call was on a client who sold farm machinery. He stayed a similar time as on his first visit and once again left the client with no clear idea of why Macleod had chosen to call on him. The third client was an importer-exporter in a substantial way of business. Here he stayed for nearly half an hour and left the client in no doubt whatsoever of what it was he wanted from him. He then went to his own offices and spent an hour giving detailed instructions to his clerk. Then, satisfied that all he could do was done, he returned home.

'How long you have been, Jean. All the time you were gone I was terrified that someone would come.'

'I'm sorry, Marie, I had to be sure no one could know what we were planning to do. If I was followed, all they will know is that I went to visit three of my clients and then spent some time at my office.'

Marie made no effort to hide her disappointment and frustration.

'Mon Dieu, you visit clients? You go to your office? This is not time for business. You said we would go to Rome yet now you ...'

'It was not business, Marie. The third client I visited is a merchant who's building up his trade in the Mediterranean. He usually has a ship a week going out or coming in. There's one that leaves for Livorno early tomorrow and he's given us passage on it. I told my clerk to wait about half an hour after I left the office and then go to the docks and arrange things. Speed in this is vital. We have to get you away before ...' but he decided not to finish the sentence. 'As I say, speed is vital.'

'Oh Jean, that is wonderful. When will we know our passage is secured?'

'Soon I hope, very soon. Now you must go and pack whatever you will need for the voyage.'

'Thank you, Jean. I am sorry I doubted you.'

'No matter. My clerk will see that supplies, bedding and all other necessaries for the journey will be delivered on board. After that he will go to the bank, withdraw money and arrange for letters of credit. Then he will come to the house with a carriage. When he does we must be ready.'

'But if they are watching?'

'Let them. We shall be out of the house, into the carriage and off to the docks before they can do anything. I hardly think they will have enough men watching the house to mount a kidnapping in broad daylight on a busy street.' Macleod felt more than a little satisfied with himself. He had been quick and he had been clever. Bentley, Lord Melford and Madame de Metz may be the agents, the ones familiar with intrigue, but had they known what he had done, they would realise that he was not without resource himself. 'Go now, Marie, and pack what you think you will need.'

Marie left and Macleod stood feeling a little deflated. He had done all that was necessary, now he could do nothing but wait.

He went to the table where his loading materials lay. He gathered them together into the weapons case from which he had laid them out and took them and the pistol to his room. He packed his clothes and other necessities into his trunk and laid the pistol and case carefully on top of his clothes. Having secured the trunk he carried it down the stairs, returned to the living room and waited.

About ten minutes later Marie returned.

'I have packed a small box. I have put it by your trunk in the hall.'

'You should have asked me to bring it down for you.'

'No, I must not be a delicate thing, a doll. Now you need a woman by you. But there is something you can do for me.'

'Name it.'

'Would you come and pray with me by Amélie? I sat with her through the night, but now we must leave her here, without benefit of priest or proper burial. She served you faithfully for many years and last night she saved my life by giving her own. There is no way we can try to repay her now except by praying for her soul.'

'Of course I'll pray with you.'

'Thank you.'

They went up to Marie's room and both knelt down by the bed. They both crossed themselves and Marie began the words of a prayer which Macleod's mother had often used with him as a child when she took him to mass on Sundays. It was a prayer for the dead. He joined in and when he did Marie stopped and looked at him.

'You know this prayer?' Macleod nodded. 'Are you Catholic?'

'Yes, though a bad Catholic these days, one who hasn't seen the inside of a church for many a year.'

'Ever since your wife and child were killed when you were away in the army?'

'Yes. How did you know?'

'Amélie told me about how they died from British cannon fire. You had put them where you thought they would be safe but it was not so. They died. She told me of your grief and how it turned to hate for the British. We talked so much about you. She liked to talk about your childhood, your wife, your child. She cared for you very much, Jean.'

Macleod was silent for a moment.

'I didn't realise.'

Marie was silent for a moment, then turned.

'Must we leave her here like this? Could we not do something?'

'No, to make any arrangements would be too dangerous.'

'I see.'

Marie hung her head and Macleod forced himself to think.

'But when we are safely on board our ship and ready to leave, I could send a note to my clerk telling him that Amélie is here and asking him to make whatever arrangements he can. To use his own judgement.'

'A mass, a requiem?'

'Amélie was shot, murdered. I cannot ask him to go beyond the law, but if he trusts me, if he is prepared to believe that I could never have ...'

'Of course he trusts you, Jean, as I trust you. He will take care of Amélie for your sake. Now we must pray for her soul. Until you can send your note it is all we can do.'

They began the prayer again and when it was finished they knelt in silence until their thoughts and prayers were interrupted by a ringing at the front door.

Macleod rose quickly.

'Come, Marie, that will be my clerk with the carriage.'

The dry clerk stood smiling at the door, beyond him was a covered wagon.

'You told me discretion was all in this matter, sir, so I used my judgement. Had I been followed then a carriage might have given a warning of what was afoot. But a wagon, sir, is no more than a wagon. Who would notice one more in the street?'

Macleod turned to Marie.

He was concerned that such a form of transport might create a repeat in her of his New Orleans experience. But Marie seemed quite unconcerned. She looked past him at the clerk.

'Tell him to be quick, Jean, to load our luggage so we may be gone.'

But the clerk needed no interpretation.

'Hi, driver, luggage here.'

And the carter climbed from his seat and began to manhandle the trunk and box into the wagon.

The clerk continued as the carter worked.

'You and the lady can go straight to the docks and board at once. I've arranged that bedding and supplies be brought on board for you. I'm afraid it will not be a comfortable journey for the lady, but I did the best I could.'

Macleod turned to Marie.

'Get your cloak and bonnet, we leave at once.' He turned to the clerk. 'You have everything I asked for?'

The clerk handed him the small leather satchel he had been holding.

'Yes, sir, all in here and just as you asked, money in gold and silver and letters of credit good at any bank in Europe.'

'Well done. I'll get my cloak and hat and we'll be on our way.'

The driver, having loaded the luggage, resumed his seat as

Marie came to the door wearing a cloak and bonnet. She allowed the clerk to assist her into the back of the wagon while Macleod pulled the front door of the house shut, locked it, then handed the key to the clerk.

'Goodbye, sir, and good luck to you both. I'll be sure and look after things here.'

Macleod climbed up beside the carter and looked down at the clerk.

'Thank you, you'll not find me ungrateful when I return, I promise you.'

'Tush, tush, sir, no need for that. Now, off you go,' and he called across to the driver, 'drive on. To the docks and make all the haste you can.'

Chapter Fifty-seven

The driver twitched the reins and touched the horse with his whip and the wagon began to move off. The clerk watched them for a minute then moved off himself in the opposite direction.

A small way up the street a figure emerged from an alleyway and watched the carriage leave. It was a stocky figure in a tall hat with large fists clenched at his side. He watched the clerk walk away from the house and then set off at a brisk pace in the direction the carriage had taken.

An hour later the same stocky figure was once again making a report to Molly, Kitty and Lord Melford.

'Sails early tomorrow, bound for Leghorn, Italy. Captain got his orders from the owner this morning sudden like. Seems he's a business client of Macleod's. Clerk did the arrangements so it looks like I watched the wrong man. They're clean away I'd say.'

'Dammit, Gregory, couldn't you have done something?'

'Like what, sir?'

'Stopped them in some way.'

'What would you suggest, sir? Hauling them out of the wagon and overpowering them on the street?'

'Don't be so damned impertinent with me ...'

'Leave it, Melford, it's no good blaming Gregory. Macleod's been too sharp for us once again. I'm damned if I can make him out. One minute he behaves like a fool and the next he's as sharp as a razor. What do you think, Kitty?'

'Well, they're running and I think Gregory's right, they're clean away. I'd say it's finished here for us and I don't see that we can get anywhere by trying to follow them. It could be days or weeks before we could get passage on another ship, and if we got one then what would we do when we got to Italy? We've no idea why they're going or what they'll do. No, they're clean away, all right.' Kitty paused a moment. 'That being the case, unless you can come up with something, Molly, I'll take what money you think is fair and be on my way.'

Molly took Kitty's words very calmly.

'Is that how you want it? I can't say this country has been kind to us. You sure staying here is better than going back?'

'I think it will be, Molly. I don't see any future for me back in London. Trent isn't the forgiving kind and I don't fancy turning up empty-handed. His idea of fair payment may have more to do with my neck than my purse. I like what I've seen here in Boston and nothing is known against me. You never know, some kind man might take a fancy to me and make an honest woman of me.'

Molly laughed.

'Don't ask for miracles, girl, they only happen in the Bible.'

Disbelief struggled with anger in Melford's voice.

'What are you two women talking about? She can't just walk out. Of course we must go after them. Dammit we are in the service of His Majesty's Government.'

Kitty gave him a pitying look.

'Service of the Government, my arse. I'm here because it was a choice between this and the rope. Molly's here for the money and why you're here, God alone knows, but whatever we were here for as far as I'm concerned it's over.' She turned again to Molly. 'Quick partings are best so I'll get my things and be on my way.'

'As you like.' Molly walked across to a drawer out of which she took a leather bag. She opened it and counted out some coins. Then she put the bag away, came back to Kitty and held out her hand. 'That's fair I think?'

Kitty took the coins and counted them.

'It'll get me started. Why not stay over here yourself? Like I say, Trent isn't the forgiving kind and you'll be going back empty-handed.'

'You're forgetting my kid.'

Kitty gave a shrug, gave Melford one last brief look and left the room. Melford watched her go then turned to Molly.

'Is that it? Does she just walk away?'

'What did you want her to do, sing a song and do a dance? She's right, we're finished over here. They're away and it would be useless to follow.'

'You mean give up?'

'I mean go back to London. We won't be the only ones looking for what Trent wants. Maybe somebody else fared better than we did. Go to the docks and find out when we can sail for England.'

'I must protest. There must be something we can do.'

'Like what?'

Melford bent his mind to the problem but without result. As a last effort he resorted to bluster.

'Our plain duty is to ...'

'My plain duty will be to give your backside a good kick if you don't do as I tell you. We're for England now and the sooner the better. Oh, and when we get there, I'll give you the honour of reporting our progress over here to Mister Trent. Like Kitty said, he's not a man who takes bad news well and he might decide to vent his spleen on the messenger. Still, you're a big strong man, Melford, and a Lord too, so Trent doesn't worry you, does he? Now shove off and get us on the first ship out of here bound for England.'

Chapter Fifty-eight

The sudden departure of Marie and Macleod from Boston wrought much the same effect on Darcy as it had on Lord Melford.

'Hell and damnation, Bentley, we've lost them.' Bentley sipped his tea showing little concern. 'It was your fault. Going in with a pistol was a mistake, and missing was a worse one. No wonder they've made off.'

'Well, one way or another they're gone so it doesn't concern us any more.'

'You're damned calm about it. What if our friends don't take such a measured view of what's happened?'

'Do you think they might not? Well, well. And if they do why should that concern you? If mistakes were made they were mine not yours.'

'And what if they choose not to make that same fine distinction but think we acted together in this mess?'

'Ah, well, in that case whatever happens to me will almost certainly happen to you.' He held out his cup. 'More tea, if you please. As I've said before, damn fine tea this. Come to that, you said you'd get me some but I don't remember receiving any.'

Darcy was standing in front of Bentley. He ignored the proffered cup and glared down at him.

'Damn and blast the tea. I tell you I won't sit still and be blamed for your blunders.'

'Then by all means stand, or sit or lie down, just as you wish but, as my host, I tell you once more I should like another cup of tea.'

Darcy hesitated for a moment then snatched the cup, refilled it and handed it back.

'Take your damned tea.'

'Thank you.' He took a slow sip. 'Now, as for this blunder of mine, as you call it. Our purpose, and I *do* say ours, was to make sure that the de Valois woman could not take her information to any agency of the American Government. One way was to kill her. Even had I been successful, ask yourself would it have been the best way to deal with the matter?'

'Well as you didn't kill her it turned out to be no way at all.'

'Now there you are wrong, Darcy. As usual you don't seem to be able to see beyond the end of your nose.' Bentley's voice took on a patronising tone and he gestured with his free hand. 'To rise in this world, as I have done, one must be aware of the world at large, the world beyond the end of one's own nose.'

His manner had the desired effect and Darcy's anger increased.

'To hell with your talk. Talk is cheap and talk won't stop her mouth. I tell you ...'

'No, but a wide ocean will.'

Darcy was about to speak, but suddenly thought better of what he was about to say.

'A wide ocean?'

'Let us assume that my shot had done its work, that I had killed her. What then?'

'Then she'd be dead and her information gone with her.'

'And we'd have a dead woman on our hands. Women of station don't get murdered in their beds in Boston. There'd have been an outcry, an investigation. Would you have preferred that?' Darcy didn't answer. 'And then what of Macleod?'

'What of him?'

'How could we know whether the de Valois woman hasn't already told him all she knew? We couldn't. So we would have had to kill Macleod and I doubt that would have proved at all an easy task. I was told he was dead in New Orleans and yet up he pops, alive and well, in Boston. I am now told that our friends in New Orleans made a try for the woman in Charleston, but he prevented them somehow. Now he spirits her quickly away, out of our reach. He's proving a very resourceful fellow is our Lawyer Macleod, and I for one am very glad that he is.'

'How so? His resourcefulness, as you call it, has taken her out of our reach.'

'Nose, Darcy, do try to look beyond the end of it. Out of our reach perhaps but more importantly out of the reach of the British agents who are here to find out what she knows. By taking ship for Italy he has quickly and efficiently removed her from any contact with the British which, for our purposes, would have probably been just as bad as contact with our own Government. He has kindly placed the Atlantic Ocean between the woman's information and Washington. Do you know what I think, Darcy?'

'No, Bentley, patently I do not.'

'Then I will enlighten you. I think he's run to keep her safe, that he cares more about her than he does about his duty. I think our friend Lawyer Macleod has been bitten in the leg by the tender passion. Not that it matters one way or another, because if they're both in Italy doing God knows what, they're not in Washington reporting to a certain highly placed individual who answers directly to the President. Now, Darcy, wouldn't you agree with Shakespeare?' Darcy looked blank. 'That what we have at the end of the day is, "a consummation devoutly to be wished"?'

Darcy didn't answer. He felt sure there was a flaw in Bentley's argument, possibly a fatal flaw, but he was damned if he could put his finger on it so he changed the subject.

'Why Italy?'

'Why not? It must have been the first ship he could get them on. He'd probably have settled for St Petersburg if it had been going there. No, believe me, Darcy, neither the woman nor Macleod threaten us or our friends any more. We keep our heads and get on with our work in hand. As I said, I have received another report and, apart from telling me of the Charleston incident, it requires you to go to Philadelphia. We had a recent setback there if you remember, nothing serious but not helpful, distinctly not helpful. Two good men lost and others sent home with their tails between their legs. Washington is getting too active, too active by half. You are to go to Philadelphia to oversee the repair work. I have the names for you.'

Bentley put his hand into his coat and threw a folded sheet of paper onto the table by his chair. Darcy picked it up.

'They mean nothing to me.'

'Good, they shouldn't. Just go to your usual contact and he will introduce you to them. Tell them what they need to know and how we operate.'

'They are completely trustworthy, I suppose?'

'God, Darcy, how would I know? As far as I know they're both Washington men planted on us by our friend, the General. I have been sent those names and told to get it organised. I must do as I am told and you, in turn, must do as you are told. Look again at those names well enough to remember them then burn the sheet.' Bentley stood up. 'And now I really must be on my way.'

'What about the British agents?'

'What about them? They've missed just as we did. Macleod and Madame de Valois are gone and they can't very well follow. I dare say they'll head back to wherever it is they came from. There's nothing further for them here. No, Darcy, our little storm is over, the teacup is once more at rest and it's back to business as usual. I'll see myself out.' He walked to the door where he stopped. 'Don't forget my tea this time, there's a good fellow.'

Without doubt he heard the teacup shatter against the closed door as he went down the stairs but he did not return to enquire what the noise had been.

Three days later Fanny Dashwood, though without a maid, and Lord Melford, still accompanied by Gregory, said their farewells to Boston and took ship for Bristol. Four days ahead of them Macleod and Marie were settling into the slow, monotonous rhythms of a long sea voyage, both heartily glad of the repetitive boredom which each day promised. As the days passed there grew in them both not only a feeling of dangers left behind but also a sense of suppressed excitement. Before them lay the Eternal City and perhaps the one man who could make them truly safe.

Chapter Fifty-nine

The late summer in London was being unkind. The wind was in the east and cold. Lord Melford had expected just such a cold and uncomfortable reception from Trent when he returned with his report from America.

That was what he had expected.

'But Melford, my dear fellow, don't take it so hard. You failed, true, but you did your best. Who could ask more?'

Melford was puzzled by Trent's manner, not only puzzled but suspicious.

'You take it all very calmly, Trent, too damned calmly I think.'

Trent grinned.

'Yes, I *do* take it calmly don't I? Which means what, do you think?'

'That the outcome doesn't disappoint you?'

Trent's grin widened slightly.

'Bravo, Melford. I hoped that a bit of action in the field might sharpen you up. I see I was right. So, if I'm not disappointed, why did I go to the trouble of sending Molly to New Orleans and make you follow her to Boston?'

Melford bent his mind to the question once more, but this time no quick answer came.

'I have no idea.'

The grin disappeared and gave way to mock surprise.

'What, none? Well, it doesn't matter. You and Molly have served your purpose, *that's* what matters. Where is Molly by the way?'

'She preferred me to bring the report of our mission to you.'

'Did she now? Why was that I wonder? She couldn't have thought that I might be upset by your supposed failure, do you? That I might vent my feelings somehow on whoever brought me the bad news? Obviously you don't think so, Melford. You, I am sure, had no reluctance to report your failure to me.' Melford was anything but reassured by the tone Trent used despite the words. 'I am not the sort of man who shoots the messenger when the news displeases me.'

'Of course you're not, Trent, but she's only a woman and you know what women are.'

'Do I? Well, let's say that perhaps I know what *some* women are. Some women are clever rogues who know how to look after themselves.' Trent smiled, but there had been a nasty edge in his voice which Melford had noted. 'As I said, Melford, I don't shoot the messenger.' The smile disappeared. 'I have other people who do that sort of thing for me.' Melford shifted in his chair uncomfortably. The smile returned. 'But enough of that, what to do next? That's the question.'

'About Macleod and the de Valois woman?'

'Great heavens no. They're of no interest. Where did you say they'd gone, Italy?' Melford nodded. 'On pilgrimage, perhaps? No, I doubt that. Maybe a desire to soak up some classical culture? No? Well, they're gone and as far as I'm concerned so much the better. Where's Kitty Mullen by the way? She didn't return with you, I'm told.'

'She stayed on in Boston, just damn well walked out on us. Molly let her go, I was against it, but Molly not only let her go but gave her money.'

'Ah, clever girls. Kitty knew she had the rope waiting for her if she came back. I could hardly let her wander about telling the world what she'd been up to could I? So, Molly let her walk, did she? Well, we'll see about that. Go and get her. Tell her it went well here and that if she comes tomorrow morning I'll pay her off. Tell her I said it'll not be as much as she'd like but enough considering her failure. That'll reassure her. I don't want Molly street-crying my business any more than Kitty.'

Melford stood up.

'I'll go at once, Trent. She'll be here tomorrow, never fear.'

'Make it sound convincing, Melford. Perhaps I haven't quite made up my mind yet whether I think *you're* still safe to walk the streets with my business locked in your head.'

Melford turned and left, glad to be out of the room.

Trent sat back and gave himself up to thought. So, Mr Macleod, you're taking your lady to see a Cardinal who calls himself a King, are you? Well, much good may it do you both.

There was a gentle knock at his door which then opened and a head appeared. Trent looked at the head.

'Well, don't just stand there, come in.'

Gregory, tall hat in hand, obeyed.

'I saw him leave so I thought I'd come along.'

'Is there anything you don't see?'

'Must be, sir, stands to reason. I can't be everywhere, can I? But there's precious little I want to see that gets by me.'

'Well, Gregory, what have you to tell me?'

'About America?'

'About anywhere. But we may as well start with Boston. Did all go well?'

'Just as you wanted, Mr Trent. The young lady who calls herself Madame de Metz or Fanny Dashwood and is Molly to her intimates was waiting for us as you said. She sent Lord Melford along to try and deal and he made a poor fist of his visit. Then they both went and did no better the second time. But they made enough show to get noticed like you wanted.'

'And made Macleod and the lady run. That was a neat piece of work. I hadn't hoped to get so much so quickly. How did they manage that?'

'They didn't, that was a gentleman, name of Bentley. He was with Mr Macleod when Molly and Lord Melford went to see him.'

'Who was he?'

'Local businessman, wealthy. Client of Macleod, important citizen and well thought of, but a wrong 'un for all of that.'

'How so?'

'The usual. A solid front but frayed round the edges if you knew what to look for.'

'And he was working for?'

'Can't be sure, sir, didn't have the time. I'd say the American Government except it didn't sit right somehow. He was good enough himself, a very confident gentleman, but his main associate, his runner, wasn't good enough for me to swallow, not if the Government was behind him, if you see what I mean.'

'Involved but probably not Government, eh? If not the Government then who, the French?'

'Could be. He did try to kill the de Valois lady.'

269

'Did he by God! A bit sudden wasn't it?'

'Very. Visitor to the house in the morning, attempted murderer in the house the same night. A very sudden man our Mr Bentley.'

'And was that what got Macleod running?'

'Maybe, but I'd lay odds there was more to it than just the attack. I'd say the lady had already given Mr Macleod a reason to leave Boston and Bentley's try with a pistol just hurried them up.'

'Why so?'

'They caught a boat for Italy. Why so far, why Italy? I doubt it was a random choice, there were other ships that would have got them away. If Mr Macleod chose Italy, then there was a reason. Leghorn was the port.'

'Thank you, Gregory. Anything else?' Gregory hesitated. 'Come on, spit it out, man.'

'About Mr Melford …'

'*Lord* Melford.'

'As you like, sir, it's all one to me.'

'What about Lord Melford?'

'He's not a very honest gentleman, is he, nor brave?' Trent ignored the question, so Gregory continued. 'I liked him. I think he'll do very well if he gets the right kind of experience.'

'It doesn't sound like he did so well in Boston.'

'No, but if you'll permit the observation, Mr Trent, he was set up not to do well, wasn't he? So you *could* say he did well after all. I think he's got an instinct for the work. Not everyone has. Put down the right hole I'd say he could start a rabbit as well as the next man. I liked him, for a not very honest, not very brave sort of gentleman.'

'Get out. I've no wish to hear your opinions on Lord Melford or anyone else.' But Gregory stood his ground and waited, his good eye fixed on a point somewhere just above Trent's head while his other roved. 'Well, why aren't you going?'

'I ain't finished.'

'Then damn well finish and get out.'

'I dare say you'll want to see the young lady to get her side of things.'

'Molly?'

'Well you won't.'

'Won't?'

270

'She scarpered. Picked up her kid and done a flit.'

Gregory waited while Trent digested the news.

'Why didn't you stop her?'

'I wasn't told to. I wasn't even told to keep an eye on her.'

'So, why did you?'

'I didn't, she came to me. Told me she was off and gave me this for you.' Gregory pushed his hand inside his hat and when he withdrew it he held a letter which he passed across to Trent. It was the letter of authorisation he had given to her before she left. 'She said to say there was nothing between you now you had that back.'

'Did you read it?'

Gregory's good eye, filled with innocence and honesty, played on Trent's face.

'It's none of my business, Mr Trent. Whatever it is was between you and her, nothing to do with me. I'm just the delivery boy.'

Trent remained silent for a second, then his manner relaxed. He put the letter in a drawer.

'Gone eh? Still, probably no harm done, Molly will know enough to keep her mouth shut. Took her child, did she?'

'Yes.'

'Well it looks like she's gone for good. She must have had a tidy sum left over from what she was given. No matter, I'll have no further use for her after this. If she'd have come back I would have had to … Well, as I said, no matter. Anything more?' Gregory stood silent. 'Then get out. If I need you I'll summon you.'

Gregory raised his tall hat and set it carefully onto his head then turned and left, and Trent put Molly, Macleod and Marie from his mind and gave his thoughts to Joseph Fouché and Cardinal Bishop Henry Stuart.

Chapter Sixty

In the monotonous weeks of their sea voyage, Macleod and Marie discussed repeatedly how they should represent themselves to the Cardinal once they had arrived in Rome. Macleod favoured a straightforward approach – they had come to enlist His Eminence's help to defeat a vile plot against the Government of America. Marie preferred a more subtle approach – they had come to pay their respects to the true King of England and Scotland.

The idea had formed in Marie's mind when, to pass the time in the first weeks out from Boston, Macleod had told her the stories he had heard at his father's knee of his Highland kinsmen. How they and his father had fought the British and the eventual fate they had shared with other Highland clans as Butcher Cumberland did his vile work. What more natural, she argued, that a son whose father had fought with the Bonnie Prince, whose uncles had died for that same Prince, whose family had suffered so much for the Stuart cause, should come and pay his respects to the man he saw as the rightful king of England and Scotland.

Macleod pointed out that it might indeed be a natural thing for such a man to do, if that man had any sort of reason for being in Rome.

Marie recognised that he was right. Without some suitable reason, her plan would not work, leaving only Macleod's direct approach available to them, an approach she felt sure would fail. They had no papers, no letters of introduction, no names which the Cardinal might recognise or accept, nothing which might support the otherwise naked claim of two total strangers.

The most obvious solution to their problem they both avoided, that they were man and wife, newly married, and making a honeymoon tour. But they had been man and wife once already and neither had happy memories of the experience. But that wasn't what made them reluctant to re-examine it under their new and altered circumstances. Their days of proximity on the ship, their talk and time together, and most of all their shared sense of safety and new purpose had combined to form a bond between them that neither was overly eager to examine too closely for fear that the feelings of one might not be the feelings of the other. But as the day of arrival drew closer and neither could think of any alternative it became obvious that one or other would have to speak.

In matters of delicacy women are more able than men, or at least more practical, so the day before the ship docked at Livorno it had been Marie who had finally suggested that, if Macleod came with a new wife, that might be their best solution, and shyly, with suitable reluctance, Macleod accepted Marie's proposal of marriage.

Having settled on being married Macleod readily agreed that they should make use of his Highland connection to find favour with the Cardinal. While in Rome on their marriage tour they had come to receive His Eminence's blessing on their recent union, as a Prince of the Church and as rightful King of England and Scotland.

So it was that, on disembarking at Livorno, Macleod bought a simple gold band and, before dinner, in a tavern where they had taken rooms, placed it on Marie's finger. For a moment there was a silence between them, then Marie, ever practical, turned away and the moment passed. In Livorno they provided themselves with all they needed. Under Marie's guidance they bought clothes and acquired suitable luggage. After a few days they could pass for what they almost were, a well-off American man of business and his pretty young wife. In their new roles they hired a comfortable carriage with driver and postillion and left the port city and began their journey to Rome.

They took a first-floor apartment on the Via Sistina in a district popular among modestly affluent foreign visitors. Their apartment was in a house beside an imposing twin-towered church at the top of a wide flight of white, marble steps and gave its name to them, the Scalinata della Trinità. These steps, Macleod counted one hundred and thirty-eight of them, led down into a fine piazza, the Piazza di Spagna. Once established in their apartment they took to walking down the steps into the Piazza and standing by the great fountain known locally by the quaint name of La Fontana della Barcaccia, The Fountain of the Old Boat, where they discussed how they would locate their Cardinal.

In many ways their situation was idyllic. The evening weather was cool, the surroundings magnificent and their apartment more than comfortable. But Macleod was worried.

He had noticed that, since being in Rome, Marie had grown strangely quiet. She was withdrawn and absorbed and had, on the morning after their arrival, slipped out early before breakfast. On her return, when asked, she said she had visited the nearby church to pray. Her manner concerned him but he put it down to the dangers she had faced continually since the murder of her husband, her subsequent flight, and the life she had been forced to endure. Now, with the interlude of their ocean voyage behind them, they were once again alone and possibly in danger. Macleod himself was feeling the strain of events, how much more, he felt, must their travails have affected a weak and vulnerable young woman like Marie? On the third evening in Rome, after dinner, he sought to offer her comfort as they sat together in the privacy of their rooms.

'You must try to be strong, Marie. So much has happened. I understand if it has taken a terrible toll on your mind and body but I have brought you this far and I swear on my life and honour I will bring you soon to safety. All we have to do is find Cardinal Henry. Believe me I will find a way. You must believe that we will ...'

Marie looked at him, her quietness all too evidently cast off.

'What are you talking about, Jean? Of course we will find him. How hard can it be to find a Cardinal in Rome? We must be careful, that is all. And what is this about my mind and body? Do I seem weak or fearful to you? I assure you I am stronger now than I have ever been. For the first time in my life I know what it feels like to be a woman ...' but here she stopped and seemed to slip once more into the strange manner that had caused him concern.

Macleod was somewhat taken aback by her sudden changes. He didn't understand them. He spoke tentatively.

'But you seem, well, quiet and worried. I thought perhaps that ...'

But he no longer knew what he thought.

'Jean, you are a good man. But you said yourself you are a bad

Catholic. That is nothing. It is natural for any man to be a bad Catholic, it is part of being a man. The Church understands such things. But a woman cannot be a bad Catholic, Jean. It is for the woman to keep the faith and pray for both. If the woman becomes a bad Catholic then both must fear the fire of eternal damnation.'

She paused and to his horror Macleod noticed tears in her eyes.

'But I don't understand, Marie.'

She looked at him with great sorrow.

'I know, Jean, that is what makes it all so terrible. We were children when we first met, naughty as children are naughty, but also innocent. But since then I have grown up and become a woman.'

Macleod was utterly at a loss.

'I'm sorry, Marie …'

'Oh don't be sorry, Jean, the fault is mine, the fault is always with the woman. The woman tempts the man, it must be so. It was so in the Garden of Eden and will always be so. Men have their appetites, appetites given by God. Women have their bodies, also given by God. The woman tempts the man with her body. She cannot help it any more than the man can help being tempted. It is always the woman's fault. It is my fault.'

And the tears came.

Macleod was utterly astounded. If he had understood her correctly she was talking about sin, that they had sinned and their sin had been sexual. But there had been no … No, he was sure, there had been nothing. Yet she was crying, distraught. She was blaming herself. For what?'

He knelt down by her and gently took her hand. She let him take it but did not raise her head.

'Marie, please, explain to me. What is it that you think we have done? What is our sin?'

She raised her head and with her free hand wiped away her tears.

'Oh, Jean, not our sin, my sin. Can you not see, my sin?'

But, try as he might, he could not. He had been married and fathered a child. He would have known.

'But Marie, we have never …'

But somehow the words would not come. He didn't know what the right words were.

'Not you, Jean, you are too good. Me, in my heart, in my heart I have …' And for her, as well, the right words would not come. But Macleod finally understood what it was she was saying. Shock and elation collided in his mind and his heart. He felt dizzy and slightly nauseous. He let go of her hand and stood up to steady himself. She looked up at him. 'Forgive me, Jean, you are right, I am weak. I should have kept it to myself, the sin is mine. I have no right to burden you.'

'Damn the burden and damn all sin. Are you saying that you love me?'

Marie lowered her eyes.

'In my heart, Jean, we are already lovers.'

'Then the least I think I deserve is a kiss. There's been precious little else in this love affair of ours as I remember.'

Marie looked up at him, shocked that he should make light of what she had said. But when she looked at his face she saw a confused and embarrassed man trying hard to deal with a situation which was almost beyond him. She stood up. Macleod took her in his arms and their lips joined. Marie had waited a lifetime for such a kiss and she put a lifetime of broken dreams and shattered hopes into it. Macleod felt the true touch of a woman's passion for the first time and, for a brief moment, the world dissolved for them both and they were alone in a place neither had ever been.

But the paradise of even the most passionate embrace is brief, and when their lips parted the gates of their private paradise, like those of Eden, slammed shut and they were once again a man and a woman playing husband and wife in rented rooms in a Rome tavern going about the prosaic business of trying to save the American Republic and at the same time stay alive themselves. Macleod stood back and Marie wiped the last trace of tears from her eyes and then smiled at him.

'What shall we do, Jean?'

'Do?'

'We play at man and wife but we are not man and wife. Will the game continue or can it be changed?'

Macleod wasn't sure what the question meant. He thought he knew, he hoped he knew, but he wasn't sure.

'Are you asking if we will get married?'

Marie laughed. She seemed wonderfully happy. Macleod didn't

understand, tears, passion and laughter crowding into so little time left him confused. Marie, as usual, became practical.

'Jean Marie Macleod, widower of Boston, will you marry Marie Christine de Valois, widow now of nowhere at all? Will you make an honest woman of me?'

No doubt remained, there it was. She was definitely asking him to marry her! He hesitated.

'Of course, at any other time, well, as I say, of course. But at the moment …' and his words gave out.

Marie looked down.

'I see.'

'Dammit, woman, no you don't. I'd marry you tomorrow if I could. Today, now. God's teeth, I've loved you since we first met in New Orleans. How I've managed to be so close to you for so long and keep my sanity is beyond my power to understand.'

'You *do* love me?'

'Of course I damn well love you.'

'But you won't marry me? Is it because …'

'It's because we're married already.' Macleod saw that she didn't understand what he was trying to say. 'How can we go out and get married when we have told people that we are on our marriage tour.'

'I see.'

Macleod took her once again in his arms.

'I hope you do, Marie. All I want is for us to marry and go back to Boston and become a normal, happy couple and live the most quiet existence on earth. But to do that we must finish what we came to Rome to do. And that means acting out our parts as a married couple.' Marie smiled and gave him a kiss. Macleod held her gently. 'Marie, if we feel about each other as we do. If we love each other and must act the parts of man and wife, could we not …'

Her manner became firm and she pushed him away.

'No, Jean, we could not. I have told you I have already sinned in my heart, I will not put our immortal souls at further at risk. We are not safe, we are still in danger. Think, Jean, what it would mean if we were to die with such a sin on our souls.'

Macleod did as he was bid, reluctantly coming to the conclusion that although he might be prepared to risk eternal flames, Marie, obviously, was not.

'Of course.'

'Tomorrow I will go and arrange to find a Father Confessor.'

'Do you know where to go?'

'Yes, I have made enquiries and there is a convent of White Nuns not far from here. They speak French there and are famous for their embroidery. They get many visitors. We can go there in the morning.'

'We?'

'You only as far as the door. Then you must wait for me.'

'How long will that be?'

'How can I tell?'

'Very well, tomorrow we will go to the nuns and find you a Father Confessor.'

Marie clapped her hands.

'Be happy for me, Jean, soon I will be free of my sin and now we know we love each other we should both be happy.'

Macleod forced a smile.

'Of course I'm happy, how could I not be?'

How indeed?

Chapter Sixty-one

The following morning Macleod and Marie made their way down the steps, crossed the Piazza and made their way through the busy streets thronged with beggars, hucksters, the fashionable and furtive, and always the black garb of religion. They passed along the fine frontages of the Via dei Condotti and turned into the Bocca de Leone which took them, after a short time, to their destination which lay on the Via Vittoria.

The convent had a large crucifix in stone over a dark, heavy street door in the middle of which was a grille. The grille in the door shot open after Macleod had pulled the visitors' bell twice. Marie exchanged a few words with an invisible face, the door opened and Marie disappeared inside. The door closed and Macleod was alone on the steps. He stood for a moment, then walked slowly away.

He had not gone far when he saw a church. Opposite the church was what he took to be a coffee house or tavern of some sort. He walked towards its door and from inside heard the sound of conversation and laughter. He turned away and crossed to the church. He wanted silence, he wanted to think.

The inside of the church was dark and silent. The daylight from the upper windows, having been filtered through either dirt or the deep colours of the stained-glass, gave a modest illumination to the main aisle and the altar, but soon dissipated among the few dark side chapels. Macleod looked at the statue nearest to where he was standing. It was a bishop. He could tell that from the mitre, the crozier and the priestly robes, but there was no hint as to who this bishop-saint might be. Yet a dozen or so candles stood lit in the sand of the tray at his feet. Devotion, a mysterious emotion whether it was to God, a saint, or to a lover.

Macleod thought about what had passed between him and Marie on the previous day. Were they truly in love or had fate thrown them together in a way that somehow counterfeited that emotion? His body wanted her, he knew that.

He glanced up at the face of the bishop saint. Its blind eyes gazed down on him with a look of blank indifference. Macleod walked back to the door of the church and went out into the sunshine. The street was crowded but he decided that he would walk up and down until such time as the convent door was opened and Marie might once again be at his side.

Macleod had spent slightly more than one hour walking back and forth in deep thought and did not notice the convent door open and Marie emerge. She saw him, went to his side and fell into step beside him.

Macleod stopped.

'Have I been so very long, Jean?'

'I didn't notice, I was thinking.'

'About us?'

'Yes.'

She linked her arm through his.

'Come, Jean, I have great news, wonderful news.'

'You have found a Confessor?'

She gave a small laugh and they resumed walking.

'That is not my news but, yes, I was introduced to an old Jesuit Father. He is Confessor to the nuns and we talked together. He will hear my confession tomorrow afternoon.'

Macleod was suddenly alarmed.

'You didn't tell him why we were really here?'

'But of course. If he is to hear my confession I could not begin by lying to him.'

'My God, Marie, you don't know him. How could you give us so quickly into the hands of a total stranger? Why tell him anything about why we're here? If you had to tell him something why not use the story we agreed?'

'But, Jean, he is a priest. He will be my Father Confessor. How could I lie to him?'

'Because our lives may depend on it. What could one more small lie matter in a world of lies?'

'But if I had lied to him today I would only have had to confess the lie tomorrow. You can see that can't you, Jean? If a confession is not a full confession it is no confession at all. You are a Catholic, you must understand.'

Macleod, reminded vividly of his childhood, was baffled by Marie's argument and her obvious certainty of having done the right thing. He could almost hear again the gentle rebuke in his mother's voice when he had questioned one of the many seemingly ludicrous Catholic beliefs she held and expected him to unquestioningly hold, "It is a mystery, Jean, we are not meant to understand. It is enough that God understands".

That Marie should reveal their most intimate secret to someone she had met for the first time was indeed a mystery to Macleod, and one which he suspected not even God might understand.

But Marie had no such qualms about what she had done. She felt she had satisfactorily disposed of the matter so moved on.

'Forget the old priest. Listen to my marvellous news.'

And as they walked up and down the street Marie told Macleod of her marvellous news.

The convent was French-speaking and many of the nuns were themselves of the nobility. It was indeed famous for its embroidery but it was even more famous as the refuge of choice for ladies of royal blood. Queen Clementina had taken shelter there during a tumultuous period in her marriage to James, the Old Pretender. The Countess of Albany, wife of The Young Pretender, Charles Stuart, had also fled there from her brutal and drunken husband. Two of King Louis XVI's aunts had stayed at the convent, having fled France and the Revolution.

Macleod listened as best he could to Marie's enthusiastic history lesson on the fate of royal ladies married and unmarried but, for the life of him, he couldn't see why or how it could be of use to them.

'But, Marie, just because these great ladies fled to this particular convent to escape a brutal husband or worse how does that help our cause?'

'Because I explained to the Mother Superior that before his death I was married to the youngest son of the Duc de Toulouse.'

'I hope to God you didn't tell her how he died?'

'No. I had to use a small lie. How could I tell the Mother Superior that he died in bed with a man at his side?'

'Or that they both were shot.'

'Oh that wouldn't have mattered, but to die in such a sin, to die in the arms of another man. I couldn't bring myself to tell her that.

But it doesn't matter because I will confess the lie tomorrow and all will be well.' Macleod raised his eyes to heaven in disbelief but Marie, not noticing, went on. 'I told her that I was newly married, I will confess that tomorrow as well, and that my husband and I were taking a tour before returning to Boston. I told her that your father had fought for Prince Charles and that your uncles had died in his service.'

'What good did you think that would do?'

'I am the widow of the son of a Duke, the Mother Superior is herself a lady. She sets store by such things. When I said we wished to ask the Prince's brother, Cardinal Henry, to give a blessing to us on our marriage she was delighted and will write a letter of introduction to the Cardinal which she will give me tomorrow. There, is that not truly wonderful news? Tomorrow we will have a letter of introduction, I will have made my confession and soon all our troubles will be over. Tell me you are pleased, Jean, tell me I have done well for us.'

Macleod's feelings were mixed, but he had to admit that, with a letter of introduction from the Mother Superior, their task had suddenly become much simpler.

'You have done wonderfully, Marie, I don't know how we would have seen the Cardinal without such a letter. Where does he live?'

The smile on Marie's face disappeared.

'Oh, Jean, I don't know. The Mother Superior didn't tell me and I never thought to ask.'

Macleod gave her arm a small squeeze.

'No matter, you can ask tomorrow.'

And they continued their walk in the warm sunshine. All of a sudden Rome seemed a happy place, full of beauty and bright promise.

They did not look back at the convent door as they walked away. If they had done so, they might have seen an elderly figure in a long black soutane and a broad-brimmed black hat leave the convent and watch them for a moment before heading off in a hurry.

282

Chapter Sixty-two

The following afternoon Macleod left Marie at the convent door and again began his patrol of the street, his mind far away in planning the forthcoming meeting with the Cardinal. Busy with his thoughts he did not see the man hurrying towards him. The man, also not looking where he was going, blundered into Macleod and a sheaf of folio papers he had been carrying spilled from his arms. Indeed it was reading one of these pages while hurrying that had caused the collision.

The man launched into an unintelligible flood of what Macleod assumed were apologies but as Macleod spoke no Italian he could not adequately respond.

'Pray, sir, don't apologise ...'

The flow of meaningless words stopped and the man resumed in English.

'Ah, an Englishman.'

'No, sir, *not* English.'

'Not English?'

'American.'

A slight breeze caught one of the pages at their feet and the man moved quickly, bent down and caught it, then started to gather and collect his papers into some sort of order. Macleod noticed one sheet gambolling away on the little breeze and, following it, picked it up and brought it back to its owner who was now standing up.

'Signore, I thank you both for your help and your tolerance.'

'Please, think no more of it, a mere accident.'

'How kind, how thoroughly American. An Englishman would have huffed and puffed and damned and blasted and God knows what. They offend too easily, the English. It is their climate I think, it sours their natures. But you Americans are ...' he paused looking for the right word, 'here in Italy or in Spain we would say, simpático. I fear you have no true equivalent in the Anglo-Saxon tongue.'

'Thank you, sir, I will not detain you further. Good day.'

But the stranger caught at his arm.

'No, please, you are offended. I am too familiar, a stranger whom you do not know. I apologise.'

Macleod felt a little embarrassed. He had not intended to be short with the man but apparently he had been.

'No, sir, upon my honour I never for a moment thought ...'

'But that also is so American, so quick to be accommodating, to be friendliness itself. Tell me, is this your first visit to Rome?'

'It is.'

'And do you make it on business or for pleasure?'

'Neither, I am here with my wife. We wanted to see Rome. We are newly married.'

'But my deepest congratulations, dear sir. May I be so bold as to suggest that, if you know no one in Rome, then please let me assist you, you and your wife of course. I would be pleased to be the one who ...'

'Thank you, no. We have no wish to move in society, we are very ordinary, quiet people.'

The man laughed.

'Good heavens, Signore, you do not think that I move in what you call society? Look at me. Do I look like a person of any consequence, someone with position or power? I am a scribbler, sir, a mere scribbler. I write pamphlets, political pamphlets, and not of the sort that would get me invited into the palazzi of the rich or influential. This is my latest effort I carry. I have just returned from the printer having discussed the cost of publication. Prices, I fear, go ever upwards. I have used him before but even he now charges ... But, excuse me, once I begin to talk about my work, time and everything else fly out of my head. I detain you. You are on your way somewhere?'

'No, merely taking a walk. My wife is occupied so I walk to pass the time.'

'Then let me make so bold as to invite you to drink a glass of wine with me. In Rome there has been, unfortunately, ample opportunity to improve one's French but less chance to improve one's English and little chance at all to note the subtle differences of American English to the native variety. Please, sir, do not hesitate, join me in a glass of wine and tell me about America.'

284

The last element of this appeal swayed Macleod, that and the fact that Marie had indicated that her confession, to be thorough and complete, would not be short. She had also said that the Mother Superior had indicated that, afterwards, she would welcome talking with someone who had experience of the New World and, as she was providing the vital letter of introduction, Marie would have to be at her service for as long as she wished. A drink with a pleasant companion would help pass the time.

'Very well, sir, I would be pleased to take wine with you.'

The man stood back a pace and gave a small bow.

'Allow me to introduce myself, Count Silviano Brutti.' He saw Macleod's surprise and hesitation and gave a small laugh. 'Please, do not be fooled by the title. The Bruttis have been Counts for several hundred years but the last one to see any real money or to own a Palazzo here in Rome was my great-great-grandfather who gambled and debauched away one half of the family fortune and gave the other half to Holy Mother Church in old age to try and save his immortal soul from hell. A waste of both time and money, in my opinion. If you stay one month or more in Rome you will find that grand-sounding titles are almost more common than churches.' Count Brutti stepped forward and linked his free arm into Macleod's and carried on his chatter as they moved off along the street. 'If no one has yet offered their services, you must let me offer my poor knowledge of my city to you and be your guide, Signor …?'

Count Brutti waited for a name.

'Macleod, Jean Marie Macleod.'

'But what unusual given names for an American.'

'My mother was French, from Paris.'

'Ah, Paris, I knew it well as a much younger man. I took part in the Revolution, not the storming of the Bastille or anything on such a grand scale, but I was there.'

Macleod was warming to this man. He was talking in the easy manner of an old friend and Macleod welcomed some sort of human contact in this strange city.

'But your title, didn't that hamper you among the revolutionaries?'

'Not at all, they welcomed me all the more because of it. Ah, here we are, a simple taverna, I'm afraid, but clean and the wine is drinkable. It comes from Frascati, not far from Rome. Do you know Frascati at all? Have you visited there?'

'No, my wife and I have not yet been out of Rome.'

It was indeed a clean and respectable-looking place with a scattering of men around the tables all decently dressed and talking quietly, drinking wine or coffee, some smoking small cigars or pipes. The man behind the bar saw them arrive and hurried out to greet them.

He rattled off something rapidly in Italian and then shepherded them to a private booth where they sat down. Macleod's new friend directed a few words to the man who went back behind the bar where he busied himself getting glasses and a carafe of white wine.

Count Brutti nodded across in his direction.

'His family once served my family in the days of my grandfather. Technically I suppose I still owe him the wages which my grandfather never paid his grandfather, but instead of that making him angry with me, he makes a fuss of me. It is the way things are here in Rome.'

The man returned and put the glasses and carafe on the table between them, bowed to the Count and then left. The Count took the carafe and poured them each a glass of wine. They lifted their glasses and drank. Macleod found the wine light, delicious and wonderfully fresh.

'You like it, Signor Macleod, our Frascati?'

'I do, sir.'

'They say that the people of Frascati keep all their best wine for themselves and what they sell in Rome is only the inferior stuff. But my friend here is from Frascati and has family there so he makes sure there is always some of their best wine kept here for me. So, my friend … I hope I may call you that?'

'If you think it appropriate on so small an acquaintance.'

Count Brutti laughed.

'But I do, I think so. You must remember you are in Rome now, the Eternal City. For thousands of years we Romans have watched people come and go, conquering Emperors, barbarian hordes, armies, people seeking wealth, people seeking the past, people seeking God and people who have no idea what they are seeking. We make friends quickly and enemies too.'

'Well, if it's a choice between one or the other I'll choose to be a friend.'

'Bravo, bravissimo, to my new friend Jean Marie Macleod and his beautiful wife.'

'Thank you for the compliment on my wife's behalf, but as you haven't seen her yet I'll accept it more as a courtesy than a considered judgement.'

'Not at all, Jean Marie, I am sure that a man of your undoubted taste will prove to have a most beautiful wife.'

'I fear you know as much about my taste as about my wife's looks.'

'Ah, now there you are wrong.'

'Wrong?'

'But of course. Of all the people in Rome whom you might have chosen as your friend, did you not choose me? That being so, how could I consider you other than a man of the most accomplished taste?'

And he sat and smiled at Macleod.

It suddenly dawned on Macleod that this meeting, so casual and yet so pleasant, had been entirely engineered by his new friend. He had no reason to feel suspicious of the man but neither had he any reason to trust him. He took another small drink from his glass and then stood up.

'I fear I must now leave you, Count.'

The Count stood up somewhat surprised.

'Silviano, please.'

'If you wish. Good-day, Silviano, and thank you for the wine.'

'But we have not talked. Must you leave so soon?'

'I must return to wait upon my wife. I do not wish her to walk alone through the streets.'

'But of course, I understand. A new wife does not like to be left alone, especially if you tell her that, rather than wait for her return, you chose to drink wine in a taverna with a rapscallion who scrapes a humble living as a political agitator. Go, my friend, and give my kindest regards to your wife.'

Macleod put on his hat and held out his hand.

'Thank you again for the wine.'

The Count took his hand and shook it.

'Remember, if you need a guide, I assure you I know all the

sights and I come at a very modest price.'

As if from nowhere, like a conjuror, the Count produced a dog-eared piece of card. Macleod took it.

'Thank you. If we need a guide we will certainly call on you.'

Macleod left the table and walked out of the taverna into the afternoon sunshine. The Count sat down and watched him go.

The man came from behind the bar and stood at the table. The Count waved away the glasses and carafe which the man gathered up and took away. The Count waited a few minutes and then stood up. He gathered his papers from the table and walked across to the bar where he dropped them in front of the man who had served them.

'Dispose of these. I have no further use for them.'

He turned and left. The barman watched him go. And there was indeed a look in his eyes, but it was one of fear, not any ancient family loyalty. He gathered up the papers, looked at them, then took them into a room behind the bar and dumped them in a basket. Later he would burn them. He would not get anyone to look at them, even though he knew at least one man who could read. The less he knew about Count Brutti's business the safer he felt. He returned to the bar. Several of the men sitting at the tables were looking at him. He gave the shrug universal in Italy which said, I know nothing and want to know nothing and neither do any of you. The eyes turned away and conversations resumed. Obviously no one in the taverna envied Macleod his newly found friend.

Macleod walked away from the taverna. It had been a pleasant meeting, a pleasant, chance meeting. But then an uneasy feeling came upon him and he stopped, turned and looked behind him. He saw nothing. No, it had been nothing but a chance meeting. He put the matter of Count Brutti from his mind. He had been careful. He had told him nothing that might put them in any danger. He had not told him where their apartment was nor that they were looking for Cardinal Henry Stuart. He had exercised all reasonable caution. But that wine, that Frascati, had been good. He would remember the name. And he continued his walking.

Marie, looking thoroughly happy, finally came out of the convent, linked her arm through his and showed him the envelope she was carrying.

'Look, I found out where the Cardinal lives and we have a letter of introduction. Is that not marvellous, Jean? He is Bishop of Frascati and he lives there. It is a place …'

'I know, not far from Rome. They say the wine is very good.'

Marie looked surprised.

'How clever of you to know. But how did you find out?'

'Somebody told me.'

Chapter Sixty-three

When walking one evening in the streets away from the Piazza di Spagna, they had suddenly come upon a waterless fountain where dirty, semi-clothed children climbed and played. They stood for a moment admiring the fountain's beauty which was half-hidden by dirt, neglect and ill-use. Macleod remarked that the sight epitomised the decaying grandeur they had found so much in Rome, even in the short time they had been there.

Frascati, when they arrived there and took comfortable rooms above a clean and respectable taverna, came as a pleasant change. The taverna occupied a corner position of a piazza dominated on one side by the façade of Frascati's Cathedral of San Pietro Apostolo, an elaborate edifice in the Greek style but with the later addition of two monumental bell-towers. In the centre of the piazza stood a substantial and ornate fountain, also dedicated to the Apostle Peter.

They spent a day becoming familiar with their immediate surroundings. They admired the clean, well-ordered streets, peopled by quiet busy locals. They lunched in the taverna and were fêted as a newly married couple on honeymoon tour by the proprietor himself. He was an incurable romantic, although married thirty years, and although they learned many things about him, his attention to them was, in truth, rather more than they cared for.

In the early evening of their first day they hired a carriage and were driven out to the Villa Piccolomini where they were made welcome by the impressive major-domo who instructed a footman to show them the magnificent gardens. They stood together to admire the wonderful Teatro d'Acqua, the Water Theatre, which was a model of the nearby Villa Mondragone.

The following day, however, they set about the business that had brought them to Frascati. Although their destination was no great distance, they hired a carriage to call at the Cardinal's

Palazzo which proved to be a very different affair from the Villa Piccolomini. The Cardinal's Palazzo seemed to them more of a fortress than a palace which, indeed was not due to their imagination, but rather because it had once been one. The old "Rocca" or castle was massive and provided with one rounded and two great square towers. Undeterred by appearances, they made their way to the great main doorway and presented their letter to the suitably ornate footman, who unfortunately spoke no English. The footman looked at the name on the letter, studied the seal, then took them into the Palazzo and promptly disappeared.

Macleod and Marie stood in a hallway about the size of a small ballroom. The floor was inlaid marble and on the ceiling was an idealised pastoral scene. From various niches busts of past bishops and other men of overwhelming dignity gazed at them with sightless eyes. Between these busts were paintings, mostly on religious themes and all in heavy, gilded frames. Macleod looked around at the splendour in which they waited and felt a vague unease. All they hoped to achieve rested on this visit.

After a short wait an elderly man wearing the black soutane edged with purple came into the hall where they waited. He spoke to them in Italian. Macleod answered in French.

'I regret, Father, that neither I nor my wife speak Italian.'

The cleric responded in French.

'I am Monsignore Cesarini, Secretary to His Eminence the Cardinal. I have read your letter from the Mother Superior. You are recently married?'

'That is so, Monsignore.'

The priest looked again at the letter.

'And you wish the Cardinal's blessing?'

The question was delivered in a tone which, clearly as words might have done, said " … but surely, as people of no importance, you know you are asking for something fantastical".

Macleod sensed that this formidable Secretary's attitude did not bode well for their hopes, and his reply was anything but assured.

'We do.'

But Marie was not hampered by any sense of unease nor any feelings of diffidence.

'My husband wishes to pay his respects not only to the Cardinal but also to the rightful King of England and Scotland. His father

291

fought in the army of his brother, Prince Charles, and his uncles died for the Prince's cause.'

'Indeed! The Cardinal, you understand, is always very busy. Many people of consequence call upon his attentions and he is much in demand both as a Prince of the Church and a man of affairs. But, for so charming a couple and for one whose family has suffered much in the glorious cause of his family, I will see if he will find a brief moment to receive you.'

'We have taken rooms at the taverna on the Piazza San Pietro. Perhaps you would be so good as to send us a message there.'

Monsignore Cesarini's look was meant to quell Marie's awful presumption but she met it and returned it with a smile.

The Monsignore coldly promised to send word to their lodging as soon as he had spoken to His Eminence and motioned to a nearby footman who approached them. The prelate, without offering any farewell, turned and walked away, and the footman held out a hand indicating the way to the door and showed them out.

Once outside the Palazzo and in their carriage, Macleod asked Marie what she had thought about their reception by the Cardinal's Secretary.

She answered that she thought it both polite and gracious.

'You didn't get the impression that we were expected?'

'Expected? How could we be expected?'

'How indeed? We arrive without warning, with nothing but a letter.'

'From the Mother Superior, a friend of royalty, a woman of consequence.'

Macleod persisted.

'With only a letter. We are seen at once by the Cardinal's Secretary. He listens politely to our request and agrees to try and arrange an audience. Wasn't it all a bit too simple?'

'Oh, Jean, you see plots everywhere. The Monsignor accepted what we told him, he is a man of God, a priest, he only wishes to help us. What have we asked for? A blessing and a chance to pay our respects, nothing more. Why should he refuse such a request?'

'And my request to acknowledge the Cardinal as the rightful King of England?'

'Well, why not? You told me yourself that is how he thinks of himself. Your family gave his brother the Prince great service, did they not? Why should the Cardinal not wish to acknowledge such service?'

'Perhaps you're right. Perhaps I see too many conspiracies.'

'No, you are right to take care. But with the Cardinal I am sure we are safe.'

Macleod helped Marie back into their carriage. He wished he could have agreed with her, but somehow he felt that safety was still proving elusive.

Chapter Sixty-four

To their great astonishment, the very next morning a note was delivered to their lodgings, carried by another splendid footman. The note told them that the Cardinal would see them in two days' time at three in the afternoon.

Marie was delighted.

'You see, Jean. All is well. And we have two whole days to enjoy ourselves. Is it not wonderful?'

'Yes. Wonderful.'

Macleod managed the words and even managed to get enough enthusiasm into them to convince Marie who at once began making plans for what they should do while they waited.

Macleod's suspicions doubly returned. An audience with the Cardinal granted so promptly and so soon. What did it mean? But, seeing Marie happy, he kept his doubts to himself and joined with her in planning their two days of leisure.

As it turned out Macleod and Marie were satisfied to pass the two days in each other's company walking and talking. They told each other of their childhoods and families. Macleod told Marie of his time in the army and the loss of his wife and child.

'It filled me with hate for the British. But there was always the problem of my father's family, the Macleods of Lewis.'

'Your father's family?'

'His Clan. How many of the men I faced on the battlefield were Scottish, perhaps Highlanders, perhaps even my own kin? I wanted to hate the British, all of them. As a child he made me swear to hate the British and be loyal to the Clan. How was I to do both, Marie?'

But Marie didn't know and could not help him. She knew nothing of Scotland and clans. That he wanted to hate those who had been responsible for the death of his wife and child she could understand. Those who take all possibility of love from someone deserved to be hated. Hate she understood well enough. But that was all she could understand.

Marie in her turn told Macleod of her own hate. How her shame and humiliation and the feeling of betrayal by her family had eaten into her very soul and how she had longed at times for death, even death by her own hand. But always the teachings she had absorbed in her childhood prevented her. Death at your own hands meant eternal punishment and she wanted no more punishment. De Valois and St Clair had provided more than enough.

They walked and talked, loved each other for the sufferings they had both endured and found comfort and peace in each other's company as they strolled through the town. Their contentment in each other's company even made Macleod forget, for a while, his suspicions.

Somehow it became known that their visit to Frascati to see the Cardinal was because Macleod's family had rendered their bishop's family some great service. That being the case, Macleod and Marie were welcomed everywhere they went. It became clear to them on those occasions when they came into any contact with the local citizens that the Cardinal was a man much loved by his people. Both knew only too well that such is not always the case with Princes of the Catholic Church.

In discussing the matter both Marie and Macleod agreed that Cardinal Bishop Henry Stuart must be a most exceptional man. Exceptional indeed.

Chapter Sixty-five

The two days of pleasant, intimate idleness ended and the appointed day of the visit came. The sun shone and despite the afternoon heat Macleod and Marie decided to forego a carriage and walk, and at three o'clock they were admitted to the fortress Palazzo by the same splendid footman. This time, however, he led them through the marbled hall where they had previously waited, into a grand salon. There they were met by Monsignore Cesarini whose manner had not noticeably changed. He gave them a polite but decidedly frigid smile.

'His Eminence will be with us shortly. He seems to anticipate this meeting with pleasure.'

Macleod felt nervous. His suspicions had returned but, more than that, he was worried about Marie. She had decided that this meeting would resolve everything for them, but Macleod felt sure that the audience would be the briefest of condescensions. A slight bow of the head, a touching of hands, a benediction, nothing more. How was he to tell the Cardinal the real meaning of their visit, and tell him in such a way as to ensure his help?

If Marie shared any such worries she hid them well. She put on her best smile and, with a white lace mantilla draped over her abundant hair, hoped that she looked sufficiently presentable. She was acutely aware of how far her attire, forced on her by circumstance of purchasing her wardrobe hurriedly in Livorno, fell short of what the magnificence of her present surroundings required. All three stood, waiting. Then, unable to bear the silence, Marie decided to speak.

'His Eminence is kindness itself to receive us.'

The Monsignor gave her another wintry smile. He also had noted the quality and cut of the dress.

'Quite.'

Macleod did not know what to say or where to put his hands so he said nothing and left his hands to fend for themselves.

The three relapsed into further silence while a pair of footmen, who seemed to Macleod to serve no purpose except ornament, stood beside the great doors at the far end of the room.

Suddenly, and without apparent instruction, the footmen opened the great gilded double doors and a figure in a flowing scarlet robe slowly entered.

Macleod was taken by surprise. Among all the magnificence, he had somehow lost sight of how old the man slowly approaching them must be. He was small, almost lost in his heavy, scarlet robe. On top of his wispy, grey hair there was a scarlet skull-cap. Macleod suddenly realised that the Cardinal must now be well over seventy years old. Monsignor Cesarini bowed to the venerable figure as the Cardinal came to a halt in front of them. Macleod stood staring but Marie salvaged the moment by falling on one knee and declaring, 'Your Majesty.'

Macleod snapped out of his trance and also fell to his knee.

'Forgive me, your Majesty.'

The Cardinal held out a hand to Marie.

'Come, Madame, rise.'

Marie took the hand and rose. She bent forward and kissed the ornate Episcopal ring on his finger.

The old man smiled and looked down at Macleod who had remained kneeling.

'Your Eminence, it is so gracious of you to allow us into your presence.'

'Please arise, Mr Macleod. I am touched, touched and heartened that as part of your wedding tour you chose to pay me the attentions that my own country is at such pains to deny me.'

Macleod arose, took the outstretched hand and kissed the ring as Marie had done.

'Not those of your countrymen who are kin to me, your Majesty. The men of the Clan Macleod were, like my father and uncles, true to your brother the Prince.' The old man's fixed smile assumed a small but unfeigned sadness. Macleod, encouraged, continued. 'And if it were possible the Highlands would still be true to you in action rather than mere words. To the Clans the name of their rightful king is still Stuart.'

Macleod silently gave thanks for the stories with which his father had filled him as a child, and the hate old Euan had tried so hard to nurture. Thanks to the stories and that hate, his fine words rang almost true.

Cardinal Henry, veteran of a lifetime of lies, deceit and betrayal, gave an equally good account of himself.

'Alas, words are all that is left to us now. We must be satisfied to resort to them alone. But I thank you for your timely reminder of the loyal and brave service the men of the Highlands have given to my family and the terrible cost levied on them for that service.' And Macleod found that he almost believed the emotion behind the words the gentle old man spoke so convincingly. 'You come to seek my blessing on you both?'

'Yes, Your Eminence.'

'Then you shall have it at once.' Macleod and Marie knelt down. Macleod felt Marie's hand steal into his own as the Cardinal raised his hand in benediction and slowly pronounced the ancient Latin formula of blessing from Holy Mother Church.

In nomine Patris, et Filii et Spiritus Sancti.

Amen.

The blessing completed they both stood.

'Now, you will take wine with me.'

Monsignor Cesarini intervened.

'But Your Eminence, the envoy is waiting. A brief blessing was what I understood ...'

Cardinal Henry silenced his Secretary with a gesture.

'The envoy must wait, whoever he is. A king's loyal subjects who have travelled from so far must come before any other business.' He looked once more at Macleod and Marie. 'We will take wine in the library.'

The Cardinal turned and walked slowly back towards the doors through which he had entered. Macleod and Marie followed him. The footmen opened the doors and the small procession passed through, leaving the Secretary watching them, angry and somewhat bewildered.

Chapter Sixty-six

In the library on a delicate dark table there were crystal glasses and a decanter of deep red wine. They sat and a footman poured wine into each glass.

The Cardinal said a few words in Italian to the footman who withdrew from the room closing the door behind him. He picked up his glass.

'It is French wine. I have suffered greatly from the French, as have many others in Rome and throughout Italy. But our Saviour demands of us that we forgive our enemies so, as you see, I forgive them, and to show my forgiveness I drink their wine. But only their best wine.'

The Cardinal held his glass and waited. To Macleod the wine meant nothing but Marie was able to do it the justice the Cardinal so obviously expected.

'But, Your Eminence, it is a truly wonderful wine. I have never tasted anything like it.'

The Cardinal smiled at her and turned his gaze on Macleod.

'And you, Mr Macleod?'

Macleod searched for words that would at least have some small ring of truth to them.

'It's tastes very red, Your Eminence, I have never tasted a wine more red.'

There was a small pause, then the old man appeared to begin to wheeze slightly and his head dipped forward. The wheezing grew slightly and Macleod and Marie looked at one another in alarm. Marie leaned forward.

'Your Eminence, are you not well? Should I call someone?'

The old man made a small, dismissive gesture with his hand and lifted his head so they could see his eyes as he looked at Macleod. At once they both realised that he was not suffering any kind of seizure. He was not wheezing, he was laughing. The laughter died from his lips but not from his eyes.

'Thank you, Mr Macleod.' Macleod didn't understand why he was being thanked. 'I cannot easily remember the last time anyone made me laugh quite so much. But please, do not do it too often, I laugh rarely and it may not be good for my health.' He lifted his glass to his lips and took a small sip then put the glass on the table. 'But now we must get to business. My Secretary will wait a reasonable time but not indefinitely. You wish to ask me for something I think, something other than a blessing?' This question was so unexpected that neither Macleod nor Marie replied. The Cardinal's manner became short. 'Come, come, Mr Macleod. You have come to me for something other than my blessing, have you not?'

Macleod looked at Marie but for once she seemed at a loss to help him, so having no other way of dealing with the Cardinal's question, he resorted to the truth.

'You are correct, Your Eminence.'

'And what is it that you wish me to give you?'

'A list of names.'

'Names? What names? Saints perhaps, to name a child if your marriage is blessed by a power greater than my own?'

'Eminence, we know of the list of names …' The Cardinal's eyes held him with a mischievous look and Macleod realised that he was being played with. His voice became firm and direct. 'You have the names of men in America who seek to subvert her lawful Government. Those are the names, Eminence, the names of traitors. I shall take those names and …'

But the Cardinal waved a hand and Macleod stopped.

'Good. I was almost sure, of course, but you must understand I needed to hear it from your own lips. You wish me to provide you with a list of names, the names of a few very highly placed gentlemen in your country who have arrived at what I shall call an arrangement with Monsieur Fouché. Am I not right?'

'Yes, Your Eminence.'

The Cardinal produced from somewhere under his scarlet cloak an envelope sealed with red wax. He held it out.

'Then take it. Although I warn you, I doubt it will do you much good.' Macleod reached out and took it. Macleod looked at it. Other than the seal the envelope was totally blank. 'You need not fear that it is not what you came to seek. Rather you should fear that having it, others may, in their turn, seek you. But it is done. You have your list.'

Marie recovered her power of speech.

'But, Eminence, how did you know the real reason we wished to see you?'

'Information comes to Rome from many sources. It is said that only the Jesuits have a better Secret Service of spies and informers than the Vatican but, as it is the Jesuits themselves who say that, one might be forgiven for doubting its veracity. I expected this visit, Madame, and expecting it, I was prepared. It is the duty of those close to the Holy See to be fully aware of, shall we say, the currents of the time. I, of course, have been aware of Monsieur Fouché's plan from the very beginning, how could I not, since it was I who was supposed to assume the throne? It is somewhat ironic, do you not think, that not only did I inherit my brother's claim to the British throne but also the same invitation he received to assume the throne of the kingdom of America?'

Marie's surprise was obvious in her voice.

'Your brother the Prince was asked to become king of America?'

'Indeed he was, Madame. It was before the American War of Independence. My brother was approached by a small embassy of senior figures who wished to see their country free of British rule. A king of their own was, they thought, one way to achieve such freedom. But, like so many projects associated with my brother, it failed to flourish. It did, however, provide Monsieur Fouché with the idea for his present endeavour.'

Macleod's voice cut in.

'I have never heard of such an approach.'

'Do you then, Mr Macleod, move in political circles where you would have expected to have been informed?'

Although the gentle Cardinal's eyes were still benign, his voice had taken on a different tone.

'All I meant, Eminence, was that as far as I am aware as an American citizen, it has never been officially admitted that such an approach was ever made.'

The Cardinal's eyes now took on a hardness and Macleod immediately regretted his original interruption. He had the list, but they were still in the fortress Palazzo.

'Perhaps that is so, but in my experience governments are so often economical with the truth.' The hardness left his eyes and the fixed smile returned. 'However, as I said, having been approached by the American agents of Monsieur Fouché I made sure I was kept well informed of the progress of the project. Your somewhat late appearance in the matter and that of Madame de Valois was an interesting but, as I thought, largely irrelevant development. It seems I underestimated the role you would play. Once you arrived in Rome I felt that providing you with the names you were seeking was perhaps the best course of action for all interested parties.'

Other than letting them know that he was well aware of their masquerade as man and wife Macleod had no idea what the Cardinal meant. It was clear, however, that he was using them both in some way.

'With the greatest respect, Your Eminence, how am I to be sure you have given me a true list of the names of those involved in Monsieur Fouché's plot against my country.'

The Cardinal held up his hand once more.

'Please, Mr Macleod, no more laughter, one good jest is sufficient I assure you.'

'I mean no jest, your ...'

'Mr Macleod, you and this charming young lady have found yourselves embroiled in something you do not nor cannot understand. That you have managed to make your way so far amazes me. Either you are far more skilled in what you are doing than I have been led to believe, or you are under the direct protection of heaven itself. Personally I believe the latter is the only possible explanation. The list you have is in my own hand and bears my signature. It is sealed with my own personal seal. Placed in the right hands its contents will certainly not be questioned. The problem now for you is, which are those right hands?'

Macleod pushed the envelope inside his coat.

'It will be placed in the hands of someone I trust and who serves the American Government.'

'If that is what you say, Mr Macleod, then I am sure that is what you intend. Now, you have what you came for so I must ask you to leave. I am a very busy man and my Secretary will already be worried that our little meeting has thrown his carefully planned schedule into chaos. He is very loyal, but he worries.'

The old man slowly began to rise but paused at Marie's voice.

'Tell me, Eminence, why are you helping us?'

Macleod wasn't sure whether he was embarrassed or grateful that Marie had asked the question.

'My child, the Macleods of Lewis suffered grievously for their loyalty to my family's cause as did many in the Highlands. Let us say that I am making some small repayment for the suffering the cause of my House has inflicted on Mr Macleod's kinsmen. I wish there was more that I could do.'

Macleod, never the diplomat, took the Cardinal at his word.

'Your Eminence, there is one more thing.'

The old man looked at Macleod, and for a brief second he was unsure. Could this man really be such an innocent, or was he very cleverly acting the part of a complete fool? But, as the Cardinal held Macleod in his gaze, he saw that he was genuinely waiting for permission to make his request, and he felt sure the man was indeed no more than a simpleton. But if that was the case, what more could this strange American possibly presume to ask of him?

Macleod completely misinterpreted the Cardinal's enquiring gaze. He took it as a sign that he should make his request and, once made, it brought a genuine smile to the Cardinal's face, one that even reached his eyes.

'Very well, Mr Macleod, I will grant your request, but I must be brief. Remember, Monsignore Cesarini is waiting.'

'Thank you, Your Eminence. I will be eternally grateful. We both will.'

A few minutes later the doors opened and the Cardinal led Macleod and Marie out of the library. A footman stood to one side impassively and Monsignor Cesarini stepped forward.

'The envoy is still waiting, Your Eminence'

Marie stepped forward and reached out her hand. The Cardinal placed his hand in hers and she bent and kissed his Episcopal ring once more.

'Thank you, Eminence.'

Macleod in his turn kissed the proffered ring.

'Thank you, Your Eminence, and may God bless and keep you, Your Majesty.'

The Cardinal ignored the words, turned away and left them. A footman stepped forward and indicated that they should follow him.

Marie and Macleod once more walked through the corridors, the salon, the marble hall and finally emerged from the Palazzo into the afternoon sunshine.

Marie slipped her arm through Macleod's.

'Come, we must go to the Cathedral and light candles for our Cardinal who is also your king.'

Macleod put his hand on the slight bulge of the letter inside his coat.

'We have much to be thankful for.'

Marie gave his arm a small squeeze.

'Jean, we have everything to be thankful for. You heard what the Cardinal said, he thinks we are under the protection of heaven itself. I think so too.'

Chapter Sixty-seven

The great doors of the fortress Palazzo closed behind them and they walked away in the afternoon sunshine without noticing its heat, full of thoughts of success and joy.

'Now, Jean, all that we must do is decide to whom we should sell our list of names.'

Macleod stopped dead.

'Sell!'

Marie paused and looked at him in surprise.

'But of course. After so much trouble, so much great danger, it is only right that we must be rewarded.' She resumed walking. 'But who is it that will reward us best?'

Macleod caught up with her.

'But, Marie, this list must go to the American Government. I have explained, have I not, that my duty ...'

Marie caught his arm and laughed.

'I know, Jean. I am happy, so I tease you. Forgive me.'

Macleod pulled her arm through his.

'Of course.'

They were about to cross the street but waited because a closed carriage was coming quickly towards them. They both stood back to allow it to pass by.

But it did not pass. It stopped in front of them and the door opened. Inside they saw a man holding a pistol. The pistol was pointing at Marie.

Count Brutti smiled graciously at them.

'Please, Mr Macleod, I would be most grateful if you and the lady would get in.'

Marie turned to Macleod in alarm.

'Who is it, Jean?'

'It is someone I met in Rome who calls himself Count Brutti. He says he writes political pamphlets.'

'But, Jean, I don't understand.'

'No, but I think I'm beginning to, my dear.'

The Count nodded at his pistol.

'Please, I do not wish to use this but be quite sure that I will if you force me. My driver, if you care to look, also has a pistol. I think you should both do as I say.'

Macleod looked at the driver and saw the business end of a pistol pointing down at him from under his cloak.

'We must do as he says, Marie. Please get in.'

Marie did as he asked and was followed into the carriage by Macleod. Brutti pulled the door shut and the carriage moved off. Sitting opposite Count Brutti was another man. He also had a pistol.

'You see, Mr Macleod, I do not take chances, but I assure you that if you both give me your fullest co-operation, neither of you will come to any harm.'

'Where are you taking us?'

'All in good time, Mr Macleod, all in good time.'

And the closed coach moved off and gathered speed.

Chapter Sixty-eight

Count Brutti's voice echoed around the great, empty and thoroughly forbidding room.

'As you can see from the iron grilles outside the windows and the solidity of the doors, the rooms of this palazzo, now alas so empty, once housed considerable wealth. But times change and one must make the best of what one has. What was designed to keep intruders out now serves just as well to ensure that as my guests, however unwilling, you will remain.'

'You cannot keep us prisoners here.'

'But why not, Mr Macleod? No one saw you arrive, that is to say, no one who would be foolish enough to make public what I choose to do in private. The wealth of my family may be gone and with it, social position, but I still maintain a reputation, although only of a certain kind. I assure you I could keep you both here indefinitely if I chose. Please be sensible and accept the situation in which you find yourselves.' Brutti looked round the large, dilapidated and rather ill-lit room. 'Below this Palazzo is a windowless pit. There have been those of my family before me who have let people slowly die in that dark place, people who had offended them or their honour. However, let us not become morbid. You have not offended me and I no longer have any honour to defend, nor would there be any profit in letting either of you die slowly in a room of any sort. In so far as my humble home is able to provide, then it is at your service. Here you see you have a table and chairs, rustic perhaps and none too clean, but serviceable. Next door a bed and bedding, only one bed I am afraid, built for humbler circumstances but again serviceable. Over there you will see that I have had your luggage brought from your lodging. I have no servants, not domestic servants that is, so I fear you must serve yourselves as best you can. You will be fed shortly and you will sleep here tonight.'

'And then?'

'And then it will be tomorrow and I will return.'

'You do not live here?'

The Count laughed and his laughter echoed around the faded walls and marble floor.

'Live here? No, I do not live here. I could say it has too many memories for me. When I told you in the taverna that it was my great-great grandfather who lost the family's wealth, I fear I lied. My father was the gambler and debauchee who managed to run through most of our money. What little he left I soon spent in trying to outdo his folly and wickedness. Yes, I could say it has too many memories, but that also would be a lie. I do not live here because it is too hot in summer and too cold in winter, and the only company are the rats. How they manage not only to survive but thrive is a mystery to me.'

One of the great doors at the end of the room opened and a man came in carrying a wooden tray. He took it to the table then left without speaking or looking at anyone. On the tray was bread, cold meats, cheese, a flagon and two pottery beakers. Count Brutti went to the table and picked up a piece of cheese, took a bite and threw it back onto the wooden plate.

'Edible. Not what you are used to perhaps, but just about edible. I regret you must use your fingers to eat, but try to think of it as if it were an al fresco entertainment. Let your imaginations suit your surroundings to this simple, peasant fare and it may not seem so bad. Now I must leave you. It has been a busy day and I have other business to attend to. I'm sure you will both forgive me for being such a poor host.'

'But what of other necessities?'

The Count, who had been about to leave, paused.

'Other necessities?'

'We must wash, and …'

'And?'

'And there are other necessities.'

'Ah, I think I see what you mean. As for cleanliness being next to godliness I fear I have left that in His divine hands. The other necessities, as you choose to call them, are provided for by a chamber pot under the bed. And now I really must go. Enjoy your meal and I hope what rest you get will be refreshing, for you will both have a busy day tomorrow.'

The Count turned and his boots echoed round the big empty hall as he left them. The door closed behind him and they heard a key grate in the lock. Then there was silence.

'Are we truly prisoners, Jean? Is there no way out?'

Macleod went to the door. He turned and pulled at the big brass handle but there was not the slightest movement. He went to the windows. They were closed and he saw no way of opening them. Not that it mattered because, beyond the grimed glass, he could make out the stout iron grilles. He went back to where Marie was standing.

'We must make the best of it, my love. Here, sit and eat.' He took the flagon and poured some wine into a beaker and held it out to her.

Marie took the beaker.

'Is there any hope, Jean?'

'I think if Brutti wanted us dead, we would be dead already.' Macleod sat down and poured himself some wine and then, as much to encourage Marie as to satisfy any hunger he felt, picked up a piece of meat and put it in his mouth. 'Come, eat. There is always hope.'

He saw from her face that his words were of little comfort but they were the only true ones he had to offer. Marie sat and picked up a piece of cheese and bit into it. Then put it down.

'But what is it he wants? He has not taken the letter that the Cardinal gave you, no questions have been asked. What is it he wants of us?'

'We will know when we are told and I'm sure we will be told soon enough.'

Macleod's mind returned to the words of Brutti, that tomorrow they would both have a busy day. He had no idea what that might mean, but he felt now was not the time to explore its meaning with Marie. No, now was definitely not the time.

Chapter Sixty-nine

The next thing Macleod knew he was being slowly shaken from side to side by an unseen hand. His head hurt and his mouth felt as if someone had stuffed an old leather glove into it. But most of all he felt an unbearable pressure on his bladder. He opened his eyes. He was sitting in a closed carriage being rocked by its movement.

He saw Marie sitting opposite looking at him. Next to her was Count Brutti. Sitting beside Macleod was a man with cropped hair, close-set eyes, broad shoulders and large, dirty hands. He looked at Macleod and said something to Count Brutti who gave a short reply.

The man next to Macleod opened the window, leaned out, looked around and then called to the driver. The coach came to a halt. The big man opened the door, got out and waited.

'Please go and relieve yourself, Mr Macleod, I have used the draught before on sufficient occasions to know how much you must feel the need. Guido will keep you company.'

Macleod got out. They were on an empty country road. Macleod walked to the side of the road, unfastened his breeches and let nature take its course. As he did so, and feeling the great sense of relief, he realised that Marie must also, at the side of some other road, have already done as he was doing, even perhaps watched by the evil-looking Guido. A sense of outraged anger gripped him, but outside the coach Guido seemed even larger than he had done inside. Realising any action on his part would be futile he allowed his anger to subside and returned to the coach.

Brutti sat looking at him.

'The wine you gave us was drugged.'

'Oh yes. You have both slept for over twenty-four hours. You were quite right, of course, I couldn't keep you at the Palazzo. I had to move you both very quickly, so I told my little story and you drank my wine and now here we all are.'

'Where are you taking us?'

'I fear we all have a long and tedious journey before us. We go to Paris. There is a man there whom I serve. He has asked me to deliver you and the letter you carry.' Macleod's hand went to his pocket. The bulge was still there. 'You see, I have not robbed you. You still carry what the Cardinal gave you. Now, you will both oblige me by listening carefully to what I have to say. I am charged with delivering you and what you carry to Paris. I would wish to do this with you both unharmed, that means I must be sure of your co-operation. I assure you that you will be delivered, although whether in sound health, or damaged, is entirely up to you. Mr Macleod, I do not doubt that you are a brave and resourceful man. To have achieved as much as you have shows me that. But do not confuse bravery with foolhardiness. Guido here could snap you in half with his bare hands. Antonio the driver has already killed four men in my service and Carlo, who sits beside him, is a most unpleasant character and has a rare talent for inflicting pain. If you do not co-operate I will have you killed and give the beautiful Madame de Valois to Carlo. Before he kills her he will enjoy himself with her. She will suffer, I assure you, and not just pain, although there will indeed be much of that.'

Macleod looked at Marie. Her eyes were filled with terror. He knew he had no choice.

'You will have my co-operation. You have my word. And may your soul rot in eternal hellfire.'

Count Brutti laughed.

'That much is already assured and I am reconciled to my fate.' The laughter left his voice. 'Do not doubt me, Mr Macleod, in certain things I do not lie. If your co-operation fails even in the slightest degree,' he looked at Marie, 'then you will find I can and will be as good as my word.'

Chapter Seventy

Lord Melford knocked on the door that divided his office from that of Jasper Trent and waited until a voice called him to enter. His manner as he stood and waited for Trent to acknowledge his presence was meant to be respectful without being subservient. Although he had stood in front of a mirror practising, he was not at all sure he had, as yet, perfected what he aimed at. His recent experiences had caused him to modify his views of his superior and he wanted to show Trent that his was a new and improved attitude.

Trent looked up from his reading.

'Well, Melford? You have something for me?'

'I have had a report from Count Brutti.'

'Brutti? What does he say?'

'He says that an American calling himself Macleod accompanied by a woman posing as his wife arrived in Rome and were asking questions about Cardinal Henry. He says he thinks they are agents of the American Government.'

'Do you believe him?'

'I don't disbelieve all that he tells us. He tells us that Macleod and the de Valois woman are in Rome and want to talk to our Cardinal. I believe that.'

'And why would Brutti want us to know that, do you think?'

'At the moment I couldn't say, not with any degree of certainty.'

'Ah, honesty and caution. Am I wrong or have you changed your attitude to our work, Melford?'

'I think I am beginning to understand a little of what our work is about.'

'Well, well, humility as well. Your adventures seem to have changed you although I'm not sure it is for the better. I rather valued your thorough selfishness, it made you predictable. I'm not sure I feel so comfortable with this new Melford.' But the new

Melford did not rise to the bait. He knew Trent wanted a reaction but he declined to respond. 'Tell me, what makes you come to the conclusion that you at last understand, even if only a little, of what our work is about?'

'The business of sending Molly running off to New Orleans then me being sent post-haste to Boston.'

'And Gregory, don't forget Gregory.'

'No, indeed, how could anyone forget Gregory?'

'So what does the business of New Orleans and Boston tell you?'

'I think it was all a bluff. I think you wanted a show of interest and activity well away from where you were really active.'

'And where would that be?'

'How would I know? I was part of a pantomime put on to attract attention. If I was taken, I knew nothing of value, neither did Molly O'Hara.' Trent smiled at him and nodded him to continue. 'If I had to guess I'd say that you knew very well what our friend in Paris was up to with the Cardinal and, if anything, you approved.'

'Approved of overthrowing the Government of a neutral State! Well, well, go on.'

'Fouché's plan would somehow resurrect the Jacobite cause. Henry claims the crown ...' Suddenly the truth dawned. 'By God, Fouché's planning to put Henry on the throne of America.'

'Bravo, Melford. Maybe you are indeed beginning to understand a little.

'A puppet king controlled from Paris.'

'A Stuart king, remember that.'

'Yes, a Jacobite, but still a eunuch of a king, a Papist priest of a king who will never sire an heir because even if he wasn't too old, he's too pious.'

'As you say, an old, weak king on an American throne, one without an heir and who cannot get an heir. An unwilling kingdom robbed of its hard won freedom and independence, kept in place by a group of self-serving politicos who, once in power, would soon fall to squabbling. What do you say, Melford, if Fouché got his king of America, would that state of affairs be such a bad thing for Britain?'

'Perhaps not, but it's a gamble, Trent, with no certainty of outcome. What if you're wrong?'

'If times changed in the coming years, if troops could be sent to aid the aspirations of a people oppressed by an alien monarch, forced on them by a foreign power, if America found itself with a choice, live under a puppet king or return to the British fold, how long would Henry sit on the throne? It would be just another small kingdom, Melford, created in treachery and no doubt kept alive by force of French troops. Fouché thinks that with a Stuart on a throne, any throne, the Highlands will rise. They won't. He thinks the Jacobite cause will be re-ignited and will force us to commit troops. It's a vain hope. That cause is dead and soon will be buried. It is France who will find it has to commit troops, troops to keep their precious Henry on his throne. Tell me, if I'm right, Melford, how long would such a kingdom last do you think?'

'Not long, Trent. I would say not long at all.'

'But it was important that our friend in Paris must not be allowed to think in such a way. He must think his plan is seen as a serious and present danger to the British war effort here in Europe. What better way to confirm his thinking than by the British trying their best to thwart his clever machinations?'

'And that role was played out by me and Molly O'Hara?'

'Yes, Madame de Metz's arrival and subsequent disappearance in pursuit of Macleod and de Valois's wife would have given the French very much the impression that we were doing all in our power to frustrate their ambitions. Fortune certainly smiled on you with the arrival of Macleod, unless of course you or Madame de Metz had a hand in that.'

'No, Macleod dropped to us straight from heaven.'

'Like manna in the desert?'

'Very like. And once you heard he'd run off with Madame de Valois no doubt you saw it as yet another piece of divine intervention?'

Trent smirked.

'Occasionally things do seem to favour one's efforts. I regard such times as just rewards delivered to the deserving.'

'Once you received Molly's report and knew where they were headed, you sent Gregory and me to Boston to put some plaster icing on your wooden cake. I was sure to blunder, you knew that.'

'I counted on it, I had every confidence that you would fail me.'

'And I realise now that I could indeed be counted on. I was brash and inexperienced and too proud to listen or learn. And you knew I would resent being placed in the position of a subordinate to a common whore.'

'A whore, yes, but not a common one. I dispute common.'

'I was bound to fail.'

'As indeed you did. You failed splendidly. I was proud of you.'

'But as the cautious man you are, you took the extra precaution of having Gregory accompany me. Was Gregory's task to see that nothing might, by some awkward chance, go right?'

Trent shrugged.

'Luckily he was not needed.'

'But if he was?'

'He would have arranged for you and Molly to be taken. You, of course, would tell them all you knew.'

'I might have resisted.'

Trent let out a loud laugh.

'If you are to understand, even only a little, of what our work is about, then lose that illusion at once, Melford. In our world no one, when questioned, resists. They may die or go mad but no one, as you call it, resists. As I said, you would tell all you knew, which was exactly what I would have wanted them to hear.'

'And Molly?'

'Ah, Molly was a different proposition. She, very sensibly, would have bargained for her life.'

'With what? She had no more information than I.'

'No, but she had a letter. A letter I gave to her which was signed by the highest authority in the land. A letter by which she could command any loyal subject of the crown. Of course it was a forgery, good enough if used well away from England, but if it fell into the wrong hands, which I admit I hoped it might, could easily enough be shown to be far from genuine if it were used against us.'

'And where is that letter now?'

'She gave it back to me. It bought her life for her. As I said, Molly knew how to bargain.'

There was silence for a moment while Melford digested all he had been told.

'Was it you who had St Clair killed?'

'No. Somebody else was responsible for that favour.'

'Who?'

'A very clever gentleman whom you had the pleasure of meeting in Boston.'

Melford mentally reviewed his visit to Boston. Only one man came to mind.

'Bentley?'

'None other.'

Melford was momentarily stunned.

'Bentley works for you?'

'No, not me.'

'Then who?'

'For a certain gentleman by the name of John Adams, lately President of America.'

'So the American Government had St Clair killed?'

'Technically, no. Adams is a private citizen now. Jefferson is the President at the moment. However, that is beside the point. The actual order to kill St Clair was given by an old military gentleman who has an office in their new capital and he used a very capable agent to carry out the execution, a man name Jones, Jeremiah Jones.'

'But you said Bentley did it?'

'In a way he did. In the same way that I tried to prevent Fouché's plan.'

'I don't understand.'

'No, you're not meant to, Melford. No one is meant to understand. That's the whole point, don't you see?'

'No, Trent. Dammit, I don't see.'

'If I had so arranged things that you could understand, then anyone might understand and Monsieur Fouché would most certainly have understood, and understood a long time ago. If that happened he would have dropped his scheme and directed his considerable energies elsewhere and that may have been at a place where some real and lasting harm might have been done.'

'So, is Bentley part of this plot of Fouché's?'

'Yes, in the same way that we all are.'

'Is he working for or against the American Government?'

'Neither and both.'

'But you said …'

But he could not make head nor tail of what Trent had said so he gave up. He had come into the room rather proud that he understood a little more of Trent's business than previously. That pride now lay in ruins. He didn't understand and he never would understand.

'I'm pleased with you, Melford. You are indeed a changed man from the arrogant semi-imbecile I sent as window dressing to Boston. Sit down and we'll take a drink together.'

'I don't understand, Trent. Why you are pleased with me?'

Trent stood up and went to a cupboard. Out of it he took a decanter filled with golden liquid and two glass tumblers which he brought to the desk.

'Because at last you show a small glimmer of promise.' He poured out two drinks and passed one to Lord Melford. 'When I sent you to Boston I doubted you would come back. Well, you came back and you seem to have made progress, small progress it is true, but progress none the less. As I say, I'm rather pleased with you and when I next see your father I shall tell him so. He thinks of you, I know, as a coward, a waster and a fool. I shall tell him you are no longer quite such a fool.' Trent sat down and raised his glass. 'Come, Melford, a toast. Confusion to all understanding, long may it prosper, long may it serve.'

Lord Melford raised his glass with little enthusiasm and drank.

'So, what do we do now?'

'Nothing.'

'What about Macleod and the woman?'

'What about them?'

'Fouché might have them. If Brutti's taken the trouble to tell us about them then it means he knows they represent no threat.'

Trent shrugged.

'If he has he's welcome to them, and if they're still free then they are of no importance. Their part in all of this is over. Forget them.'

'But they went to see Cardinal Henry. What does that mean?'

'I neither know nor care. The business is over for us and if Fouché has them he may do as he pleases with them.' Trent threw off what was left in his glass. 'Now, drink up and leave. I have other work to do.'

Jasper Trent watched as Melford finished his drink, rose and left. He was not displeased with the way his dealings in the matter of Cardinal Henry Stuart had turned out. Whether Fouché would manage to bring off his plan he doubted, he doubted it very much. The Americans were indeed divided and there were senior men in America, very senior men, who had played on those divisions for their own ends. But the divisions in the country were not yet sufficient to be in danger of setting them all at each other's throats. That day might well come, Trent felt sure of it, but if it did it was still a long way off. No, Fouché had played a clever game but had overplayed his hand. Still, it had kept him from other things while his powers to harm the Crown were at their height, so it was all to the good. Soon enough he would find other more pressing problems, not least among them the ambitions of Napoleon. And cracks in *that* relationship were already well advanced. Well advanced indeed.

Chapter Seventy-one

Macleod and Marie presented a sharp contrast to their surroundings. They were tired and shabby, whereas the room to which
they had been brought was alive with light, colour and decoration.
They stood in front of an ornate, lapis-lazuli-topped desk. Behind
the desk sat a man whose appearance was also at some variance
with their surroundings. He was plainly dressed and somewhat
nondescript. Nondescript that is, except for the intensity of his
eyes.

They had arrived in Paris in the morning but had not been
brought to Government offices as they had expected but to this
private house. Even the cursory glance at the exterior told them
that this was the house of an important man, a man of consequence
and a man with undoubted power. Nonetheless, it was still a
private residence.

The room in which they stood appeared to be a large study.
Count Brutti stood behind them, silent, while the man behind the
desk gazed at them.

Then the man reached out a hand and Count Brutti's voice
came from behind Macleod.

'M'sieur Fouché requests the Cardinal's letter.'

Macleod did not respond to the outstretched hand or Brutti's
words.

The man at the desk put his hand down.

'How disappointing. I had hoped for a little intelligence, that
crude violence would not prove necessary.'

He was about to make a sign to Brutti but Marie interrupted.

'Give it to him, Jean. If you do not he will only take it from
you.'

Fouché gave her the smallest of smiles.

'Thank you, Madame.' He once again held out his hand. 'The
letter, M'sieur.'

Macleod put his hand inside his coat and withdrew the

envelope. He stepped to the desk and threw it down. Fouché took it up and examined the seal carefully before breaking it and opening the envelope. He took out and unfolded two sheets of paper which he read. Then he placed them face up side by side in front of him and stood up.

'Allow me to properly introduce myself. M'sieur, Madame, I am Joseph Fouché, Duc d'Outrane and until recently Chief of Police to the French Republic.'

He waited.

Macleod felt Brutti's finger poked into his back.

'I am Jean Marie Macleod of Boston and this is my wife, Marie.'

Brutti gave a harsh laugh but stopped as Fouché's eyes fell on him.

'You may leave us, Count.'

'But, Your Excellency ...'

'Yes, Count Brutti?'

'Nothing, Your Excellency.'

Brutti went to the door of the study and left. Fouché came round from the desk and indicated a table on which there was a decanter with wine and three glasses.

'Please, will you sit down? You have suffered a long and tedious journey under the most trying circumstances. But now you have arrived safe and well, so there is no longer any need for severity of any kind.'

Macleod and Marie looked at the wine and then at each other. Fouché smiled and walked to the table, poured himself a glass of the wine took a long drink, then put the glass down.

'If the wine has been tampered with then we will all suffer the same consequences. Your luggage has been placed in a room in my house and all facilities will be available to you once we have spoken. But first some wine.' He poured two more glasses then re-filled his own. Macleod and Marie waited until he picked up his glass and once more took a drink. When he had done so they both drank, grateful for the taste of the wine. 'Now, before I can play the host I fear I must play the interrogator. As I said, I no longer hold the position of Chief of Police so my enquiries are completely unofficial. If you choose not to answer any of my questions you are, of course, at complete liberty to do so.'

'And are we at liberty to leave if we choose to do so?'

'Ah, so very direct, M'sieur Macleod. No, I regret you are not at liberty to leave, but I assure you that is entirely for your own protection. Were I still to hold my office I could have let you go wherever you wished and offered you assurances of security during your stay in Paris. Without the force of my late office I have to tell you that were you to leave this house, your safety would be far from assured.'

Fouché waited for a moment. Macleod wasn't sure what to say, so it was Marie who asked the next question.

'But if we chose to accept whatever risks to our safety Paris might hold, could we then leave?'

'Most assuredly, Madame. You are not in any sense prisoners here.'

Macleod put down his glass and stood up.

'Then, sir, we choose to leave.'

'Wait, Jean. At least let us hear why Monsieur Fouché has brought us here.'

'Bravo, Madame, beauty and sense combined, you are a lucky man, M'sieur Macleod.'

Macleod reluctantly sat down.

'As you seem impatient to be free of my hospitality I will be as brief as I can. Do you know what is in the letter the Cardinal gave you?'

Macleod's response was immediate.

'Yes.'

Marie's qualification was more gentle in delivery.

'We know some of it.'

'And that would be?'

'The Cardinal told us the letter contained a list of names. You know the connection in which those men whose names are on that list stand to you and also to the Government of America. We have no knowledge as to what more may be in the letter.'

'I see. I wish I could believe you.'

'The seal was unbroken, you saw that for yourself and, as we were kidnapped almost as soon as we left the Cardinal, we had no way of tampering with it.'

'Yes, Madame, I realise that. The seal was, as you say, unbroken. But I have no way of knowing whether the Cardinal had not already told you what the letter contained.'

'He did not, M'sieur.'

'Then of course I take your word, Madame.'

Macleod interrupted once more.

'Why go on with this farce, Fouché? You're beaten.'

'Farce, Monsieur? Beaten?'

'If as you say you are no longer Chief of Police and the Cardinal is prepared to reveal the names of the plotters in America what hope is there for your plan now?'

'Wait, Jean.'

'Wait? What for?'

But Marie ignored his question. Her attention was on Fouché.

'I think, M'sieur, you had already anticipated that the Cardinal's list of names would fall into someone's hands. I think you were waiting for it to happen.'

'What?'

Fouché ignored Macleod, his attention was on Marie.

'Madame, I salute you.'

'Thank you, Monsieur Fouché, and I salute you on the success of your plan.'

'Merci, Madame, from someone as perceptive as yourself such praise is most gratifying.'

Macleod forced himself back into the conversation.

'Success, what success?'

But both ignored him.

'What will happen to us now?'

'That depends on how much you know, Madame.'

'We know nothing, I assure you, nothing that is for certain. It is merely that we have made assumptions. We could, of course, be wrong.'

'Made assumptions? Dammit, what assumptions have we made?'

'Yes, Madame, I join with your husband. Please tell me your assumptions.'

'We assume that it was never your intention to put Cardinal Henry on the throne of America.'

'What!'

'Please, Jean, let me finish.'

'Yes, M'sieur Macleod, I beg of you, let Madame finish.'

Macleod lapsed into a reluctant and sullen silence.

'The Cardinal is an old man and frail. Also I believe he is a good man. I think this because I know his people love him. What sort of king would he make and for how long?'

'He claims the English throne, he claims that he is already a king.'

'He honours his father's and brother's memory, no more.'

Macleod broke out of his silence.

'But for God's sake, Marie, if Fouché never intended to put him on the throne, then what the hell was it all …'

'Indeed, Madame, as M'sieur Macleod asks, if not the throne then what?'

'To get the list of names written in the Cardinal's own hand and sealed with his seal, as for the rest …'

She paused.

'Yes, Madame, as for the rest?'

'Our assumption is that it is a short declaration by the Cardinal rejecting any arrangement whereby the throne of America would be offered to him and identifying the men in the list as those who had sponsored such an proposal.'

'Bravo again, Madame.'

'I see, M'sieur Fouché, that I am right.'

Fouché stood up.

'Substantially. You differ from the actuality in details only.' He walked back to the desk and rang a small bell. 'I truly regret, Madame, what it is that I am about to do.' The door opened and Count Brutti re-entered. 'Take them to La Force. They are to be held as "Specials", you understand, no charge, no records, no names. They are to communicate with no one, no one at all you understand? In secret. And no food or water until I give the order.'

'At once, Excellency.' The Count went back to the door and gestured to someone outside. Two men entered. 'Those two to La Force in a closed carriage under your guard. If I find they have spoken to anyone before they are confined you will both suffer for it.'

The two men marched across the room. One grabbed Macleod and one grabbed Marie. Macleod made a brief struggle.

'Damn you, Fouché, you can't do this.'

'Oh, but I can, M'sieur Macleod.' He turned to Count Brutti. 'If either resists in any way, be sure to kill them both.'

Macleod ceased his struggle and they were taken away followed by Count Brutti.

Fouché returned to his desk and looked at the Cardinal's papers in front of him.

'Well, Mr Trent, we have both played the game. Soon we will see which of us has won.'

Chapter Seventy-two

La Force was not a particularly horrific prison, not by Bastille standards.

Situated in the Rue du Roi de Sicile, the building had originally been the home of the Duc de la Force. A few years before the Revolution it had been converted to a prison and, although it could not be said to be comfortable, La Force was provided with well-ventilated shower areas and, apart from some excesses during the early years of the Revolution, was not a place whose name instilled fear into people. However, in what had been the Duc's wine cellars there were a few cells where "Specials" were brought and lodged. Such inmates were never allowed any contact except with carefully selected guards. No sound ever emanated from these dark, damp cells into the main prison, and for that the more fortunate inmates were heartily grateful.

Macleod and Marie had arrived at La Force in daylight but no light penetrated their damp, dark cell. The floor was stone not relieved even by straw and there was no form of bedding. They could not see each other and neither spoke, for both shared the same thoughts, that from this place, if they ever left it, it would only be to be taken to a place of execution. Once the door had slammed shut they had found each other's hands and sat together in silence.

Neither had any idea how long they had been there, possibly a night and into the next day. But in such a place, how did one measure time?

Suddenly they heard the door of their cell open and the light of a lamp flooded into the dark stone chamber. A harsh voice behind the lamp gave a command.

'Come.' Marie's grip on Macleod's hand tightened. The voice spoke again. 'You heard, come out.' They stood up and Macleod spoke to the unseen figure behind the light.

'Where are we being taken?'

'Come, or I'll have you dragged out.'

In the lamplight Macleod saw Marie turn to look at him. He knew what she thought awaited them.

'Marie, whatever happens remember that I love you.'

'And I love you, Jean.'

And then, with as much nobility as they could, they emerged from the damp, filthy cell into the damp filthy stone passage.

Their gaoler led the way with the lamp and they followed. Marie slipped her hand into Macleod's and he pressed it as if to say, have courage.

They were led up a flight of wet stone steps, on through further dark stone passages until finally they emerged through a heavy door into what looked like a guard room. Two uniformed soldiers, each with a musket resting butt-end on the floor, stood and watched them as they entered. Their time spent in the total darkness of the cell made it difficult for Macleod or Marie to adjust to the well-lit room and, looking at what they both assumed to be their final escort, neither noticed the other man present until he spoke.

'M'sieur Macleod, dear Madame, please accept my apologies. It has all been a most unfortunate mistake. Monsieur Fouché would not have wished this to happen for the world, I assure you.'

Macleod focussed his eyes and looked at Count Brutti blankly. Marie was the first to manage a question.

'We are not going to be executed?'

'But, my dear Madame, what could have put such a thought into your pretty head?'

He tried to give a light laugh which broke through Macleod's momentary confusion.

'Because it was that swine Fouché who had us thrown into that stinking hole. That put the thought into our heads. That and his orders to kill us if we resisted.'

'But, my dear Mr Macleod, he did not speak literally. It was merely a manner of speech.'

'A manner of speech!'

'Monsieur Fouché would be desolate if any harm befell either of you.'

'Good God man, you'll be telling me next it was only his little joke. I've a good mind to take you by the neck and throttle the damn life out of you.'

The two soldiers had stood impassively throughout the exchange but Macleod's words and his menacing manner caused them to pick up their muskets and point them casually at him. Marie saw what they had done.

'Jean, please, what has happened is past. What matters now is that we leave this place and try to leave it unharmed.' Macleod saw her look at the soldiers and became aware of the muskets. 'We must go with this man and see what Monsieur Fouché intends to do with us.'

Count Brutti gratefully greeted his new ally.

'Dear lady, how very sensible.' Brutti made a quick gesture to the soldiers one of whom opened a door. Brutti, still talking, led them out of the guard room into a well-lit corridor. 'I assure you M Fouché regrets wholeheartedly what has happened. There is a carriage outside. You, Madame, will be taken to some ladies who will assist you in your toilette and provide you with suitable attire and anything else you require.' They passed through a large hall which had once been a grand reception area, where prisoners now stood or lounged about the walls. On the far side of the hall two soldiers stood on either side of a pair of heavy, ornate doors. Into one of these doors had been set a smaller, plain door. On seeing Brutti approach, one of the soldiers, who had been in conversation with an inmate, stepped to this door, unlocked it and pulled it open. Brutti led Marie and Macleod out. Standing in the street by the door was a closed carriage. Brutti pulled open the carriage door and offered his hand to Marie who took it and got in. Brutti stood to one side and smiling, gestured for Macleod to follow her. Once in the carriage and moving Brutti resumed his flow of conversation as if they were old friends sharing a pleasant ride. 'If, once we have made arrangements for Madame, you would accompany me, M'sieur Macleod, you also will be provided with all attentions. Afterwards, Monsieur Fouché invites you to dine with him. There will be with him a friend of yours who wishes to meet you both again. Your friend will join you for the meal.'

'A friend?'

'Indeed, that was what I was told.'

'What friend?'

'Alas, no name was confided to me, but it is always pleasant to renew old acquaintances, is it not? You will be refreshed and restored, meet an old friend, and then you will dine well, I promise you.' He gave a small laugh. 'So, all is well and we can put all this,' he waved a deprecatory hand at their stained and cell-scented clothing, 'unfortunateness behind us.'

Chapter Seventy-three

Everything was as Count Brutti had promised. Macleod, after being cleansed, dressed and generally refurbished next saw Marie when she entered the splendid room in Fouché's house where he had been taken to await her.

She was wearing an evening gown of dazzling beauty looking like someone who had not, nor ever could have known, a care in the world. She was fresh, bright, cheerful and more lovely than ever. As for Macleod, from head to foot he was simply a fashion plate. Had the late Monsieur de Valois been able to cast an eye over him and see him now, he would have unhesitatingly approved and passed him fit for the best company in the land. Marie crossed the room straight to where Macleod, self-conscious and deeply uncomfortable, stood captivated by the vision that was Marie.

'But, Jean, is it you? You are magnificent. Have they given you a title? They must at least have made you a Duke, for you to look so very grand.'

'Please, Marie, don't mock me. I objected, I argued, but as you see here I am once more playing the primped-up dandy and feeling more like a tailor's dummy than anything human.'

Marie reached up and gave him a small kiss on the cheek. Then spun round.

'And me, Jean, do I also look primped-up, like a tailor's dummy?'

Her dark hair was gathered up on to her head and held in place at the back with a jewelled comb. Her dress shimmered under the light of the two candelabra and round her neck was a jewelled necklace the pendant of which pointed down to where the cleavage of her bosom showed above the low cut of the dress.

Macleod was unable to speak for a moment, his eyes guided by the pendant and his mind in a turmoil. He had forgotten what Marie looked like when she dressed as he had first known her.

A door opened and Fouché entered.

'My dear Madame de Valois,' he came and took her hand and kissed it, 'you look like a queen.'

'I hope not, Monsieur, that title is an unfortunate one in France.'

'A Duchess then, and remember, I speak as a Duke.' Fouché turned to Macleod. 'I hope you bear me no ill will, M'sieur. A man in my position cannot always regard his own wishes. For myself, I have found you both to be charming and under other circumstances …'

Macleod cut him short.

'The circumstances were as they were.'

Fouché gave him a nasty smile and a small bow.

'I am so glad that you understand.'

'I was told there would be a friend here.'

'There will be. He will arrive very shortly.'

'Who is this friend?'

'It is a Monsieur Bentley. He comes from Boston and claims to know both of you very well.'

'Bentley!'

'You do not know him?'

'I know him.'

'Do I detect in your tone that he is perhaps not regarded by you as such a friend?'

'Friend! If he dares to show his face to me again I'll break his damned neck.'

Marie put a hand on his arm.

'Jean, please, remember where we are.'

'I don't give a curse for where we are or who we're with. I'm fed up with being no better than a ball on a billiard table poked round by anyone with a confounded stick. I say if that blackguard so much as shows his face …'

And as he spoke the door opened and Bentley entered. He walked straight across to Marie.

'Madame de Valois, looking, if I may say so, more beautiful than ever. My compliments, Madame.'

And as he took her hand and bent to kiss it Macleod stepped forward and his fist crashed into the side of Bentley's head. Bentley uttered a cry, staggered sideways, fell over a chair and tumbled to the floor.

Marie gave a small scream and Fouché uttered an oath.

Macleod ignored them all and glared at Bentley.

'Get up damn you, I'm going to thrash you.'

Bentley sat up rubbing the side of his head.

'In that case, Macleod, thank you for the offer, but if you don't mind I think I'll sit this one out. My brawling days are too far behind me to enjoy a rough and tumble just at the moment.'

'Get up I say or I'll thrash you where you …'

Marie screamed again but louder this time and Macleod felt the point of a knife pressed into his neck just below his ear. He tried to turn his head but the knife only pressed harder.

All eyes were on Macleod, but it was Bentley who spoke.

'Careful, Fouché, remember our agreement. If your man kills him then you know what will happen.'

All of Fouché's charm of manner had returned.

'Have no fear, M'sieur Bentley, I rarely kill my dinner guests and certainly never before they have dined.' He turned to Macleod. 'If M'sieur Macleod tries to cause any more trouble, Count Brutti will merely disable him, no more.'

Count Brutti held the knife where it was but reduced the pressure.

Bentley slowly got up.

'You still carry a punch, Macleod.' He straightened his coat. 'And your temper hasn't improved with age. But I dare say you feel yourself to have been provoked. Well, perhaps you were. And that being the case we'll consider the matter closed. Now, Fouché, I thought I had been invited to dine not roll around on the floor among your furniture.'

'What about M'sieur Macleod? He seems to be a somewhat unwilling companion.'

Bentley gave Macleod a grin.

'Not at all. He always greets people in that manner, it's how he gets so much custom. You know that after you've met him for the first time things can only get better.' He walked over to Marie and took her hand once more. 'Permit me, Madame, a moment ago I was interrupted.' He kissed her hand. 'Now, Fouché, get rid of your friend with the stiletto and lead us to our meal and if the food and wine are half as agreeable as the company', he smiled at Marie then looked at Macleod, 'or as diverting as the entertainment I

331

shall be well pleased.'

Fouché waved away Count Brutti who lowered his knife and withdrew.

'Come, please, the table is ready.'

'Macleod, I claim the privilege of an old comrade in arms to offer my arm to Madame de Valois.'

Marie took the proffered arm.

'Merci, M'sieur.'

And they walked together towards a door that had opened showing a dining table laid and ready for guests with liveried servants waiting. Fouché stood beside Macleod.

'Come, M'sieur Macleod. I hope you like the menu my chef has chosen for us. He has no knowledge of American food in general, and none at all of Boston, but he has done his best, and in Paris his best is considered equal to any chef, even that of our glorious First Consul himself.'

And Macleod, utterly at a loss to understand what was going on, allowed himself to be led in.

Chapter Seventy-four

Macleod took no pleasure in the meal. The food and wine were, he supposed, excellent, but he ate only because he was hungry. The polite conversation that went back and forth across the table was closed to him by both temperament and choice.

Marie, however, was vivacity itself. She was a veteran of many such evenings where, as an unwilling hostess or unwilling guest, she had played the part required of her, just as she played it now.

Bentley was also playing a part, the gay and diverting guest, not at all the man who, in Boston, had tried to kill Marie and had succeeded in killing Amélie.

Fouché assumed the role of the polished and urbane host and there remained no trace of the man who, in this very house on the previous day, had ordered them both killed if they offered any resistance.

Macleod alone at the table acted no part, but either no one noticed his dogged silence or they all chose to ignore it. So it was that the evening ran its course until the performance was over and the curtain finally came down.

They returned to the room in which they had first assembled where Bentley took it upon himself to make their farewells.

'My compliments to your chef, Fouché, an excellent dinner.'

'Merci, and made all the more excellent by the company.'

'Well then, even the pleasantest of evenings comes to an end and we must now take our leave.'

'Of course, M'sieur Bentley. Your carriage is at the door.' Fouché took Marie's hand and kissed it. 'Madame, such beauty, wit and brains have not graced this house for a very long time.'

Marie smiled a formal acknowledgement of the compliment.

The door opened and a maid entered with Marie's cape together with two footmen who carried the cloaks of Bentley and Macleod.

Fouché waited until they were ready.

'So, M'sieur Bentley, it is as you wished, you are safely

reunited with your friends.'

'It is as we agreed, Fouché.'

'In that case I bid you all adieu.'

He gave a small bow, Bentley returned it and Marie gave the slightest of curtsies. Bentley then turned and led them from the room to the front door, outside which his carriage waited.

The carriage rumbled through the dark streets but the carriage lights shone in through the windows enough for the passengers to see one another. Marie looked at Bentley.

'Tell me, M'sieur Bentley, are we now safe?'

'Safer than you were, but not yet, I regret, as safe as I would wish. Nor will you be, either of you, so long as you are in Paris or even in France.'

'Paris! I wish I'd never seen the place. A curse on it. And a curse on Fouché and on you, Bentley, in fact on all damned foreigners and all false intriguers.'

And, having delivered his judgement on Paris, his late host, his carriage companion, and foreigners in general, Macleod lapsed once more into sullen silence.

'I'm afraid, Madame, that Macleod is in a poor mood and not, I suspect, open to any conversation I might wish to have with you both. We have much to talk about, and much to arrange, but it had better wait until the morning when our growling bear has rested. Let us hope he wakes up in a more receptive frame of mind.'

Marie sat back and they all continued the journey in silence, each busy with their own thoughts.

The carriage rolled on through the dark streets and stopped at a large house in a fashionable part of the city behind the Place Vendôme. A maid answered the door and Bentley led them to some comfortable and well-appointed rooms where Macleod and Marie found their luggage waiting for them, their clothes unpacked, and everything laundered and carefully laid out.

Bentley looked around the room to satisfy himself that all was as it should be.

'I trust you will both be comfortable. If there is anything you want please ask the maid. Now I must leave you but I will return tomorrow morning and try to explain everything.'

'Thank you, M'sieur Bentley.'

Bentley turned to Macleod who stood stolidly silent.

'Well then, goodnight.'

But Macleod ignored the offered hand and said nothing.

Once Bentley had gone Marie came to Macleod and kissed him gently.

'Jean, what will happen to us? Are we safe now?'

'I don't know.'

'Bentley cannot really be our friend, can he?'

'I don't know.'

'But nothing more can happen tonight?'

'No, I don't think so.'

'Jean, we have played the part of husband and wife so many times. Whatever happens tomorrow, tonight we will not play any more.' Macleod looked at her and, realising what it was she meant, took her in his arms and they kissed again. 'Go now and when I am ready I will come to you.'

Macleod needed no further encouragement. He went at once into the bedroom, pulled off all his modish clothes and threw them into a corner of the room, got into bed and lay, still and excited, all thoughts driven from his mind, except that Marie would come to him at last and they would share the love that had grown so great between them.

It was not really so very long before Marie quietly and shyly entered the bedroom and in the darkness crept naked into the bed.

'Jean, I am here, I am ready.'

But her soft voice received no reply. Macleod had lain waiting, tired but at last content. He had closed his eyes and given himself up to thoughts of Marie naked and in his arms. As his mind and body, so sorely taxed for so long, felt at last the comfort of ease, his happy thoughts turned rapidly, but imperceptibly, to happy dreams of Marie lying beside him ready to show her love, and Macleod slept.

Chapter Seventy-five

Marie was up and dressed before Macleod woke and, when he did wake and dress, to hide their embarrassment, both behaved as if nothing at all had happened, which, of course, it hadn't.

Bentley returned at half-past eight and both Marie and Macleod were glad that he had called so early. The morning had not been easy for either of them. When he entered Macleod ignored his greeting but Marie was less reserved.

'Please, M'sieur Bentley, will you sit down? May I ring for some coffee?'

But Bentley dismissed the offers.

'Nothing, thank you, there is not time. Madame, and you are included, Macleod, black looks or no, your situation here remains, as I said last night, perilous. You understand that?'

'How very mysterious you are, M'sieur Bentley. Are you trying to frighten us?'

'A little fear for your present situation might not go amiss.'

Macleod at last came to life.

'If you have something to say, Bentley, be so good as to say it. We want none of your intriguer's games.'

'Very well. This afternoon you both go to Le Havre where you take ship tomorrow for Boston. You're going home Macleod, I hope you're pleased.'

Macleod failed to keep the surprise from his voice.

'If that's true then I am glad, heartily glad.'

Marie, however, was more cautious.

'And I would also be glad, M'sieur Bentley, if I could be sure that what you say is true. Yesterday you said you would return and explain. Today you return and say we are to go to Boston. But you do not explain.'

'If I had the words to convince you, I would explain. But, as you both know words are a much debased currency in the world in which you have found yourselves. Deeds alone, I think, can

336

convince.'

'Dammit, man, if that's so then less words and more deeds.'

Bentley turned angrily.

'Macleod, you are and always were a pig-headed fool and God alone knows why you're still alive. If it were you alone I had to deal with I'd happily leave you to the tender mercies of our friend Fouché. However, as there is Madame de Valois to consider I will do my best to save your lives and get you safely back to America.'

Macleod was also angry and his fists were clenched. Marie looked at the two men and feared a repeat of the violence of the previous evening.

'We want no favours from you, Bentley, damn you and your explanations and your ships to Boston. Get out of here before I finish now what I should have finished last night.'

For a moment they stared at each other. Then Bentley sat down heavily on a chair.

'I give up. You're too much for me, Macleod.' He pulled a white handkerchief from inside his coat and held it up. 'I surrender.' He turned to Marie. 'But I surrender to you, Madame, not to this madman. I throw myself on your mercy.'

Marie also sat down.

'I accept your surrender, sir.' Macleod looked from one to the other. 'Sit down, Jean. M'sieur Bentley is going to explain.'

'Yes, Macleod, sit down. We're both too old for fisticuffs even if I had the time.' Macleod reluctantly sat down. 'Macleod, upon my honour, I never thought that you would become involved in the way you have. You were meant to play the smallest of parts. Somehow, God knows how, for I certainly don't, you were drawn into this thing and Madame de Valois was drawn in alongside you.'

'And this thing, M'sieur Bentley, what exactly is this thing?'

'Dammit, Marie, we don't need to be told.' Macleod faced Bentley with a look of triumph. 'We know all about it, Bentley, it's a vile plot. Fouché intends to put Cardinal Henry Stuart on the throne of America and is in league with men in America of sufficient influence to bring about such an abomination. The Cardinal himself handed me a list of the traitors.'

Macleod sat back satisfied with his bombshell.

Bentley looked at Marie.

'Is that what you think, Madame?'

'I think there is a plot but I do not think that Cardinal Henry ever had any intention of allowing himself to be used as Jean has suggested.'

'No, Madame?'

'No, and I think Monsieur Fouché is too clever to put his trust in such a plan.'

'May I ask why you think that?'

'Cardinal Henry did not appear to me as a man with such great ambition for himself.'

'He already claims one throne.'

'True, but he does not do that for himself, he honours the memory of his brother, no more. He is a good man, his people love him. They spoke of him with affection and told us with great bitterness how he had lost all his money when the Revolution came to France. They said that what little he had left he gave to the Pope to free him from imprisonment by Napoleon. Does that sound like the kind of man who would plot to gain a kingdom for himself?'

Bentley looked back at Macleod. The triumph Macleod had felt had left him.

'I don't understand. Are you saying, Marie … well, what is it you are saying?'

But Bentley spoke before Marie could answer.

'Madame is saying nothing. She is thinking out loud and they are idle thoughts, of no consequence. It would be better to put such thoughts from you, Madame. For your own safety I strongly suggest it.'

'If you say so, M'sieur, then it is already done.'

'Well then, I said I would explain and now I will, in so far as I am able. I am here on Government business.' He held up his hand to silence Macleod whom he could see was going to challenge his claim, 'I merely tell you that to explain why I am here. Whether you believe me or not is immaterial. On arrival I find that you and Madame de Valois have fallen foul of Monsieur Fouché and are in Paris, detained in unfortunate circumstances. I arranged for your release. My arrangement will hold good for no more than thirty-six hours at the very most. If you are still in France after that, you will both most assuredly die.' Bentley stood up. 'A carriage will call for you at one o'clock. If you choose to take it you will travel to Le

Havre where an American merchantman will take you both to America. If you choose not to take it then …' and Bentley shrugged his shoulders.

Marie stood.

'M'sieur Bentley, if you did indeed arrange for our release then Jean and I thank you from our hearts. I would very much wish to believe that you did arrange it. If that was so I might begin to believe you were our friend. But there is one thing that stands in the way of my belief. Was it you who tried to kill me in Jean's house in Boston? Was it you who killed Amélie?'

'Great heavens, Marie, what makes you think …'

'Jean, who else wanted me dead? Think, Jean. The British agents wanted my information not my death. Who else was there?'

They both turned and looked at Bentley who tried to give them a conciliating smile.

'Believe me, dear lady, I did not intend to kill anyone, but I had to act. Darcy would have suspected me of a double game if I had done nothing and I couldn't risk that, so I went to the house and found your room. I meant to put my shot somewhere in the wall, that was all, but that damned old housekeeper rushed in and pushed past me, and I had to get a shot off as best I could. I simply fired at random, unfortunately I hit the woman. I wouldn't have had it happen for the world, I assure you, although it did wonders in convincing Darcy that I had fully intended to kill you. I'm afraid Amélie was an unfortunate incident, accidental damage shall we call it?'

'No, M'sieur, we will not call it accidental damage. We will call it the death of a loyal and loving friend.'

'Madame, I assure you …'

'Please, M'sieur, no more. It is done and cannot be undone so I must accept it.'

But from the tone of her voice Bentley rather thought she didn't and he felt he couldn't really blame her.

'Madame, I salute your good sense, so for your own safety please use it to try and persuade this blockhead here to take the carriage. If he refuses then I do truly urge you to go without him. You should have had no part in all of this. And now I really must leave. There are calls on my time I can no longer postpone. I am sorry, Madame, that your visit to Paris has been so brief and unsatisfactory.' He turned to Macleod. 'Good day, Macleod. If time and circumstances permit I will be at Le Havre to be sure you get away safely. Both of you I hope.'

He held out his hand. Macleod looked at it then stood up and took it.

'You never did work against the Government, then?'

'No, never, but there were people who needed to think that I did. And now I really must go. The carriage, sharp at one, mind.'

Bentley left and Macleod stood for a moment after he had gone.

'I still don't understand. Whose side is the Cardinal on and why ...'

Marie put a hand on his arm.

'Stop, Jean. Think of it as if you were a child again asking a question about your faith.'

Macleod thought of it as a child.

'That it's a mystery?'

'Yes, it is something you are not meant to understand. It is enough that, if not God, then someone understands and, because someone understands, we are alive and tomorrow we will leave France and set sail for America.'

Macleod thought about it and came to the conclusion that what Marie had said made more sense than anything else he had heard that morning.

'If you say so.'

And she kissed him.

Chapter Seventy-six

Macleod was walking with Bentley on the deck of the ship as the crew busied themselves in making ready to sail. Marie was below seeing to their cabin arrangements.

'Tell me, Bentley, and the truth now. What was my part in all of this?'

'It was never meant to be a very big part. I needed you out of the way because of the Darcy business, that is all. Jeremiah arranged it for me. You were to go to New Orleans and, well, really do no more than draw attention to yourself.'

'Draw attention to myself!'

'Yes. It was Jeremiah's idea. A very able man, Jeremiah. A very brave man.'

'Damn Jeremiah. I can't believe that all I've been through was for no better reason than to draw attention to myself.'

'Sorry, Macleod, but there it is. You were supposed to be a person of no importance, a side-show. Circumstances, however, decided it should be otherwise and things got somewhat out of hand. It happens. Our business is not an exact science.'

'And what exactly is your business?'

Before Bentley could reply, if he intended to reply, Marie rejoined them.

'All is made as comfortable as possible.'

'I'm glad to hear it, Madame.'

'Tell me, M'sieur Bentley, is it all over now for us? Are we free of your plots and intrigues?'

'Quite free. Once this boat sails you may both forget all about plots and intrigues.'

'Then I thank God for that.'

But Macleod was not as ready to let the recent past depart. 'But there *was* a plot? Just because we are free, the plotting and intrigue doesn't stop, does it?'

'No, I fear that never stops, nor ever will.'

'Leave it, Jean, it is now nothing to do with us.'

'But I can't leave it, Marie. I may have been a side-show, as Bentley calls it, but I was involved and if I know nothing else, I know that there is a threat to my country. How can I leave it?'

'Macleod, it's over, can't you just be grateful you've come out of it alive.'

'No, I damn well can't. I know my country is threatened. I wasn't supposed to know, but now I do. I can't just sail away to safety and forget it ever happened.'

'Hell's teeth, you're a stubborn bastard, Macleod. It's over, there is no threat, at least not from any plan of Fouché's. His game is finished and Monsieur Fouché will find out that those names on the list are no longer any good to him. In fact he will find they are a two-edged sword and it is France, not America, which will be cut and bleeding. That is why it was so urgent that you both leave France. Fouché made a bargain. I got you both away and, in return, I would give him the name of an agent of the American Government he had long suspected was inside his organisation. I'm afraid it proved a bad bargain on his part for the name I gave him will soon enough prove to be false. Fouché will not be a happy man the day he realises he's been duped.'

'And the names?'

'We have had those names for some time, but we decided that it was best to leave them where they were until we were ready to use them.'

'Use them how?'

'That need not concern you. Suffice it to say that very soon those names will be used to good effect. America is safe I assure you, as Fouché and others will soon find out.'

'So, the General beat him!' Macleod felt like giving a great hurrah. 'Great heavens, the General was too much for the French bastard. He had his hand inside their vile plot and was pulling the strings all along.'

'No, Macleod, not the General.' Bentley paused before going on. He knew that what he was about to say would wound Macleod as much as any musket ball. 'I regret that the General's name was on that list. In fact, it was his name right at the top.'

Macleod almost stood back in shock

'I don't believe you. The General would never betray his country. You're a damn liar.'

'I wish I was but I regret I am not. The General was from the South and believed the North was out to take all the real power, financial and political, into its own hands, leaving the South like a poor, rural cousin, entirely dependent on the North. He wasn't going to let that happen to the land he'd fought for. He was the leader of the whole thing. It was he who would have come forward if the plan had succeeded. He was to be their figurehead to unite and save the country.

'Fortunately, almost from the beginning, I was able to place my own man close to the General as his aide and by the time the General realised what had happened it was too late. He could not act against my man without revealing his own involvement.

'It was through the General that I was able to recruit the others and palm them all off on to …'

Bentley stopped, but too late.

'That you recruited?' Bentley remained silent. 'But you said you never worked against the Government.'

Marie spoke gently.

'Nor did he, Jean.'

'But you heard. From his own lips.'

'Leave it, Jean, forget it all, their plots, their intrigue. It is no longer our affair. Why should it matter to us who started the plotting or why?'

'Listen to her, Macleod, I tell you solemnly she's giving you very good advice.'

Marie heard the threat in Bentley's voice and looked at Macleod with concern.

'We were not part of any plan, we were like Amélie or de Valois, my husband, accidental damage.' She turned to Bentley. 'When we are back in Boston we will forget this nightmare, forget it completely. You have my word.'

'Good, I hope you do.'

Macleod had overcome his shock and the truth of the General's treachery seemed, among so much treachery, just as possible as all the rest.

'But what's it all for, Bentley, all this scheming, secrecy and betrayal?'

'Where one government leads all others must follow suit. They work against us and we, in our turn, work against them. What you have witnessed is a very small piece of a very large canvas.'

'But if one government stopped, couldn't it all be stopped? Just because it has begun, must it continue?'

Bentley paused for a moment before replying.

'I have a friend who trades with the East. He told me of a saying they have. The man who rides the tiger cannot dismount.'

'Which is supposed to mean what?'

'That once begun it cannot stop.'

Voices started calling across the deck.

'The captain is making ready. I must go ashore. There is one last thing, Macleod.'

'Yes?'

'I am an old-fashioned Protestant and Boston is an old-fashioned Protestant town, and this lady is, well, this lady is too fine to be … damn you, man, do the right thing and make an honest woman of her.'

'M'sieur Bentley, are you asking Jean to marry me?'

'No, I'm damn well ordering him to marry you.'

'But I cannot marry him.'

'Cannot? Why?'

'Because we are married already. We were married by the Bishop of Frascati, by the Cardinal himself. It was the briefest of ceremonies but I assure you it took place and that we are now man and wife.'

'Good God! Macleod, either you're the best agent I've ever met or the best counterfeit of one. You've done it again, you devil.'

'I don't understand. Done what?'

A voice cried out from somewhere on the ship.

'All ashore that's going ashore.'

Two sailors stood by the gangplank waiting, one called across to Bentley.

'Come along, sir, unless you want to go to Boston.'

Bentley took Marie's hand and kissed it.

'Goodbye, Madame Macleod. I hope the voyage is kind to you.'

He then held out his hand. Macleod took the offered hand and shook it warmly.

'Goodbye, Macleod. Go back to Boston and settle back down to your lawyering and being a good husband.'

Bentley walked across to the gangplank and stood on the quay. The two sailors pulled the gangplank on board and the noise and activity increased until finally the ship began to move.

Macleod and Marie looked at Bentley who lifted his arm in a gesture of farewell and shouted something. But amongst the noise on the deck Macleod could not catch the words.

'What did he say?'

'I am not sure, Jean, but it sounded like "Welcome to the tiger".'

Chapter Seventy-seven

PARIS 1802

September 5th

The Office of Maurice de Talleyrand, Foreign Minister to the French Republic.

The magnificent doors of the office of the Foreign Secretary of the French Republic opened and Monsieur Talleyrand stood to greet his visitors. Robert Livingston, the American Ambassador, entered and strode purposefully to the large ornate desk and faced Talleyrand. Behind him, limping but doing his best to keep up, was a young man who walked with the aid of a stick. Talleyrand waited until the young man had arrived beside the Ambassador.

'M'sieur Livingston, it is, as always, a pleasure to greet you.'

'Thank you, Minister, but if you don't mind I would like to dispense with the usual formalities.'

Talleyrand could see that Ambassador Livingston was in no amiable frame of mind, in fact his mood seemed decidedly black. He cast his mind around to try and remember what, in particular, he might have done to bring about a visit of this gentleman in such a disagreeable humour, but could think of nothing.

'As you wish, Mr Ambassador, I am, as always, at your disposal, with or without the usual formalities.' He indicated the chairs opposite his desk. 'Would you and the young man care to sit?'

'I would not, sir. I would care to leave.'

'Indeed! To arrive so suddenly and leave so soon? I confess myself at a loss.'

'This,' and the look he gave the man spoke volumes, 'this gentleman,' and here he paused to dissociate himself from the courtesy of the title, 'will make any necessary explanations. He has been sent by my Government. I have been asked to bring him here and present him to you. As it is the wish of my Government, I do so. M'sieur Talleyrand, Mr Jones.'

Talleyrand looked enquiringly at Mr Jones whose countenance, apart from the smallest of polite smiles, remained blank. Receiving no communication from that quarter he moved his enquiry back to Robert Livingston.

'And Mr Jones is?'

'I have no doubt that Mr Jones himself will communicate that information to you, sir. As for myself I will, with your permission, withdraw.'

'Of course, M'sieur Ambassador, as soon as you wish.'

Livingston turned on his heel, marched to the door and left.

Talleyrand gave his full attention to the young man in front of him.

'Well, M'sieur Jones, is it you or I or some other party who has sent the Ambassador into such a black humour? I confess I can think of nothing on my part which might have brought about such an unfortunate state. Nothing recently, that is.' The young man remained silent. Talleyrand began to get an uneasy feeling about his visitor. 'However, as our esteemed Ambassador has withdrawn, please sit down and tell me to what I owe the pleasure of this meeting so urgently requested by Ambassador Livingston?'

The young man lowered himself into a chair and they sat looking at each other across the wide, ornate desk.

'M'sieur Talleyrand, a Special Envoy, Mr James Monroe, will soon be sent to Paris to assist Ambassador Livingston in the purchase of the Louisiana Territories. I have been given the task of ensuring that this purchase will be satisfactorily completed no later than the spring.'

'Indeed?'

'Yes, Your Excellency, indeed.'

Talleyrand's unease increased. He did not like this young man's manner, it was confident and quiet, the manner of one who is sure of the outcome before he begins his business.

'And how do you propose to set about the task you have been given?'

'By declaring war on France.'

Of all the answers that might have been made, the Foreign

Minister expected this one least, and liked it less.

'You personally, M'sieur Jones, or will you declare war on the French Republic with friends?'

'No, Monsieur, not I personally, nor even with friends. The American Government will formally declare war on the French Republic on the day that war resumes between France and Britain.'

'France and Britain are at peace.'

'And today it is not raining in Paris.'

'Which means?'

'That one day I think it will most certainly once again rain in Paris.'

Talleyrand's manner lost some of its charm.

'Mr Jones, I am a busy man and have no time for conundrums. If you have a message to deliver to me then deliver it.'

'The Government of France has, over a period of time and under the direction of Joseph Fouché, until recently your Chief of Police, undertaken a plot to overthrow the legitimate Government of America. It has suborned senior politicians, businessmen and others of power and influence who are American citizens. It has used French and American nationals as agents on American soil to bring about this treason. This plot is active and continuing. Only a short while ago a letter was carried from Rome to Paris by Fouché's agents, American agents, and delivered to M'sieur Fouché in person. We both know from whom that letter came. The letter contained, among other things, the names of those traitors Fouché has involved in the plot. The American Government has at its disposal, I assure you, ample evidence of this plot and two courses of action lie open. One is to arrest those American citizens involved, together with certain agents working for the French Government, and put them all on public trial. If they are found guilty, and the involvement of the French Government proved thereby, it will be regarded by the American Government as confirmation of an act of aggression by a foreign power. When hostilities resume between France and Britain, the American Government will declare itself an ally of the British in response to this French aggression, and declare war on France. To aid our British allies, American troops will march into the French Louisiana Territories.'

'I beg your pardon, Mr Jones, but those Territories are the

Spanish Louisiana Territories.'

It was a weak argument and Talleyrand knew it.

'Then I am sure France will be happy to let Spain defend its Territories if it wishes.' Talleyrand did not respond. 'Needless to say, whatever the outcome of the war in Europe, America will not cede back to France, nor even to Spain, whatever lands are taken. They will become a part of the American Republic.'

'I see, you are telling me that your Government intends to fabricate a plot involving the French Government in order to violate the sovereign territory of another power?'

'M'sieur Talleyrand, you are perfectly aware that no fabrication will be necessary. M'sieur Fouché has provided my Government with more than enough evidence for it to proceed as I have outlined.'

Talleyrand waited for a moment, but Jones remained silent and he was forced to ask the question.

'And the second course?'

'As I said, a Special Envoy, Mr James Monroe, will arrive early next year to negotiate alongside Ambassador Livingston for the purchase of the Louisiana Territories. The American Government has no wish to go to war with anyone despite such acts of provocation as I have already mentioned, but one way or another America will expand. I believe Ambassador Livingston has been at pains to make that very point to you. For some time he has been trying to persuade the French Republic, through you, to consider the sale to America of the Louisiana Territories.'

'I see. You wish to buy the Territories at the point of a gun? That is not diplomacy. I fear it is more akin to piracy or highway robbery.'

'I do not of course speak officially on behalf of the American Government, Monsieur Talleyrand, I am here merely as a messenger to place information before you. Information which I think you might be well advised to consider.'

'But still at the point of a gun?'

'It is not the policy of the American Government to indulge in the diplomacy of violence favoured by the Barbary Pirates. In fact, to show our displeasure at such methods, our fleet is currently blockading their ports. They would not negotiate, they preferred that our differences be decided by force of arms. As we speak they are regretting that decision.'

'And what is it that you suggest?'

'Believe me, Your Excellency, the American Government has no wish to extract an unfair price by the threat of violence nor the appearance of any threat. Special Envoy Monroe will be told to negotiate the best price possible, but it will be the best fair price. We are not brigands, Your Excellency. Mr Monroe will not be aware of what I have told you and will be negotiating in good faith. I trust as much will be said for yourself on behalf of the French Government. My role is simply to place information before you to ensure that you are aware of what the American Government sees as its options should the negotiations fail to produce a satisfactory outcome, satisfactory, that is, to both parties. And now, as you have pointed out to me that you are a busy man, I will leave you to your business. I think I have made clear the reason for my intrusion into your valuable time.'

Jones slowly rose.

'Am I to take it, M'sieur Jones, that you think this matter closed?'

'By no means, Monsieur Talleyrand, I consider this matter only just opened. Good day to you, Your Excellency.' The young man turned and limped to the door which opened. 'It has been a great pleasure to have met you, sir. I have long been an admirer of your methods.'

And the door closed behind him.

Talleyrand's secretary came in through another door.

'You heard?'

'Yes, Excellency.'

'What did you think of the young man Jones?'

'A very capable and confident young man.'

'I knew that one day they would send someone who would force me to listen, but I confess I was surprised at both the man and his argument.'

'I'm afraid, Excellency, he has studied your methods too well, that the secret of successful negotiations is to have them won before they begin.'

'How true. How very true.

'What do you wish me to do?'

'Begin to let it be known that our First Consul does not have the same interest in protecting our possessions in America since our recent losses in the Caribbean.'

'And?'

'Once that story has achieved some circulation let it be known that Napoleon wishes to raise money, a large sum of money, to increase our forces here in Europe. That he is prepared to consider the sale of foreign assets.'

'The British will take that as a signal that we are preparing for a return to war.'

'By the time the story gains purchase we will almost certainly *be* preparing for war, and monies from the sale of the Louisiana Territories will, without doubt, be spent to that end.'

'I cannot believe that anyone will be taken in by either story. Neither sounds so very convincing to me.'

'No, nor to me. If, before the new envoy comes, I can think of something better all well and good. If not, then we must make the best of what we have and leave it to history to decide what shall pass as the truth.'

Postscript

On Saturday 30th April 1803, without a shot being fired (officially), Ambassador Robert Livingston and Special Envoy James Monroe signed the treaty by which America came into possession of the Louisiana Territories, a tract of land of some 828,000 square miles covering what is today fifteen US states and two Canadian provinces. The price was 60 million French francs or 11,250,000 US dollars, roughly 3 cents per acre. Announcing the Purchase, President Thomas Jefferson said:

We have lived long, but this is the noblest work of our whole lives ... From this day the United States take their place among the powers of the first rank.

Spain immediately challenged the boundaries of the Territories and this dispute rumbled on until 1819 when both countries signed the Adams-Onis Treaty whereby the US acquired Florida and the boundary between the US and New Spain (from 1821, Mexico) was established.

Needless to say it didn't end there.

Henry Adams (1838–1918), whose grandfather and great-grandfather had both been US Presidents, described the Louisiana Purchase as trebly invalid, claiming that if the Territories were French, Napoleon had not the right to sell them without Government approval. If they were Spanish, the French couldn't sell them at all. And if Spain had first refusal of any sale under the Treaty whereby France had acquired them, the sale to America became worthless.

In his book *The Lies My Teacher Told Me* the sociologist and historian James Loewen (1942–) pointed out that all the US could buy from France was their claim to the Territories as the land actually belonged to the tribes who lived there.

And so it goes on, it never ends, it can't.

And the others?

The General, along with several other men of note, some few

from inside the Government, retired into private life where two committed suicide, one died under ambiguous circumstances and three left the US and settled in Europe. The General died of natural causes on his plantation aged seventy-three. None left any words for posterity.

Cedric Bentley replaced the General as Comptroller of the Contingent Fund of Foreign Intercourse, effectively the head of the American Secret Service, answerable directly to the President. He appointed Jeremiah Jones as Deputy Comptroller.

Napoleon was defeated at Waterloo in 1815 and exiled to St Helena where he died. Talleyrand survived to serve the restored French King, Louis XVIII, as Ambassador to the UK from 1830–34. He died on 17th May 1838 and was buried near his castle, the Château de Valançay.

Jasper Trent continued in his role and Lord Melford continued in his service.

Molly O'Hara's whereabouts could not be established although Jasper Trent instituted enquiries.

Kitty Mullen stayed in Boston where she took domestic service.

Joseph Fouché died in exile in Trieste in 1820.

Also by James Green

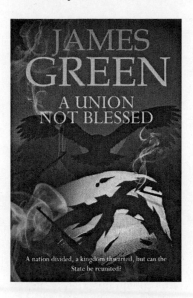

A Union Not Blessed

1804. America is a Union at peace and about to enter a golden age. The Louisiana Purchase has opened up the West to American settlement. America has crossed the Mississippi and the march to the Pacific can begin.

Spain is deeply involved in European war and reluctantly allows American settlers to develop its land.

America watches as Spain tries desperately to stem the tide of independence. War will come, but only when America is ready, meanwhile all is diplomacy.

But there are those in America who have their own plans for New Spain, not least ex-Vice President Aaron Burr. Burr's political fortunes are in terminal decline. He has made too many enemies and, having mortally wounded Alexander Hamilton in a duel, has been dropped by Jefferson from the presidential ticket. But Burr is nothing if not a man of guile and resource...

April 2013   **ISBN 978190826912**

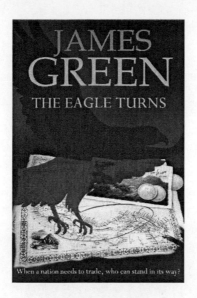

The Eagle Turns

1848. America has acquired Upper California and the Oregon Territories. The new American West needs a safe and short route from the populous East Coast for settlers and for trade Washington turns its eyes urgently towards Panama. But America is not alone.

Other nations see the almost unlimited power of owning a viable route which would open the west coast of the Americas and remove the need for shipping to risk the Roaring Forties of Cape Horn. Panama is a region of newly independent La Gran Colombia which would not willingly give away such a valuable asset.

America needs to possess Panama, or more accurately, that narrow strip of Panama on which a link between the Pacific and the Atlantic could be constructed. A way has to be found, and American Intelligence has a vital part to play ……

August 2013   **ISBN 978190826936**

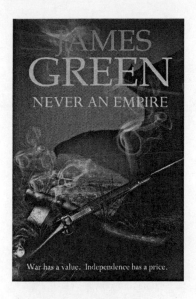

Never an Empire

1898. The Peace Treaty ending the Spanish-American War ceded Cuba, Porto Rico and the archipelago known as the Philippine Islands to the United States. America had become a colonial power! But the Philippines were already in a state of revolution against Spain and with its defeat the insurgents declared independence.

America had to fight or withdraw. She chose to fight. The American forces were victorious but at a cost beyond human life. They met with force a subject people's aspiration for freedom and independence .

America finds itself at the beginning a new century as a colonial power and its Intelligence Services have to cope with a different kind of conflict …

April 2014   **ISBN 978190826967**

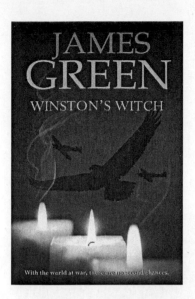

Winston's Witch

1944. The USA is a superpower and its Intelligence Services are vital both in defeating the Nazis and preparing for the Cold War with the Soviet Union. The mighty CIA is soon to be born.

On the south coast of England the greatest armada the world has seen is being assembled to invade Nazi-occupied Europe and face Hitler's Atlantic Wall. Security and intelligence is everything, all resources are poured into making sure the great invasion force is ready and that its landing beaches remain secret.

No, not quite all resources. In a London office a British Intelligence Major is given an unusual order, to see that Helen Duncan, a spiritualist medium, is put out of harm's way until the invasion has begun and is well underway.

So begins the odd chain of events that led to the trial at the Old Bailey, under the 1745 Witchcraft Act, of Helen Duncan, the woman who became known to the world as The Callander Witch.

August 2014   **ISBN 978190826981**

361

Accent Press Ltd

Please visit our website
www.accentpress.co.uk
for our latest title information,
to write reviews and
leave feedback.

We'd love to hear from you!